Witchful
Thinking

BY H. P. MALLORY

THE JOLIE WILKINS SERIES
Fire Burn and Cauldron Bubble
Toil and Trouble
Be Witched (novella)

THE DULCIE O'NEIL SERIES
To Kill a Warlock
A Tale of Two Goblins
Great Hexpectations

Witchful Thinking

A Jolie Wilkins Novel

H. P. MALLORY

BANTAM BOOKS
NEW YORK

A Bantam Books Mass Market Original

Copyright © 2012 by H. P. Mallory
Excerpt from *The Witch Is Back* copyright © 2012 by H. P. Mallory

Published in the United States by Bantam Books, an imprint of The Random House Publishing Group, a division of Random House, Inc., New York.

BANTAM BOOKS and the rooster colophon are registered trademarks of Random House, Inc.

ISBN 978-0-345-53145-2
eBook ISBN 978-0-345-53155-1

This book contains an excerpt from the forthcoming book *The Witch Is Back* by H. P. Mallory. This excerpt has been set for this edition only and may not reflect the final content of the forthcoming edition.

Cover design: Eileen Carey
Cover illustration: Anne Keenan Higgins

Printed in the United States of America

www.bantamdell.com

9 8 7 6 5 4 3 2 1

Bantam mass market edition: March 2012

For my son, Finn

ACKNOWLEDGMENTS

My extreme gratitude goes to the following people:

My husband for your love and support
My mother for all your valuable input
My editor, Shauna Summers, for helping me make this book so much stronger
My agent, Kimberly Whalen, for all your help
Klaasje Helgren and Mercedes Berg who both won my "Become a character in my book" contest. I hope you enjoy your characters!
And to all my readers, thank you! I would not have come this far without your support!

Prologue

"So, no more ghostly encounters?" Christa, my best friend and only employee, asked while leaning against the desk in our front office. She was referring to the fact that the previous evening I'd seen my first ghost.

I shook my head and pooled into a chair by the door. "Maybe if you hadn't left early to go on your date, I wouldn't have had a visit at all."

"Well, one of us needs to be dating," she said, knowing full well I hadn't had any dates for the past six months.

"Let's not get into this again . . ."

"Jolie, you need to get out. You're almost thirty . . ."

"Two years from it, thank you very much."

"Whatever . . . you're going to end up old and alone. You're way too pretty, and you have such a great personality, you can't end up like that. Don't let one bad date ruin it." Her voice reached a crescendo. Christa has a tendency toward the dramatic.

"I've had a string of bad dates, Chris." I didn't know what else to say—I was terminally single. It came down to the fact that I'd rather spend time with my cat or Christa than face another stream of losers.

As for being attractive, Christa insisted I was pretty, but I wasn't convinced. It's one thing when your best friend says you're pretty; it's entirely different when a man does.

And I couldn't remember the last time a man had said it.

I caught my reflection in the glass of the desk and studied myself while Christa rambled on about all the reasons I should be dating. I supposed my face was pleasant enough—a pert nose, cornflower-blue eyes, and plump lips. A spattering of freckles across the bridge of my nose interrupts an otherwise pale landscape of skin, and my shoulder-length blond hair always finds itself drawn into a ponytail.

Head-turning doubtful, girl-next-door probable.

As for Christa, she doesn't look like me at all. For one thing, she's leggy and tall—about five-eight, which is four inches taller than I am. She has dark hair the color of mahogany, green eyes, and rosy cheeks. She's classically pretty—like cameo pretty. She's rail skinny and has no boobs. I have a tendency to gain weight if I eat too much, I have a definite butt, and the twins are pretty ample as well. Maybe that made me sound like I'm fat— I'm not, but I could stand to lose five pounds.

"Are you even listening to me?" Christa asked.

Shaking my head, I entered the reading room, thinking I'd left my glasses there.

I heard the door open.

"Well, hello to you," Christa said in a high-pitched, sickening-sweet, and non-Christa voice.

"Afternoon." The deep timbre of his voice echoed through the room, my ears mistaking his baritone for music.

"I'm here for a reading, but I don't have an appointment—"

"Oh, that's cool," Christa interrupted, and from the saccharine tone of her voice, it was pretty apparent this guy had to be eye candy.

Giving up on finding my reading glasses, I headed out in order to introduce myself to our stranger. Upon seeing him, I couldn't contain the gasp that escaped my throat. It wasn't his Greek-god, Sean-Connery-would-be-envious good looks that grabbed me first, or his considerable height.

It was his aura.

I've been able to see auras since before I can remember, but I'd never seen anything like his. It radiated from him as if it had a life of its own—and the color! Usually auras are pinkish or violet in healthy people, yellowish or orange in those unhealthy. His was the most vibrant blue I've ever seen—the color of the sky after a storm when the sun's rays bask everything in glory.

It emanated from him like electricity.

"Hi, I'm Jolie," I said, remembering myself.

"How do you do?" And to make me drool even more than I already was, he had an accent, a British one. Ergh.

I glanced at Christa as I invited him into the reading room. Her mouth had dropped open like a fish's.

My sentiments exactly.

His navy-blue sweater stretched to its capacity while attempting to span a pair of broad shoulders and a wide chest. The broad shoulders and spacious chest in question tapered to a trim waist and finished in a finale of long legs. The white shirt peeking from underneath his sweater contrasted with his tanned complexion and made me consider my own fair skin with dismay.

The stillness of the room did nothing to allay my nerves. I took a seat, shuffled the tarot cards, and handed him the deck. "Please choose five cards and lay them faceup on the table."

He took a seat across from me, stretching his legs and resting his hands on his thighs. I chanced a look at him and took in his chocolate hair and caramel eyes. His face was angular, and his Roman nose lent him a certain

Paul-Newman-esque quality. The beginnings of shadow did nothing to hide the definite cleft in his strong chin.

He didn't take the cards. Instead he just smiled, revealing pearly whites and a set of grade A dimples.

"You did come for a reading?" I asked.

He nodded and covered my hand with his own. What felt like lightning ricocheted up my arm, and I swear my heart stopped for a second. The lone red bulb blinked a few times then continued to grow brighter until I thought it might explode. My gaze moved from his hand up his arm, and settled on his eyes. With the red light reflecting against him, he looked like the devil come to barter for my soul.

"I came for a reading, yes, but not with the cards. I'd like you to read . . . me." His rumbling baritone was hypnotic, and I fought the need to pull my hand from his warm grip.

I set the stack of cards aside, focusing on him again. I was so nervous, I doubted any of my visions would come. They were about as reliable as the weather anchors you see on TV.

After several long uncomfortable moments, I gave up. "I can't read you, I'm sorry," I said, my voice breaking. I shifted the eucalyptus-scented incense I'd lit to the farthest corner of the table and waved my hands in front of my face, dispersing the smoke that seemed intent on wafting directly into my eyes. It swirled and danced in the air, as if indifferent to the fact that I couldn't help this stranger.

He removed his hand but stayed seated. I thought he'd leave, but he made no motion to do anything of the sort.

"Take your time."

Take my time? I was a nervous wreck and had no visions whatsoever. I just wanted this handsome stranger to leave so my life could return to normal.

But it appeared that was not in the cards.

The silence pounded against the walls, echoing the pulse of blood in my veins. Still, my companion said nothing. I'd had enough. "I don't know what to tell you."

He smiled again. "What do you see when you look at me?"

Adonis.

No, I couldn't say that. Maybe he'd like to hear about his aura? I didn't have any other cards up my sleeve . . . "I can see your aura," I almost whispered, fearing his ridicule.

His brows drew together. "What does it look like?"

"It isn't like anyone's I've ever seen before. It's bright blue, and it flares out of you . . . almost like electricity."

His smile disappeared, and he leaned forward. "Can you see everyone's auras?"

The incense dared to assault my eyes again, so I put it out and dumped it in the trash can.

"Yes. Most people have much fainter glows to them— more often than not in the pink or orange family. I've never seen blue."

He chewed on that for a moment. "What do you suppose it is you're looking at—someone's soul?"

I shook my head. "I don't know. I do know, though, that if someone's ailing, I can see it. Their aura goes a bit yellow." He nodded, and I added, "You're healthy."

He laughed, and I felt silly for saying it. He stood up, his imposing height making me feel all of three inches tall. Not enjoying the feel of him staring down at me, I rose too and watched him pull out his wallet. I guess he'd heard enough and thought I was full of it. He set a hundred-dollar bill on the table in front of me. My hourly rate was fifty dollars, and we'd been maybe twenty minutes.

"I'd like to come see you for the next three Tuesdays

at four p.m. Please don't schedule anyone after me. I'll compensate you for the entire afternoon."

I was shocked—what in the world would he want to come back for?

"Jolie, it was a pleasure meeting you, and I look forward to our next session." He turned to walk out of the room when I remembered myself.

"Wait, what name should I put in the appointment book?"

He turned and faced me. "Rand."

Then he walked out of the shop.

One

Queen.

I'm not even really sure what to make of the word.

And the worst part is that it's not a detached, unfamiliar, or unthreatening word. Nope, Queen is an up-close-and-personal sort of thing, as in I'm going to be living and breathing it. Some would say being Queen is my destiny, I don't know about that but what I do know is that Queen is now my reality.

I am Queen of the Underworld.

Jolie Wilkins, Queen of vampires, werewolves, and other creatures you wouldn't want to invite to dinner.

Somehow the title just doesn't fit me. It's like trying to wear a pair of shoes that are way too big for my size eight feet. I'm not a Queen, I never wanted to be a Queen, and I definitely don't have the makings of a Queen. I'm just me—a witch with some magical abilities, one of which is the power to reanimate the dead. But Queen? Not by a long shot.

One of the lessons I learned when I first became involved with the Underworld (less than two years ago) is that whatever the Underworld wants, it gets. It's like the mob—once you get in, ain't no gettin' out. And I'm in—up to my neck.

So how did I become Queen? Was there a royal celebration? Were Prince William and Harry in attendance?

*Was Kate Middleton pissed? No, no, and no. My entry
into the royalty of the Underworld was more like trial
by fire—I'd been in the middle of a war; Gwynn (the
bitch) had just run me through with a blade in return for
destroying her lover; I'd died and then I'd been on the
receiving end of reanimation, myself.*

*The crowning glory of the whole battle came when
Mercedes Berg, the supreme witch of all witches (also
known as the prophetess), basically shell-shocked everyone with a magical burst of energy that lit up the entire
sky. It was like God's television had short-circuited.
Everyone just stopped in their tracks, as if their brains
had gone dormant. No one had been able to function.
As if waving their white flags of surrender, everyone laid
their weapons on the ground and just stared at one another dumbstruck. And that was the end of that.*

Well, for them. For me it was just the beginning.

*After Mercedes put the kibosh on our little war (a war
for independence against the tyranny of the witch Bella,
who wanted to be Queen), she informed me that I was
now the Queen of the Underworld. And it wasn't like I
ever submitted my résumé for the position. It had come
completely out of left field, and the craptastic part of the
whole situation was that I couldn't say no. Mob, remember?*

*So now I'm Queen and I want nothing to do with the
position.*

*About now, Diary, I imagine your head is spinning.
Crap, my head is spinning and I'm the one who lived
through all of it. In a fit of desperation, I decided to
write it all down—to document how absurd my life has
become in an effort to make sense of it all.*

*Actually, this is my first journal entry. I never really
got into diaries because my life didn't warrant record-
ing. It was a quiet, mundane existence fixed in routine,
but I liked it well enough. I had a best friend, Christa,*

*who never ceased to amuse me with her frivolous talk
about sex, sex, and more sex. I had my cat named Plum
and I owned my own business—a tarot-card-reading
shop. My skills, though limited, included reading people's fortunes through cards as well as detecting auras to
determine if someone was sick or healthy by glancing at
the colors reverberating off them.*

*The day Rand Balfour walked into my life, he changed
it forever. Rand is a warlock and the first to inform me
of my witchiness. He taught me pretty much everything
I know . . . not to mention, I'm also head over heels in
love with him. But more about Rand later.*

*At this point the important things to know are: First,
the Underworld is polarized in a battle of good (Rand's
side, which includes me, a handful of witches, a few
hundred vampires and werewolves, and the entire legion
of fairies) versus bad (the evil witch Bella and her min-
ions, including an equal number of vampires and werewolves, none of the fairies, but all of the demons).*

*They say religion is at the core of most wars. Well,
that wasn't the case with this one. This war began over
me—and I'm not saying that to sound vain or to make
you think I have an inflated sense of self-importance.
Trust me, I'm really not that great. But once word
spread throughout the Underworld that I could reanimate the dead, all the creatures went into a tizzy because
no one before me had ever been able to do that. Bella, in
true Bella form, wanted me on her side because like
most villains, Bella sought power—power over all the
Underworld species. I guess I was a sharp arrow to have
in her quiver.*

*As with any other war, what happened was heart
wrenching—vamp fighting vamp and witch fighting
witch. Of course, I didn't get to observe too much—just
as I was impaled by Gwynn's blade, I was whisked back
in time to Alnwick, England, in the year 1878. There I*

met the prophetess, Mercedes Berg. Well, as it turned out, she'd been the party responsible for sending me back to 1878 in order to save me as well as herself. To put it bluntly, Mercedes needed a ride back to the future to avoid her own untimely death, and I played the part of bus.

As I mentioned earlier, Mercedes ended the war by raising her hands and causing that big ol' magical burst, looking like a conductor leading the orchestra of the skies. After Gwynn stabbed me, Mercedes brought me back to life and I learned that she was the only other person besides me who could reanimate the dead.

And now? It's only been about two hours since Mercedes stopped the battle. Now I find myself sitting in a cottage, alone, in a fairy village in the middle of the Cairngorms Forest in Scotland, waiting for I don't know what. After the war ended, we took care of the injured and the dead, while also taking Bella's remaining forces captive. Oh yeah, I forgot to mention our victory— Mercedes was on our side . . . thank God.

So here I am, camped out in this room, with not a whole lot to occupy myself, just waiting for word on what our next course of action will be.

PRESENT DAY
FAE VILLAGE, CAIRNGORMS FOREST, SCOTLAND

At the sound of a knock on the wooden door, I lifted my gaze from the parchment in front of me where I'd scribbled my journal entry. I laid my pen on the oak desktop and stood up, catching a glance at my outfit as I did so, and I had to laugh.

One fact about the fae and fae communities in general was that magic ruled. When you were in a fae village and if you happened to be female, fae magic dictated you be dressed in what looked like Renaissance garb. My dress had an empire waist and was so long that it skimmed the ground. The material was light and gauzy, off-white, and bedecked with pink ribbon piping around the waist, the bust, and the wrist-length sleeves. I didn't even have to look at my hair to know it was three times its usual length, now grazing my butt in a mass of golden sausage curls, kissed by pink cherry blossoms.

I'd gone into battle dressed in stretch pants and come out of it looking like Rapunzel.

I pulled open the door and found Rand standing before me. His chest was bare, revealing ripples of sinuous muscle. Rand's physique is nothing short of awe inspiring, but his muscles aren't the type you'd find in the gym. He's not into lifting five hundred pounds and grunting as loud as he can to make sure everyone knows he's lifting five hundred pounds. No, Rand's physique was sculpted from hard work and training with werewolves, master vampires, and fae kings.

I couldn't help but stare as my eyes trailed his beautiful upper body and rested on his blue-and-green-tartan kilt. While fae magic bedecked women in gowns, the same magic endowed men with kilts. It was like living in the book covers of every Highlander romance in existence.

Rand still wore the filth and misery of the war—blood and dirt staining a face that surpassed all others in its beauty. Well, maybe the master vampire Sinjin Sinclair (who just happened to be Rand's detested ally—long story) could compete with Rand's good looks, but at the moment I wasn't thinking about vampires. No, instead, I was getting drunk on the beauty of a warlock.

Rand is tall enough, maybe six-two or six-three, but he appears even taller by the proud way that he carries himself. He has chocolate-brown hair, cropped short. If you took that same chocolate, melted it, and added just a touch of cream, you'd have the color of his eyes. His complexion is what could only be called sun-kissed, without interruption by freckle or mole. And his face is pretty angular—a strong jaw, cleft chin, and high, sharp cheekbones. The beauty of his lips—full and plump under his strong nose—is on par with his gorgeous eyes. When he smiles, his dimples light up his entire face until you would swear you were beholding someone heaven-sent.

Neither of us said anything for a second or two. We just stood there, staring at each other as if we were from different planets and unable to communicate. And it made sense because, although we definitely loved each other, the best way to describe our relationship was as an emotional roller coaster. As such, I still didn't know where we stood—whether we were together as in boyfriend–girlfriend or . . . not.

Jolie.

It was Rand's voice in my head—complete with his thick English accent—a form of communication he and I have shared ever since we first met at my shop in Los Angeles two years ago.

"Rand." I said his name out loud and suddenly his arms were around me, holding me tightly. I felt the heat of his skin against my cheek as he pulled me close. He smelled like spice and sweat, the scent of masculinity, the embodiment of Rand. I closed my eyes and inhaled deeply, wanting nothing more than to fill myself with his very essence.

"I lost you," he whispered with a strained voice. He was referring to my death, when Gwynn's blade had pierced my stomach. He pulled away from me, and his eyes were glassy. "I will never forget the pain of watching you die. It will stay with me forever."

I didn't want to think about pain. I'd known my fair share but I also couldn't deny him the ache in his eyes.

wanted nothing more than to soothe him, to promise we would never be apart again. "Mercedes brought me back," I began. I'd only really been dead for a second or two, so did it really even count?

He crushed me against him, almost as if he was trying to remind himself I was truly flesh and blood, and not some figment of his imagination. He held me incredibly tightly, as if he could erase the past twenty-four hours by smothering me.

"I don't know whether to be indebted to Mercedes or furious with her," he said. I wasn't sure where my feelings leaned on the subject either. I had a damn good hunch that Mercedes knew beforehand that I was going to die—there didn't seem to be much of anything she didn't know. But at the same time, she was the one who brought me back to life, so how mad could I be?

"Let's put it behind us now," I whispered.

"You said Mercedes was the prophetess," Rand continued. "Are you sure?"

I nodded. If I was sure of anything, it was that Mercedes was the prophetess—the fabled and legendary witch to end all witches. The prophetess was rumored to be able to change history, something Mercedes had artfully demonstrated by pulling me back to 1878. Her magic was so potent, it was scary.

"Yes, I'm positive." The image of her manipulating the sky came to mind. "Didn't you see how she ended the battle?" I mean, hello, if that wasn't proof I didn't know what was.

He nodded but didn't say anything else, just continued to hold me, stroking my head like I was a child. Finally he spoke, and his voice was soft.

"And what is this about you being Queen?"

That was a tough subject, and I could read lots more into Rand's question than the mere fact that he asked it. Rand wasn't crazy about any form of monarchy, no offense to the Queen Mum. He'd rebelled against Bella's plans to become Queen of the Underworld, and even though he and I were allies and I was as different from Bella as day is from night, I couldn't imagine he'd be any more eager to see me ascend to the throne. No, Rand believed in the ideals of democracy and justice. Even though he was as English as tea and crumpets, he could easily have been an American revolutionary from the eighteenth century based on his feelings about equality, liberty, and freedom. And he did make a mean apple pie.

"I don't know," I answered, which was sort of the truth. I mean, I didn't know what Mercedes had in mind for me, and although Rand had been there to witness everything she had to say about me becoming Queen, there hadn't been much. In fact, as I recall, she said I'd become Queen and it was my destiny to unite the creatures of the Underworld, and that had been that.

"Mercedes made it sound like prophecy," Rand continued, eyeing me as if he thought I knew more than I was letting on.

"You heard everything I did," I answered simply. "I don't know what to make of it or what it means, but I imagine Mercedes will fill me in at some point."

"You have freedom of choice, Jolie. If you don't want to be Queen, you don't have to."

How ironic—this was the first time "freedom of choice" had ever been mentioned with regard to the Underworld. Freedom really wasn't something that came easily to Underworld creatures. Their society wasn't structured like ours—a lesson I'd learned the hard way.

"Mercedes assumes I have no choice in the matter." I sighed, not really wanting to shatter the beauty of the moment with thoughts of my new career path. "She said it was my destiny to unite the creatures. And if it is my true destiny, how can I avoid it?"

Rand was quiet for a second or two before he shook

his head. "Let's not think about it right now," he said, pulling me closer. "We can figure out all of the details later." He kissed the top of my head. I closed my eyes as I held him, but it was a false sense of security. As if foreseeing my own future, I realized Rand would most likely oppose me if I chose to follow my destiny to become Queen. It wasn't a reality I wanted to face.

The sound of cheering and laughter broke my reverie. I was suddenly aware that our alone time was nearing its end.

"What's going on out there?" I asked, although I wasn't really all that interested. Instead my mind was teeming with all the discussions I needed to have with Rand—centering on a turn of events in 1878. So much had happened, and unfortunately what happened in 1878 couldn't stay in 1878.

"A celebration, Jolie. That's why I came to get you—to escort you to the festivities," Rand answered absentmindedly, as if the last thing he was interested in was celebrating. He and I were on the same page.

A celebration. I hadn't even considered it. The overall tone after the gruesome battle was one of mourning and charity as our soldiers cared for their fallen, separating our dead from the maimed and injured and bringing them to this fae village.

One of the benefits to having me on Rand's side was the fact that I could reanimate all of Rand's deceased soldiers. It was going to be a long and arduous job, but I had promised I would do it, to myself as well as to our legion—those soldiers who had stood beside us from the beginning and vowed their loyalty to Rand. And it was something I wanted to do—something I needed to do. As far as I was concerned, death was no longer permanent; it was merely an inconvenience to be overcome.

"How many are dead?" I asked in a hollow voice.

"No final count yet," Rand responded in the same barren tone. He secured a stray tendril of hair behind my ear and grazed my cheek with his fingers. "Everyone is asking after you—apparently word of your death spread, causing quite a bit of anxiety. I want to prove to everyone there isn't anything to be worried about." He paused, and a sweet smile lit his face. "I know you're exhausted, but it is important for both of us to make an appearance. Will you oblige me?"

I really had no choice but to oblige him. Rand was the captain of our legion and as such, he had to be there, congratulate his men, and play his role as their leader. And so would I. I needed to promise the family members of the fallen that I would bring back their dead. I'd have to hobnob with Mercedes and introduce her to everyone as the prophetess, the highest of all witches. Most suspected she was only a legend. Little did they know.

"Yes, of course," I answered with as sincere a smile as I could muster. The truth of it was that I was beyond exhausted, physically and emotionally. And times like this called for nothing more than an amaretto sour and an early night.

The war and reanimating our fallen legion weren't thoughts I wanted to address at the moment. Not when I was in the arms of the one man I loved with all my heart. And, more so, there was so much I had to tell him.

Before my little excursion back in time, things with Rand had been strained. Although we loved each other, our relationship had never been an easy one. Rand had begun our affiliation as my benefactor/employer and consequently, he restrained his carnal feelings for me, fearing he'd be taking advantage of the situation. As that became less of a problem, we were faced with the issue of bonding.

Ah, bonding . . . what a bitch.

When witches love each other, they form a bond tha

is like a marriage on crack. Bonding lasts forever—there's no divorce. And witches live longer than humans, by a few hundred years at least, so bonding is definitely a long-term commitment. When witches bond, their powers increase tenfold, but so do their vulnerabilities. So if one bonded party dies, the mate also dies. And bonding isn't something you can actually choose—it's as if your body decides for you, usually right about the time you're getting hot and heavy. And I know this from personal experience. Talk about a buzz kill . . .

Prior to the war, when I was still in the present time, Rand and I had succumbed to the heat of the moment—and just when he'd been ready to seal the deal, he'd freaked out and proceeded to take a cold shower, literally. Later he explained that we'd nearly bonded, which in turn freaked me out. And scared as I must have appeared, Rand looked like he'd just gotten up close and personal with the headless horseman. Needless to say, all sexual bets were off and we were relegated to star-crossed lovers who couldn't get it on.

To say I'd been sexually frustrated for the last two years of my life was the understatement of the century.

Sexual frustration or not, this is where my story gets even more complicated. Part of the reason Rand was so freaked out about bonding with me was the fact that he'd bonded with a witch in his past and had nearly died because of it. It had taken Mathilda, the wisest and oldest of the fairies, to keep Rand sane and alive. Little by little, she nursed him back to health, using her magic to make him forget the details of the witch he'd bonded with until he could no longer recall her face, name, or anything else about her. He survived, but only by a thread, and the fact that he endured the "death" of his bond mate was testimony to Rand's incredible strength and stamina.

But there's more. On my tour de 1878, I met Rand

during his initial steps in warlock training. To make a long story short, we both fell madly in love and bada bing bada boom, we had the best sex ever and yep, you guessed it, we bonded. Our happy little tryst didn't last long, though. Before I knew it, Mercedes insisted that I return to my own time, saying I had to save the world or some other such crap, and I reluctantly had to leave my Rand of 1878 behind.

If you're following my story, you probably just figured out the whole thing. If not, let me spell it out . . . *I* was the witch Rand bonded with, and my departure nearly killed him. It was a truth that had been hard for me to digest . . . one I had to share with Rand.

"What happened out there, Jolie?" Rand asked as he glanced down at me. "Where did Mercedes come from? And why were you wearing my mother's ring?"

It was the same question he'd asked me when I died on the battlefield. God, it felt weird to say that. I didn't imagine I'd ever get used to it.

I swallowed hard and glanced down at my hand, where I still wore his mother's ring. Suddenly I wanted to cry over the injustice of it all: Rand had once loved me and given himself to me and I to him. He'd also asked me to marry him and I'd said yes, although I knew all along that I would have to return to my own time. He'd given me his mother's ring and forced me to promise him that he and I would reunite in my own time. Even as I made him that promise, I'd wondered if I'd be able to keep it; if I'd be able to convince the Rand of today that we were meant to be together.

"Something amazing happened," I said simply and racked my brain, trying to figure out the best way to explain.

Sometimes the best route is the direct one. "I traveled back in time, Rand," I said slowly, hoping the words would sink in.

"And?" he prodded, as though my comment was completely understandable. That was one thing I could appreciate about Underworld creatures—nothing really surprised them. When you got hairy during a full moon or had a hankering for O negative, it only made sense that what might be considered unusual by some standards seemed little more than commonplace and ordinary.

"I traveled back to 1878. Mercedes is the one who orchestrated it."

He nodded but didn't seem to get the gist of what I was saying, so I figured I should start from the beginning.

"It was wintertime, Rand, in England. Even though it was summer when the battle here began—"

"About that," he interrupted in a scathing tone. "You knew I didn't want you anywhere near that battle, Jolie."

Yeah, that was true. But I was stubborn and I'd made up my mind to fight even though Rand had forbidden it. I was determined if nothing else. I'd also been smart about it, though, realizing I would need some form of false identity in order to deceive Rand into letting me participate in the battle. With the help of Mathilda, I had managed to drum up a spell that changed my outward appearance so Rand wouldn't recognize me. I fought alongside him, alongside our legion, and none of them was the wiser. That was before I nearly died. Once that happened, and I'd been transported back in time, all my careful spell preparations had been for naught because my false identity was stripped from me. Upon my return to my own time, with Mercedes in tow, I was again sans my disguise, and of course Rand had recognized me instantly.

"Rand, that's in the past," I reminded him, not up for

being chided about something that really didn't matter now.

"If you had listened to me, none of this would have happened." His tone wasn't angry, more wistful than anything, as if he were imagining a completely different outcome, one in which he'd been spared from witnessing my death.

I shook my head and smiled up at him. "No harm, no foul."

"So stubborn." He chuckled. "Jolie." He tilted my chin up and gazed down at me lovingly. "It's been too long since the last time I kissed you."

Before I could even respond, his warm and sumptuous lips were on mine and I melted into him, feeling my body wilt against his. He chuckled and held me more firmly, running his hands through my hair as I felt his tongue enter my mouth. Suddenly, in my own mind, I was transported back to 1878 when Rand loved me freely and neither of us had to hold back. The thought depressed me so much I thought I might start crying. So I pulled away, thinking I should focus on the rest of my story. I had to get it out in the open, just to get it over and done with.

"I nearly froze to death when I arrived in 1878 but two maids helped me. One was named Elsie."

Elsie had been one of the attendants at Pelham Manor, the same manor Rand now inhabited and owned. But in 1878, it had belonged to Rand's best friend, William Pelham. Upon Pelham's death, William had bequeathed his property to Rand. Either way, the name Elsie wasn't ringing any bells in Rand's head. I could tell by the blank look in his eyes.

"It was Pelham Manor, Rand," I admitted finally. "Mercedes was responsible for bringing me back in time to Pelham Manor."

He blinked for a few seconds and then eyed me inquisitively. "Pelham died in 1878. I was in residence at the manor."

Hmm, about Pelham dying—that was another issue I had to address with Rand, but it wasn't at the top of my list. I'd sort of taken it upon myself to heal Pelham while I'd been his guest. As it was told, Pelham had died of cholera, but the ailing man I'd cured seemed to be dying of something else; his symptoms were different from those of a cholera patient. Well, I'd have to shelve that subject for another day. Now I had more serious stuff to get off my chest. Big stuff.

"Yes," I said firmly. "You were there."

"I was there?" he repeated, his eyes narrowing as he considered my words.

"You gave me your mother's ring."

He shook his head as if he was finding it difficult to believe. "I have no recollection of any of this," he said and pulled away from me, beginning to pace as he always did when agitated. "When I first met you in your store, there was nothing that seemed in any way familiar about you."

I nodded, but I had no clue what the laws were about time travel either. "I don't know what to tell you. Maybe I didn't seem familiar because you didn't know me yet at that point? Maybe technically you hadn't met me yet?"

"But if you traveled to 1878, we had already met—over one hundred years earlier."

I shook my head. Somehow I had to tell him that we'd bonded. But suddenly it was like a figurative light switch went off in my head. Rand and I were no longer bonded. Of that I was convinced, because when you're bonded with someone you're one with them—you can feel the same emotions they do, hear their thoughts. And I couldn't feel any of Rand's emotions. Nor could I hear his thoughts, and it didn't appear that he was cognizant of mine. In traveling back to my own time and Rand nearly dying, the bond between us had to have been destroyed . . . We were two separate beings. With this discovery I felt nothing but an isolating numbness.

I swallowed hard as I further considered it. There was a big chance that Rand might not take news of our bonding very well. Bonding had nearly killed him, and I didn't imagine that would be easy to swallow, especially since over the past one hundred years he'd carried with him the void of believing that his partner had died. So, really, wouldn't it be better not to tell him, better not to dredge up something that was so incredibly painful to him? I mean, we weren't bonded anymore, so maybe it was better just to let that conversation die and focus on the future? Focus on a fresh start? Besides, Rand had made it pretty clear that he wasn't interested in bonding again, not after the first time around nearly killed him.

"Rand," I began.

"Rand an' Jolie, where be ye?" The voice boomed from outside and seemed to rattle the walls of my makeshift cottage room.

"Odran?" I asked Rand with a smile, referring to the fact that the baritone voice could belong to none other than the King of the fae.

Rand nodded with a sexy grin. "You and I have a party to attend. Are you ready?" He held out his arm and I took it with a nod, pushing thoughts of bonding conversations to the deep recesses of my mind.

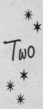

Two

Rand escorted me out of my room in the fae village. As we walked down a dirt pathway, the sound of birds singing and insects humming was thick in my ears. It was almost as deafening as the echoes of laughter and merriment. Festivalgoers reveled all around us, but I didn't feel like celebrating. Instead I could feel my heart swelling with anxiety like a water balloon expanding beyond its limit. My mind refused to relinquish the possibility that Rand might not react happily to the news of our bonding. What if he hated me? What if this whole bonding thing sabotaged any chance of us being together? Was I to blame? I mean, yes, I knew that sex between us could lead to bonding, but I sort of got carried away in the heat of the moment and the rest is history. So maybe it was my fault? Of course, on the flip side, maybe Rand would be thrilled to know I was the woman he bonded with. Maybe it would come as a relief . . . hmm, maybe. And maybe not.

As we entered the cobbled courtyard, I looked around and drank in the beauty of the fae. The flowers surrounding the courtyard were as tall as I was—in hues of vibrant yellow, pink, red, blue, and violet. A canopy of tree branches stood even taller, enveloping us in a lush hug. The sun's rays leaked through the branches, warming my skin and making me wish they could heat the coldness in my soul. But not even the beauty of the fae sun could vanquish the emptiness there.

"Lass!"

It was Odran, and although he was far from my favorite person in the world, he had such warmth in his smile that it chipped away at the ice inside me, ate at the knot of worry in my stomach. It's funny what being on the brink of death will do to you—it makes you happy to see just about anyone.

Odran broke away from a crowd of fae women who'd no doubt all been clamoring to hear his battle stories. Then, like the great leader he was, he ambled toward Rand and me, his extreme height and expansive build impressive by anyone's calculations.

Physically, Odran is very striking. The first thing you notice about him is that he's built like a bull, exuding strength with not even an ounce of fat—nope, just rock-hard muscle. Next you might notice his long mane of slightly wavy, golden hair that trails to his butt. Then you would probably notice that his facial features resemble those of a lion—solid, angular planes with a strong jaw. His eyes are deep set and wide, the color of amber. He's definitely a sight to behold, but he's also a complete and utter man whore.

"Odran! Congratulations!" I said with a heartfelt smile.

Odran smiled broadly, reaching out to envelop me in his beefy arms. As if a hug wasn't enough, he spun me around in the air.

"I thought ye were dead," he said, bringing me back to the ground and pulling me against his massive chest. I felt like I was hugging a wall.

I eyed Rand, a little worried he might not be taking Odran's familiar greeting very well. Rand never trusted Odran and always tended to be overprotective where I was concerned. But not today. Today there was a smile etched on his face that I didn't imagine anything or anyone could remove. Well, scratch that—the vampire Sinjin probably could have wiped the grin right off his face.

Thinking of Sinjin, I had to swallow my sense of foreboding. Sinjin had been there on the battlefield—he'd watched Gwynn run me through with her blade, and then he'd destroyed her. When I subsequently died from the mortal wound, Sinjin vanished, and I hadn't seen or heard from him since.

And that bothered me, because complicated though it was and as much as I didn't want to admit it to myself, I cared about Sinjin—a lot.

"Jolie?" Rand asked, seeming to realize that I'd completely zoned out, my thoughts consumed with Sinjin Sinclair.

"Sorry?"

"Do you know where Mercedes is?" Rand asked with an arched eyebrow.

What, pray tell, is on your mind, Miss Wilkins? His voice entered my head, and I faced him with surprise, not sure which question to answer first.

"I don't know where she is but I imagine she's here somewhere," I replied, glancing between Rand and Odran. "Mercedes brought me to my room this morning."

"I wouldna like ta miss an introdooction to the prophetess," Odran said in his thick brogue and then winked at me. Hmm, it appeared Odran was back to lusting after me again. For a while there he'd been pretty freaked out over the fact that by touching him, I'd been able to see glimpses of his future—of him on the battlefield. But now it seemed as if that fear had been replaced with his inexhaustible need to rut. Just great.

I took a step closer to Rand, who clasped his hand in mine, which was fine by me . . . anything to curtail the sexual interests of the King. "I'll make sure to introduce you."

Are you going to answer my question?

I faced Rand and smiled. *There's really nothing to say—and since when do you call me Miss Wilkins?*

The Rand of 1878 had referred to me as Miss Wilkins in the first week or so of our acquaintance, when he'd wanted nothing more than for me to leave Pelham Manor. Rand, both now and in the past, was suspicious as well as protective of those he loved. In this case, he had thought he was protecting Pelham from me, a gold digger. In the end, though, 1878 Rand's tune had changed as far as I was concerned—but it's not like it had been an easy task. It had taken a spell from Mathilda to allow 1878 Rand to have the same feelings for me that modern-day Rand felt. That's when he'd warmed up to me, considerably. That's also when we had sex and bonded. Sigh.

My heart was suddenly even heavier and I felt like I needed to sit down—like I couldn't carry it around anymore, lest it fall right out of my chest and shatter into a million pieces at my feet. But I couldn't sit down because we were still standing at the mouth of the courtyard, caught up in a conversation that prevented me from leaving.

We never got to finish our discussion about you traveling back in time, Rand's voice in my head pointed out.

I glanced at Odran and was suddenly relieved by the fact that I had a diversion—that this celebration wouldn't allow for a detailed conversation.

We'll find time, I answered simply.

"The legion will want ta see ya, lass," Odran said and turned toward the great expanse of open courtyard, facing our throng of soldiers, who stood huddled in small groups, laughing and patting one another's backs with obvious pride. The surviving members of our legion filled the courtyard of the smallish fae village, and the more I observed them, the more I realized their attention kept working its way back to our small circle as they smiled and laughed, raising their cups of ale in toasts to us.

These people, for lack of a better word, were my family now. Prior to Rand walking through my door and changing my life forever, the only family I had was a mother whom I rarely saw and Christa, my best friend. Luckily, Christa had moved to England with me so I still counted her among my family members. On the other hand, I found myself growing steadily distant from my mother. She was a very religious woman and, as such, had no idea who and what I was. I was able to keep our conversations limited to trivialities—the weather and the latest television shows. It wasn't an ideal situation but it was better than nothing.

So now the Underworld had become my family and I was proud of them—proud of the fact that we had risked everything to fight against the tyranny of Bella and won.

"Ready?" Rand asked, smiling down at me.

I nodded. Flanked by Odran and Rand, I entered the courtyard while the soldiers cleared the way for us as if we were royalty. I felt a few pats on the back and heard lots of whispering over the fact that I wasn't dead along with more conjecture over who would be reanimated and in what order.

Once we'd made our way through the crowd, Rand stood before our soldiers and held up his hands to quiet everyone.

"In honor of our victory," he began, but he was drowned out by cheers and hollering. He managed to get everyone under control again and continued. "I invite you to celebrate—eat, drink, and relish the fact that you are free—that you fought for your freedom and you deserve this victory! Bella's power has been quashed, and none of us will ever call her monarch!"

Another round of cheers while Rand smiled and

waited for everyone to quiet down again. "I have heard much talk concerning whether or not Jolie Wilkins died," he said, turning to me. "Well, as you can see, she is very much alive." He held up my hand, which was firmly clasped in his. The crowd broke into raucous laughs and claps. I just smiled, my eyes cast down.

"We heard she died," someone from the audience yelled.

"Yes, she did." Rand nodded. "But as you can see, that is no longer the case."

"How is that possible?" shouted someone else.

"Jordans said he heard there was a prophetess?" called out an old man right in front of us, wobbling with his cane like he was about to keel over right then and there.

Rand glanced at me with eyes that echoed the same doubts rampaging through my mind. Where was Mercedes? It hadn't really dawned on me to look for her— I'd just figured she'd show up at the celebration. When she left me in my room, I hadn't been in the mood for a long-winded conversation about her itinerary.

"There is a prophetess," I began, but I was apparently too quiet because there were a few "what did she say"s going through the crowd. "Mercedes Berg is the prophetess," I shouted.

There was momentary silence and then hushed whispers as people expressed their shock. The prophetess had always been a legend according to most people— sort of like the Underworld version of Santa Claus, only Mercedes didn't pack a bag full of presents and I wouldn't exactly describe her as jolly.

"Where is she?" asked the old man in front of us with a look of impatience in his eyes.

I swallowed. "I don't know." Hey, I wasn't her keeper.

"She is here."

I recognized Mercedes' voice and turned to my right,

finding her standing before me—that is, before us. She moved forward and the crowd seemed to double back on itself, almost as if they were afraid of her. I couldn't blame them—there was definitely a part of me deep down that shared their fear. That little voice reminded me that no one knew what Mercedes was truly capable of . . . that she was incredibly powerful.

Yes, Mercedes was the poster witch for power. Hers was a power that vibrated from her—you could feel it coming off in rivulets of energy. She was dressed in the color of royalty, wearing a deep purple velvet gown that tickled the ground as she walked. Her brown hair was pulled back into an array of ringlets and purple ribbons that cascaded down her back. When she glanced at me, her stunning green eyes radiated an almost unnatural beauty.

Mercedes is centuries old but you'd never guess it—she looks like she's thirty-two, tops.

"Way to make an entrance," I said with a smile.

Mercedes beamed at me and took my hand—the one that wasn't currently engulfed in Rand's. She glanced at Rand, who said nothing but continued to watch her placidly. She nodded to him in silent recognition before facing the crowd of soldiers.

"I am Mercedes Berg. Some of you refer to me as the prophetess."

The crowd was completely silent. They stayed that way for a few seconds until I began to wonder if she had put some sort of charm on them. Then the little old outspoken man in front began to clear his throat.

"And how can we be sure you are who you say you are?"

The creatures of the Underworld are a suspicious bunch.

"I believe every one of you witnessed Jolie and myself

put an end to this war?" Mercedes asked before glancing at me again with a warm smile.

The little old man nodded and stepped back into the crowd, apparently satisfied with her answer. Of course, witnessing the big stunt Mercedes had pulled would have been enough for me. I would never have questioned her in the first place.

"I am the prophetess, yes." Mercedes' voice rang out loudly and seemed to broadcast her ancient wisdom. "But I am also the advisor to your Queen, Jolie."

Rand shifted uncomfortably, and I didn't dare look at him. The crowd broke out in whispers, seeming to echo his discomfort. They'd all come damn close to having a Queen thrust on them in the form of Bella; I could imagine that having another Queen pushed down their throats wasn't exactly welcome.

"This is our fate, our destiny," Mercedes continued. "Jolie Wilkins has powers not even she fully recognizes yet. She will be responsible for reuniting our kind and bringing peace to the Underworld. What she needs now is your allegiance, not your questions and your doubts."

I had to wonder if Mercedes had been a public speaker at some point in her long career—maybe a politician. She definitely had the gift of persuasion because soon the crowd was nodding in agreement. Or maybe she'd just charmed them into acquiescence.

I glanced at Rand, even though I knew I shouldn't have. His jaw was tight and he did nothing but stare straight ahead, focusing on the horizon. He didn't appear to be listening, and it seemed like he wanted to be anywhere but here.

Rand. I thought the word even though I wasn't ready to get into this conversation. I still wasn't convinced I was the right person for the position of Queen. And I could only imagine that the more I talked to Rand, the more he would try to talk me out of my supposedly destined role.

Let's not worry about it now. The tone of his voice was sweet, unconcerned, but underneath the apparent levity was a weighty and serious issue. Now might not be the time to discuss it but that time would come—it was as obvious as the rigidity of his posture.

It's the elephant in the room, I argued.

He chuckled and finally looked at me. *There is too much to be thankful for—too much to celebrate. We'll figure out the details later. For now, I just want to enjoy the fact that the woman I love is standing next to me and . . . alive.*

I had to swallow the lump in my throat.

The woman he loves. Me.

I didn't even know what to say, much less what to think. I didn't say anything and, instead, squeezed his hand reassuringly and tried to focus on the faces of our legion. I tried not to worry that I might destroy that freely given love as soon as Rand realized I was planning to follow my destiny to become Queen. Well, at the very least, I hadn't completely abandoned the idea. And if that issue didn't destroy our chances of being together, I had to imagine the little tidbit about our bonding might do the job just fine.

A few hours and countless tankards of ale later, I felt footloose and fancy-free. The same couldn't be said for Rand. It seemed the drunker I got, the more serious he became. I'd always known Rand could handle his liquor; now I had to wonder if it was warlock magic that assisted him, because I could have sworn he'd drunk twice as much as I had.

"So you say you were a resident at Pelham Manor in 1878?" Rand questioned Mercedes with narrowed eyes.

"Yes," she answered simply.

"Then why don't I remember you?" Rand continued, taking another sip of his ale while eyeing her like a hawk.

"Mathilda erased all memories of my visit from your mind," Mercedes said. I nearly choked on my mouthful as I worried she might venture into unwelcome territory.

"So where is Bella?" I interrupted, uttering the first thought that came to my mind.

We had just finished dining on ham, turkey, a variety of breads and cheeses, and a cornucopia of fruits and vegetables. As we sat beneath the stars at a long wooden table that accommodated our entire legion, the soldiers chorused an old Scottish ditty, "Aiken Drum."

There was a man lived in the moon
Lived in the moon, lived in the moon
There was a man lived in the moon
And his name was Aiken Drum.

"The witch is in coontainment 'ere in this village, lass," Odran answered before joining in on the song. His deep baritone pealed through the cloudless sky, and I couldn't help tapping my toe to the beat as he sang.

And he played upon a ladle
A ladle, a ladle
And he played upon a ladle
And his name was Aiken Drum.

"Bella is under surveillance by two fae guards, Jolie," Rand confirmed. He just shook his head in wonder as Odran suddenly rose up like a snapping anglerfish and grabbed the waist of a fairy woman who'd sauntered too close. He carried her into the courtyard and set her back on her feet, embracing her with a kiss. I'm not sure if what happened next would be considered dancing or an indecent public display.

I glanced at Rand, who smiled before turning to Mercedes again, his jaw tightening.

"Jolie said you brought her back in time?" he asked. Mercedes simply nodded. "Why?"

Mercedes glanced at me with slight annoyance before returning her gaze to Rand. "Simple—she was about to be killed, so I saved her."

"Yet when you sent her back to the present, she was immediately killed," Rand pointed out while I swallowed the last three gulps of ale and refilled my empty mug with just a thought.

Mercedes' lips tightened into a white line. "I had no control over the exact moment we would return and it just so happened that my timing was off . . . a bit. But may I remind you I brought Jolie back from the dead."

Rand nodded. "Yes, I'm well aware of that." He was quiet for another three seconds. "Why did you need to bring Jolie back into the past in order to save her?"

Mercedes arched a brow as if to say that she didn't appreciate being interrogated. "I did not do it just to save Jolie. I also needed her magic to help transport me into the present."

"Ah," Rand said, a smile void of humor pasted on his full lips. "In reality, then, you were using Jolie's powers to help yourself?"

"Rand, if she hadn't escaped 1878, she'd have been killed by Lurkers," I interrupted, becoming increasingly uncomfortable with Rand's persistence.

"Lurkers?" Rand repeated in a dubious tone, although he knew only too well who the Lurkers were—a group of humans who were part vampire and thus possessed incredible strength but could tolerate daylight. The Lurkers' sole purpose was to destroy the creatures of the Underworld. They often lacked any sort of unity, though, so they were more like marauding guerrillas than soldiers, killing our kind whenever the opportunity arose.

And, no, their attacks weren't limited to vampires. Any sort of Underworld creature was fair game. Apparently they had posed a big enough threat to Mercedes to make her flee 1878.

"Yes," Mercedes interjected while offering me a grateful smile. "I saw the Lurkers kill me in a vision. When I realized I could harness Jolie's energy and powers to help me out of my predicament, I acted on it."

"And you call yourself the prophetess?" Rand prodded, his tone revealing his disbelief and, furthermore, his impression that she must be a charlatan.

"I do not call myself anything. Your kind chose to give me that title."

Rand, can't you see her aura? I thought the words.

As I mentioned earlier, I have the ability to see people's auras. Humans usually have pink or violet glows about them; yellow or orange for those who are sick.

While witches might have more distinctive auras than humans, Mercedes' was a rainbow of colors that billowed off her in blues, purples, yellows, oranges, and reds. It was spectacular to say the least.

Yes, of course I can.

Then why don't you believe her?

"Because it is Rand's nature to distrust," Mercedes said, answering my question.

I gasped in a mouthful of air. So Mercedes could hear our telepathic conversations . . . She was the prophetess and then some.

"You would have us blindly accept that you are who you say you are?" Rand demanded, apparently unimpressed by rainbow auras and telepathic eavesdroppers.

Mercedes shook her head. "One of life's lessons is to learn how to trust in the things over which we have no control."

"Good luck," I snickered, thinking Rand wasn't exactly the blindly trusting type.

Rand said nothing as he downed his cup of ale. Mercedes' attention shifted back to me.

"You have much to learn as Queen, Jolie."

"Such as?" I glanced at Rand, trying to decipher whether or not he would argue against my being Queen. But he merely sipped his ale and watched Odran. The fairy King continued to engulf the poor fairy woman in a wet, urgent kiss, looking like he was trying to swallow her in one shot.

"Magic, history of all creatures, leadership, and propriety." Mercedes itemized, ticking off the list of my lessons on her fingers.

"Whoa, what?" I questioned. "Propriety?"

Mercedes nodded. "If you are to represent the Underworld, you must do so with the utmost grace."

This job was looking worse and worse by the minute. "What about freedom of choice?" I started, remembering Rand's words. "What if I don't want this job?"

Mercedes seemed indifferent as she answered. "There is no choice, no free will. There is only fate and destiny. And this is your fate."

Rand stood up and turned to me with a frown. Before I could say anything, he simply walked away. I wasn't sure if I should follow him and was toying with the idea when I felt Mercedes' hand on mine. I glanced at her in surprise.

"There is unharnessed power inside you, Jolie. You have no idea what you are capable of. It is up to me to direct that power and shape it."

I didn't know what to think. Yes, I constantly amazed myself as I learned more about my powers, but this did seem over the top. And I still hadn't exactly decided whether or not I liked the idea of being Queen.

"When does my training begin?" I asked in a small voice.

"Immediately," Mercedes replied. "As soon as we return to Pelham Manor."

So "we" were returning to Pelham Manor. I could only wonder what Rand would think about that little arrangement.

"Rand will want you to be close to him, and if I am part of your entourage, there will not be much he can say," Mercedes finished with a self-impressed smile.

I glanced at her in surprise. "What, you can read my mind too?"

She shook her head and laughed. "No, I can read your expression. And I can hear any thoughts you ideate."

"That's why you could hear my conversation with Rand? Because I was broadcasting it?" I asked, trying to fathom the extent of her powers. She just nodded, which was a relief. I mean, who in the heck would want to have their innermost thoughts and secrets overheard? Not me.

Now it was my turn to throw a wrench into Mercedes' plans—a wrench named Christa. "My next stop is Australia, not Pelham Manor," I said with finality.

"Australia?" Mercedes repeated, and the surprised look on her face was an absolute Kodak moment. It was a shame I didn't have my camera.

"Yep, I have to go get my best friend."

Before the battle with Bella had started, Rand had arranged for Christa (who lived at Pelham Manor and acted as Rand's assistant) and me to travel to Australia, out of harm's way. Also, if Bella was victorious, Christa and I could have lived there off her radar.

When I rebelled and insisted on fighting in the battle rather than chaperoning my best friend, I had to charm Christa to go on by herself with the promise that I'd come get her as soon as the battle was over. If I was still alive.

Well, the battle *was* over and I *was* still alive.

"It is too dangerous." Mercedes shook her head as if to emphasize the point. "You are a Queen now, you cannot concern yourself with such commonplace trivialities."

Anger started boiling up inside me, which, mixed with countless pints of ale, was enough to give me a stomach-ache. "My best friend means more to me than being Queen."

Mercedes shook her head again like I wasn't getting it. "It is not about her being more important to you—you have a duty to the creatures of the Underworld. Only you have the ability to unite them against a threat larger than Bella."

"A larger threat?" I repeated, wondering what the hell she was going on about.

"The Lurkers, Jolie."

"Bah." I waved my hand at her dismissively. "They aren't a threat at all." To me, they were more like a bunch of half-vampires with fang envy. A massive problem? I didn't see it.

"Lesson one: Never underestimate your enemies," Mercedes said in a harsh voice. "Your duty now is to your people."

"My people," I repeated, standing up, and throwing my hands on my hips as I thought about free will, which I still believed in. Just as Rand had said earlier, this was my choice. I didn't have to succumb to a destiny that was thrust upon me. I could resist it. "I have no people— I'm not a Queen and I've never wanted to be one." I took a deep breath before facing her again in all my anger. "I'm done with this farce."

Then, dramatically, I spun on my heel in a great display of outrage and walked away, wondering if it could possibly be that easy to leave the title of Queen behind me.

Three

What to write about today . . . Well, since I can't seem to get him off my mind, I might as well talk about Rand . . . gosh, where do I even start? I've already mentioned that he's an incredibly gifted warlock. His magic is probably among the strongest out there . . . well, of the witches and warlocks anyway. One time I watched him spar with Odran and Rand held his own. He is probably more equally matched against Sinjin, who has an ungodly amount of strength and speed. As a vampire, Sinjin can bewitch his prey just by looking at her, but luckily for me his powers don't work on witches. And unluckily for me, my powers don't work on vampires.

I wouldn't say Rand is the strongest force out there—I know some fairies who could rival him, namely Mathilda. Really, Mathilda taught Rand everything he knows. And I think Mercedes could make short work of him. Well, she could make short work of just about anyone.

I think I also might have mentioned the fact that Rand is absolutely beautiful. Even though he's one of the handsomest men I've ever seen, it's not even his looks that intrigue me anymore—it's the man inside. Rand is the noblest, most loyal and honorable person I've ever met. He is fair, honest, and responsible. He would make the best husband and an equally fantastic dad.

And there's the rub. A huge part of me suffers when I think about it—about a white picket fence and the little house on the corner with two kids running through the yard while I bake brownies and Rand comes up behind me, surprising me with a kiss.

The problem is that Rand and I will never have that little fairy tale. And I'm not even talking about problems like whether or not Rand will support me as Queen or what he'll think about the fact that we bonded. What I'm talking about is the fact that witches have an incredibly difficult time carrying a pregnancy to term. As I understand it, this is only the case in witch-to-witch unions. I wouldn't have a problem carrying a fairy baby or a were baby or a human baby. Vampires can't procreate so that isn't even something worth considering— although strangely enough the idea has crossed my mind . . . casually of course. But witches and warlocks successfully having offspring together is very unlikely, which is why our race is dwindling.

I still haven't figured out where the witch gene was in my family. Rand said there must be a witch somewhere in my lineage because the gene was passed down to me. It didn't require that my mother or father be in any way witch-like, which must be true because neither of them is, or in my father's case was.

Idealistic family life aside, I always seem to find myself in a quandary where Rand is concerned. He has this pervasive sense of morality, and while I love him for it, he can also be beyond frustrating. Sometimes I wish he would just give in to his desires and act on them rather than analyzing everything into the ground. But Rand wasn't always like this—in fact, he used to be pretty different.

What I've realized is that I'm in love with two men— the Rand I met in 1878 and the Rand I know today. And although I love the modern Rand more, a part of me bemoans the loss of my 1878 Rand. I can't help but flood my mind with memories—memories of a Rand who was less complicated, who acted on his desires, and who wasn't familiar enough with magic to worry about its consequences.

I play that stupid game of "what if" with myself all the time. What if I were offered the option to return to 1878 and live out the remainder of my years with 1878 Rand? Would I take it? I don't honestly know that I would. I mean, if it were just a question of love, maybe I would, but as silly as it sounds, then I'd miss my modern Rand. Besides, there's so much I have to do in my own time, I doubt I'd be able to bail on the here and now. And then there's Christa, my best friend. I could never leave her behind—yes, I would miss her and all that, but more important, I don't know that Christa could really take care of herself. 'Course, she does have her werewolf boyfriend, John, to keep her company and out of trouble. But even so . . .

I guess none of it really matters anyway, and thoughts like these are just a waste of my time. I'll never be able to go back to 1878 Rand, and for that I am sorry.

I couldn't get Rand out of my mind, thoughts of him in 1878 running headlong into one another. There was something inside me that was broken, something that yearned for the love we'd shared in the past. And while I couldn't send myself back to 1878, I could re-create my memories.

I wasn't sure if it was warranted but I felt guilty as I held my hands up, palms facing each other. Guilty about the fact that I shouldn't have been living in the past, shouldn't have been focusing on memories that could never be anything other than reruns.

A whitish light began to build between my hands. The more I focused, the brighter the light became, until could barely make out the outline of my fingers. I closed my eyes and forced myself to remember, forced myself to bring to life a memory of a time long gone.

When I opened my eyes, I smiled, but there was a sadness in me as I focused on the images wavering between my hands.

It was Christmas in 1878 and Rand had just appeared in Pelham Manor like Santa Claus himself, laden with an enormous bag of presents. Pelham had been alive at the time, and together with his sister, Christine, the four of us had celebrated the best Christmas I'd ever had. I smiled as I watched the images of merriment made possible by my magic. It was with a sad heart that I continued watching, as Pelham and Christine left Rand and me alone. I knew well what would happen next, but I couldn't tear my gaze away from the reel playing out before me. In watching it, I felt as if I were there, experiencing the same feelings all over again . . .

"We shall be along momentarily," Rand said in response to Pelham, as his friend turned to inquire if we would follow him into the dining room.

Rand dropped his head and kissed me. I wrapped my arms around him and returned his thrusting tongue. He pulled away from my embrace and reached for his coat, which he'd draped over the coatrack. Flakes of melted snow wetted the stone hearth. He fished inside the coat pocket and returned with a small gift, wrapped in silver foil.

He handed the gift to me and I reached out, accepting it. I tore the paper off, letting the silver foil fall to the ground. Rand lowered himself to one knee at the same time that I flipped open the box to find a ring. It was a brilliant sapphire encircled by white diamonds that reflected the firelight onto the walls, like a prism.

"I love you, Jolie. And I want you to be my wife."

I shut my eyes to stifle the pain that suddenly overcame me. God, if only I could stay with him and play full-time homemaker. If only I could enjoy him warming my bed each night and sharing the rest of our lives together. But I knew it was useless. I couldn't stay here. Not when so much depended on Mercedes and me returning to the present.

"Rand," I started.

He took the ring out of the box and slid it onto my finger. It fit . . . perfectly. "It was my mother's. And now I want you to wear it."

"It's beautiful, Rand, but . . ."

He stood up and kissed me again, erasing my concerns with his urgent lips. When he pulled away, his face was flushed. "No more talk of returning to your own time, Jolie. Not when you would be endangering yourself. I simply will not hear of it again."

"Rand . . ."

"If ever your safety is in jeopardy, that is enough for me to refuse."

"I can't stay here," I protested softly. Rand's attention focused on my hands, which he clasped in his. I tightened my grip as I felt new tears rolling down my cheeks. "I have to go, Rand, and I have to bring Mercedes with me. There is too much at stake if I remain here."

"What is at stake aside from your safety if you return?"

I swallowed hard. "Rand, Mercedes will die if we remain."

He gazed with an expressionless face toward the fire. He didn't answer but remained staring intently at the flames as they crackled and hissed. Finally he turned to me with a face full of pain. "Then we could send her back alone," he stated, almost desperate. "I cannot lose you, Jolie."

I shook my head. "Mercedes is the prophetess and it

was my mission to come here and take her back with me. We have a master plan to fulfill. I can't abandon my responsibility."

"Jolie—" Rand started when Pelham suddenly appeared in the doorway.

"Cripes, old man, are you joining us?"

Rand nodded, but continued to stare at me. "Momentarily."

Pelham returned to the dining room.

"Will you consider my proposal?" Rand asked.

I nodded and marveled at the ring on my finger as it gleamed, representing a life of happiness—the life I'd always wanted. Dammit all, for one moment I'd pretend this could really be. Just for one moment. "Yes, of course."

Rand held out his arm and I ran my hand over the fine material of his sleeve, allowing him to escort me into the dining room. Yes, I'd pretend that Rand and I really could be a couple. That Christmas was truly a time for miracles.

Silver linens covered the table, where a huge centerpiece of red roses, oranges dotted with cloves, and pine boughs dominated. Tall red tapers illuminated the great length of the table, which contrasted with the snow plastering the windowsills outside and the fire crackling in the hearth inside. It was a Christmas scene to end all Christmases, bar none. I sat opposite Rand, beside Christine, who seemed to be studying us intently. Once she caught sight of the ring on my finger, her grin grew exponentially. She picked up my hand and inspected it, suddenly addressing her brother.

"It seems congratulations are in order," she began while displaying my hand in the air for Pelham to see.

Surprise was his only expression and he thumped Rand heartily on the back, beaming. "Balfour! You are *a sly fox after all." He hugged Rand, eyeing me. "You will have the loveliest bride in all the shires, old man."*

Rand regarded me and nodded, his eyes deep pools of chocolate brown. "I am quite aware, Pel, I am quite aware."

The images began to fade away and the white light between my hands slowly died, until all that was left between them was air. I couldn't help the smile on my face, but it was bittersweet.

Two days had passed since the celebration, and now we (as in our entire legion) were stationed at Pelham Manor again to figure our next steps. It was like old times. Prior to the battle, the legion had been based at Rand's English estate so that the soldiers could train with one another, sparring in practice for the battle. And now here we were again; it was like we'd come full circle.

The reason Rand had wanted everyone to return to Pelham Manor was twofold. First, he wanted all of the creatures to have a say in what their futures would entail—and that would require lots of meetings. Second, we had to rebuild our army. Many creatures had died on the battlefield and needed to be reanimated, and it was easier to take roll when all the creatures were assembled in one area. As to the deceased, we had buried them on the battlefield of Culloden, knowing when the time came for me to reanimate them, their bodies would merely disappear, resurrecting themselves into live flesh and blood at my behest.

As we sat around the expansive mahogany table in Rand's dining room, I was proud. Proud of Rand, proud of our side, and proud of myself. We had fought and died alongside one another to protect ourselves and future generations. And now I could give back. It felt good to be able to do so—to offer the gift of life, or in my case, re-life.

Because not all of the creatures stationed at Pelham Manor could fit into Rand's dining room, each race had elected officials to represent their interests. Seated at the table were Rand and me, who represented all witches; Mathilda and Odran, who stood for the interests of the fae; Mercedes, representing herself; Trent, a were, who represented other shape shifters (and unfortunately for me also happened to be my ex-boyfriend); and Varick, who stood for the vampires. Varick was a master vampire and one of the oldest. He was also Sinjin's employer.

Employment in the vampire world was pretty different from a boss–employee relationship in the human world. For starters, an employer, such as Varick, was usually much older than his protégé and therefore much stronger. Although Varick wasn't Sinjin's creator, Sinjin had been assigned to the older and stronger vampire in order to train and learn. If Varick was ever killed, Sinjin would take his place.

Speaking of Sinjin, he was still nowhere to be found, and as the days passed I became more and more worried. It was bizarre that he wasn't in attendance, that he wasn't at Varick's side, especially when the two had always worked in such close proximity.

"Have you heard from Sinjin?" I whispered to Varick, leaning into him so I wouldn't pull any attention away from Rand, who was in the middle of an uninteresting discussion with Odran.

"I have not," Varick answered in a monotone. As stunningly sexy and attractive as Sinjin was, Varick was anything but. He had the look of a carrot—tall and skinny with pasty white skin and flaming orange hair. Still, he possessed the aura of power that seemed to accompany all vampires.

"The last time I saw him was on the battlefield," I

began, feeling the worry eat away at my gut as I remembered the expressions of disbelief, anger, and sorrow in Sinjin's eyes as I died right in front of him. "He watched me die, Varick, and then he just disappeared. And I haven't seen or heard from him since."

"Neither have I," Varick answered in the same indifferent voice.

His apathy angered me. How could he be so callous, so uninterested, when he and Sinjin had worked together for hundreds of years? How could he care so little?

"Aren't you worried?" I demanded in a harsh voice. Varick turned his full attention to me, and something feral in his eyes warned me not to upset him. I had to swallow my trepidation. "I mean, aren't you worried that maybe he's in trouble?" If I'd been a dog, my tail would have been firmly planted between my legs as I circled Varick's feet and begged for a good scratching right between the ears.

"In trouble?" Varick responded with a chuckle that revealed anything but humor. Nope, Varick was someone you didn't cross. It was like he was just aching to rip out your throat. But he also had to know that messing with me wasn't a good idea—not with Rand and Mercedes in the room. One lunge at me and they'd open up a can of whoop-ass on Varick faster than he could say "bloodsucker."

"Isn't it kind of crappy that you're so nonchalant about the fact that Sinjin is MIA?" I asked, feeling stronger in my own skin.

"And perhaps you would care to enlighten me as to why you are so interested?" Varick retorted in the same monotone that grated on my nerves.

"Sinjin is my friend," I replied with narrowed eyes. "And I care about my friends. If he's in trouble, I want to know."

Varick raised both brows as if he didn't quite believe the whole "Sinjin is my friend" story. I held my tongue but didn't look away. Finally, Varick realized I wasn't about to admit anything else, and he dropped his patronizing expression.

"Sinclair is not in trouble. He is most probably causing it."

Yeah, I had to concur with him on that one. Sinjin was a troublemaker, if nothing else. I leaned back in my seat and sighed, hoping the nervous energy in my stomach would dissipate. But I didn't imagine it would until Sinjin was actually standing in front of me, in his usual attire of black on black, with that flirty smile I'd come to know so well. Only then could I assure myself he was okay.

"I can feel him in my veins," Varick whispered, leaning closer to me. The cold of his body pierced my skin, making me shiver. I resisted the urge to pull away because if anything, that's what he wanted me to do. He glanced down at the goose bumps that were now covering my forearm and smiled in sincere amusement. It was obvious that he enjoyed his immense power.

"But—" I was ready to argue that if Sinjin was okay, he'd be sitting around this table probably playing footsie with me while I attempted to rebuff his advances.

"Set aside your concerns," Varick interrupted, shaking his head as if to say the conversation was over.

Hmm . . . jerk though Varick obviously was, his words brought me some sort of relief. The more I thought about the fact that Varick could feel Sinjin in his veins, the better I felt. That meant Sinjin was alive . . . well, as alive as a vampire could be. Yet if Sinjin was alive, why wasn't he here at Varick's side? Was Varick irritated by Sinjin's absence? Would he hurt him?

I glanced at Varick again, trying to decide if anything seemed amiss about him. He definitely appeared to be irritated, but that was probably the result of my interrogation. Besides, Varick seemed perpetually vexed—as if living for hundreds of years gave him little or no patience for dealing with people like me.

"Have you created a list of all of the creatures who are in need of Jolie's talent?" Mathilda suddenly piped up, her eyes traveling around the table. They settled on me and she frowned, probably annoyed at the fact that I'd been carrying on my own conversation with Varick rather than paying attention.

"We are in the process," Rand answered succinctly. "We've filled a ledger with the names of the survivors and are comparing it with the original list of all of the soldiers in our legion, making note of those who cannot be accounted for."

"And we were careful to collect a piece of clothing from everyone so it will be easier for me to bring them back," I added, hoping it might seem like I'd been involved in the conversation all along.

In order for me to reanimate the dead, I have to touch something that belonged to the deceased—either a piece of clothing or something that was in some way connected to the person. Up until now, I had actually only ever reanimated two people. My first was Bella's father, Jack, and that had been a mere accident.

When Bella and Rand were on significantly better terms than they are now, she hired Rand to solve the mystery of who killed her father back in Chicago in 1922. So Rand began searching for a witch powerful enough to help him cast a spell that would re-create the scene of Bella's father's death. That's how he found me.

After he made me an offer I couldn't refuse, we flew to Chicago, to what had once been Bella's father's home. In conducting the spell, I managed not only to find out who had murdered him—his wife—but to reanimate him.

Later, I found out that Bella, upon finding her father alive again, had promptly killed him . . . Yeah, that had been my first hint that she was a complete nut job. Once she knew about my secret talent, she became desperate to control and possess my abilities and would stop at nothing to get what she wanted. She had even kidnapped me; if not for Sinjin, who betrayed her and helped me escape, who knows where I'd be now?

The only other person I'd reanimated was Trent, my werewolf ex. And sometimes I doubt that decision. Well, I shouldn't say that because it isn't nice, but what I can say is that he turned out to be a player in every sense of the word. Although his antics never broke my heart— which firmly belonged to Rand—I wouldn't say I was fond of the werewolf . . . at all.

Are you all right, Jolie? Rand's voice penetrated my thoughts.

I glanced up in surprise to find him looking at Odran, clearly in the midst of another conversation. I've never understood how he could multi-task so well.

Yeah, I'm fine, why?

It looked as if Varick was upsetting you. Perhaps you'd care to sit beside me?

When he looked over at me, I just shook my head and offered him a sincere smile. *I'm okay. Thanks for looking out for me, though.*

He nodded but didn't smile. His gaze was piercing, as if he were reading my mind with just the intensity of his stare.

I would prefer to have you beside me.

I arched a brow, trying to decide if he was flirting with me. *And why is that?*

I do not care for vampires, and besides . . . His voice trailed off, probably because he was trying to pay attention to whatever Odran was saying.

Besides, what? I prompted.

I quite like the way you smell.

I laughed and shook my head as I stood up and walked around the long table, taking the empty seat beside him. I noticed a few people staring at me, probably wondering why I'd suddenly burst out laughing when no one was talking to me, but I couldn't be bothered to care. If Rand wanted to smell me, who was I to stop him? Rand didn't take any notice of me when I settled in next to him, continuing his role of chairing the meeting.

"And what do you propose we do with Bella?" he asked.

Bella was currently being restrained in one of the guest rooms at Pelham Manor. Mathilda and Mercedes had cast a spell that kept her imprisoned, and Rand kept two guards stationed outside her door twenty-four/seven. Overkill anyone?

Before I knew it, the feel of Rand's hand was warm on my thigh. At first he just laid it there, but after a few seconds he began stroking, stopping at my knee and then coming back up.

Ah, so you were really after a cheap thrill? I thought. Although my tone might have sounded level and in control, my heart was pounding through my ears.

His chuckle pealed through my mind. *I hadn't intended to touch you but I can't stop myself.*

Why do I have a feeling this was your plan all along?

Would you prefer I stop?

Hell, no, I didn't want him to stop.

No.

Then stop complaining.

I'm not complaining.

A wide smile overcame him even though he was looking at Trent, whose conversation had something to do with Bella. When Trent saw Rand's bizarre expression, he stopped talking and turned to face Odran, confusion etched in his eyes.

Pay attention to the conversation. I grasped Rand's hand, which was still massaging my thigh. *You're scaring everyone around the table.*

I'm having difficulty focusing on anything but your body.

A shudder vibrated through me at his words, and the errant thought that Mercedes might be overhearing us crossed my mind. But I honestly didn't even care. Instead my entire body was tuned to Rand's hand as it began to inch its way back up my thigh. He squeezed me gently and I nearly jumped out of my seat.

"Aye, we shouldna allow 'er ta live," Odran said, nodding in agreement with Trent's last comment—which, by the sound of it, had something to do with killing Bella. For all I cared, they could have been talking about aliens abducting Bella. No, my only interest was the current program titled "Jolie Is Finally Getting Some Action."

"I don't think we should kill her," Rand argued. I was surprised he was still paying attention.

"She will never be our ally," Varick announced.

"But is that any reason to kill her?" Rand countered.

"I don't think we should kill her either," I concurred in a voice that sounded breathy and hurried. No one glanced at me, though, so I figured the secret that Rand's hand was now at the North Pole was still mine to keep.

"This can be resolved at a later date," Mercedes interrupted. "For now, I believe we should concentrate on rebuilding our army."

Rand nodded and began drumming the fingers of his other hand against the wood table. I noticed that his hand had relaxed and was no longer massaging or squeezing my leg. He was fully focused on the conversation. Bummer, but it had been fun while it lasted.

"Once the ledger of names is confirmed, we can begin

bringing our dead soldiers back," Rand said, offering me a smile.

Mercedes nodded and turned to me. "I will assist you."

Ah, yes, I had momentarily forgotten about the little fact that Mercedes could reanimate the dead—a talent she'd demonstrated when she so artfully brought me back to life. Between the two of us, I hoped the task would be expedited. Even though I hadn't seen the tally, I had a feeling there were many creatures in need of our . . . abilities. And it wasn't like bringing back the dead was easy. It took intense concentration and it sometimes didn't work on the first, second, or even third attempt. So depending on how many dead there were, Mercedes and I were about to be very busy.

"We must rebuild the legion quickly," Mercedes continued, as if she'd been reading my mind. "Jolie's role as Queen will soon require her complete attention."

I could see Rand's lips tighten. "As far as I understand it, Jolie hasn't decided if she wants to be Queen."

"It is her fate," Mercedes said simply, meeting his gaze. Her eyes were just as piercingly defiant.

"I believe the prophetess, Rand," Mathilda said in her bell-like cadence. "The child is gifted, you have known that from the beginning."

Rand nodded. "Yes, Jolie is gifted, and yes, I trust her entirely, but that's not to say I believe in fate. No, I believe in the freedom of choice. As Jolie's protector, I insist she be given the right to choose."

"If it is ordained," Odran started, "it cannoot be denied."

Rand stood up and slapped his palms loudly on the table before him, leaning forward. "This is another subject that won't be resolved today." He paused for a moment or two and then added, "I think we've discussed enough."

At Rand's less-than-subtle indication that the meeting was over, everyone stood and started for the door.

"Jolie, can you stay for a minute?" Rand asked me. As I turned around to face him, he smiled encouragingly, as if to say it would be a pleasant conversation. Hmm, half of me had been hoping I was in trouble—I could use a good old-fashioned spanking over his knees.

I nodded, resuming my place at the table. "Am I in trouble?" I asked with a smile.

He returned it. "It depends. Do you want to be in trouble?"

So he was still flirting with me. That was a good sign. "What's my punishment?"

He chuckled and shook his head, dropping the charade. Instead he approached me and set both his hands on my shoulders, massaging them with his strong fingers. "I wanted to talk to you about when you traveled back to 1878."

I nodded and felt my stomach rise up into my throat. I was suddenly suffused with panic. It was at that moment that I decided what Rand didn't know about us bonding wouldn't hurt him. We weren't bonded now and that was all that mattered. It was better not to rehash the past, better not to tell him I was the reason for his brush with death.

"Where should I start?" I asked with trepidation in my voice.

He stopped massaging my shoulders and took the seat next to me, reaching for my left hand. He looked it over, no doubt taking in the fact that I was still wearing his mother's ring. "You said I gave this ring to you?"

I nodded while fingering the band, then slid it off my finger. I probably shouldn't be wearing it—not when things were still at an impasse between us, or at the very least undecided. "Do you want it back?"

He wrapped his fingers around mine and pushed the

ring back onto my finger. "No," he said, curling my fingers back into my palm. "If anyone should wear it, it's you." I didn't even have time to digest that statement before he was off on another. "And if I gave it to you, it belongs to you now."

"Thanks," I said, feeling heat in my cheeks.

"What was it like traveling to the past and meeting Pelham and me? And Christine?"

Besides Mercedes, Christine had been my only friend.

"It was surreal. At first the only people who were nice to me were Mercedes, Pelham, and Christine."

"And how about me?"

I regarded him with a frown but couldn't keep my smile to myself. "You were less than nice. *Rude, argumentative, and surly* might be a better description."

He chuckled deeply. "But of course, in true Jolie Wilkins fashion, you must have won me over."

I nodded and sighed as I thought about it. I remembered winning him over, remembered how amazing it had felt when we finally admitted our feelings for each other. And how incredible he had felt inside me.

"Yes, I did finally win you over, but it wasn't an easy feat," I said with a laugh that sounded sad even to my ears. "It took a spell from Mathilda for the old you to have the same feelings you have for me today."

He nodded and glanced down at the table before returning his chocolate-brown eyes to me. "Ah, so I fell in love with you, did I?"

Even though I was surprised by his admission, I just nodded because it was the truth. The old Rand had fallen in love with me and it wasn't a false love, spurred on by the convenience of Mathilda's spell—every thought, every feeling Rand bore toward me was genuine, real, based on his feelings for me in the here and now. It was the new Rand that I had to be sure about now. I reached for his face, trailing the soft skin of his temples down to the roughness of his cheek, where the beginnings of a shadow were starting. "Are you in love with me, Rand?"

"Yes, very much so," he answered without hesitation. "But my love for you isn't why I asked you to stay behind. I need to know what happened in 1878, Jolie. Why did I give you my mother's ring? What were the circumstances?"

"Rand—" I swallowed down a huge lump of nervousness. Something that felt like angst began to well in my gut and before I could even fathom what I was doing, I was already doing it. I stared into Rand's eyes and felt the words swirling through my head, felt the chant ricochet through me, recognizing the duplicity in my actions but seemingly unable to do anything about it.

I can't discuss the facts of 1878 with you, Rand. Focus on another topic—ask me about any other subject in the forefront of your mind.

It hadn't even occurred to me that maybe Rand, being the powerful warlock he was, would be immune to my magic, and luckily for me it didn't appear that he was. Instead his eyes took on the same dreamy expression I'd witnessed whenever I used witchcraft to influence someone.

"Do you intend to become Queen?" he interrupted. I felt my entire body deflate with relief, even as guilt started eating me from the feet up. The relief was a mere respite, though, because the subject of whether or not I intended to become Queen was about as welcome as the bonding conversation.

"I don't want to deter you, Jolie, but I want to ensure this is what you want and that you aren't just acting as Mercedes' puppet."

"I . . ." I didn't know what to say.

"Mercedes is very demanding, and I want to make certain someone is looking out for your best interests," Rand finished.

And that was Rand to a T. He was always looking out for my best interests, making sure I was taken care of—that I was safe.

"I don't know what I'll do," I said finally, looking down at my hands where his mother's ring sparkled up at me. I almost felt like I should take it off again—offer it back to him. Because the truth of the matter was that I had no right to wear it.

He nodded. "I want you to make the decision for yourself—not because Mercedes is breathing down your neck or because you feel like you owe it to the creatures of the Underworld. On the other hand, don't deny yourself the title if it's what you truly want."

I glanced up at him, pushing all of the worried thoughts from my mind. "And if the throne was what I wanted, would you support me?"

Rand dropped his gaze and chewed his lip. "You know my thoughts on the subject, Jolie. I cannot abide by any form of monarchy."

"I know," I was quick to respond.

Rand's smile was unexpected and secretive. "Have I ever told you why?"

Hmm, come to think of it, he hadn't. I'd always figured it was just one of those things that made Rand Rand. Sort of like his deep brown eyes and his dimpled smile.

"No, you haven't."

He nodded and, standing, took a few steps away from me, crossing his arms against his chest before turning back to face me again. "In 1870 I was appointed ambassador to the United States by Queen Victoria."

I felt my eyes widen in surprise. "You were?"

Rand chuckled. "I'd already lived a full and colorful life before you came into it, Jolie."

"Go on."

"In my position as ambassador, I spent quite a bit of time with your president at the time, Ulysses Grant."

"Grant as in the Civil War hero?" I asked, my mouth dropping open again.

Rand laughed. "It appears your knowledge of history is quite good. Yes, your Civil War hero." He took a deep breath. "In the three years that I represented British interests where America was concerned, I developed a keen admiration and love for the American way—for the emphasis placed on equality and justice for all men." He sighed, and his gaze settled on the vista outside the window. "I thought perhaps England could adopt some of the American values I had come to believe in, but of course that was entirely impossible due to the fact that my country had always been a monarchy." He turned to face me again, and there was fire in his eyes. "But when I realized the Underworld didn't have to follow the path of monarchy, my hopes for a republic were born. And I've never given up on my beliefs that the society of Underworld creatures should be governed by and unto themselves, not overlorded by a monarch."

I nodded and sighed. His feelings were obviously carved in stone. Crap and a half. "So if I do become Queen, things will be over between us?"

"I didn't say that."

But he didn't have to. Realistically, how could he love me and be with me if he didn't condone my day job? It would tear us apart; I could see it as clearly as if I were peering into a crystal ball.

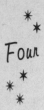

Four

"Jolie?" Rand's voice accompanied a strong rap on my door.

I stood up from my position of sloth on the couch and turned down the volume of the television. The clock above the TV announced it was eleven thirty at night. Wondering why he could possibly be visiting so late, I pulled open the door and found him before me, dressed in loose-fitting dark jeans and a white T-shirt that glowed in the rays of moonlight behind him.

"Is everything okay?" I asked.

"Yes, yes," he said dismissively and eyed the inside of my house with what appeared to be longing.

"Do you want to come in?" I held the door open wide and stepped aside.

"If you aren't otherwise engaged, yes please."

"I'm not."

He walked inside and eyed the surroundings of my house as if he hadn't seen it before, as if this was the first time he'd ever viewed what once was the butler's quarters of Pelham Manor. I closed the door behind us.

"I couldn't sleep and found nothing entertaining on the telly," he started and ran an agitated hand through his hair that told me he was uncomfortable or, at the very least, nervous. What he had to be nervous about was anyone's guess. But really, that was just Rand. He could never be described as predictable.

"Oh," I said, not really knowing what else to say.

"I, uh, thought perhaps you might like some company."

I shrugged, attempting to give the idea that I was cool, calm, and in control of my emotions when the truth of the matter was that I could think of nothing more appealing. "Sure."

Secretly I wondered if he might resume the last conversation we'd had—about what would happen between us should I become Queen. Of course it wasn't a conversation I wanted anything to do with, so it wasn't like I was about to bring it up. And hopefully neither would he. I just wasn't in the mood for a long-winded and difficult discussion.

"I wondered if perhaps you might be interested in a magic lesson?"

"Now?" I asked, my tone echoing my surprise.

Rand chuckled, a deep, harmonious sound. In fact, I never tired of Rand's laugh—it was one of those sounds I couldn't help but love.

"Tonight is a waning crescent moon," he started.

"Huh?"

He laughed again. "When the moon enters the waning crescent lunar phase, just prior to becoming a new moon, the impetus for magic is at its highest."

I glanced outside my window at the sliver of moon, which looked more like the white top of a French-manicured fingernail. "That sounds like an important detail," I said, glancing back at my warlock. "How come I'm just learning it now?"

Rand shrugged. "It's taken me over one hundred years to amass all the knowledge I have today, and yet I'm still a novice."

"Great. I have a long-ass time to look forward to then."

Rand cocked a brow and just smiled.

"So what lesson am I in for tonight?"

"Astral projection."

"Astral what?" I asked and eyed him suspiciously. I couldn't exactly say I was in the mood for a magic lesson. Wasn't there something to be said for just chilling on the couch and watching *Come Dine with Me*? Throw a few makeout sessions in there and it would prove to be the best evening I'd had all week.

"Yes, astral projection."

"I'm hardly dressed for it," I said, glancing down at my Victoria's Secret cotton PJ pants and my oversized pink sweatshirt. I didn't even have on any shoes.

Rand nodded and any nervousness he'd had before was gone. In its place was a cool assurance. He took a few steps toward me until my body was maybe a foot from his. Then he brought each of his hands to my shoulders and smiled down at me.

"Astral projection can only be successfully attempted during the waning and waxing crescent phases of the moon, so why not take advantage of the opportunity nature has presented us with?"

I sighed. "Want to explain what it is first?"

He nodded but didn't remove his hands from my shoulders. Instead he tightened his hold and wore a funny little smile, like he was getting some sort of kick out of this whole thing. "Astral projection has been associated with out-of-body experiences, near-death experiences, and the afterlife."

"Great," I said with a frown. "That all sounds really reassuring."

His smile deepened. "It's the separation of the soul from the physical, corporeal body."

I gulped. "This is sounding worse by the minute."

He brought his finger to my face and traced from my temple down my cheek to my jawline. I felt my breathing increase as my heart began to pound.

"I would never endanger you, you realize that, Jolie?" His voice was low, gruff.

My own voice had packed up and moved out so I just nodded dumbly.

"Your skin is so soft," he whispered, and before I could worry about separating my soul from my physical body or the wax-on, wax-off cycle of the moon, his lips were on mine. I closed my eyes and relished the feel and taste of him. His lips were so incredibly full and soft. He gripped my neck and pulled me into him as his tongue breached the closure of my lips.

He pulled away and gazed down at me with a serene expression. "I apologize."

"Um, what?"

He chuckled. "For derailing your lesson."

Lesson? What lesson? "Oh, it's okay."

He pulled away from me with a smirk and shook his head; why, I wasn't sure. Then he glanced down at my feet.

"Should I put on some shoes?"

"No, we aren't leaving your house."

Out-of-body experience, separation of the soul from the corporeal body . . . yeah, I guess the fact that we wouldn't be leaving the house made sense. I mean, it was all about soul travel. Hmm, speaking of soul travel, I had to wonder if it was possible for one to astrally project oneself to the grocery store?

"So start 'splainin', Lucy," I said with a smile.

Rand just responded with a cockeyed expression that told me he wasn't familiar with *I Love Lucy*. Still, he didn't seem to be very concerned; he just approached the window and gazed at the moon.

"You start by focusing on the moon," he said as I

moved up next to him so as not to appear the inattentive student. "Allow the magic to penetrate you, soak in the lunar rays, and then allow yourself to project."

While his directions didn't exactly answer the myriad questions floating through my head, I kept my concerns to myself and simply watched as he closed his eyes. There wasn't any sort of expression on his incredibly handsome face. Instead he looked like he was meditating—the square lines of his jaw relaxed and tranquil.

There was no indication that anything of a magical nature was happening but, with regard to the Underworld, looks usually were deceiving. Continuing to study Rand, I almost missed the reflection of something shimmery and white from out of the corner of my eye. I glanced outside and could faintly detect the outline of a man as he walked among the trees. There was a whitish glow about him; inside the glowing outline, his body was transparent, like a ghost.

I glanced back at Rand and found he looked exactly the same as he had—like he was still sound asleep. Before I had the chance to look out the window again at our ghostly visitor, Rand took a deep breath and opened his eyes. Then he released his breath and smiled.

"Did you see me?"

I nodded. "You looked like a ghost."

"Astral projection."

"And let me guess, now it's my turn?"

He chuckled. "Quite astute of you, Jolie."

I sighed and turned squarely in front of the window in the hope that I could fully maximize my ability to soak in the lunar rays. I needed all the help I could get.

"Close your eyes," Rand said in a soft voice. I did as I was told and felt his breath against my cheek; my skin responded with goose bumps. "Feel the magic soak into you, Jolie, allow the power of the moon inside you."

He lifted the curtain of my hair from my neck. That, combined with his announcement that I should let the moon "inside me," was enough for me to demand that we forget all this projection stuff in favor of some sex stuff. But I managed to maintain my cool. Point for me.

I focused on the darkness of my eyelids and imagined the light and magic of the lunar rays soaking into me, filling me up with their powerful tide.

"Okay," I whispered.

Rand's breath was now on my neck. I could feel his body as he moved closer to me, pulling me backward and into his arms.

"Allow yourself to walk through the trees. Imagine smelling the crisp air outside, feeling the soil beneath your toes, the chill of the wind."

I concentrated, imagined the things he'd just envisioned for me, and it felt as if I were suddenly weightless—merely a thought, floating through space and time. It was a lightness I've never experienced before—I was no longer subject to gravity. Instead I was like the air itself. I opened my eyes and found myself outside. I could feel the branches and leaves on the forest floor. The rays of the moon seemed to embrace me in an otherworldly hug.

"Come back to me, Jolie."

Rand's voice sounded far off, almost like he was whispering into the wind.

"Pull yourself back in."

I nodded and glanced up at the moon again, telling the great white goddess that I needed to return to my body. My time here was up.

And as suddenly as if I'd been hit by a truck, that light-headed, weightless feeling was ripped away from me. In its place I felt heavy, dense. My knees buckled at the same time that Rand caught me with a chuckle. I opened my eyes and with my heart beating frantically in my chest, glanced around my living room.

"Did I do it?"

"Yes, you did," Rand answered. He sounded proud.

I held on to him and allowed my head to rest against his chest as my heartbeat calmed. I still felt wobbly, though, like a newborn giraffe.

"You never stop amazing me." His voice was soft as he kissed the top of my head. "Your magic, Jolie, is incredibly strong. I sometimes forget how powerful you truly are."

But I didn't want to hear how powerful I was. All I wanted was to lose myself in the feel of Rand's arms around me, in the way he smelled of spice and something deeply masculine. I didn't say anything but tightened my arms around him, wishing this moment would never end.

Five

Even though I put up a good fight, in the end I didn't fly to Australia to retrieve Christa. Mercedes kept insisting that it was just too risky for the Queen of the Underworld to be flying around the globe in these "uncertain times." She may have perceived the times as uncertain, but I was more than certain this Queen business was seriously cramping my style.

I would have continued to argue my case for retrieving Christa if her boyfriend, John, hadn't happily offered to take the task upon himself. And after talking to him, I sensed that he'd also prefer to do it alone. And I didn't blame him—if I'd been separated from Rand for more than two weeks, I'd also prefer some one-on-one time. Pun most definitely intended.

Either way, Christa was safe and sound and back at Pelham Manor. Although, she wasn't too thrilled with the fact that I had charmed her into traveling to Australia on her own.

"I had to do it, Chris," I said with a hopeful smile.

It was early evening and we were sitting on my couch in the living room of my small house—about two miles from Pelham Manor. It might seem strange that Christa lived in Rand's home and I didn't (but really, what counts as strange when we're talking about witches, vampires, and werewolves?). Anyway, when Christa and

I first moved to Alnwick, England, to live with Rand (due to the fact that Rand said I needed protection once I'd been introduced to the Underworld, and he could offer said protection), we both lived alongside of him in Pelham Manor. But as emotions between Rand and me got more confused and even more frustrating, I decided I needed my own space, so I moved out. Christa had continued to occupy Pelham Manor, employed as Rand's assistant. And as for jealousy? It actually wasn't an arrangement that bothered me at all, mainly because Christa had a boyfriend and Rand had put a spell on her that made her feel only brotherly feelings toward him.

So tonight was girls' night. I'd given express instructions to everyone to leave us alone. Anyone or anything with testosterone was most definitely not invited. No, tonight was going to be about reconnecting with the one person who was closer to me than anyone on the planet, and we had lots to catch up on.

"It wasn't fun sightseeing by myself," Christa whined, her lower lip protruding in a pout as my cat, Plum, jumped off my lap and sashayed over to her, rubbing up against her and begging for a chin scratch. "You know I hate being by myself."

If John hadn't told her I was supposed to be her tour guide in Australia but had chosen to battle Bella's legion instead, she never would have found fault with the situation. Yes, I believed in honesty being the best policy and all of those other poignant idioms, but come on, John could have thrown me a bone on this one . . .

"Well, to make up for it, I have a lot to tell you," I offered and then paused, hoping Christa would go for the bait. If there was anything Christa loved, it was gossip.

She pulled the cork from our second bottle of wine—this one a Shiraz—and beamed a grin that told me all of my transgressions were forgiven. "Okay, that does make it better. Shoot."

So I did. I told her about how I'd fought in the battle, and most important, how I'd killed the vampire Ryder, which had been one of my prime motives for joining the fight in the first place. Ryder was someone who just had to be killed. Not only had he betrayed Rand by pretending to be on our side, but he'd also kidnapped me and taken me to Bella, aka the Wicked Witch of the West. And that wasn't his last or even his least offense—after kidnapping me, he'd fed on me, nearly draining me, and had then come even closer to raping me.

Needless to say, when I delivered the fatal blow and Ryder morphed into ashes at my feet, relief became my constant companion. That is, until all of this business of being appointed Queen was thrust upon me.

"Wow," Christa said, shaking her head in wonderment before her smile vanished and was replaced by a curious expression. "But I thought your magic was useless against vampires?"

I nodded. "It is, but . . ." I wasn't sure how to tell her the next part because it was top secret and, therefore, taboo. After another few seconds of wondering how to phrase it while watching Christa start to fidget, I finally blurted out: "I drank Sinjin's blood."

Drinking the blood of a master vampire, such as Sinjin Sinclair's, had enabled me to even the odds when I battled Ryder. Without Sinjin's blood, I would have been defenseless against Ryder's extreme strength and speed. I knew this from past experience—prior to killing Ryder, the bastard had been teaching me self-defense, and to say I was helpless to protect myself against his attacks would have been an understatement.

"Sinjin let you drink his blood?" Christa asked in a tone of utter disbelief, her mouth open in a perfect O.

"Yes," I answered and suddenly worried Christa might

blab this information. She did have a big mouth. But, apparently, so did I. "You can't tell anyone. It has to remain confidential. You can't even tell John." As a master vampire, Sinjin never should have allowed anyone to drink his blood. It still surprised me that he'd awarded me such a privilege. Truthfully, without Sinjin's blood, I never could have killed Ryder, because Christa was right—my magic was effective on everyone in the paranormal community except for vamps.

"Sinjin must be in love with you." Christa shook her head, apparently still shocked by the news.

"No, he isn't," I replied quickly as I contemplated the idea of Sinjin being in love with anyone, me included. Love or any emotional attachment seemed inappropriate to the six-hundred-year-old vampire. I couldn't imagine him dropping his guard long enough to love someone. He was too concerned with his own well-being to ever allow himself the weak dependence of affection.

"Sounds like love to me. What would you call it?"

I shook my head. I didn't know what I'd call it, but definitely not love.

"Maybe just curiosity," I said, thinking that was probably the best description. Even though Sinjin was a complete mystery and I constantly found myself second-guessing his motives, the one thing I did know about him was that he was motivated by his own sense of importance. He seemed to enjoy playing God—allowing circumstances to unfold while he stood back and watched like an unconcerned spectator. But if the situation ever became too heated or turned in a direction that didn't suit his plans, he'd bring his thumb down and squash whoever or whatever happened to offend him, and he'd do it with the same cool, calm countenance in which he did all things.

"Where is Sinjin, anyway?" Christa asked while pouring herself another glass of wine. She glanced up at me and held up the bottle in a charade of *Want more?*

I shook my head as I returned to the whereabouts of my favorite vampire. Worry began gnawing away at my stomach again. "No one knows where he is."

"Did he die in the battle?"

"No." I then explained how Varick was able to feel Sinjin in his veins, which made me believe he was unscathed. Before I knew it, I'd spilled my guts about time-traveling back to 1878, Mercedes, falling in love with Rand, and, finally, how I'd been chosen to be Queen.

"So Rand doesn't want you to be Queen?" Christa asked, her left eye beginning to droop like it always did whenever she got drunk.

"No," I said, settling my gaze on a willow tree that was swaying outside my living room window, its leafy foliage dancing almost playfully. "He doesn't believe in monarchy, he's made that much crystal clear."

"He'll have to come around," Christa said with a smile before gulping the last drops of her wine and wiping her forearm against her lips. "I mean, if the prophetess exists, which she obviously does, and she says you're supposed to be Queen, Rand sort of has to get on board, you know?"

I nodded, even though I knew it wasn't that simple. "Yeah, but you know how Rand is. If he doesn't believe in something, he won't support it."

"You gotta do what's right for you, Jules." Christa patted my hand consolingly. The cat apparently became irritated, because she hopped off Christa's lap, plodded into her cat house, and fell back to sleep.

"You can't let other people hold you back," Christa finished. Her compassionate expression coupled with the facts that I was holding on to an empty glass of wine and there were two empty wine bottles on my coffee table made me feel like I was on the receiving end of an Alcoholics Anonymous intervention.

"But!"

"It sounds like you're meant to be Queen, Jules," Christa interrupted. "This is your calling."

"What if it's a mistake, Chris?" I asked, placing my empty glass on the side table. "What if Mercedes has the wrong person? What if I'm not really meant to be Queen?"

Christa shook her head. "I'll bet the prophetess made sure you were the right person before she announced it to everyone. I mean, think of what a disaster it would be if she realized you were a total loser or something? Besides, one of the things I learned in Australia is that when something feels right, you just have to go for it."

I couldn't help but smile. And Christa did have a good point—I couldn't imagine Mercedes making a mistake on anything, let alone something this huge. "You learned that in Australia?"

She nodded. "Yeah, I was walking down Market Street in Sydney just doing my own thing and minding my own business"—she eyed me with an expression that implied, *Since you left me on my own*—"and I was suddenly overcome by this crazy feeling that I should glance over my shoulder. So I did, and would you believe it, I saw the cutest pair of red stilettos right there in a shop window. You know how I've been looking for a pair of red ones forever?" I nodded just to placate her and she continued. "Yeah, well, now I own a pair."

"Seriously, Chris?" I asked incredulously. "You're comparing a pair of shoes to me being Queen?"

She frowned and stuck her tongue out at me. "I'm just using the stilettos as an example, Jules. You have to be ready for whatever life throws your way. When you don't take risks, you don't find red stilettos."

I laughed and shook my head at the absurdity of this

whole conversation. If only my life could be as simple as buying a pair of shoes. "You have a very unusual way of looking at things."

"I'm an unusual girl," she said with a candid smile, her eyelid's droop now increased by another thirty degrees. "What were we talking about again?" she asked, reaching for a third bottle of wine. "Ah, I remember. So Rand is having a little conniption about the thought of you being Queen?"

"No, not so far," I said and sighed as I thought about Rand's general discouragement about the whole Queen bit. He hadn't asked me not to accept the role, but I knew that's what he wanted. "In fact, I haven't seen him at all yesterday or today."

It had been two days since our little discussion in his dining room and in true Rand form, he'd vanished for a couple of days, probably tending to the legions stationed at Pelham Manor. Hopefully he wasn't just avoiding me. "So, what, is he pissed again? He always seems to disappear when he's mad at you," Christa slurred.

"No, I think this time he's honestly busy."

Christa nodded and took a sip of her nth glass of wine, arching her eyebrows at the bottle in what appeared to be silent appreciation. She poured the remaining wine from the bottle into my glass and handed it to me. "What was he like back in the, what was it, sixteen hundreds?"

"Um . . ." I tried to hold back a giggle but failed miserably. "Rand wasn't alive in the sixteen hundreds, Chris."

"Whatever." She waved me away. "The eighteen hundreds, then. What's the difference?"

"Aside from the Industrial Revolution, you mean?" I replied with a smile.

"Blah, what year was it that you met Rand?"

"Eighteen seventy-eight," I answered and then took a

second to think about what Rand had been like back then. "He was wonderful," I finally admitted, sighing. "He didn't trust me at first, but once we got past that, he was amazing, Chris. He allowed himself to love me and he even asked me to marry him."

"He asked you to marry him?" she squealed. "So are you engaged or did you actually get married?"

I shook my head and suddenly felt sick—I wasn't sure if it was from the thought that I missed out on marrying the love of my life or if all the wine was finally making a statement in my gut. I leaned back against the couch and closed my eyes. "No, I mean, I said yes, but he knew I'd have to return to my own time. He just made me promise that he and I would be together again in the here and now."

"But you aren't?"

I sat up straight again and opened my eyes, not feeling any better. "No."

She shook her head and offered me an expression of annoyance—like it was my fault that Rand and I weren't together. "So you need to make it happen—to keep your word to . . . ancient Rand."

"Ancient Rand," I repeated with a laugh before returning my thoughts to the subject at hand. "It's not as easy as it sounds."

"Rand will get over this whole Queen thing. I mean, otherwise, off with his head, right?"

"There's a lot more to it than that." I took a deep breath. "Remember when I told you that Rand had bonded with a witch in his past?"

She nodded and glanced at the empty bottle of wine, then started exploring the perimeter of my living room with her eyes, probably in search of more bottles. Not finding any, she faced me again with a sigh before apparently remembering that I'd asked her a question. "Yeah, and her death nearly killed him?"

I nodded but didn't say anything for a few seconds, not really sure how to say what I needed to. "That was me, Chris."

"What was you?"

"The witch he bonded with."

She looked perplexed. "How can that be? You aren't dead." Then her face paled. "Oh my God, are you dead, Jules? Did you die in the battle?" She stood up and gawked at me. "Are you a ghost?"

"No." I shook my head.

"Because if you are a ghost, I don't think I can handle that. I've been afraid of ghosts my whole life."

"No, Chris, I'm not a ghost." I glanced up at her and frowned; the color still hadn't returned to her face. "I'm not dead, Chris! Jeez."

She sat back down next to me, but at the far end of the sofa. "Well, what did you expect me to think?"

"I didn't expect that!" I announced before returning to my story. "The woman Rand bonded with never died—she just time-traveled."

It took her a second to compute the meaning of my sentence—I think she was still stuck on the ghost thing, and the haze of alcohol wasn't helping. Once my words sank in, she stared at me in total shock.

"No freakin' way, Jules," she said, shaking her head at how crazy this whole situation was. "Rand bonded with you!"

"Bingo."

"So what did Rand think about that? The look on his face must have been priceless."

I sighed again and couldn't escape the feeling of guilt that immediately descended upon me. "That's the other part of the story . . . I haven't told him yet."

"What?" she squealed. "What do you mean, you haven't told him yet? That should have been the first thing you said." Then she stood up and faced the wall, her arms extended before her until she looked like she was about to deliver Hamlet's soliloquy. "Um, hi, I'm back from time-traveling the world, and by the way, you and me got it on like Donkey Kong and I was the chick you bonded with, capiche?"

She looked at me while I clapped. Well, it wasn't "To Be or Not to Be" but it was a close second. "Got it on like Donkey Kong?"

"Well, you did, didn't you?" she asked as she eyed me approvingly. If there was one subject besides gossip that Christa loved discussing, it was sex. And due to the fact that my sex life had been anything but interesting, she had to be eating this up.

I nodded as thoughts of sex with Rand infiltrated my head. "Yeah, we did, and it was amazing."

"And it can be amazing again, Jules. You just have to tell him the truth."

I nodded but it was unconvincing. "I've decided not to tell him."

"Why?"

"Because I think it's better that he doesn't know—I mean, it's not like we're bonded anymore . . . and, besides, I think the news could really hurt him."

She shook her head. Suddenly noticing that my glass of wine was still full, she reached for it, the expression on her face saying she needed it. "Why would bonding with you upset him? It just means you're meant to be together. That's like a better love story than *The Princess Bride*." *The Princess Bride* just happened to be Christa's favorite movie of all time, so she was really saying something. "Jules, that is seriously romantic."

Look out Romeo and Juliet, Tristan and Isolde, Mr. Darcy and Elizabeth Bennet, because here come Rand and Jolie. Somehow I just wasn't feeling it.

"Well, I guess Rand could take it well," I began, but I couldn't say I believed it. It was really more of a concession to Christa. "Or he could just freak out when he realizes that he nearly died because of me."

She was quiet for a second or two. "Hmm, I hadn't thought of that angle." Silence for a few more seconds. "But you didn't know you were going to bond with him, right?"

"It crossed my mind."

"But as soon as you saw his hot, naked bod, you must have been like *Bond, what bond? Oh, you mean bondage?*"

I laughed, suddenly feeling so grateful. Yes, Christa had her shortcomings, but she was the greatest friend in the world and I loved her. "Yeah, it went something like that."

She nodded and swigged the last of her wine, er my wine, before facing me again blankly. Then a smile spread across her lips. "Well, when you tell him, just leave out the part about you guessing you two might bond. Just make it sound like it totally took you by surprise and you never expected it."

"I don't know, Chris, I think it's better to just avoid the whole thing . . ."

"You're just going to have to spit it out, Jules. The longer you hold it in, the more upset he's liable to get because he'll want to know why you didn't tell him sooner."

I woke up and I wasn't sure why. It wasn't like I'd been having a nightmare. I opened my eyes and blinked a few times, trying to adjust them to the light of the yellow moon that was beaming through my bedroom window, interrupting the monotonous dark of night. I loved the feel of the cold air as it tried to breach the warmth of my covers.

The mischievous breeze ruffled my curtains, allowing them to billow out in a sensuous dance. Finding the visual reassuring, I started to close my eyes again. But something in my peripheral vision stopped me. There was a darkness at the far end of the room—a blackness that hinted of something more sinister than just night. I opened my eyes in alarm as I watched the darkness that was too dark twitch.

I bolted upright and didn't have time to scream before I felt a cold swish disrupt the air. Then within a split second he was directly in front of me—a speed that characterized his race. Just as suddenly the fear pounding through me faltered and was replaced by a calming ocean of relief.

"It is true, then," he said in a hoarse voice, his English accent thicker than I remembered it.

"Sinjin," I answered, and before I could even fathom what was happening, the vampire's mouth was on mine, his arms around my shoulders. His smell, which was somewhere between the clean scent of soap and the spice of an exotic aftershave, hit me like a truck. Memories of another kiss we shared while en route to Culloden Battlefield in Scotland hijacked my mind.

I cared for Sinjin—it was as obvious as the fact that I was finding it difficult to pull away from his embrace. But I had to pull away because even though there was a part of me that could recognize my attraction to Sinjin, kissing him didn't feel right—not after what I'd been through with Rand.

I pulled away and smiled up at him somewhat nervously as a flood of emotions welled up within me, threatening to choke me. Sinjin was okay. The relief almost made me want to cry—I wanted to reach out and touch him, run my fingers down the velvet perfection of his skin, but I wouldn't allow myself.

"You are alive," he said while continuing to stare at me, his hands still on my shoulders. I gently escaped from his hold and pushed the duvet back as I stood up, wrapping my arms around myself. I was dressed in a long-sleeved Victoria's Secret nightshirt that ended at my knees. Even though my nightshirt wasn't terribly revealing (okay, I was showing a little leg), Sinjin beheld me with his wolfish stare from head to toe, making me feel as if I was as naked as the day I was born.

Then he smiled and it was a smile I remembered too well—a smile that could only characterize Sinjin—something racy and bold, yet secretive. "I could not believe you were alive though I felt your very life blood pulsing within me."

Sinjin had drunk my blood months before when I was attacked by a werewolf and had nearly become hairy, myself. He sucked the poison from the wound and, while saving me from becoming lupine, he'd also given me about ten orgasms . . . Anyway, owing to the fact that he'd swallowed my blood, he could track me.

I shrugged, not knowing what to say. I didn't know if I should wrap my arms around him and tell him how worried I'd been and how incredibly happy I was to know he was okay. In the end, because our relationship was purely platonic, I opted for a more casual response.

"Yep, I'm alive," I confirmed, not knowing what else to add. Truth be told, I was still reeling from the fact that Sinjin was in my room and we'd just shared a very . . . good kiss.

"I watched your life end," he said in a hollow voice that sounded pained.

"It did end." At Sinjin's curious expression, I continued, "The prophetess brought me back to life."

In an instant his attention was riveted. "The prophetess, you say?"

I nodded, wondering why the prophetess held such interest for him—she always had. In fact, prior to the battle with Bella, Sinjin had been teaching me how to take on Ryder. In return, he only asked that I attempt to locate the prophetess telepathically. Of course, I hadn't been successful at the time because she'd been stuck in 1878.

"What happened to you, Sinjin?"

"I am more interested in what happened to you, poppet. I have relived your death too many times—until I thought perhaps I would go mad."

I shook my head, dismissing Sinjin's flair for the dramatic. What I wanted to know was why the hell he'd just vanished like that. I could remember it like it was yesterday—Sinjin standing with his back to the battlefield—the tightness of his lips and the glossiness of his eyes.

"And thanks, by the way, for not doing a damn thing when I died."

"What would you have suggested I do?" he demanded with narrowed eyes, his muscular arms wrapped across his chest.

I shrugged. "I don't know—you seemed to have some tricks up your sleeve when that wolf attacked me."

He nodded and glanced down for a second or two before his ice-blue gaze met mine again. His eyes weren't quite so narrowed and his jaw had relaxed. "You were much closer to the gates of heaven, love, than you were when the wolf attacked."

"You could have done something," I insisted even though I didn't entirely believe my own words.

He swallowed and his eyes suddenly steeled again. "All that was left to me was turning you into one of my own kind, and that is a choice I could never make." He turned away from me and faced the window, allowing me to appreciate the expanse of his shoulders and back. His shoulders were broad and then tapered into an athletic waist and a tight rear that topped an incredibly long pair of legs. Sinjin was very tall—probably six-five or thereabouts. And as I'd come to expect, he was clothed entirely in black—a black sweater with a black undershirt and black slacks.

He turned toward me again and I couldn't help but swallow, gulping down the thoughts of how incredibly beautiful he was.

"I would never condemn you to live this way," he whispered.

Surprise echoed through me. If anything, I would have thought Sinjin would have no problem turning me or anyone else into one of his kind. He seemed to parade his vampire status around as if it was the be-all, end-all in the Underworld community—like driving the newest, coolest car in town.

"Where have you been, Sinjin?" I asked, no longer feeling comfortable with the direction this conversation was headed.

"Have you been worried about me, pet?" His tone reminded me of the old Sinjin, the joking and never serious, but seriously sexy, Sinjin.

"Yeah, I have," I said without a trace of humor. "I've been wondering what the hell happened to you. Where have you been?" I repeated.

He nodded but didn't say anything for a few seconds. "I have been everywhere and I have been nowhere, love."

"Don't screw around with me," I snapped. "Where, specifically?"

"I have been traveling, poppet. You could say I have been doing some soul searching."

"And is Varick going to be upset with you?" I asked, remembering how irritated Varick had seemed the other evening. I didn't know if there was something overly protective about me but for some reason I did tend to be a mother hen where Sinjin was concerned.

"I care not, love." He approached the window, his long and slender physique highlighted by the moon. "I

understand congratulations are in order?" he asked,
blinding me with his incredibly charming smile.

"Congratulations?" I repeated. At my bewildered expression, he merely bowed slightly, so formally that I felt
like I was back in 1878.

"You are Queen, as I understand?" he asked, standing
up straight again.

"Well, I haven't exactly . . . ," I started, about to argue
the point that I hadn't abandoned myself to my apparent calling.

"I am your loyal and faithful subject, my Queen, to do
with as you please."

And the way he said it dripped with sensuality.

"Thanks," I said, but wasn't sure I meant it.

Six

Mercedes Berg. The prophetess . . .

It's almost as if I can see her power emanating from the very letters of her name.

I can't help but think back to the day of the battle, when Gwynn ran her blade into my gut and then I blinked and found myself in the middle of a snowbank and was like WTF *just happened? It was so cold, I nearly froze to death and would have if it hadn't been for Mercedes. She was the one who dragged me in from the snow. Of course, she knew I was coming all along since she was the one responsible for bringing me there in the first place, but I guess I still owed her gratitude for preventing me from becoming a Jolie Popsicle.*

At the time, I sure as hell didn't regard the scullery maid with the beautiful green eyes as anything extraordinary. Of course, I had to wonder when she lifted me over her shoulder and carried me into the house like she was some sort of woman wrestler souped up on steroids. And if that wasn't enough, she was also able to restore my frostbitten toes to their former glory just by wrapping her hands around them. So the clues had been there; I just hadn't possessed my full faculties to really add everything up. (I mean, I had been on the brink of a very cold death. Who can really blame me for not paying much attention to anything else?) And even if I had added everything up, I would never in a million years have reached the conclusion that I'd just met the prophetess.

A few months ago I wasn't even convinced the prophetess was real. She was more like an urban legend that everyone halfheartedly believed in, some more than others. Any disbelief stemmed from the fact that pretty much no one could boast that they'd ever set eyes on the prophetess, until now.

Sure, Bella has always been convinced that the prophetess exists. Looking back on it now, I'm convinced Mercedes was the reason Bella wanted me on her side to begin with—so I could reanimate the prophetess and Bella could benefit from her power. As a matter of fact, Bella forced me to try to reanimate some old woman whom she believed to be the prophetess, but of course, the old woman wasn't.

Nope, Mercedes Berg is the prophetess. And even though she's this omniscient being, I can't say I completely trust her. It's not as though she's ever done anything that would make me not want to trust her, it's just that with all-powerful beings, you can't help but wonder what their deal is. I keep asking myself if Mercedes really exists merely for the good of our society. Couldn't it be possible that she falls victim to the same vices we all do—fame, power, and greed, to name just a few? What does Mercedes get out of making sure I unite all the creatures of the Underworld and become their Queen? Maybe it's just a sign of my sinful humanity that I'm even doubting her in the first place.

Truth be told, Mercedes worries me—her power is so extreme, no one really seems to know how strong or how powerful she truly is. And I believe Rand questions her for the same reasons. I guess I shouldn't doubt her, since she's never done anything other than insist I'm the

savior of our kind. Most people would probably be in-
credibly grateful to her. Just call me an ingrate I guess.

And speaking of this whole savior stuff, Savior is a
really big title to wear. And so, for that matter, is Queen.
Really, if Rand would just stop playing the part of revo-
lutionary, he'd make the perfect King. He's kind, honest,
and just. What more could you want in a King? Oh, and
he's incredibly hot. Hmm, and if I married him, that
would make me Queen by default. Wonder if Mercedes
would go for that . . .

Who am I kidding? Rand would no sooner become
King than befriend Sinjin. So where does that leave me?
The same place I'm always left when it comes to this
subject—square one. And square one is getting old fast.
Regardless, Mercedes seems to think I've accepted my
fate as Queen because she keeps going on and on about
my lessons and when I'll be Queen this and when I'll be
Queen that.

I just have this gut feeling that if I do follow my "call-
ing" and become Queen, I'll lose Rand. And that's a big
gamble to take.

I opened my front door, shivered in the night wind,
and beeped my remote, unlocking the doors of my silver
Range Rover Freelander. The SUV had been a gift from
Rand after my relocation to England.

But back to my present mission. There was lots of important stuff I needed to discuss with Rand—chiefly,
when to start reanimating our legion. It seemed like it
was taking Rand an eon to compile his list of the deceased. Really, I was itching to get started—to be able to
give back to the soldiers who had given their lives for
our cause.

I drove the two miles to Pelham Manor in silence.
Once I arrived, I didn't make any motion to undo my
seat belt; I just sat there instead, staring up at the stone

edifice. I almost felt intimidated by the ancient walls. I turned off the headlights and melted into the darkness, shivering despite myself. I stepped outside to face the wide stone staircase that graced the front of Rand's majestic home, leading to a pair of dark, heavy, wooden doors.

With the weight of the Underworld on my shoulders, I trudged up the stone steps and rang the doorbell. A few seconds later the door flew open and Christa appeared in her cowboy-and-Indian PJs, a pint of ice cream in one hand and a spoon in the other.

"Hi, Chris," I said in a somewhat dejected tone.

"Hi, Jules, what's up?" She rammed her spoon into the hard ice cream and seemed to wrestle with it before a smile of victory lit up her mouth, which she then opened wide to make room for the heaping spoonful.

"I came to see Rand," I said as I walked in through the open door.

She nodded but said nothing as she spooned another heaping bite of what looked like chocolate ice cream with red cherries and hunks of fudge into her mouth. There was probably a third left. "He's outside trying to finalize the list of dead guys," she said, not bothering to swallow first.

"Is the list almost ready, then?"

She shrugged and dug in for another mouthful. "I don't know but hot damn, it seems like it's taking forever."

She didn't wait for my response but turned around and headed down the hall to the kitchen, which led to the back gardens of Pelham Manor. I couldn't help but glance around Rand's house, wondering if anything had changed since I'd moved out. Everything seemed to be in the exact same place. I wasn't sure why, but for some reason that little familiarity made me happy.

Even though the outside of Pelham Manor boasted its

seventeenth-century beginnings, the inside was the epitome of modernity. A large black leather sofa dominated
the living room, which had oriental rugs on the floor
and abstract oil paintings on the walls. But the most
outstanding centerpiece of the room, and the feature
most commented on, was Rand's fireplace, which was
easily as tall as I am. What I loved most about Pelham
Manor, though, wasn't the priceless art or the ginor-
mous fireplace, but the way it smelled—it shared the
same clean spiciness that put me in mind of Rand.

"Did you hear Sinjin is back?" I asked, in an effort to
force myself to think of another subject.

Christa glanced over at me in surprise, pausing only
momentarily before she dived back in again, looking
like an archaeologist chipping away at a fossil. She'd
probably come across a nut.

"Where did you see him?"

I knew my answer was going to sound bad but there
really wasn't any way around it. "He showed up in my
house last night."

She nodded, not daring to pry her attention from the
excavation of an almond. "Did you get it on?"

I just shook my head—I knew that would be the first
thought to cross her mind. "You seriously think about
sex way too much."

She freed the almond and spooned it into her mouth,
smiling at me as she did so. "And you think about sex
way too little."

I wasn't sure if that was true but I also wasn't in the
mood to argue. Instead I stayed silent and followed her
through the hall and into the kitchen.

"So where the hell has Sinjin been?" she asked, dropping the empty ice-cream container in the trash can on
the way to the back door. How Christa could eat the
way she did and yet manage to keep her awesome figure
was beyond me. I teetered on the line between "athletic"

and "could stand to lose five pounds"; it was a constant struggle. I did find, however, that living within the Underworld had taken about ten pounds off me. So I guess I was off the diet seesaw . . . for the time being, anyway.

"He refused to tell me," I answered, remembering how Sinjin had deliberately avoided the subject of his location.

After our reintroduction, I'd sent him on his way so I could get some shut-eye. I was convinced he'd just hung out in my house, though, because I kept waking up to strange sounds I couldn't place—sounds that had probably been coming from the TV. I hadn't really minded. Somehow, with Sinjin in my house, I actually felt safer, as ridiculous as it sounds, since he could easily rip my throat out.

Before I had the chance to comment any more on the subject, I noticed a pool of mist appearing just over the staircase. The more I watched it, the more it morphed into the shape of a man, resplendent in nineteenth-century breeches and a waistcoat.

"Um, what are you looking at?" Christa asked and turned in the direction of my gaze. Of course she couldn't see the ghost, Pelham, the original owner of Pelham Manor.

"I'm looking at Pelham," I answered as I smiled and waved at the ghost in question.

Ah, you have decided to return and grace me with your beautiful presence. I could only hear Pelham's voice in my head.

"Hi, Pel," I said with a warm smile.

Christa glanced at the staircase, back to me, and back to the staircase again before letting out a deep sigh. "Spooky. Anyway, Jules, why don't you tell your invisible friend that we were in the middle of a conversation before he interrupted us?" She folded her arms against her chest and tapped her fingers on her elbow as if she was irritated.

"He can hear you," I said and threw her a frown.

Pelham just smiled at me and tipped his head as if to say yes, he could hear her and he apologized for interrupting us.

"I'll come and visit soon, Pel," I announced.

Very well. I have missed you. Then he just disappeared into the stairwell.

"Do you still want to see Rand?" Christa asked.

"Yes," I said and followed her down the hallway to the kitchen, which, in turn, led to the back garden area.

"There's your man," Christa said with a smile as she pointed at Rand, who stood beside Odran and Trent. All three of them were staring at a piece of paper on a picnic table. I assumed the paper in question was the ledger of names of the dead soldiers who needed to be reanimated.

Behind them, as far as I could see, were the tents of our legion. The glow of their campfires cast shadows and flickering lights against the tents, making it look like a campsite of ghosts.

"Thanks, Chris," I answered with a grin before starting forward. The three men were probably twenty feet or so from us, all hunched over the table, scrutinizing whatever was on the sheet. At my approach, all three looked up, but it was Rand who smiled first.

"Is everything all right?"

Christa mumbled something about it being too cold outside and returned to the house but I didn't turn to watch her leave. I couldn't tear my eyes away from Rand. I smiled and nodded even though the answer to his question was a definite no. If anything, it felt like my world was crumbling down around me and it was all I could do to grab hold of a loose brick or two.

"Yeah, I just wanted to find out when you thought we should start the reanimations," I said.

Rand nodded and glanced at the sheet of paper in front of him, flicking it with his long index finger as he stood up straight and beamed at me. "I think we're ready."

"And I am quite certain the dead soldiers would thank you if they could."

All four of us turned to the sound of Sinjin's voice as he stepped out from behind a massive pine tree. My heart leapt into my throat and I wasn't sure if it was because Sinjin had just appeared out of nowhere and scared me half to death, or because he was standing in front of Rand. The two hadn't seen each other since the battle and whenever they came within a few feet of each other, it was a prescription for conflict.

"Sinjin," I said without realizing I'd spoken his name.

Sinjin bowed and smiled, his fangs reflecting in the moonlight. He was dressed, as always, in black, and he looked as elegant and handsome as ever with his longish black hair curling over his ears in gentle waves, in contrast with the iciness of his piercing blue eyes.

"Greetings," he responded, his tone dripping with sensuality.

It was like slow motion as my gaze shifted from the vampire to Rand. And Rand's expression was not a happy one. His eyes were narrowed and his lips were tight, his jaw even tighter. The color had completely drained from his face.

"You bloody bastard," Rand started and before anyone could stop him, he lunged forward, pulled back his fist, and delivered a clean blow to Sinjin's cheek. The vampire took a step back and appeared to be slightly off balance. For a split second I thought he might fall down, but he regained control and stood stock-still.

"Blooody 'ell," Odran exclaimed while restraining

Rand with his mammoth arms when it appeared the warlock was going to go for round two. Rand said nothing but shot daggers at Sinjin with his eyes as his chest rose and fell with his belabored breathing. If Odran released him, he'd be at Sinjin's throat in a split second.

The tension in the air was so thick, I felt like I didn't want to breathe. I didn't want to inhale the negativity— enough pessimism was floating through me as it was.

Glancing at Sinjin, I was suddenly worried he'd lash out at Rand, but he didn't appear to be in a fighting mood. Instead he just wore a smile that was ironic considering the blood still trailing from his lips. After another second or two, Sinjin wiped his sleeve across his mouth.

"That was not quite the greeting I expected, Randall." Sinjin had a tendency to call Rand "Randall" even though that wasn't Rand's name and Sinjin knew it.

Rand made an attempt to break out from Odran's grip, and Trent and I stepped in between Rand and Sinjin. I glanced at Trent with a frown but said nothing, instead turning my attention to Sinjin.

"I don't want either of you to fight," I said in a tight voice.

"Fear not, my love, I come bearing tidings, not ill will," Sinjin said, taking a step toward me until we were separated by only two inches. I swallowed hard as I looked up at him, wondering what in the hell he was doing here, and why, no matter where he went, he always brought trouble.

"What the hell," I began, but my voice died away as he brought his fingers to my mouth and shushed me.

"Don't touch her," Rand seethed, fighting to release himself from Odran's stranglehold. "You do not fucking touch her."

Sinjin dropped his fingers from my lips and turned to face Rand, a smirk on his face. "Ah, Randall has become quite territorial, has he not?" he asked, facing me again with a wink.

"It's your bloody fault she died," Rand ground out in a hoarse voice.

"Enlighten me, Balfour, how was that my fault?"

A bluish light engulfed Rand and grew brighter until Odran winced. Realizing Rand was using magic to try to release himself, Odran began glowing yellow in response, using magic to fight magic. The blue of Rand's light blinked a few times more before dying out as Odran reinforced his hold on Rand with a bullish roar.

"Release me, dammit!" Rand yelled at Odran.

"There will be nay fightin'," Odran said in a low tone that echoed the warning.

"I won't touch him," Rand responded while staring Sinjin down. Odran must have believed Rand, because he dropped his arms and Rand stepped away.

"Jolie," Rand said, reaching for my hand and pulling me close behind him. He squeezed my hand reassuringly— as if to say he'd make sure the scary vampire would soon be on his way.

Sinjin laughed. "You think I would harm her?"

"You care only for yourself." Rand spat the words. "You allowed Jolie to fight in the battle, you fucking bastard. It's your fault I watched her die."

"It wasn't his fault," I interrupted, stepping out from behind him. He refused to unlock his eyes from the vampire, so I grasped his chin and forced him to look at me. "Fighting was entirely my idea, my plan. If you're mad at anyone, it should be me."

Rand shook his head. "Sinjin helped you when he should have known better." He faced Sinjin again and the anger in his eyes increased tenfold, his aura swelling as purple began to eclipse the blue. "As far as I'm concerned, it started with Sinjin and it will end with Sinjin."

Sinjin nodded, not appearing to be fazed in the least.

"Yes, I aided our lovely witch. But you know how persuasive she can be. And you also know of my weakness for a damsel in distress."

I wasn't in the mood to listen to Sinjin taunt Rand all night. We needed to cut to the chase. "What do you want, Sinjin?" I demanded.

Sinjin brought his attention from Rand to me, and a smile slithered over his mouth. His eyes seemed to glow as he eyed me up and down. "Is that not obvious, pet?"

"I want you off my property," Rand said but Sinjin just smiled at him. Then Trent suddenly took a few steps forward, as if to say he would see to it the job was done. They were poorly matched—Sinjin could make mincemeat of Trent in . . . hmm . . . I'd say three seconds flat.

"Rand," I said, thinking he was taking this whole thing a bit far. Yes, Sinjin could be a jerk, and yes he and Rand had never had a good relationship, but Sinjin was on our side and always had been. In truth, Rand blamed Sinjin for something that I'd orchestrated, and I wasn't about to stand by and let Sinjin take the blame.

"You are no longer our ally, Sinclair," Rand lashed out, refusing to look at me.

"This isn't his fault," I repeated.

"Shhh," Sinjin interrupted. "Do not defend me, poppet. I have come to declare my loyalty and, as I mentioned last night, my supplication to the Queen."

"Last night?" Rand questioned, his gaze traveling from Sinjin to me. His eyes were both murderous and pained. "What the bloody hell does that mean?"

Just as I was about to reply, Sinjin did it for me. "I visited our lovely witch last evening, just as she was dropping off to sleep. She does appear ever so innocent when she sleeps, does she not?"

"Jolie?" Rand repeated, his eyes begging me to disaffirm Sinjin's announcement.

I shook my head, panic enveloping me as I realized

how incredibly bad this looked. "Rand, nothing happened." As soon as the words left my mouth, I realized they were the three worst words I could have said. Why is it that "nothing happened" screams just the opposite—that everything happened and then some?

Rand shook his head but the anger remained in his expression. "Why the bloody hell did you allow him into your house?"

"Well, I didn't really have a choice," I said, remembering how Sinjin had just appeared in my bedroom. "He just sort of showed up."

"In your bedroom?" Rand demanded. Not only were Trent and Odran completely quiet, but they'd been moving farther and farther away from us, which was just as well because I really didn't want an audience.

"The lovely poppet speaks the truth, Randall. I was not invited," Sinjin finally admitted, allowing me to find my breath again.

"If you so much as laid a finger on her," Rand started, his voice full of fire and anger. He turned to me, and the fury in his eyes was frightening. "Did he touch you?"

"He didn't touch me," I said although there had been that whole kiss—a kiss that now plagued me—a kiss I wanted nothing to do with. I glanced at Sinjin and warned him with my eyes not to betray me by admitting he'd stolen a kiss. That would send Rand over the edge.

Rand nodded and appeared to be slightly relieved before he turned to face Sinjin again. "Where the bloody hell have you been?"

Sinjin shrugged and offered me a smile that said our secret was safe. I didn't return the smile because I was suddenly angry with him—angry that with Sinjin everything was a big game. He enjoyed pushing Rand's buttons, but we didn't have time to deal with this now—not when we had so much to accomplish with regard to our legion.

"I have been keeping a low profile, as they say," Sinjin replied.

"Doing?" Rand continued.

"He won't admit anything to you," I answered, not wanting a repeat of last night. I turned to Sinjin and allowed my angst and irritation with him to seep into my voice. "Why don't you make it easier on everyone and just tell us the truth?"

"Because that would be too noble for Sinjin," Rand interrupted, reaching for my hand and wrapping it in his own.

"When is it a crime to merely take some time for oneself?" Sinjin asked with a chuckle as his gaze settled on our clasped hands. "Are you trying to impart some information regarding Jolie and yourself?"

Rand nodded. "Yes, I'm imparting the information that you need to stay the hell away from her or else you'll have to answer to me."

"You are such a spoilsport, Randall," Sinjin said with a grin although I could have sworn Rand's actions had somehow thrown him off. There was something in Sinjin's eyes that hadn't been there before, maybe just the slightest inkling of doubt?

"Wherever you've been, I suggest you return," Rand said.

"On the contrary, my good man," Sinjin replied, laughing. "As our legion is stationed here, so should I be."

"I don't have time to deal with you." Still holding my hand, Rand turned around and started for Pelham Manor.

"Then perhaps Jolie should deal with me instead. I enjoy her company much more than I ever did yours," Sinjin said as he easily caught up with us and hovered beside me.

Rand stopped walking and faced him, his aura now entirely purple. "I want you out of here."

"I am part of your legion. When the legion leaves, then so shall I. You would not want me to accuse you of playing favorites?"

Rand shook his head. "I won't accuse you of anything except being an absolute bastard."

"And besides," Sinjin continued, "I believe you are no longer in command here, and my orders herewith must come from our lovely Queen."

I didn't glance at Rand because I didn't really need to. I could feel the fury radiating from him.

"As long as you are stationed at Pelham Manor, you'll answer to no one but me, do you understand?" Rand demanded.

Sinjin arched a brow and smiled. "I understand perfectly well."

Somehow, I didn't think he was referring to the conversation.

Seven

After the altercation with Sinjin, I followed Rand back into the house. I wanted to talk to him about the fact that he couldn't blame Sinjin for allowing me to fight in the battle against Bella and also that Sinjin was and always would be our ally. Somehow I had to make him realize that we needed Sinjin—he and Varick basically controlled the vampires, so it was important for them to be on our side. And Rand needed to rein in his temper where the vampire was concerned.

Approaching the back door, Rand catapulted himself up the steps and stomped through the hall, a frenzy of nerves and bad temper. I followed and stood at the entrance to the kitchen, watching as he began rifling through his cupboards. He was so preoccupied with whatever it was he was doing, he didn't even realize I was there. I took a seat on one of his stools, leaning my forearms against the black granite countertop of the bar as I watched him open a cupboard and, not finding what he was looking for, cuss and slam it shut. He opened another cupboard only to slam it shut again.

"Whoa, someone's in a bad mood," Christa announced. I glanced over at her. She was lying on the couch watching *True Blood* while working on something that looked like an Excel spreadsheet. Probably something Rand had tasked her with. She arched her brows at me, turned off the TV, and stood up, placing the bundle of pages beside her and her highlighter on top of the pile.

"Who the heck burst your bubble?" she asked.

Rand looked at her and must have seen me out of his peripheral vision, because he offered a quick nod of his head in salutation. Facing Christa again, he frowned.

"A fucking vampire burst my bloody bubble."

She didn't say anything more but threw me an expression of pity and vacated the living room, disappearing down the hallway.

Rand turned around to face me again and offered an apologetic sigh. "I thought I had some bloody coffee in this bloody kitchen."

I smiled, I couldn't help it. "Why don't you just bloody magick some?"

He shook his head, the beginnings of a smile on his lips. But his foul mood must still have been raging because just as quickly as it had appeared, the faint smile fell off his lips. He started running his hands through his hair, then approached the counter and leaned against it.

"I can't seem to best Starbucks," he said.

I shrugged. "They have made coffee their life's passion."

He chuckled and then studied me for a few seconds. Looking at him, my eyes were drawn to a few drops of blood that stained his light brown sweater, Sinjin's blood. He followed my gaze and, seeing the blood, tore the sweater over his head. His white T-shirt underneath rode up, gifting me with a view of his six-pack. He glanced at me again, pulling his T-shirt down to hide his beautiful torso.

"Fucking vampire," he grumbled as he inspected the bloodstains.

"They come out with cold water," I offered.

He wadded up the sweater and threw it on top of the

metal trash bin in the corner of the kitchen. Apparently cold water might remove the blood but not the vampire himself.

"I'm sorry you had to witness my foul mood," Rand said, looking down at me with a slight smile on his full lips.

I shook my head. "It's not a big deal."

"That bastard Sinjin just rubs me the wrong way."

I nodded and chewed on my lip. "That's what I came to talk to you about."

Rand eyed me with a wary expression and a heartfelt sigh as he backed away from the counter and reached his arms behind his neck, expanding his chest, as if he needed to alleviate some stress. Probably a good idea. The sleeves of his T-shirt bunched in his armpits, revealing the peaks of his biceps. I forgot to breathe for about five seconds.

"I'm not in the mood for a lecture," he said, dropping his arms.

I shrugged. "Well, you're going to get one anyway."

He glanced at me in surprise and started chuckling. It was a deep, rich sound. "Am I?"

I jumped off the stool and walked around the bar until I was standing right in front of him. He towered over me and seemed to be amused by the fact that I was going to lecture him, all five-foot-four of me.

"Yes, you are," I answered, propping my hands on my hips to warn him not to argue with me. "Would you like me to deliver your lecture here or somewhere more private?"

"Would *you* prefer to deliver your lecture in a more intimate environment?" he asked, raising a brow as a shameless smile stole across his lips.

I shrugged again. "I can reprimand you anywhere—it makes no difference to me."

"Very well," he said and offered me another quick,

flirtatious grin before leading me from the kitchen and up the grand staircase. "I prefer to be chastised in the privacy of my own bedchamber, thanks for asking." He took the stairs two at a time and reached the second floor while I was still halfway up the stairs.

"If I didn't know better, I'd say you were looking forward to this," I said.

"Perhaps I am," he answered as he started down the long hallway that merged into Pelham Manor's master chamber, his bedroom. He opened one of the double doors and held it for me. I entered and immediately felt embraced by the room, as if I were coming home again. It was a strange feeling that sort of threw me because I really hadn't spent that much time here. Although the memory of a time I'd gotten drunk with Christa suddenly plagued me. In my drunken stupor, I'd fallen asleep on this bed. At the time, Rand was out of town, and when I awoke the next morning I found him smiling down at me, no doubt wondering what the hell I was doing in his bed. To make matters even more embarrassing, there was also a framed photograph of him wedged beneath my chin, and my drool was all over his pillow.

As I glanced around his private chambers now, I realized that nothing in his bedroom had changed. It was still the orderly (as in bordering on OCD) space it had been before, nothing out of place. Rich mahogany wood furniture complemented the hunter green of the walls. The dark oak floors gleamed around an Aubusson rug that reiterated the earth tones of the bedroom.

I inhaled deeply and filled myself with Rand's spicy scent, suddenly light-headed. I grabbed hold of one of the bedposts for extra stability—feeling like I might just keel over right there.

The sound of the door closing behind me made me turn around. I faced Rand as I realized we were now completely alone. And he was ungodly gorgeous and I had suddenly become ungodly horny. But I hadn't come here to have sex with him . . . although for the moment my mission had completely escaped me. It took me a second to wake my brain the heck up. Then I remembered. I was here to reprimand him.

"Let the scolding begin," he said with a deep and sexy chuckle.

I laughed and, shaking my head, took a seat in one of the armchairs beside the fireplace. He just watched me but made no motion to take the other chair. Instead he stood there in his jeans and white T-shirt, which contrasted so nicely against his tan skin. His arms crossed over the wide expanse of his chest as if he were now entering defensive mode.

"Well?" he prodded. I swallowed my embarrassment with a gulp when I realized I'd just been zoning out, staring at him and probably looking like a total moron.

"Um, you really need to get your temper under control, Rand," I began, again trying to remember what in the hell I'd come up here to talk to him about. It definitely hadn't been his incredibly sculpted cheekbones or his biceps that bulged out as he leaned backward and braced himself against the wall. And I definitely hadn't come to talk to him about the fact that I could see the slightest movement of something . . . male from underneath his pants every time he shifted.

If Rand had any idea that I was standing here trying not to stare at his . . . um, male part . . . God, I was no better than Christa, the sex freak.

"I suppose you're referring to my . . . reaction to Sinjin?" he asked, sighing as if the last thing in the world he wanted to discuss was the vampire.

I nodded and internally slapped myself. I had to focus. "Yes, I am. Whether you like it or not, he's on our side."

Rand shook his head and frowned. "Sinjin wants you

to think he's on our side but he's on no one's side but his own."

I couldn't argue with that, so I didn't even try. "Put it this way, he's more on our side than on Bella's. And furthermore, we need him."

Rand narrowed his eyes, and there was a sudden stiffness to his composure. "And why is that?"

"You know why," I started and stood up, approaching him. "Sinjin is a master vampire—"

"I know that," he barked and then frowned. "I didn't mean to snap at you," he added in a small voice.

I waved away his concern and continued. "Sinjin and Varick have all the vampires in their control, and we need them to help us keep the vampires in line. We can't afford to fall out with either of them."

Rand nodded. "I have no issues with Varick."

"You can't afford to have issues with Sinjin either." I took his hand and held it. I really couldn't help myself—I had to touch him, to feel that incredibly soft and warm skin.

He shook his head and seemed ready to argue the fact but then squeezed my hand, folding his fingers over mine. "Sinjin wants something from you, Jolie, and I don't like it." He paused for a second and glanced down at our interwoven hands before lifting his eyes to me again. "I hate the way he looks at you and I hate the way he flirts with you."

"You've gotta get past that, Rand," I said. "It's all an act—it's just how Sinjin is. I'll bet he's like that with every woman he comes across."

Rand laughed, but it was a humorless, hollow sound. "No, he's not like that with other women." He gazed down at me and shook his head. "He has some sort of fascination with you."

"And that's why you dislike him so much?"

He held my hand up closer to his face as he inspected

my fingers, rubbing his own along my nails. "It's just one of the many reasons I dislike him. I don't trust him and I don't want him anywhere near you."

"I can take care of myself, Rand . . ." I started to pull my hand away but he held it tightly and pulled me against his chest, wrapping his arms around my waist as he gazed down at me.

"I know you can, but I also know you're good-hearted and you like to give everyone the benefit of the doubt. Sinjin deserves none of your kindness, though." He was quiet for a few seconds. "I just wish you could see him the way I see him, in his true colors."

"I'm not fooled by him, I know he has an agenda. I just don't think he's anywhere near as . . . threatening as you make him out to be." I paused, wondering if maybe he was right—maybe I did tend to give everyone the benefit of the doubt. What if Sinjin was as bad as Rand made him out to be? But somehow, deep down inside, I couldn't believe that. I just didn't think Rand knew him as well as I did. "I don't think Sinjin is a bad person."

"I suppose on that point we can agree to disagree," he said and shrugged. "I just don't ever want to see Sinjin hurt you and I'm afraid he will."

"He can't hurt me, I haven't allowed him to get close enough for that." Even though I said the words, I wasn't exactly sure I believed them. If it did turn out that Sinjin was merely out for himself and our friendship meant nothing to him, then yes, that would hurt me.

"I hope you never do."

I smiled up at him, loving the feel of his large arms around me, the heat of his body that was now enveloping me. "At any rate, I do hope you see my point that we need him as our ally, that we need him on our side."

Rand was quiet for a few moments. "I don't agree."

"Then we'll agree to disagree," I said furtively, drawing attention to the fact that this conversation was over.

"I also want you to realize that Sinjin wasn't responsible for me fighting in the battle against Bella. That was all me."

He shook his head and dropped his arms from around me. Hmm, guess this subject really bothered him . . . He took a few steps away before turning back around to face me with a tight jaw.

"You will never convince me that Sinjin didn't have a hand in that, and I will never forgive him for it."

"I asked him to help me. He was doing me a favor."

He took a few more steps away from me. His eyes were angry as he turned them on me. "It was a favor he never should have granted you. He should have kept you away from the battle at all costs."

"He knew I had to kill Ryder, Rand. He knew it was something I had to do."

"I would have killed Ryder."

"No, it had to be me," I was quick to interject. "It was my anger and my revenge."

Rand just shook his head again. "Sinjin risked your life." His hands were now fists at his sides. "I will never stop damning him to hell for doing it."

Okay, so he wasn't going to budge on that one. I guess I could live with that. I smiled and sighed, figuratively waving my white flag of surrender. "Well, aside from the battle, I hope you'll try to keep better control over your temper where Sinjin is concerned?"

Rand inhaled deeply but said nothing so I continued. "He just likes to push your buttons, you must see that?"

"Of course I do."

"Then why do you get so flustered?"

He shrugged. "I can't help it. I suppose I wear my emotions on my sleeve."

I arched a brow at him and smiled. "I guess so." I took a few steps for the door, feeling triumphant. I'd hit two out of three, which wasn't bad. At least Rand had come around to the realization that Sinjin was our ally and, equally important, that we needed him to be on our side. And if he never forgave Sinjin for assisting me in combat, well, I guess I'd have to live with that.

"Wait just a minute," Rand said with the hint of a smile as he took two purposeful strides and inserted himself between the door and my body, blocking my exit. "Now it's my turn."

"Your turn?" I asked in surprise.

"I have a few questions for you."

I shrugged and stepped away from the door as he approached me.

"You have questions for me?" I repeated.

"Yes, I do." He brought his hands to my shoulders, gently pushing me until my back was up against the wall. My heart started thudding in my chest as he pinned me between his outstretched arms, his face directly in line with mine.

"Why hasn't Sinjin realized you want nothing to do with him?" he asked, his eyes burning with what appeared to be jealousy.

"What do you mean?" I asked innocently.

Rand smiled, signifying that he was on to my game. "What I mean, Jolie, is that I believe Sinjin confuses your kindness with . . . interest."

"Are you trying to say I'm leading him on?"

Rand shook his head and chuckled although the fire still flared in his eyes. "No, that's not what I'm saying, although that's what it sounds like." He paused for a second and glanced down, as if trying to prepare what he really meant to say. "What does Sinjin mean to you?"

I smiled. "Why, are you jealous?"

He shrugged and the playfulness was absent from his expression as well as his voice. "Should I be?"

"Sinjin knows what the situation is between us."

"And what, pray tell, is that situation?"

"That he and I are just friends because . . ." My voice died in my throat. I was suddenly afraid to admit my feelings to Rand. Well, not so much afraid of admitting my feelings as admitting them knowing I still had the burden of our bonding situation on my shoulders.

"Because?" he prodded.

"Because I'm in love with a warlock who can't control his temper."

Rand laughed and leaned down until the end of his nose touched mine. "And does this warlock love you?"

I shrugged, trying to appear casual, although inside I felt like I was suffocating. I could feel Rand's breath against my lips and see his pulse quickening in his throat. Not only that, but I could feel him hardening against my thigh.

"I think so," I answered breathlessly.

He chuckled and brought his lips to my cheek, caressing my skin with the lightest of kisses. He pushed himself against me, crushing my breasts against his chest. "I think I know this warlock of yours . . . ," he started.

"Do you?"

"Yes, and I can say he loves you very much." His lips worked down the soft skin of my ear until they met my neck. "He loves the way you laugh, the way you smell." He inhaled deeply.

"What else does he love?" I whispered and closed my eyes.

I felt Rand pull away from me so I opened my eyes and found him smirking. "He loves your eyes and the way you taste."

Before I could respond, his lips suddenly met mine and our tongues circled in a carnal dance. He ground his hips into me, as if he thought he needed to draw attention to the throbbing erection in his pants. He didn't . . . holy enormous hot dog, he didn't.

"Rand," I breathed.

"Tell me Sinjin means nothing to you." His whisper was raspy and coarse.

"Sinjin is my friend and I care about him," I said even though I knew he didn't want to hear that. I just couldn't lie. Sinjin did mean something to me and probably always would. "But," I continued, "you mean the world to me, Rand. It's you I love."

"Say it again," he said and his hands were suddenly beneath my shirt, fondling my breasts, teasing my nipples.

"I love you," I groaned out.

"Tell me you're mine," he ordered and pulled my shirt up to my chin, his eyes fastened on my breasts. Before I could think another thought, he had one breast in his mouth, his tongue teasing the delicate nub.

"Say it," he demanded again.

"I'm yours."

He suddenly pulled away from me, and there was a frenzied look in his eyes. "I need to make love to you, Jolie."

I was unsure what to say since it felt like the floor had just been ripped out from underneath me.

"Rand," I began, hesitantly, thinking about the fact that I still hadn't told him the truth about our bonding, a truth I'd decided to cover up. I didn't think I could deal with possible bonding episode number two. "What if we bond?"

"I don't care," he responded and tugged on the waist of my pants, unbuttoning my jeans as he unzipped them. Before I could say another word, his fingers were at the junction of my thighs, poised, perched, and ready.

"Rand, we can't." I heard myself say the words and was shocked they'd come from my mouth because my brain was basically begging his fingers to take the plunge.

He stood back and looked at me with a strange expression on his face. Maybe one of surprise mixed with rejection.

"I want you," I said, worried he might take this the wrong way. "God, I want you more than anything in the world."

He nodded and smiled, wetting his lips, as he pulled away. "I understand, Jolie. There is too much up in the air right now."

There was that too.

"Rand—"

He interrupted by pulling me into his chest and holding me as he kissed the top of my head. "You're right. This isn't the time."

"I don't want you to think . . ."

"Shhh," he said and silenced me with a kiss.

Eight

JOURNAL ENTRY

So I witnessed something . . . interesting last night. After my little tryst with Rand, I went in search of Christa to say good night. Well, even though I was hoping to get in and get out, instead I found myself on the receiving end of Christa's hour-long tirade about how John thinks she wants sex too often! Yes, this is what my life has been reduced to! And just the conversation I wanted to get into . . . Especially when I might as well become a born-again virgin for all the exercising my equipment gets.

Anyway, when I'd heard all I could stomach about Christa and her insatiable sexual appetite, I found myself staring out her bedroom window, wishing I could relocate myself by clicking my heels three times and muttering, "There's no place like home." I mean, if I had to listen to one more word about role-playing, fuzzy handcuffs, or warming liquid, I was going to put myself out of my misery.

Apparently God was feeling sorry for me too, because wouldn't you guess what happened next? Well, Diary, you can't guess because you're an inanimate object so I'll just tell you . . .

I saw Sinjin having a heated discussion with Mercedes in Rand's rose garden. At first, I thought maybe I was just delusional and my brain was creating interesting images in order to woo my thoughts away from Christa's description of John's phallus. (By the way, apparently weres are endowed with an average of two inches more than human men in that area—who'd have thunk?) Anyhow, after convincing myself my brain wasn't trying to escape to its "happy place" and Mercedes and Sinjin really were outside verbally sparring, I said good night to Christa and ran downstairs and outside, pretending to search for a lost cell phone.

Upon seeing me, Sinjin immediately stopped talking, cleared his throat, and smoothed down the front of his shirt so you know something had to have been going on—and something he didn't want me to find out about. I mean, I have never seen Sinjin do anything even remotely hinting that he was uncomfortable. Mercedes didn't give anything away—she looked just the same as she always did.

After I announced that I was searching for my cell phone, Sinjin made a big fuss about helping me find it and accidentally (or not) brushed up against me a few times and then said he hoped I hadn't gotten into "trouble" for his antics earlier in the evening. And as much as I wanted to be angry with him (because he is the quintessential troublemaker), there is just something about Sinjin that allows him to get away with murder. I can't stay angry with him. And he knows it, the smug jerk.

So I basically just ignored him, my mind racing with thoughts about what in the heck he and Mercedes had been talking about—and even more, about why Sinjin had almost seemed to panic when I interrupted them. The vampire was up to no good; that was as obvious as the fact that Christa needs a sex therapist.

The more I thought about it, the more I had to wonder why Sinjin has always had this preoccupation with the prophetess. There were all those times when he'd been training me for battle and asked me to try to locate *her telepathically. And as if that weren't enough, when I first met Sinjin and he was pretending to be on Bella's side, he showed more than just a casual interest in my few attempts to reanimate that old bag whom Bella thought was the prophetess.*

Yep, Sinjin definitely has something up his sleeve, and I've decided to make it my personal mission to find out what that "something" is.

And I also can't help being disappointed by the fact that I can't completely trust him. I don't know why exactly but I like Sinjin—I always have. It's actually hard not to like him—he's incredibly charming and funny. And yes, incredibly good-looking too. I just wish he would tell me the truth. Even though I know Rand is the one for me, or at least I hope he is, it would be nice to know if Sinjin really cares about me or if I'm just a means to an end. I can't help but think I'm a pawn on his chessboard, nothing more.

After obviously not finding my supposedly missing phone, Sinjin excused himself, saying he was hungry and had to go find a willing donor. Then he hightailed it out of the courtyard as quickly as he could.

When I asked Mercedes what they'd been talking about, she was vague and just told me he was interested in where she'd been, how she was able to bring me back to 1878, and what her plan was. Did I believe her? Yes, Mercedes really has no reason to lie to me—especially not to protect Sinjin. But even though I believed Mercedes, I definitely didn't believe that Sinjin just happened to be curious about those things.

Back to Mercedes . . . apparently she thinks I'm an incredibly powerful person. I have noticed that she never refers to me as a witch, which I find increasingly interesting . . .

And that brings me to my next thought. When I was Bella's abductee, and I attempted to resurrect the old woman whom she thought was the prophetess, the old woman said something that I'd never quite understood. When I touched her, she reeled back from me then announced I wasn't a witch—and that I had no idea what I was. Then, poof, she died. Yeah, talk about bad timing . . . Even back then, I thought the old woman's words were strange and just a little ominous but I sort of dismissed them as the ravings of a sick, old woman on the brink of death. But maybe I was wrong . . .

What if I'm not a witch? What if I'm a totally different creature or something no one knows about? What if I'm like a mermaid or something nuts? Of course, I've never sprouted a tail in the shower and I don't particularly enjoy The Little Mermaid. But that aside, wouldn't my being something other than a witch explain the fact that Mercedes won't refer to me as one—and wouldn't it also explain that old woman's comments?

I hate having unanswered questions.

I'm probably just spinning my wheels, though, because if I'm not a witch, who in the hell would know exactly what I was? Maybe Mercedes? Note to self: Ask Mercedes if I'm something other than a witch and if so, what that something is.

So leaving that subject alone for a little bit, the other interesting thing that Mercedes mentioned last night was that as Queen, I'll have to find a suitable home. And this was the part of my evening that kept me up all damn night. I'm happy in my butler's quarters—I'm happy living in the shadow of Pelham Manor and knowing Rand is only two miles away if I ever need him. I don't want to move.

When I told Mercedes as much, she wouldn't even listen to me. She said it was out of the question for a Queen to be living in a servant's quarters. So then I sort of freaked out and said I didn't want to be Queen and she went on and on about how it was my destiny and how

it was an honor I should stop resisting. Then she pro-
ceeded to tell me that if I didn't rise up and accept my
role as Queen and unite our species, wars will continue
to be fought and creatures will continue to die.

Talk about a guilt trip.

The more I think about it now, the more I'm starting
to realize this might actually be my destiny and some-
thing I can't run away from. And really, if I run away
from my so-called responsibility and our society falls
victim to our enemies, I would never forgive myself,
even if it costs me the love of the one man I adore with
all my heart.

I wasn't sure why but I woke up.

I glanced at the green glow of the clock just beside my
bed and noticed it was three a.m. Groaning to myself, I
rolled onto my other side and closed my eyes, willing
myself to go to sleep. But there was something keeping
me from losing myself to unconsciousness. A worry that
had started in my gut and was quickly building momentum, boarding my bloodstream and traveling throughout my body.

I sat up and glanced around, taking in nothing more
than the moon as it reflected through my windows, battling to breach the wall of my curtains. The night air
was chilly and calm, quiet and relaxed. So why wasn't I?

I took a deep breath and that was when I felt it—like
the worst headache you can ever imagine—the uglier
sister to a migraine. I grabbed my head and reeled back,
dropping myself against my pillows as I cradled my
forehead in my hands, willing the pain to go away. As a
witch, I can cure myself of most maladies, but even
though I was sending reinforcing white light to the center of my forehead, the apex of the pain, nothing was
happening. Instead the pain was beginning to throb,

reaching out its tendrils of agony until I felt like my eyes might explode.

Panic began welling up within me but I held it at bay and focused my energies even more resolutely, imagining the white light of my power battling whatever this pain was.

Still nothing.

As fear began wending its way through me, the pain behind my eyes started to dissipate into a gentle drumming before it vanished completely. I felt my heart rate decrease as relief flooded me. But the relief was short-lived once I tried to open my eyes and found they were locked down . . . tight. It was as if I had no control over my own body.

Suddenly there were images floating before me, the black of my eyelids acting as a canvas. I didn't fight the images; instead I focused on them, allowed them to cluster into a movie, a story unfolding. And what I witnessed frightened me.

It was open land, as far as my eyes could see—devastated and barren. The brown of the hills was the same color as the sky and it looked as if a bomb had gone off and decimated what I had to imagine was once verdant farmland. I could only concentrate on the dinginess of the sky and hills for so long, though, because my vision slowly began to take in the rows and rows of lumps, mounds of more lackluster color. The more I focused, the more the shapes delineated themselves, revealing them to be people. People facedown in muck, others on their sides, and some facing the malodorous sky. All were dead.

That image was suddenly yanked from my mind's eye and another dropped in its place. It was a throne, empty. A scepter and a crown stood unattended at either side of the golden chair. It was as if they were both awaiting the return of their monarch, of their King or Queen. And before I could take another breath, that image was plucked away and I was again gazing at the barren landscape. Only this time, the people weren't dead yet. No, they were fighting. And the enemies they were fighting were like nothing I'd ever seen before. Even though they appeared to be humans, they were fast, lightning fast and just as strong, hurtling their foes left and right, the glow of their mini fangs glinting in the moonlight.

The more I watched the two sides battle against each other, the more I realized the losing side were Underworld creatures—weres, vamps, and witches. But they were outnumbered and outskilled. Not only were the creatures attacking them stronger and faster, but there was something about them . . . something magical. Light radiated off them, wove in and around them as they delivered their death blows.

Lurkers.

The word suddenly infiltrated my head and it wasn't like I'd thought it myself. It was as if someone had fed me a clue, someone had placed the word inside my head. And with the dawning realization that the creatures before me were the biggest threat to the existence of the Underworld, I was suddenly keenly aware of the fact that not only were they vampire-like with their strength, speed, and fangs, but they were also magic.

The Lurkers possessed magic.

Reeling with that observation, I again attempted to fight against the images, to gain control over myself. I'd seen enough. But the vision wouldn't release me. Instead pictures of the empty throne returned, and as I watched, the crown and the scepter began melting into the base of the golden chair. Something inside me again started panicking as I watched the scepter and the crown meld into the throne and it, too, began dripping into a puddle of gold.

Fear shot through me and I pushed against the images

with my mind, fought them with the glow of my own power, and little by little they began to fade into the darkness of my closed eyelids. I took a deep breath and blinked, found myself surrounded by the blackness of night. My heart raced within my chest and when I attempted to stand up, I had to lean against the post of my bed. I was exhausted, weak.

Even though I was at a complete loss as to what I'd just experienced, the thing I was sure of was that I'd just had a premonition of the future. I had just seen a brief window into the destruction of the Underworld at Lurker hands. Whether it had been a mere vision concocted of my own power or whether someone had sent it to me, I had no idea. But I absolutely knew that the only way to stop this vision from becoming reality was for me to take the throne. I mean, what else could the empty throne mean?

I took another deep breath and steadied myself against my bed.

I was going to accept my role as Queen because if I didn't, the destruction that I'd just witnessed would become real. If I didn't become Queen, the Underworld would perish.

"Jolie!" I heard Rand's voice outside accompanied by the sounds of his fists banging against the door.

I took a step forward and, finding my strength returning, forced myself into the living room. Before I could reach the door, Rand opened it with a burst of magic and faced me, his expression betraying his worry.

"What the bloody hell happened to you?"

I shook my head. "I don't know but I . . . I . . . ."

He closed the door behind him and, seeing me leaning against the couch back, strode up to me. "I could feel your distress and when I tried to contact you, I didn't get any response."

I was surprised that he could feel me, considering I'd

convinced myself that we weren't bonded. But that was a subject for another day. At the moment I was more curious to find out what the hell *had* just happened to me.

"It was like someone took control of my body," I started. I tried to take another step forward but I was too weak and gripped the back of the couch again. Rand caught me in his arms.

"Why can't you stand?"

"I don't know," I answered weakly.

Rand shook his head and I could tell he had a million questions floating through his mind as he set me on the couch and sat beside me. "You're safe now, Jolie," he said in a soft voice, pulling me into his broad chest. "But I need you to tell me what happened. Start from the beginning."

So I did. I told him everything I could remember.

"I think it was a vision," I finished. "A sign that I'm meant to be Queen in order to stop the Lurkers from destroying us."

Rand shook his head like he wasn't convinced. "We don't know that for certain."

"What else could the images mean, then?" I demanded, feeling suddenly exhausted again.

Rand sighed deep and long and his gaze settled on my window as he absently stroked my upper arm. "I don't know."

It was the evening after I'd witnessed the horrible images of the Lurkers destroying the creatures of the Underworld. Rand had scheduled a meeting at Pelham Manor to discuss the future of our legion and, more important, the future of the Underworld in general. Like last time, there were representatives of each race. In attendance were Rand, me, Odran, Sinjin and Varick, Mercedes, Mathilda, and Trent.

With the help of Rand, I'd just explained the experience of the night before, describing in vivid detail everything I could recall about the vision. Everyone seemed dumbstruck, their expressions revealing shock and concern.

"The Lurkers have magic," I finished.

"Perhaps they do," Mercedes said and offered me an unenthusiastic frown.

"I saw and felt it," I argued.

She shook her head. "We do not know anything for certain. Yes, you had a vision, but as you well know, Jolie, visions can be flawed. They can reveal part of the picture, but not necessarily the whole thing."

"We must consider them possessing magic as a possibility," Mathilda offered.

I glanced at her and smiled. She lowered her head and faced Mercedes again.

"Of one thing I am certain . . . the Queen will require protectors," Mercedes announced, addressing the entire room. She was sitting next to the fireplace, and the fire burning in the hearth highlighted the strong planes of her face, making her look like an omniscient deity.

At the mention of "the Queen," I glanced at Rand. His attention was riveted on Mercedes' face, but he wasn't allowing any reaction to show. It was like he was trying to imitate a statue and doing a damn good job.

"Protectors?" Trent repeated and raised his eyebrows in an expression I didn't know how to read. As I mentioned earlier, Trent and I had a history, although not exactly a deep one. We dated until he told me he was too dangerous and basically dumped me. Then a week later, I saw him sporting some werewolf girl on his arm. Later I had the displeasure of meeting up with him at an Underworld function chaired by Rand, where Trent tried to get back together with me. Of course I told him where he could shove that idea and then, to make a long story short, he got pissed off, accused Rand of trying to be with me, and then sucker-punched him right across the face.

I guess it was kudos to Rand that Trent was even sitting at the table this evening—Rand could be forgiving when it suited him. Although I imagine he'll never forgive Sinjin for . . . being Sinjin.

Mercedes faced Trent and nodded, her lips drawn in a tight, stern line, her expression one of *Don't question me, you peon, I'm the prophetess.*

"Yes, we will need to assemble a band of soldiers dedicated solely to the Queen's protection," she said with finality.

"I offer my protection," Sinjin said. When I glanced at him, wondering if he was joking, he wouldn't look at me. Instead he faced Mercedes resolutely, looking every bit sincere.

"No," Rand answered at the same time Odran began chuckling.

"Perhaps I could have protected her from the vision," Sinjin started.

"No one could have protected me from it," I intercepted. "I believe it was just a vision, an unbelievably lucent one but a vision all the same."

Sinjin nodded but by the twinkle in his eyes, it didn't seem he'd given in. "Regardless, I will protect our Queen."

"Aye, boot who will protect 'er against your advances?" Odran then erupted into another hearty laugh, which Trent echoed. In fact, it had come to my attention that Trent had recently taken up the position of Odran's shadow. They reminded me of a poorly cast Batman and Robin—just missing the tights.

"Odran is right," Rand offered. "Sinjin would be the worst person to protect Jolie."

"The child would be vulnerable in the day," Mathilda added in a soft voice.

"Would you prefer to take the task upon yourself?" Mercedes demanded of Rand, seemingly ignoring Mathilda's comment for the moment.

Rand narrowed his eyes but said nothing more, merely leaned back in his chair and crossed his arms against his chest, looking pissed off. Instantly my stomach seemed to drop to the ground as I wondered why Rand didn't champion my cause—why didn't he stand up and announce that, yes, he would defend me, that he would continue protecting me as he always had?

"I offer my complete and total loyalty to our Queen," Sinjin continued, now looking at me. "It is true that I cannot protect her while the sun commands the sky, but I will arrange for others who can."

Mercedes nodded. "I believe that solves the issue." She glanced at Mathilda. "Mathilda?"

Mathilda merely nodded as Sinjin cleared his throat, returning our attention to him.

"And as long as my employer does not find fault with the arrangement, I dedicate myself entirely to the Queen's preservation."

Varick seemed to weigh the subject for a few seconds before he nodded. "I find this arrangement to be quite satisfactory."

"Very good." Mercedes slapped her hands together. "Sinjin, I will leave it to you to assemble a force strong enough to protect your Queen."

Sinjin bowed his head in what appeared to be humble acceptance and then glanced at me, the beginnings of a smile working on his lips. It was an expression of triumph and I had to wonder why being named my protector would cause him to feel victorious.

Rand exhaled deeply and then pushed himself away from the table to walk to the opposite side of the room. He was dressed casually in loose, dark jeans that hinted at the athletic lines of his butt and legs. He wore a chocolate-brown polo-necked, short-sleeved T-shirt, and I tried to pull my attention away from his incredibly shapely arms, ignoring how his biceps seemed to pop whenever he shifted.

"I believe we should release the legion from Pelham Manor," he said. I wondered if I was just imagining it or if he was making eye contact with everyone but me.

"Your ledger is finalized, then?" Varick asked.

Rand nodded and crossed his arms against his chest, leaning against the wall. He still refused to look at me.

"Yes, and our soldiers are eager to return to their families. If all of you agree, I will dispatch them and tell them to await further instruction." He paused for a second or two and then faced Sinjin with razor-sharp eyes. "In fact, I will require everyone to vacate Pelham Manor by tomorrow evening."

Sinjin arched a brow and relaxed into his seat, as if to say he wasn't going anywhere. "Agreed, Randall, though any soldiers deployed in the safety of the Queen must remain . . . with the Queen."

"No," Rand said quickly, almost cutting Sinjin off. Rand's voice was rough, like a raspy file grating on cement. "You are most certainly no longer welcome here."

Sinjin dropped his smile but didn't lose the intensity of his glare, which was aimed at Rand. If looks could kill . . .

"I am the Queen's sworn protector—I go wherever she goes."

"Which brings up another issue, Rand," Mercedes interrupted. "I informed Jolie yesterday that she will need to make her home elsewhere—somewhere more suitable for a Queen."

Rand didn't say anything but shook his head and started pacing from one side of the room to the other in usual perturbed-Rand form. I personally hated the fact that I had to move, and seeing the anger chip away at Rand's face made the subject even harder to swallow.

Finally Rand stopped pacing and faced Mercedes. "I do not support a monarchy," he said simply.

The silence in the room seemed to pound against my mind with fists of mute frustration. I tore my gaze from Rand's face and looked around the table, noting the surprise in everyone's eyes.

Odran cleared his throat. "Ye have noo choice," he said.

"This is preordained, Rand." Mathilda glanced up at him with eyes of understanding. Aside from me, Mathilda really was the only other person in the room who cared about Rand. I thought of her as his surrogate mother in some ways.

"I don't care," Rand answered, shaking his head. "I couldn't tolerate the idea of Bella being Queen, and although I care deeply for Jolie, I can't support monarchy in any form."

I suddenly felt sick to my stomach, like I might vomit right then and there. This was what I'd been afraid of all along, though I'd known it was coming all the same. Really, I should never have expected otherwise—Rand was too stubborn, too dedicated to his ideals of democracy to ever sway from them. And for that, I actually admired him.

"Rand," I started but was drowned out by the voices of everyone else around the table. It was suddenly a cacophony of dissidence—questions tumbling over comments of surprise and anger.

"This is Jolie's destiny." Mercedes quieted everyone in an instant. It was as if she could control sound, so that only her voice could be heard. It sort of freaked me out.

"I believe in freedom of choice, not destiny," Rand responded, his voice constricted and tight.

"Jolie's fate is to become Queen and unite the creatures of the Underworld. Without her, our society's existence is perilous," Mercedes said.

Mathilda nodded and I glanced at Rand as the sick feeling returned. He was still avoiding my eyes. I felt like I was a ghost, just observing a conversation in which I had no part. I was losing him—I could almost feel him ripping away from me and I wanted to cry. Scratch that, I wanted to scream. But I couldn't argue with Mercedes because I knew that this *was* my destiny. And in accepting that there was a greater purpose for my life, I had to sacrifice Rand's love.

"Then if he isn't with us, he's against us?" Trent continued, his voice laced with anger.

"Rand is not against us," I said in a vacant voice.

Rand was silent for a few seconds, staring at me as if he'd only just remembered I was in the room. I said nothing in return and met his stare, our eyes having a conversation of their own.

Finally he smiled sadly. "I will never be against you. I am merely opting out. I have always been a renegade so I'll go back to being a renegade."

And that was the truth. When I was first introduced to this world and learned that newbies needed some type of protector, Rand hadn't been exactly keen on the idea of becoming mine. Instead he'd informed me that he lived outside the rules, that he was a renegade. But once Bella made it known that she wanted to be my protector—for less-than-noble reasons—Rand really had no choice but to take the task upon himself.

"No one should exist outside the rules of the kingdom," Varick said pointedly. "If we are to have a Queen over our society, we must come to terms with the fact that rules must exist for everyone. Otherwise, there is no difference to how things used to be."

"Yes, there would be a difference," Rand began. "A

monarchy would be in full effect but I would not consider myself an enemy of the state, merely a bystander."

"I doona like the idea," Odran said and shook his head.

"Frankly, I don't care," Rand answered.

I couldn't help but notice that Sinjin hadn't said anything. I was glad. I didn't want to know what was going through his head. But I did want to know what was going through Rand's.

It can be different, Rand, a different form of rule than you're imagining it to be, I thought and glanced up at him, my expression hopeful.

This goes against everything I believe, Jolie, everything I stand for.

Even though I knew it was fruitless, I couldn't help but fight back. I had to try to convince him his idea of monarchy was old school, that the Underworld Queen of the twenty-first century could be as different as night is to day.

It doesn't have to contradict your values, Rand. We can shape this role to be anything we want it to be! And for the first time, I realized what my goal was, my hope in taking the so-called throne—I didn't want to rule the Underworld alone. I wanted to lead with Rand by my side. The problem was that Rand was too stubborn to see it.

By its very nature, this goes against every fiber of my being, Jolie. I don't believe any creature should be subjugated to a ruler, whether Bella or . . . you.

Rand, please. Just give me a chance.

"As I understand it, there are creatures who are waiting to be brought back to life?" Mercedes asked, focusing on Rand again. I had to wonder if she'd been eavesdropping on our conversation or if she had just realized it was time for a change of subject matter.

Rand was quiet for a few seconds and then nodded. "I am ready if you and Jolie are."

Mercedes nodded and faced the table again. "I believe we should start with ten deceased at a time."

"Ten?" I asked in surprise, pushing all thoughts of being Queen to the back of my mind. "Um, I've only ever reanimated one person at a time, Mercedes."

"Jolie has a point," Rand said, shaking his head. "Ten seems overzealous."

Mercedes gave a smile that said she knew something we didn't. I've learned to hate those types of smiles.

"With the three of us, it will be an easy feat," Mercedes said. "Let us reassemble here tomorrow morning."

I just nodded although I had to wonder how in the hell I was going to reanimate ten of our fallen soldiers at the same time.

Later that evening, I couldn't sleep. Memories of Rand assaulted my mind and I couldn't seem to force them down. I sat up in my bed and sighed deeply. Sometimes I felt like I was living in the past—like I just couldn't allow the memories of my best moments with Rand to live in eternity as they were meant.

But tonight my memories were alive. And they centered on the moment when Rand had first told me he loved me. It was the evening before we were due to go to war with Bella, and Rand and I were in the midst of a telepathic conversation . . .

Rand was quiet for a moment or two. *Have you been crying?*

Yes, I've been so worried and I couldn't stomach the idea of you going to war and being angry with me.

I wasn't angry with you, Jolie. I was hurt.

I'm sorry.

There is something I've wanted to tell you for a while.

I'd hoped to tell you before tonight and I could kick myself for my own bloody foolish pride . . . but I want you to know there has never been a day I haven't thought of you. Sometimes I drive myself mad with debating over whether we should be together or not. I've never acted on my feelings because I've convinced myself I'm not in your best interests.

His comment amazed me. Not in my best interests? As if to say I was too good for him? *How could you not be in my best interest?*

Because you are special, Jolie. You're unique and someday you'll realize the extent of your powers. You're not like any Underworld creature I've ever seen before and I've kept you at arm's length because I feel such an incredible need to protect you.

Rand . . .

It's my own foolishness that has made me unable to tell you, but now we might never see each other again. I . . . I just want you to know . . .

He paused for such a long time, I wondered if I'd lost him. I was about to prompt him, to make sure he was still there but he beat me to it.

I love you. I've always loved you.

Nine

JOURNAL ENTRY

Enemies of the State

Diary, I've been thinking a lot about my vision of the Lurker attack and the fact that Mercedes is convinced that if I hadn't accepted my role of Queen, the Underworld creatures would continue to battle against one another and our society would become more and more vulnerable. Maybe even more important, we'd become easy targets and our enemies could infiltrate our ranks when we're at our weakest. The more I think about that somber possibility, the more I realize just how lucky we were that the Lurkers didn't ambush us when we were in the midst of battling Bella and her followers.

Even though I once thought the Lurkers weren't much of a force to be reckoned with, Mercedes has changed my mind. I think the main reason I never really took the threat of the Lurkers seriously was because I didn't entirely understand who or what they were. Sure, I'd heard of them taking out a few vamps, witches, and weres here and there, but they hadn't seemed all that intimidating. And no one knew that much about them.

The fact that no one knows much about them really disturbs Mercedes. In her words: "The first lesson you must learn as Queen, Jolie, is to keep your friends close but your enemies even closer. The fact that we know very little about the Lurkers is a problem and a problem that could devastate our society."

Needless to say, I got the hint and have decided to outline this great threat to our existence—to catalog all the things I do know about the Lurkers.

1. Lurkers are human half-breeds, part vampire and part human. Their history dates back to the seventeen hundreds in Graz, Austria. They began their existence as a band of human villagers who, realizing vampires were living among them, decided to act the part of pest control.

   The humans attacked the vamps but as you can probably guess, the vamps made short work of them. They fed on them and left them for dead. Apparently, in the chaos of the moment, a few of the villagers ended up ingesting some of the vampire blood, which not only ensured their survival but also endowed them with superhuman traits such as the strength and speed of a vampire and the ability to outlive their ordinary human counterparts. As I understand it, the average age of a Lurker is two hundred years. And Mercedes believes a few of the Lurker elders (who are still alive) were among the original massacred villagers, which means they have first-generation grudges in full effect.

2. Their race has been expanding over the centuries while ours has been dwindling. Due to the multitude of squabbles among the creatures of the Underworld (all the races tend to stick together with very little cross-breeding, and as mentioned earlier, witches have trouble procreating with one another so our race has been hurt the most), our community lacks the unity required to preserve it. Meanwhile, the Lurkers can procreate by breeding like ordinary humans, a huge boon to their power and number.

3. The Lurkers have only ever attacked us in guerrilla-style one-offs, giving the appearance that they lack any sort of accord or sophistication. Mercedes is convinced this attack style was meant to throw us off, to make us doubt them as a legitimate foe. And apparently their strategy worked.

4. Lurkers have attacked all Underworld creatures in general, giving the appearance that they want to banish anything otherworldly from the face of the earth. As to the whys of it, no one really knows. It sounds to me like they're seeking revenge, and I guess I can't blame them for hating vampires. I do find it ironic, though, that they want to banish something that's inherently a part of them. I have to wonder if they detest that part of themselves? Who knows. And really, does it matter?

5. The Lurkers possess magic. Even though I can only base this opinion on the vision I witnessed, I'm convinced there is more to the Lurkers than meets the eye. I could so clearly see and feel their magic when I was struck with that vision of them destroying our kind, I know it must be true. And that makes me wonder what their weaknesses are. Do they have any? Furthermore, how do we uncover their weaknesses? Even scarier, what if they don't have a chink in their armor—what if they are all-powerful? Somehow that seems impossible to me—if that were the case, they would have obliterated us a long time ago.

That's basically all I know. Mercedes advised us to put together a special task force whose only responsibility is researching the Lurkers and I gave this idea my blessing, so she's moving forward with it.

Really, the only other enemy of our state is Bella. Many of her followers died, and we're not about to reanimate them. Of those who survived, the majority *immediately took an oath (accompanied by a charm to ensure they didn't break it) pledging themselves to our side.*

What was interesting was the fact that of the twenty or so who seemed more hesitant, eighteen were demons. I don't have much experience with demons. In fact, the first demon I ever saw was on the battlefield, and I hadn't really known what to make of it. But according to Rand, demons can be law-abiding citizens of the Underworld so we had to offer them amnesty as long as they were willing to abide by our laws.

After some time and some gentle prodding, the demons also took the oath. In an ongoing attempt to ensure the loyalty of our followers, we started implementing truth serums. A truth serum is basically a liquid of some kind (we used apple juice) charmed with a loyalty oath. Any creatures in question drink the serum, and if they're guilty of allying themselves with our enemies, the truth serum begins to burn as soon as it hits their tongues. They usually can't handle it and after gagging, they vomit it all back up again.

Honestly, I'm not sure what I think about the truth serums—it seems a bit Clockwork Orange or Big Brother but I guess desperate times call for desperate measures and we need to know who is with us and who is against us. Oh God, I sound like Mercedes . . .

But back to Bella . . . Bella is most definitely not on our side and she poses a big risk to all of us. She wants nothing to do with the truth serums or oaths of allegiance and I have a feeling she'll continue to be a problem. Do I think she should be put to death? No, even though there are many among us who think death would be the best solution for her. What do I think should be done with her? I haven't decided.

I actually paid her a visit early this morning. I wanted to make sure she was being treated properly. Although she isn't allowed to leave her room in Pelham Manor—she has a comfortable room, three meals a day, a TV, and plenty of reading material (all Christa's old *Vogue* magazines, which I found humorous; why, I'm not really sure).

Anyway, Bella was less than friendly and accused me of coming to gloat. Of course I instantly denied it because it just wasn't true. Instead I told her I wished she'd join our side and that I bore her no ill will. She turned her back on me and told me to leave, that she wanted nothing to do with me. So I left. But before I went, I made sure to remind her I wasn't her enemy.

Yep, she's going to be a tough nut to crack. But I really do hope she comes around, because it would go against everything in my being to put her to death. It would not be right. And I know Rand would be opposed to it as well.

Rand.

I don't even like to think about what happened last night when he declared he didn't support the monarchy and intended to be a renegade again, living outside the rules of the kingdom. I know this whole Queen bit is going to drive us apart—I just don't see any way around it, and it breaks my heart every time I think about it.

I completely understand his angst toward a monarchy. Prior to the war with Bella, he'd outlined a plan for an ideal republic. It had been a good, solid plan, precluding the existence of a monarchy, since all creatures were endowed with the freedom of choice. Rand had designated covens around the world, and each creature would belong to the coven closest to it. Members would elect magistrates who would represent their interests. Rand even delineated a panel of thirteen elders, each elected by a coven as their representative. These leaders would meet monthly to discuss problems and find solutions.

Rand's republic was an exercise in weights and measures, everything and everyone being equal.

And really, I approved of this plan and still thought we could put it to use, just with me as the figurehead, since it was still necessary to ensure the creatures of the Underworld were unified. The problem, though, was that Rand couldn't seem to see my point of view or, if he did, he didn't believe it was possible.

Regardless, it's now ten o'clock and I've got a date with Mercedes and Rand so we can start reanimating our legion. At least we're all in agreement on that subject.

Mercedes decided we should do our reanimations outside since those who needed to be reanimated might be a bit dirty and bloody, having died while in the midst of a battle. That seemed to be fine by Rand, who didn't argue. I almost wanted to smile as I imagined us reanimating these first ten in Rand's living room and then watching them bleed all over his couch or bump into his priceless art pieces.

But my sense of humor didn't last long. Things were still strained between Rand and myself. I'd tried to talk to him after our meeting last night but he'd been barraged by questions from Odran, Varick, and Trent.

This morning I just felt like being alone and writing in my journal. Now I was face-to-face with him and although he was as polite as he always was, there was something hesitant about him, something reserved. Yep, I'd been exactly right—this Queen stuff was a huge elephant in the room, stomping and showing off her enormous tusks.

"Morning," I said to Rand with a weak smile.

"Hi, Jolie," he said with a smile that attempted to ignore the situation breaking us apart. "I hope you slept well?"

"I slept okay," I lied and dropped my attention to the ground, hating the fact that we were doing the whole small-talk thing. God, there was so much I wanted to say to him but I didn't want Mercedes to be our audience. I figured if I tried our mind connection, she would overhear it. Nope, I'd just have to wait for a better time, even though waiting basically sucked.

"So what do you want us to do exactly?" I asked Mercedes as a cold breeze rustled the elm trees and enveloped me in an unwanted hug. I shivered in the morning air and wrapped my arms around myself, hoping this little adventure wouldn't take very long. However, I couldn't imagine it would be a quick task to reanimate ten creatures, especially when in the past it had taken me the better part of a day to reanimate just one.

I felt a drop against my cheek and glanced upward, watching the dark gray clouds swirl and grumble above me as they threatened to swallow up the sky. A storm was coming, and by the looks of things it was moving in fast. Another cold wind rattled through the trees as two more drops spattered against my cheeks. I had to wonder if this was some sort of sign—it was as if the heavens didn't approve of us getting involved in the cycle of life and death.

"Hold Rand's hand," Mercedes said and glanced at me pointedly, like she was annoyed I was so preoccupied with the weather. I didn't say anything; I just nodded and turned to face my warlock. I reached for his hand at the same time he reached for mine and when our skin met, an electric pulse shot through my hand and blazed its way up my arm. It was the same feeling I got whenever I touched Rand—it was basically his energy, his power traveling into me. Sometimes it seemed stronger than others; today it was especially powerful, almost as if the electrons in the air were somehow recharging it.

I felt another drop on my hand and glanced at it,

watching it wind its way down my fingers and pool in the crevice of Rand's thumb and index finger. I couldn't help but focus on his strong hands—how large and capable they were, with long, slender fingers and the lightest dusting of dark brown hair at his wrists.

Rand squeezed my fingers, and I glanced up at him in surprise. He gazed at me, looking almost detached, like he was watching a movie.

Don't ever think I don't care about you, Jolie. It was his voice in my head. *No matter what happens, nothing can change my feelings for you.*

Rand, it doesn't have to be so black and white, I tried, my heart reeling at his confession. I wanted to, no, I *had* to convince him that the problem of the monarchy was something that could be resolved. It didn't have to be all one way or all the other.

We could still create your republic, I thought.

"Are you ready?" Mercedes asked and glanced at me impatiently. If I wasn't convinced she could magick me into oblivion, I would have bitch-slapped her silly for her bad timing.

"Yeah," I mumbled as Mercedes reached inside a big ziplock bag and produced a handful of cloth scraps. It looked like she was about to give us a lesson on quilting.

"Three for you," Mercedes announced as she handed me three squares of cloth: one red, one pink, and one black. I glanced down at them and fingered the cottons, figuring Mercedes must have cut the clothing supplied to us by our legion into smaller pieces so they'd take up less space. These three pieces of clothing represented three lives that were cut short—three lives we were about to give back.

"Very good," Mercedes said, once she'd handed Rand his three squares and she clutched the remaining four. "I believe you both know what to do next?"

I glanced at Rand as I remembered the previous two

occasions on which we'd reanimated creatures of the Underworld. Yep, I knew what to do now, and it was the hardest part of the whole process.

"Focus, focus, and then focus some more," I muttered. Rand chuckled and I glanced up at him.

You'll do fine. Don't worry, Jolie.

I didn't have the chance to respond before Mercedes took my hand and Rand's and then closed her eyes. I allowed myself one more drawn-out look at Rand then followed suit.

"Yes, focus," Mercedes began. "Empty your thoughts and try to concentrate on the emptiness within your mind, on nothing."

I tried but focusing on nothing is basically impossible— well, for my mind anyway. In fact, I was concentrating on the blackness of a void when remnants of my conversation with Christa and her sexual issues started sneaking into my head—images of furry, leopard handcuffs punctuated my thoughts until I wanted to scream. I clenched my eyes even tighter and instead was met with the image of John dressed like a pirate and muttering "Aye, where be the warmin' liquid?"

"I can't do this!" I opened my eyes in an instant, hoping I hadn't been permanently blinded by the images in my mind's eye.

"Jolie." Mercedes' tone was that of a teacher reprimanding an unruly child.

"Focusing on nothing is just dumb," I spat out, afraid to close my eyes again lest the sexual pirate John make another appearance.

"Let me try," Rand said to Mercedes. Not waiting for her response, he pulled my other hand from hers. He faced me and, taking both my hands in his, smiled down at me. "Close your eyes."

I did and felt like I wanted to cry, I was so overwhelmed with the need to tell him I was the woman with whom he'd bonded. It suddenly seemed like a very good idea—maybe Christa had been right when she said he'd be happy to know the love of his life had been me all along. In fact, maybe he'd be so thrilled, we could put this monarchy stuff behind us.

"Focus with me, Jolie," he whispered and began massaging my hands with his much larger ones. His energy seemed to reverberate through me, encompassing me in a cocoon of power. "You're surrounded by darkness— night is all around you. Picture that darkness, Jolie. It's limitless. You can't see where it begins or where it ends."

Rand's voice flowed through me, seeming to reach out to every molecule of my body and soothe me, blanketing me with his calming baritone. And suddenly I could see the darkness, I was enveloped by it. I felt Rand shift and my hand was engulfed in Mercedes' much smaller one. Her power rippled up my arm. With Rand's on the other side, I felt like the middle of a power sandwich.

Then I heard something faint—the smallest sound of chinking metal against metal. I opened my eyes. I was still surrounded by darkness, only the moon's glow showing me that I was in the midst of a battle. All around me creatures fought—the sounds of their screaming and cries of pain thick in my ears. Beyond me stretched flat grassland, for miles, with only a few groves of trees interrupting the otherwise monotonous green. On my left side, I noticed a few enormous stones, some standing and some on their sides. Beyond them were small rocks piled high atop one another. There were rows and rows of them, creating circular patterns that I immediately recognized as the Clava Cairns—the Scottish burial mounds.

We were in Scotland, then, near the battlefield of Culloden, fighting against Bella. I glanced around me in shock, suddenly worried I might be in the line of fire.

Then I remembered that in this altered state of reality, I was a ghost; nothing could hurt me.

Recalling that I was here to find the ten people whom we were to be reanimating first, I glanced over both of my shoulders, wondering where the hell Mercedes was. Rand never seemed to be able to transport himself whenever I went on one of these reanimation excursions, so it wasn't a big surprise that he was absent.

But I was surprised that I didn't see Mercedes anywhere. I glanced down and noticed I was clutching all ten scraps of fabric in my right hand. I didn't remember Rand or Mercedes transferring them to me—not that it mattered now. Obviously I was on this mission alone.

Before I could think another thought, it was as if some unseen force suddenly pushed me forward. I found myself walking, then running straight ahead, aiming for two men who were thick in the heat of battle. One was a were, and I could feel his ability to shift radiating off him. The other was a vamp. The were was fighting a losing battle against the vamp and I could see his skin beginning to ripple—he was preparing to shift.

My palm started to burn. When I glanced down, a dark green piece of cloth had begun to tremble as if there were a tiny creature burrowing underneath it. I watched as a light built from underneath the fabric until it engulfed the entire square.

The dark green material began to roll into itself like one of those fortune-reading fish and I realized it was singling itself out—it had been the object that pulled me toward these two men. And that was when it dawned on me that one of these men was about to die and I had to intervene in order to bring him back to life. I just had to figure out which one . . .

No sooner did the thought cross my mind than the vamp lunged at the were before the were had the chance to shape-shift. The vamp caught the weaker man in the throat with fangs that glinted in the moonlight. I felt myself lurch forward, and just as the vamp tore away from the were, flesh hanging from his teeth as blood pulsed from the open wound, I grabbed the were's hand. And instantly he was gone.

As soon as I made contact and the were disappeared, I felt something ricochet through me, something that felt like my magic separating from me. I fell back and hit the ground, panting as my heartbeat raced in my chest. This had never before happened when I'd attempted to re-animate someone—it was like touching an electric fence, almost as if my magic had misfired. But if that were the case, where had the were gone?

I glanced around, realizing that all of the swatches of fabric littered the earth beneath me. Suddenly afraid the vamp might attack me, I jerked my neck up but then remembered I wasn't really there and was, therefore, safe. The vamp glanced down at the ground beside me and then turned around and disappeared into the throng of fighting soldiers. He didn't act as though he'd just watched his enemy disappear in front of him, so I had to imagine that in his parallel universe, the body of the were was still lying in the blood-soaked earth.

I forced myself to my knees, trying to shake off the headache that nagged at me. I grabbed the pieces of cloth I'd dropped on the ground and stood up, waiting for the next piece of cloth to lead me to my next crea-ture, all the while still wondering if my first attempt had been successful.

I didn't have to wait long. A piece of pink cloth began to quiver while a dull, pinkish glow emanated from it. I felt compelled to turn to my right so I allowed my feet to follow, to bring me through the throng of fighting sol-diers. Once on the other side, my eyes immediately fell upon a woman, a fairy, who was on the ground, battling a creature I had little experience with—a demon. It had the body of a man but a long red tail extended from its backside . . . like a coiled snake ready to bite, the barbs in the tail had embedded themselves in the fairy woman's thigh as she wailed in pain.

The creature had her pinned on her stomach, its gargantuan mouth biting into the nape of her neck as she begged for release and blood soaked the dirt beneath her. The demon ripped its barbed tail from her thigh and reeled it around like a fishing line, only to embed it into the fairy's side. The woman yelped in agony before collapsing, just as the demon prevented her from falling against the ground by wrapping his arm around her middle. With one hand, the creature fondled her breasts and I realized the bastard planned on raping her before killing her.

So I did what any woman would do—I ran full bore at the demon and kicked him in his gut. And of course, it didn't faze the demon at all because I was, for all intents and purposes, a ghost. Instead I just flew right through the demon and landed on my ass. That was when the ugly realization dawned on me—I might have to witness this creature having its way with the woman before it killed her. After all, the only window I had to reanimate her was at the point of her death. And that reality sickened me.

I stood up and turned around to face the demon as I watched Odran hurl himself into the creature, prying it off the fairy woman with a roar that would scare Satan himself. Odran then lifted the demon above his head WWF style and threw the ugly bastard about ten feet into the air. Then, bringing his hands out in front of him, Odran magicked a lance in a split second. In a flash the demon hit the ground and Odran wasted no time impaling the demon with the lance, straight into its gut. The creature groaned as a forked tongue snaked out of its mouth; then it collapsed in a dead heap at Odran's feet.

When Odran and I turned to the fairy woman to see if she was all right, she was already dying. Why, I had no idea, but her eyes had gone slack and I could see the pulse in her throat slowing. I had to wonder if the barbs on the demon's tail were poisonous—or maybe just poisonous to the fae. But at the moment I couldn't be concerned with poisonous barbs. I did what I'd been trained to do and dived down, touching her just as Odran lifted her into his colossal arms. And she disappeared.

And the same exact feeling of electricity pounced through me as soon as I made contact with her. Only now it was accompanied by a sense of weakness, of exhaustion. I leaned over and panted, bracing myself against the ground on all fours. I felt like I'd just sprinted at top speed. I felt like I was going to throw up.

I pushed the feeling aside and rolled onto my butt, forcing myself to sit up. Whatever the hell was wrong with me, I had more creatures to reanimate, eight as a matter of fact. And how I was going to get through eight more was beyond me.

After what felt like an eternity, I was left with one scrap of fabric in my hand and one creature left to reanimate. I'd already reanimated four weres, the fairy woman, three vamps (which was a curious subject because I'd never been sure that the undead could be reanimated considering they weren't alive to begin with), and one witch. And to say I was tired was an understatement. With each reanimation, the feeling of electricity coursing through me was stronger, and after each session I was left weaker. Yet I had no choice but to continue forward, to get through the list of ten.

I took a deep breath and glanced down at the final piece of black cloth in my hand. It glimmered into a subtle glow and vibrated as I allowed it to lead me to my final rescue for the day. That was when I made the mistake of glancing to my right and seeing . . . myself. It was like I was having an out-of-body experience as I just stood there, watching myself. I glanced down at my legs as if to make sure I was still standing there and not some ethereal being, but no, I was still me, still corporeal.

I couldn't say I heard or felt anything at that moment. Instead I thought I was mired in quicksand, unable to pull myself away from the visual unfolding before me. Gwynn, wearing an expression of agony mixed with pure rage since I'd just cremated her lover and creator, Ryder, pulled back her arm and rammed her blade into my gut. I watched myself fall as my gaze moved down my body to the hilt of the dagger. My eyes revealed only disbelief.

Sinjin stood by my feet and in an instant he was on Gwynn, ripping her head off, not even watching as she exploded into dust before him. Instead his eyes were riveted on me with an expression on his face I'd never seen before—something that looked like terror.

Mercedes was also there, standing next to Rand. But all I could focus on was Rand—as he held me and tears bled from his eyes, Rand crooning to me and begging me not to die.

But I did die—I knew it now as well as I'd known it then. And watching yourself die is the most macabre, bizarre feeling in the world. I literally just slouched in Rand's arms as he dropped his head against mine and sobs racked his entire body.

I watched Mercedes lean down, place her hand on my forehead, and close her eyes. Instantly my eyes blinked open, wide with confusion and panic. My chest rose as the breath of life filled my lungs. But I couldn't even focus on myself, not when the smile on Rand's face was the most glorious, beautiful thing I'd ever seen.

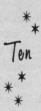

Ten

After watching myself die and Mercedes bring me back to life again, I somehow managed to seek out the last creature on the list, a witch, and brought her back to life, albeit absentmindedly. I mean, I was still reeling over the fact that I'd just witnessed my own death and was sort of in a haze.

Then I observed a bright flash of light followed by a moment or two of total darkness. I must have passed out because the next thing I knew, I was lying on the ground outside, my face and cheek up close and personal with the rough dirt. I rolled over to find Rand and Mercedes leaning over me with concerned expressions while the ten recently reanimated creatures looked on in what appeared to be shock, something we had in common.

Surprisingly, I had managed to reanimate all ten creatures in one day, and I'd never felt worse. I was exhausted, but more than that, I still felt nauseous. When I asked Mercedes where in the hell she'd been during the reanimations, she'd replied rather dismissively that this was my gift, not hers . . . WTF?

Of course, I was quick to point out the fact that she'd played the part of the Energizer Bunny well enough when I died on the battlefield and she subsequently brought me back to life. Her reply? Reanimating me had only been possible because I was part of the equation—I had to wonder if that meant that if I had been someone else, I'd be pushing up daisies right about now.

Well, I'd just been through hell and back so I didn't feel like arguing or digging any deeper into a subject she clearly had no interest in pursuing, so I left it at that. Thinking I definitely deserved the night off, I wasn't exactly thrilled to learn that Mercedes had arranged for my first lesson as Queen to begin that same evening!

Worst of all, my first lesson was ballroom dancing (by default due to the fact that my other tutors weren't available on such short notice) . . . blah, blah, and blah again. If I could be described in one word, it would be *clumsy*, so I was looking forward to this lesson about as much as a stick in my eye.

Mercedes took exactly two minutes to introduce me to my instructor, Herr Strauss. Then she promptly disappeared, saying she needed to leave me to my lessons. Really, I think she just wanted to escape Herr Strauss because he appeared to be as interesting as a wall.

"Ven you are dancing zee Valtz, you must feel zee Valtz, taste zee Valtz, and zee zee Valtz in order to love zee Valtz, yah?"

My instructor (who must have been German or maybe Austrian) had the physique of a flagpole with long, skinny legs and arms; his posture was just as rigid. He was a were but unlike most weres, he wasn't at all burly and his skin was so translucent white he looked like he could be the descendant of a turnip. His hair looked like white straw and matched the white of his trimmed mustache to a T. He looked like a praying mantis someone had doused in flour.

"Come zen," he said, holding out his long, scarecrow arms, motioning for me to come closer, as I responded by taking a step backward.

We were in Rand's ballroom—yes, Pelham Manor had

a ballroom, though this was the first time I'd ever been inside it. The floors were dark oak with cream-colored walls. Floor-to-ceiling windows boasted panoramic vistas that included a grove of elm trees bisected by a running creek. A carpet of bluebells decorated the grass, making it seem as though you were viewing some exquisite painting rather than the grounds of Pelham Manor. Inside the room, crown molding accessorized the junction of the walls and the ceiling; suspended from the center of the ceiling was the most ornate chandelier I've ever seen, its prismatic crystals reflecting rainbows all around the room.

"Like zis," my praying mantis partner said, holding his stick-insect arms out before him as if he were blindly groping for a light switch.

I held my right arm like I was pretending to hug a tree and put my left arm directly in front of me, which I'm sure made me look like I was about to pull a *Matrix* move on him, Keanu Reeves style. The praying mantis scrunched up his face in what appeared to be disgust and dropped his elegantly draped arms down to aid my less-than-elegant ones.

"Zis and zis," he said as he angled my arms appropriately. "Zen you follow mine steps like a box. A one ztep, a du ztep, a tree ztep, and four!" With that he whizzed around me, his feet in a perfect box step while I just observed in wonder.

"Now you," he said. I tried my best to imitate him but as soon as I saw scrunchy face number two, I realized I'd failed.

Master Strauss didn't get the chance to lambaste me further because we were interrupted by the sound of deep chuckling and clapping. We both turned to face the source. I frowned as I saw Sinjin emerge from the doorway, a smile of amusement lighting his handsome face.

"That is no way to teach a lady to dance," he said,

arching a brow at the stick insect who merely "har-umphed" in response. Sinjin strode right past him until he stood directly before me.

"My Queen," he said with a lascivious smile. With a quick bow he took my left hand in his and pulled me in so close, my stomach touched his groin. Then, as if the fact that my stomach against his groin was of no conse-quence to him, he laid the palm of his other hand flat onto the small of my back. He glanced down at me and winked before facing Herr Strauss again.

"You must hold her closely enough that she can feel your body tightly against her so that she may copy your moves." Sinjin dropped his attention to me, and his eyes were piercing as he gazed down at me. "You must glide with her, become one with her."

I swallowed hard. I couldn't help it.

"Zir, I have been teaching zee Valtz for zirty years," Herr Strauss spat out, his eyes livid as he folded his tree-branch arms across his prepubescent chest.

"And I have been dancing the Waltz for hundreds of years," Sinjin said flatly. Before Herr Strauss could argue further, Sinjin was suddenly gliding across the floor and I was moving with him. His feet swayed so lightly and gracefully, I had to glance down to ensure we were still touching the ground.

"Never take your eyes from your partner, poppet," he whispered and I brought my eyes back to his ice-blue ones. "Your gaze must never leave mine. All you need to do is follow the lines of my body, allow me to lead you."

I just nodded and smiled up at him, finding huge relief in Sinjin's arms after my disastrous experiences with Herr Strauss. Just the idea of touching the praying man-tis had been enough to turn me off dancing for the rest of my life.

"This is a very simple dance, really," Sinjin continued. "I begin with my left foot and I execute a forward half box." He completed the half box. Then he stepped backward and did the same thing. "The next step is the same, only in reverse. And you, my very lovely poppet, begin with your right foot and execute a backward half box, followed by a forward half box."

"You lost me at box," I said with a smile.

Sinjin chuckled and pulled me in closer, until I could feel the swells of his thighs as they shifted against me. I'd never realized how . . . sensual dancing could be—how feeling the motion of a man's, of Sinjin's, body against mine could be such an . . . erotic experience.

I heard Herr Strauss mutter something angrily before stomping out of the room. After dancing with Sinjin, and feeling the expert way he whisked me across the floor, the idea of dancing with the stick insect was . . . unappealing to say the least.

"Just follow my lead, love," Sinjin said as I obediently stared into his eyes, forcing myself not to second-guess my own feet. Strangely enough, they seemed to be doing a good job on their own.

"If I didn't know better, I'd say you vampired me into knowing how to dance," I said with an elevated brow, wondering if I hadn't succumbed to some form of vampiric persuasion.

Sinjin didn't respond but just smiled in an amused sort of way as he twirled me around the room so deftly, I didn't even feel like it was me dancing with him. It was almost as if I'd had an out-of-body experience, and was watching a woman who looked like me—someone with long blond hair, blue eyes, and freckles across the bridge of her nose. But no, it was most definitely me, and I'd basically just mastered the waltz with Sinjin's help. Feeling suddenly courageous, I decided to tread into dangerous territory.

"Sinjin?"

"Yes, my love?" he asked.

"Why have you always been so interested in the prophetess?" I asked with a sweet, innocent smile, as if I were merely curious and not burning with the need to know. "What do you have up your sleeve?"

He chuckled but didn't lose a beat. Instead he twirled me in front of him and then pulled me back into the cocoon of his body. I almost lost my breath as I bounced against him and found myself so close I could feel the silkiness of his shirt against my cheek and his breath on the top of my head. Somehow I didn't think we were dancing the waltz any longer. No, this felt more like the "forbidden dance," whatever that was. I felt my heartbeat increase as blood rushed to my head.

"Interested, my pet?" Sinjin asked as he leaned into me, inhaling deeply, and smiled to reveal his fangs. "I make you nervous."

I shook my head but I realized it was stupid to argue the point. He did make me nervous. I never knew what he was thinking, or what his intentions were. And he had a tendency to want to . . . touch me all the time.

"You're a vampire and I'm full of blood," I answered dismissively.

"That is not why I make you nervous."

"Let's talk instead about your fascination with the prophetess," I said, pulling away from him, giving my feet a well-deserved rest and hoping some air might clear my head. I took another two steps back.

"I have no fascination with the prophetess," Sinjin said and shrugged as if to reinforce his response as casual, unconcerned. "I believe the only person you could accuse me of having a fascination with would be you, poppet."

I laughed and shook my head. "Only because I've got a crown over my head."

Sinjin wetted his lips and narrowed his eyes as I felt my heart drop again. It was the expression of someone who was about to pounce on his prey, about to take whatever it was he wanted.

"Not quite, my love. You know I have sought you from the beginning." He paused for a second and then took the two steps that separated us. "Yes, from the very first moment you sauntered into my life, dressed in your little tutu"—I'd gone to a costume party dressed as a fairy—"my interest in any other females was forever quelled."

"Why do I find that hard to believe?" I asked, eyeing him suspiciously, propping my hands on my hips. Sinjin's libido was quelled? Yeah . . . No. Sinjin was the most sexual creature I'd ever met—he even rivaled Christa, and that's saying something.

"I do not know, love," Sinjin said as a secretive smile spread across his lips. "Did my heart love till now? Forswear it, sight. For I never saw true beauty until this night." He ran his fingers down my cheek and chin and smiled again. His fangs were noticeably longer, and I'm sure I was just imagining it but they also looked sharper.

"Nice, Romeo," I said with a hesitant smile although I had to admit there was something . . . romantic about an incredibly handsome man quoting lines from *Romeo and Juliet*. But romantic or not, I had to ponder why Sinjin appeared to have such an . . . attachment to me. Of course, whether or not that perceived attachment was legitimate was anyone's guess. Regardless, I wasn't the type to lead him on.

"Sinjin," I began in a serious tone. "I hope this is all a big joke to you because you know we can never be anything other than friends . . ."

"Shh, love," he interrupted, bringing his fingers to my lips. "I know you imagine yourself to be enamored of the warlock."

I didn't respond because I wasn't entirely sure what to say. "Enamored of the warlock" didn't really even begin to describe my feelings for Rand. Then it suddenly occurred to me that maybe I should tell Sinjin I'd bonded with Rand in 1878—maybe then he would understand how deep my love for Rand really was. As soon as the thought sprang into my head, I rejected it. Somehow word would get out. Rand needed to hear about our bonding from me firsthand, not from the vampvine.

Sinjin dropped his fingers but not the soul-searching gaze in his eyes. "I am well aware of the rules of this game, poppet," he whispered. "Therefore, let us have just one more dance."

And so I did. I abandoned my hang-ups about Rand as well as my questions about what the hell Sinjin wanted from Mercedes. Instead I just allowed Sinjin to hold me tightly, guiding me around the room. I allowed myself to enjoy the feel of a man's hands around me, Sinjin's hands, and pretended that maybe in an alternate universe somewhere, maybe in the vicinity of Kurt Vonnegut's planet of rolling tires, Sinjin and I could have our day.

It had to be midnight. Well, I wasn't sure what time it was exactly, but judging by the pitch black outside, I assumed it must be the dead of night. I found myself in Rand's living room, awaiting the arrival of Varick and Sinjin who had gone out feasting . . . On whom, I had no idea. Odran and Trent sat on Rand's leather couch while Rand stood on one side of the fireplace and I stood on the other, trying to thaw the perpetual chill that had lodged itself in my bones. I never could get used to cold English nights.

Rand seemed to be doing his utmost to avoid looking at me and I was doing my utmost to avoid looking at him. It was silly but obligatory because it wasn't like we could now get into the mega-conversation that we kept evading. It seemed that lately there was just too much going on for us to reconnect. I was either in dance lessons or otherwise preoccupied with equally fun tasks while Rand was . . . well, Rand was Rand.

Mercedes stood at the front door, searching for any sign of Sinjin or Varick. She turned to face us again, letting out a sigh as though she were eager to start our emergency meeting. Apparently, an hour or so earlier, someone had arrived at Pelham Manor bearing the news that the Lurkers had struck in Vermont. They'd killed twenty Underworld creatures—actually the entire population of Underworld creatures who made their homes in Vermont—eleven weres, two witches, and seven vamps.

After another minute or so, Varick and Sinjin appeared in the doorway and Mercedes hurriedly ushered them into the living room. Upon seeing me, Sinjin smiled and bowed low, whispering "my Queen" in salutation. My heart rose up into my throat and my pulse thundered in my ears. I didn't smile but just glanced away, suddenly feeling uncomfortable about our dance. For some reason, it almost seemed indecent to me—indecent that we had danced so closely and even more indecent that I'd allowed it.

I was meant to be with Rand—I convinced myself of that when he and I had our moment in 1878. Now I was doing a damn poor job of keeping my promise that he and I would be together again in the here and now. While I didn't have the luxury of time when it came to picking a suitable moment to talk to Rand, dancing with Sinjin certainly hadn't moved me any closer to my goal.

None of that mattered now, though. What mattered was the twenty of our own who were now dead.

"What happened?" Rand demanded. I couldn't help but notice his gaze as it traveled back and forth between Sinjin and me. I almost wondered if his question was aimed at us or at Mercedes.

"I only know what the messenger shared with me,"

Mercedes said. Evidently, the so-called messenger had come across the death scene in Vermont and immediately boarded a plane to England and Pelham Manor. He'd announced the dire news to Mercedes, who just happened to be the first person he encountered.

"And where is this messenger?" Sinjin asked nonchalantly as he settled himself in an unoccupied armchair just beside me. He stretched out his long legs and crossed them at the ankles, looking comfortable and dashing in his customary black attire.

"He seemed a bit . . . flustered . . . so I charmed him to sleep," Mercedes answered with a smile. That had to mean the poor guy was so frazzled after seeing his friends and/or family massacred and then traveling half a day, he probably had a meltdown. I know I would have. And luckily for him, he had Mercedes instead of Tylenol PM.

"But upon my instructions, he was able to procure this." Mercedes reached across the tabletop behind her and produced a bloody, wadded-up piece of clothing that appeared to be a shirt or maybe a skirt. I thought the fabric was pink, or maybe all the blood had just turned it pink.

"I guess we're on again tonight?" I asked, realizing Mercedes planned another reanimation for whomever the clothes had belonged to, and that she'd probably intended for us to do it immediately. But the thought of attempting to reanimate anyone else left me nothing but worried. I wasn't sure I had the strength to go through it again. Not after what had happened last time.

"That was my intention," Mercedes said with finality.

"I don't think I can handle ten more," I said hesitantly, biting my lower lip. "Something happened to me with the last ten."

"You are not aware of your own strength," Mercedes said dismissively but Rand interrupted her.

"What do you mean, Jolie?"

I shook my head. "I don't know what happened but it was as if I lost some of my power with each reanimation. I was exhausted like I've never been before. It was like . . . like electricity went through me or something."

"It is a difficult feat to reanimate more than one creature," Mercedes started.

"If Jolie isn't feeling well," Rand interrupted.

But I knew we'd have to reanimate at least one of the dead in this most recent incident. Otherwise, how would we ever find out exactly what had happened?

"I think I'm okay," I said with an insincere smile at Rand.

He just frowned and cocked a brow before facing Mercedes again. She held up the tattered piece of clothing she'd managed to obtain from the messenger and studied it before facing us all expectantly. "This is a sign, I hope you all realize."

"Ah sign?" Odran repeated, reminding me that he and Trent were still in the room. It's funny how whenever Rand and Sinjin were in attendance, everyone else seemed to fade into the background.

Mercedes nodded as she faced the fire, appearing to lose herself in the dancing flames. Worry gnawed at her features, and I had to wonder what was going through her head. Suddenly realizing she had an audience, she cleared her throat and faced us again.

"I imagine our enemies know what our weaknesses are—that our population continues to dwindle while theirs continues to increase. We are on the precipice of a disaster that could wipe us out entirely."

"And what do you propose we do?" Rand asked with tight lips. I glanced at him, despite my attempt to keep from looking at him all night. Seeing him did me no good. Instead it made me all nervous and flustered inside and increased my body temperature by about five degrees.

"We need to continue reanimating the entire legion," Mercedes said.

"We're already doing that," I pointed out, in a *duh* sort of tone.

"No." Rand shook his head as his eyes found mine. "We're reanimating our side, not Bella's."

Mercedes nodded as if to say Rand had hit the nail right on the head. "Perhaps we should reanimate both sides, ours and Bella's."

There were lots of hushed tones as everyone reacted to the idea of reanimating our enemies. The more I thought about it, though, the more I realized there was no way around it. If the Lurkers really were growing in numbers, it was possible that they could wipe us out. Especially if we couldn't discover their weakness or, worse yet, if they didn't have any weaknesses. And as to whether or not our magic would work against them . . .

"Mercedes, does witch magic work against the Lurkers?" I asked.

She shook her head. "I do not know." She seemed uncomfortable with that fact.

"Bella's soldiers could take the loyalty oath with truth serum to ensure they are on our side," I said in a small voice, basically admitting that I agreed with Mercedes.

"It is a risk," Rand interjected as he started to pace back and forth. And he was right—it would be a risk because it would mean that half our proposed legion had once been loyal to Bella. In effect, we'd have a legion that was already polarized, already divided against itself.

I glanced at Rand again and noticed he was wearing a long-sleeved, white T-shirt and dark jeans. It looked as if he was in need of a haircut because his chestnut waves stuck out from behind his ears. I actually preferred his hair long like this—it gave him a rugged sort of look. But it wasn't like Rand—*unkempt* wasn't part of his vocabulary.

"Bella's soldiers would recognize the Lurkers as a bigger threat to their future than us," Trent pointed out. "That could be enough to get them on our side."

"Aye," Odran concurred. I glanced at him, wondering why he'd been so quiet throughout the meeting—it wasn't like Odran. However, seeing he was almost passed out on Rand's couch, I guessed he was just tired. Hmm, had someone had a busy evening?

"Regardless of whether we decide to reanimate Bella's legion, we're forgetting a major issue. We don't have time to reanimate more creatures," I interrupted, suddenly very aware of how long it would take to reanimate another two hundred soldiers.

"If we reanimated Bella's soldiers, that would bring our number of soldiers to five hundred," Mathilda said quietly.

"Is that enough to take on the Lurkers?" I asked, somewhat surprised to know we would only number five hundred. Of course, I guess it made sense: If Underworld creatures numbered in the hundreds of thousands, the society of humans would not exist as it currently did. The entire world would be subject to the powers and abilities of the Underworld beings, who were much more powerful than humans.

Mathilda cocked her head to the side as if she were considering my question. "I do not know."

"How many are on their side?" I asked, glancing at Mercedes.

She shrugged. "I believe their numbers are close to one thousand."

"One thousand?" I repeated. "How is that possible? That sounds much smaller than I'd imagined. I thought they had no issues with procreating?"

Mercedes shook her head. "The females are only fertile for a short time before they become Lurkers, that is, before their fangs set in."

"But you said they were expanding at an alarming speed?" I argued.

"Their rate of procreation is faster than ours, that was my point."

"How do you know this?" Rand asked.

Mercedes frowned at him. "I have learned all I know of the Lurkers through visions and brief encounters with them over the hundreds of years of both of our existences. I admit my knowledge of them is hardly exhaustible." She paused for a few seconds. "What I do know is that in order for us to defeat them, we will need Bella's legion."

Everyone was quiet as they mulled over the possibilities of reanimating Bella's legion. Before I could think of a solution for the time issue, I was plagued with yet another troubling thought. "We don't have any pieces of clothing or anything personal from Bella's soldiers, which prevents us from being able to reanimate them in the first place."

"We'd have to get Bella on board," Rand answered, sighing as if that task would be even harder than reanimating her entire legion. He was probably right.

"That's virtually impossible," I said, remembering how less than happy she'd been to see me when I'd visited her. No, she would relish having us at her mercy and would love telling all of us to shove it.

"There would be no other way," Rand argued as he started pacing back and forth again. "She must have created a ledger or something of that nature bearing the names of all her soldiers."

"I don't see Bella helping us," Trent said.

"I think he's right, Rand," I said.

"We're not offering her a choice," Rand interrupted,

stopping mid-pace as he focused on me. "If we don't give her a choice, she can't refuse."

"Leave Bella to me," Sinjin said with authority. I turned to face him and found him staring at me. I frowned, remembering that he'd befriended Bella on false pretenses once before. When he and I had met, he'd been pretending to be allied with her and had also been boffing her, both of which made me feel ill.

"If anything, she hates you more than anyone else, given the circumstances," I said in response.

"Is not the line between love and hate very thin?" he asked with a devil's smile. I just shook my head.

Mercedes glanced at him and nodded. "Do what you must," she said, ending the conversation.

"I believe step number one is to bring our victim back to life," Mercedes announced and reached for the item of clothing again. She handed the clump to me, and I was immediately captivated by some sort of perfume that smelled like lilies. The scent was light but sweet and I guessed this victim was a woman. I glanced at Rand and offered one hand at the same time Mercedes took the other. Now the fun would start.

"Do you want me to help you focus, Jolie?" Rand asked.

I closed my eyes and shook my head. I concentrated on the black of my closed eyelids as I attempted to tune out the room around me and everyone in it. The darkness began to swirl and I felt as if I were floating in a sea of black nothing, riding the swells as reality began to erode into surreality.

My feet landed on something hard that felt like concrete. I opened my eyes to find that I was standing in the backyard of a one-story house. Surrounded by a forest of trees, I noticed that there were no birds singing or insects chirping. Instead screaming deafened my ears and appeared to be coming from the house. I wasn't sure what to do so I took a few steps forward, nearly tripping over a woman lying prostrate before me. A man stood above her, staring down at her lifeless body. I figured he must be a family member.

I knelt to ensure she was dead when I noticed that the man above her was suddenly wielding a wooden stake. The man smiled and revealed the tiniest fangs—almost like sharpened Chiclets.

As I suddenly realized the woman wasn't dead and this jerk was about to finish her off, I lurched forward and dived for her. The Lurker brought the stake down in a split second, his speed and strength impressively fast, vampire fast. I felt a handful of the woman's hair in my palm. When I opened my eyes, she appeared to be fading, disappearing into the air. I glanced down at myself and noticed that the same thing was happening to me.

I don't think I passed out this time—the transition between reality and alternate reality was much faster than it had been earlier. I blinked and found myself in Rand's arms as he, Mercedes, and everyone in the room focused on the woman who was huddled on the floor before us.

She seemed to take a deep breath and then stood up on wobbly legs, glancing around herself as if wondering where the hell she was.

"Where . . . what . . . ," she started in an American accent, a Texan drawl to be more specific. Her eyes fell to Sinjin and she heaved a sigh of relief.

"Sinjin Sinclair," she said and paused for a second or two. "Why do I have the feeling I just died and you really are the devil himself?"

Eleven

Even though Sinjin merely chuckled at the woman's accusation, it was safe to say that the rest of us were shocked. It seemed as if even the fire in the fireplace was taken aback because it hissed, hurling a few sparks against the screen.

"Ah, we meet again," Sinjin said in his sexiest voice as he looked her up and down appreciatively.

"Well, I can't say I'm really all that bothered by the fact that I'm dead," she replied with a coy laugh as she approached him. I think the rest of us were too mummified by what happened next to even make a sound—she simply leaned down, placed her hands on either side of Sinjin's face, and kissed him! Then, in the next split second, she pulled her hand back and smacked him right across the face.

"And that's for taking off and never leaving word about where the hell you went, you son of a bitch!" she shouted angrily, fangs indenting her lower lip.

And Sinjin, in true Sinjin form, didn't budge or resist. He merely allowed her to attack him and relaxed back into Rand's armchair, unfazed. "I apologize, love, but I was much younger then and could not be tied down," he said with a self-satisfied smile. Jerkwad.

"As if you could ever be tied down," the woman replied, some of her femme fatale wiliness sinking back into her tone.

"So are you going to introduce your . . . friend, Sinjin?" I asked, not meaning to sound so put out. I even let my arms drop from across my chest in an attempt at indifference, as though knowing these two had a past didn't bother me in the least.

The woman turned to face me and I realized how pretty she was. She had long dark hair that reached the middle of her back, blue eyes, and a smile that seemed contagious.

"I apologize," she said, shaking her head almost as if she were embarrassed. "I'm Klaasje Helgren, it's nice to meet you." She pronounced her name *Klasha*—like *Tasha* with a *Kla*.

She offered me her hand and I shook it, figuring that since I was the one to bring her back to life, I should probably act the part of the good hostess. Of course, the one who knew her better than any of us was Sinjin, who was evidently responsible for the wham, bam, thank you, ma'am, but whatever.

"I'm Jolie," I began, smiling while motioning to Rand, who merely tipped his chin in acknowledgment. "And this is Rand Balfour, owner of this manor. Mercedes Berg, the prophetess." I turned to face Mercedes.

"The prophetess?" Klaasje repeated with her wide eyes fastened on Mercedes. "I always thought you were just a fable."

"Luckily for me, that is not so," Mercedes said with a little laugh. I was so unaccustomed to her making jokes that I didn't even really know how to respond. Instead I hurriedly continued with my introductions.

"This is Odran, King of the fae," I began as I suddenly realized I had no clue what Odran's last name was. Did the fae even have last names? Odran Fairy? Hmm, that sounded . . . well, it didn't sound good. "And this is

Trent, head of the weres. And you probably already know Varick?"

Klaasje just nodded and flashed Varick a quick smile. He dropped his head in much the same way Rand had, but somehow with Varick it seemed ice cold and unfriendly.

"And you obviously already know Sinjin," I finished and frowned at the vampire in question as he beamed up at me, playing the part of an innocent.

"Yes, Mr. Sinclair and I are well acquainted," Klaasje announced as she presented Sinjin with another flirtatious smile.

"How do you two know each other?" I was quick to ask, trying to sound like I was just making conversation.

Klaasje glanced at Sinjin once more before turning her full attention on me. "Oh, Sinjin and I . . . well, we go way back, don't we?"

Sinjin nodded and crossed one leg over the other. "I do believe it was August 1875 in Salado, Texas, when we met, love?" he asked. I wasn't sure why but the fact that he had now called her "love" twice irritated me . . . a lot.

Klaasje nodded, a broad smile glowing on her pretty face. "That's right, Mr. Sinclair, the gentleman from Britain." She had a faraway look on her face like she'd just been transported back to 1875 and probably just met the debonair Mr. Sinclair. That is, before he left her and continued on his merry way, into some other woman's bed, no doubt.

"Did Sinjin turn you?" Trent asked.

Klaasje laughed at his apparent stupidity. "No, I never did get that honor." She rolled her eyes at Sinjin, as I realized her response was drenched in sarcasm.

"You flatter me, love," Sinjin said and shook his head, apparently not picking up on the fact that she was kidding. Or, more likely, he was disregarding her sarcasm.

"Did I ever tell you how jealous everyone got once you started coming around?" Klaasje continued, sounding sincere this time. Sinjin laughed and leaned forward but before he could reply, Rand cleared his throat and looked more annoyed than I probably did.

"There are many subjects we still need to discuss," Rand started. After frowning at Sinjin, he turned to face Klaasje. "More specifically, what happened to you in Vermont?"

Klaasje looked a bit confused and glanced at Sinjin as if her answer lay with him. Her eyebrows furrowing, she returned her gaze to Rand. "I think it's pretty simple—some bastard staked me."

I glanced at Rand and shook my head when it seemed he was about to bombard her with myriad questions.

"She might not realize what happened," I suggested and faced Klaasje. "You might want to sit down."

She took a seat on the leather sofa beside Sinjin's armchair. "If you're asking me to sit, this must be some story." She tried to sound jovial but there was an undercurrent of worry in her voice.

I nodded. "You did die, Klaasje, but I brought you back to life."

"You what?" She looked at me like I'd just sprouted another head.

"I brought you back to life," I repeated. "I'm a witch and—"

"Jolie is also Queen of the Underworld," Sinjin interrupted. Klaasje raised her brows as she appeared to re-examine me. Then she dropped her head in deference and stood up to curtsy before facing me again.

"May I ask you a question?" she asked. It was almost as if she'd had a personality switch—the garrulous and confident woman now concealed by someone more humble and unsure. And it was all because Sinjin had just dropped the monarchy bomb on her.

I nodded. "Of course." Not appreciating the fact that I was now being treated differently from everyone else in the room, I turned to face them all and sighed. "I don't want to be put on a pedestal. I'm Queen, yes, but to me, it's only a title—a mission I must fulfill in order to unite our people."

Mercedes humphed her disagreement but didn't argue with me. Point for her. I returned my attention to Klaasje and she nodded, clearing her throat.

"When you say I died . . . ," she started.

"You were attacked by someone we believe to be a Lurker," I answered.

Klaasje seemed to be taking all of this extremely well—based on the fact that she wasn't yelling, crying, or passing out. She looked at Sinjin, and he gave her a smile that seemed to comfort her.

"Thank you." She glanced up at me again. "I will be forever grateful."

I nodded but before I could say anything else, Rand was back to his line of questioning. Guess he was impatient.

"Do you remember what happened in Vermont, Klaasje? Do you remember how many Lurkers attacked you?" His questions were in sync with his pacing. I wasn't sure about Klaasje but he was definitely making me nervous.

"My housemates?" Klaasje asked. Mercedes merely shook her head. Klaasje's eyes narrowed and she dropped her attention to the floor, looking like she was trying to summon up any strength she still possessed.

"Do you recall anything?" Mercedes added.

Klaasje was quiet for a moment or two. Then she seemed to remember what had happened to her—her lips began to tremble and her eyes glassed over.

"There were maybe six of them, I'm not sure. All I can remember is hearing my housemates screaming from the backyard. When I ran outside to help them, there was a . . . a human, I think, with incredible strength. I mean, he just lifted me up over his head and threw me to the ground. Before I could say one word, he had me pinned." She glanced up at me. "How could a human have pinned me?"

"Because they are descendants of vampires," Sinjin answered as he examined his nails.

"Descendants of vampires?" Klaasje repeated. It suddenly struck me that some Underworlders didn't even know who or what Lurkers were, didn't realize the threat they presented, Klaasje being a case in point.

"They are called Lurkers," I said. Once I had her attention again, I continued. "They're basically vampires, only they can walk in the daylight and they don't drink blood."

"That is a far cry from a vampire," Sinjin said derisively. I almost felt like apologizing. But I didn't.

"Quite so," Varick agreed but I merely ignored him.

"Will you reanimate my housemates?" Klaasje asked, facing me.

I glanced at Mercedes to redirect the question to her. She nodded to Klaasje. "In time."

"Can you tell us anything else about the Lurkers, Klaasje?" Rand asked. Leave it to him to keep the conversation on track.

She glanced at him and shook her head, sighing deeply as her attention fell to her hands in her lap. She looked up again and eyed me, as if she wasn't comfortable talking to Rand. Given the fact that he was pacing the room like an expectant father, I didn't blame her for seeking attention from someone who seemed less stressed out.

"I didn't really have the chance to find out anything about them," she said with a shrug. "I just remember hearing screaming and then running outside. I remember seeing one of my housemates dead but there were other bodies, too, people I didn't recognize. I couldn't think much on it, though, because before I knew it, I was getting . . . staked."

I nodded and offered her a smile of consolation. It was a huge bummer that she couldn't tell us anything more about the Lurkers, but at least it sounded like her roommates had been able to kill a few Lurkers in the process. If only we had something that belonged to them—of course, I had to wonder if it was even possible to reanimate a Lurker.

"And we have nothing that could have belonged to the dead Lurkers?" I asked Mercedes, who just shook her head.

Not wanting to focus on that letdown, I decided to see if there were any other pertinent facts we could get out of this woman, anything that might help us paint a picture of what happened and how.

"How many of you shared your house, Klaasje?" I asked.

"There were seven of us."

"All vampires?" I continued, feeling the heat of Rand's eyes on me. I glanced up and he immediately looked away.

Returning my attention to Klaasje, I pondered the fact that the house had been full of vampires. But weres and a witch had also been killed. "Did all the attacks happen at the same time?" I asked Mercedes.

She shrugged. "As far as we know."

I nodded and chewed on my bottom lip as I tried to piece it all together—trying to draw a picture of what had happened. If the Lurkers had attacked the vampires and the other creatures at the same time, it must have been choreographed.

"The Lurkers must have been staking out the victims before they attacked. The whole thing was planned," I said.

"Aye," Odran said. I had a feeling he'd dozed off through the majority of our meeting.

"It could be that the point of the attack was to send a warning," Rand added.

"What do you mean?" Klaasje asked, frowning.

He shrugged. "They've drawn a line in the sand and now it's up to us to figure out how we're going to respond."

"Before we even contemplate our response, we must increase our numbers," Mercedes argued. Her expression dared us to challenge her.

"We need to finish reanimating our soldiers and then we need Bella's," I agreed, realizing the success of any future reanimations rested entirely with me.

Once the meeting was over and everyone disbanded, I started for the door but Rand's voice stopped me from leaving.

"Jolie, do you have a minute?"

"Sure." I turned back to face him and watched as he approached me with a smile. "What's up?"

He shrugged and pointed to the couch so I took a seat, watching him walk to the fireplace.

"You haven't finished telling me exactly what happened when you traveled back in time."

And my mind suddenly went blank. Why was he asking me this? Hadn't I put a charm on him to redirect his thoughts? Why was this coming up now?

"Jolie, what happened in 1878?" he asked.

"Well," I started, searching for something to say. I couldn't admit that I'd bonded with him. Not now, not after I'd kept it from him for so long. "I healed Pelham, Rand," I confessed.

"Healed him?" Rand repeated.

"You said Pelham died of cholera but when I met him, he didn't seem to be ailing from that. His symptoms just didn't fit." I paused for a second and then shook my head, wondering if this next bit would upset Rand. "I know I shouldn't have, but I healed him."

Rand shrugged and seemed unconcerned. "Pelham died from cholera. I was at his bedside and I witnessed his passing."

I shook my head as I considered it. "How can that be?"

"Because sometimes people are meant to go. Sometimes they've finished their life's mission and it's just their time."

"But—" I started.

He took a seat, leaning against the back of the leather sofa, crossing his arms against his broad chest. "I'm certain you did heal him, but later he simply came down with cholera and it killed him."

"I guess that makes sense," I said with a nervous laugh.

"Jolie, tell me how it came to be that I gave you my mother's ring."

Well, there really wasn't any way to get out of it and I wasn't about to rely on my magic to throw him off again. Maybe it would be a good thing to have the bonding discussion . . .

"You gave me your mother's ring because uh . . . um . . ."

I took a deep breath and steadied myself. "You gave me your mother's ring because you asked me to marry you." Surprise lit up his eyes and I dropped my gaze to the floor for a few seconds before bringing it back to his handsome face again. "And I said yes."

He furrowed his brows, then nodded, seemingly not upset in the least. "Did we wed then?"

"No," I said and a tremor of anxiety started churning in my gut until I felt like I wanted to throw up. The anxiety spiraled up my stomach, traveling north until it felt like a frog had taken up permanent residence in my throat.

"But there's more, I daresay?" he asked and stood up.

"Rand." I took a deep breath. "You and I were very much in love and we . . . we . . ." *Ah, spit it out, Jolie!* "We had sex!"

Rand took a step back as if I'd just punched him. His expression was unreadable.

"We had sex?" he repeated.

I just nodded, not sure what else I could say.

Rand took a deep breath and faced me with furrowed brows. "And let me guess, we bonded?"

Hearing the words come from his mouth caused a flurry in my stomach. There was nothing in his eyes or demeanor that said he was angry, but there also wasn't anything that said he was happy.

"Yes, Rand, it was me. It's been me all along. I was your bond mate." The words just sort of fell out of my mouth. My heart was hammering so hard, it echoed in my head until I couldn't hear anything beyond the pounding in my ears.

He glanced at me again with an expression of someone who'd been deceived, as if I'd just told him I wasn't who he thought I was, that all along I'd been his enemy. And the pounding in my ears was now deafening. A feeling of nausea had also taken residency in my gut.

"Rand." I took a step forward.

"No," he said as he held his hand up. "I . . . I need to wrap my head around this, Jolie."

"Talk to me, please," I begged.

He shook his head and ran his fingers through his hair as he did whenever he was upset. "Why can't I remember any of this?"

"Because Mathilda erased everything from your mind when I left."

He frowned at me. "Why don't I remember Mercedes?"

I gulped. I didn't know what the answer was, but I could guess. "Mathilda probably had to erase anything from your mind that would in any way remind you of Mercedes or me. Maybe remembering Mercedes would remind you of me or would remind you that something was missing from your memory."

He shook his head and started for the door. Then he paused and turned to face me. "I . . . need some time to think about this."

"Rand, talk to me," I begged, sobs choking my throat.

He shook his head. "Please, Jolie, just go."

Tears burned my eyes but I did as he requested and started for the door. I paused at the threshold but, realizing there wasn't anything more to say, left him to his solitude.

Twelve

JOURNAL ENTRY

I've had a rough last couple of days, Diary, and it has everything to do with Rand's reaction to our bonding news. And to make matters worse, I haven't talked to him since that night. Sure, we've seen each other, but Rand is formal and stiff, and since Mercedes is always with us I can never get any alone time with him. But that's only part of my rough last couple of days. The other part is the fact that I actually haven't been able to reanimate anyone else since Klaasje. It's almost like whatever ability I had is exhausted, gone. Mercedes and Rand have been patient with me but I can see the distress and worry in their eyes—which, really, is nothing next to my own sense of foreboding. What changed? What happened between the last time I was able to perform and now? The only thing I keep returning to is that strange dream-vision I had of the devastation at Lurker hands and that empty throne. What if something happened to me when I had that vision? What if somehow, that vision was more than just a vision and it emptied me of my abilities?

Mercedes didn't seem to think that was the case but she also didn't seem to have a plausible reason as to why I've failed in my abilities. She charmed me with a relaxation spell, something meant to release all my internal stress, but so far I don't feel as if it's done anything for me, really. I guess the true test will be when we attempt reanimations again, something that will happen in the near future. But for right now, I have some well-deserved time off.

Since my life completely sucks lately, I was actually pleased when Mercedes approached me this morning and told me we needed to start searching for my permanent home. Although I hadn't previously embraced the idea of moving away from Pelham Manor, given recent events I think it's the best freaking idea I've heard in a long time.

What it comes down to is that I need to stand on my own two feet—I need to step out from underneath Rand's shadow and be the independent woman I know I am and the sovereign woman I have to be as Queen. I have to follow Mercedes' example and set my own personal heartache aside in order to focus on uniting our species and building a kingdom. I have a destiny, a fate, and that is what will see me through this pain and misery. What I feel in the bottom of my heart is that Rand and I won't be able to fix things . . . or maybe that's just me feeling sorry for myself, I don't know. I just can't help but wonder if maybe I was wrong all along and we aren't meant to be together. Maybe the path I am meant to walk will take me in a completely different direction, a direction away from Rand . . . It's a thought that feels like acid eating me from the inside out.

Paths and destinies aside, I do think it will do me a world of good to put some distance between Rand and myself, especially if he decides he can never forgive me. He can go back to his reclusive ways and play the part of renegade and remove himself from the monarchy and I won't have to suffer through it, living only two miles from him. Now I'll have my own space and I'll be able to start a new life for myself.

So, Diary, with those feelings inside me, Christa, Mercedes, Odran (whom Mercedes asked to accompany us in order to provide protection—against the Lurkers, I'd imagine), and I spent the better part of the day looking at homes. Well, really, "homes" doesn't do them justice. They were more like manor houses, castles, and mansions befitting a Queen of the Underworld. I did insist that our search should include only southern Scotland and northern England, mainly because I like this area and it feels like home. And, yes, there is still a part of me that somehow wants to be close to Rand, and the idea of living hours away from him just hurts me too much. Even if we never speak to each other again, just knowing he's somewhere nearby is enough to help see me through the long days and even longer nights.

Mercedes seemed to glom onto the idea of Scotland for my Queenly headquarters because she thought living in Scotland would be a nice way to appeal to the fairies (since Odran, the King of the fae, is Scottish). And incidentally, the fae just happen to be a huge subset of my kingdom. And of course Odran was in complete agreement. It's also interesting to note that the fae had singlehandedly provided the income required for my Queenly headquarters, the fae being the wealthiest of all creatures. Now that I think about it, I guess it made sense that Odran was in attendance while I searched for a home—seeing as how he was basically acting as my benefactor. At first I felt weird about it, like I shouldn't accept such a large gift, but Mercedes informed me that my comfort—and more to the point my expenses— would be the responsibility of my subjects; each faction of Underworld creatures would be responsible for gifting me my various necessities. So I've accepted this reality because, really, I have no other choice. When in Rome, I guess. After searching for hours as far south as the Lake District in England and as far North as St. Abbs, Scotland, we eventually found the most in-

credibly beautiful manor home in Eyemouth in the Scottish Borders. Eyemouth is only a forty-five-minute drive from Pelham Manor so I didn't feel as if it was too far out of my comfort zone. The town itself is a traditional fishing village, fairly small with very narrow streets. What struck me the most about Eyemouth, though, and what made it stand out among all the other towns we visited was the coast. The Eyemouth coastline is stunning, with high cliffs overlooking clear water and sandy coves. Everything about the village is picturesque, with buildings and harbors that just beg to be memorialized on canvas. According to our real estate agent (who couldn't stop staring at Odran—and of course the King ate it up, prancing around like a peacock), the Eyemouth coast also offers "excellent opportunities for bird-watching" and although I've never really been into birds, I could see myself investing in a pair of binoculars.

Given my love for the town and the rocky coastline, imagine my excitement to find that the manor house we toured was just as magnificent. The house is called Kinloch Kirk and it's a decent trek from the town. It really is a study in privacy because there is not another soul around for miles, only thrushes, redwings, and blackbirds for neighbors. Kinloch Kirk is perched on a cliff overlooking the ocean. On either side the Scottish moors seem to go on for miles, the green of the grass only interrupted by lavender splashes of wild heather. I was just waiting for Heathcliff to make an appearance.

The entryway to the house is—in one word—spectacular. It has a cobbled drive maybe one hundred feet long, and on either side of the drive are towering pine trees bordered by endless miles of uncropped pasture. The entryway boasts double doors with a great flight of stairs leading up to them. The stairs are framed by two stone statues, one of a lion and the other of a unicorn, symbols of the United Kingdom. I have to wonder what the original owner of this magnificent house would think of a Yank living within its walls!

And the house, itself . . . sigh. It was first built in the early sixteen hundreds and has, through the years, been remodeled and renovated until it's now a sprawling estate. It's three stories high and I lost count of the bedrooms and bathrooms. It would basically give Pelham Manor a run for its money and that's really saying something.

The outside of Kinloch Kirk is white stucco, but covered in beautiful green vines that look as if they've been there for hundreds of years (the entire house is nearly covered). Inside, you're immediately awed by the incredibly high ceilings (they must be forty feet tall in the entryway) and the great expanse of distressed-maple floors. The only interruption in the wood flooring is the kitchen and bathrooms, which are tiled in something that looks like travertine. The walls throughout Kinloch Kirk are a creamy white, all with crown molding. A tall, elegant chandelier greets guests as they enter the foyer, and opposite the room is a picture window revealing the craggy coastline of Eyemouth.

The floor-to-ceiling windows in most of the rooms give the house a great open, expansive feel. The sunlight brightens the entire space, making it seem like there's no roof to keep the sunshine out. And every room has magnificent views of either the rugged cliffs and the ocean beyond or the haunted Scottish moors.

Kinloch Kirk was so unbelievably picturesque; I could most definitely see myself living there. Christa was dumbstruck throughout our tour and barely said two words. She wore a perpetually open mouth in response to every room and its associated view. Mercedes never stopped smiling and nodded every time we ventured into a new room, remarking on how much she loved the house. At the end of the tour, she was basically beaming when I said Kinloch Kirk was my favorite of all the properties we'd viewed. I thought she might break into song and dance right there in the driveway.

After affirming my intentions to move forward with the property, Mercedes was quick to get the agent to call in with our offer. While the agent was busy with the task of submitting Mercedes' offer and Christa was busy with Odran, asking him about birds or something, I found the perfect opportunity to grill Mercedes.

I told her about the old woman I'd tried to reanimate under Bella's direction who had said I wasn't a witch, but she had no clue what I was. Mercedes was quiet as I recounted my story and then she merely nodded in that mysterious way of hers and said the old woman had been correct—I'm not a witch. But Mercedes wouldn't tell me exactly what I am—she only admitted that I'm capable of incredible things. She was also adamant about telling me it would take time to employ all of my powers and fully understand the extent of my own abilities.

What I've realized is, Mercedes is like watching Wheel of Fortune. She's willing to give me some consonants in order to figure out the damn phrase but I've got to pay up for the vowels. I think she delights in giving me only half of the puzzle pieces in an effort to force me to figure out the rest for myself. I know it's probably for my own good and all that crap about teaching me to fish versus giving me a fish and blah blah blah . . . But sometimes I just wish someone else would finish the puzzle and show me it's really a great image of the Eiffel Tower, or whatever.

The more I think about it, the more I have to wonder if Mercedes even knows what I am. Maybe she's just as clueless as me. Well, even though I'm not any closer to knowing exactly what I am, I'm glad I might be some-

thing more than a witch. It feels pretty cool to know you're a powerful person, capable of great things, even if I'm currently an Underworld orphan with no clear understanding of my lineage. Now if I could just get Rand to forgive me—scratch that, talk to me—things might start looking up.

Three days later we purchased Kinloch Kirk. Well, Mercedes did. She also hired a multitude of construction workers to fix anything that was "subpar" (her word); we made plans to take possession of Kinloch in one week's time. That was fine by me, because I couldn't get out of my butler's quarters at Pelham Manor fast enough. Rand still refused to talk to or even look at me.

Over the last three days, we'd attempted to reanimate more creatures but as with my last attempt, nothing. Mercedes still didn't seem entirely concerned; or if she was, she did a good job of hiding it, instead telling me to sip some potion she concocted and to basically meditate and focus on "unblocking my negative pathways," which she imagined were inhibiting my abilities.

Maybe in an attempt to pull attention away from the fact that I was beginning to freak out over my inability to reanimate anyone, Mercedes scheduled a lesson for me. This one was on magic, and my teacher was Mathilda.

"Mercedes informed me that you are having difficulty resurrecting your gift, child?" Mathilda questioned in her clear voice.

I sighed deeply. "I don't know what's wrong with me."

She nodded and took my hand, leading me across the manicured rose gardens of Pelham Manor.

"You have much going on, Jolie," she said softly. "Mercedes sent me to help you through it, to coax your magic."

I smiled and accepted her outstretched hands. She closed her eyes and her lips twitched; I imagined she was chanting something to herself. When she opened her eyes, gold flecks appeared for a mere instant then melted back into hazel.

"You are troubled, I can feel it in you," she whispered. "Tell me why."

"Rand." It was the first thought that came into my head. "He knows I was his bond mate."

Mathilda smiled, and it suddenly occurred to me that maybe this was news to her as well. I never had gotten the whole story when it came to whether or not Mathilda remembered me from 1878.

"Did you know I was his bond mate?" I asked.

She shook her head and smiled knowingly. "No, though I did suspect."

"But you were the one to erase his memory of me?"

Mathilda nodded slowly, as if this were a long and complicated subject that required just the right words. "I knew only that I had to help Rand through the loss of his beloved. I did not know why, or who she was. Mercedes must have imprinted those instructions upon me, and in the process I believe I erased not only Rand's memories but mine as well."

I nodded, thinking her response made sense. Mercedes was a secretive person, and it seemed she did everything according to some grand plan that existed in her head. I guessed this was no different.

"And Rand's reaction to your news?" Mathilda asked.

"He didn't take it well."

Mathilda tightened her hold on my hands. "You must understand, child, how difficult it was for him upon your departure. He wanted nothing more than to remember you, to preserve the memories of your time together, but little by little those memories began to eat away at his sanity. Before long he was ill, deathly so.

Even though I did not have the wherewithal to understand his pain, nor for whom he lamented, I did what I was instructed to do and nursed him through the darkness, brought him to the light again. He nearly died in the process."

I felt something burst inside me and felt like I wanted to cry. I'd never heard Mathilda's side of the story before; listening to it now left me empty.

Mathilda closed her eyes again and her lips started quivering. "I can feel a block within you," she whispered.

"A block?"

She nodded, then clenched her eyes shut even more tightly as she continued moving her lips in time with her thoughts. When she opened her eyes, they were narrowed, angry. "Someone has shielded you."

"I don't know what that means."

"Through magic, someone has blocked your ability, put a stopper on your magical flow."

"But—" I started, my thought disappearing into the air.

"Has anything out of the ordinary happened to you recently? Perhaps a stranger you came across, a dream you had?"

I felt my heart rate increase. "That vision," I said and glanced down at her with wide eyes. "I had that bizarre vision about the Lurkers, remember?"

Mathilda merely nodded. "You believe the Lurkers possess magic . . ."

"I'm convinced of it."

"Perhaps you are correct, child. Perhaps it was their magic that dampened your abilities."

"So how do I get my powers back? How do we reverse the shield?"

Mathilda smiled and stroked the surface of my hand gently. "Close your eyes and focus with me, Jolie. I cannot do this alone; you must force your magic to the forefront, allow it to overcome the block."

"What if I can't, what if it doesn't work? What if I have no power or magic left?" My tone increased in urgency as terror began to spiral through me.

"Jolie, calm down," Mathilda said forcefully, her lips tight. "It is merely a block, that is all."

I nodded and closed my eyes, willing my fears to retreat. "What do I do?"

"Summon your power, allow your magic to flow like a river throughout your body, replenishing you, flowing freely through you."

I focused and imagined my magic and power building in a furious momentum against the shield, pushing against it, forcing it to loosen. I could feel heat rising within me as beads of perspiration broke out along my hairline. I clenched my eyes tighter and imagined the light of my power, of my magic growing brighter and stronger, overcoming the pebble of dissidence within me.

"I can feel your power building, child."

I tightened my hold on Mathilda's hands and continued my thoughts, imagined myself screaming from the very bottom of my soul, screaming out against the shield, screaming out against the wall that was holding back my abilities. I could feel fury rising within me, cresting and riding the tide of my magic, building and growing until power emanated through me. Electricity sprang from my fingertips, bouncing off Mathilda's own powerful aura.

"Now, Jolie, destroy the block now."

I felt my power almost go on autopilot as it surged up within me. I imagined the flow roaring through me, busting through the shield and dissolving it into a million pieces, only to consume it in a whirlwind of power.

I opened my eyes and found myself panting.

"You did it," Mathilda beamed up at me, her smile wide. "I do not feel the shield any longer."

"Then my ability to reanimate our soldiers has returned?" I asked, winded.

"I believe so," Mathilda said with a grin. She then dropped my hands as she started for the house again. I easily caught up with her and walked alongside, wondering if she was right.

"I feel as if a weight has been lifted off my shoulders," I said.

"It has."

I was quiet for a few seconds as I considered the fact that my magic lesson for the day had just been derailed. "Is Mercedes going to be upset with you that we didn't have a lesson?"

Mathilda glanced up at me in surprise. "Oh, but we did."

"We did?" I repeated.

She nodded. "I just taught you how to reverse shields."

"Ha, two birds with one stone."

She just smiled knowingly.

Once we entered the house, I felt myself subconsciously searching for Rand. The need to see him was almost suffocating. From past experience, I expected to find him in his library, so I decided to check there first.

I hurried up the stairs, a flurry of butterflies in my stomach as I wondered exactly what I'd say to Rand once I found him.

The library was at the far end of the hall, and I jogged the rest of the way. In my urgency I didn't even knock on the door, just threw it open, and immediately I noticed Rand sitting in one of his armchairs. He was staring into the fireplace even though there wasn't a fire. Regardless, he looked tired, as if he bore the weight of the world on his shoulders.

At my brusque intrusion, he glanced up at me and

swallowed, but said nothing. I closed the door behind me, steeling my courage and begging my heartbeat to slow as I turned to face him again.

"We need to talk," I said in a strained voice.

"Very well," was all he said. I approached him and thought about sitting in the chair just beside him; then I thought better of it, since I had too much nervous energy to sit. Instead I stood behind the leather armchair and held on to its stiff back, my stomach now in my throat.

"I'm tired of you ignoring me," I began.

"I haven't been ignoring you," he interrupted.

"What would you call it? Avoiding me? That works too."

He shook his head. "I've needed time to think, Jolie, to digest everything you told me."

"Well, I hope you've had plenty of time to think about our . . . bonding."

He stood up and sighed as he walked over to the mantel and leaned against it. He ran his hands through his hair and let his attention drop to the floor before looking at me again.

"I have thought about it a great deal, yes." He paused. "It seems to be the only subject occupying my mind lately."

"Then why haven't you at least paid me the courtesy of speaking to me?" I asked, wanting to cut to the chase.

"Because I'm angry," he said curtly and his eyes burned with it.

Just then something inside me burst. A dam that I'd been erecting to hold back my emotions gave way and tides of pain and anger roared into me.

"Why are you angry?" I demanded, crossing my arms against my chest.

"Exactly how long were you going to wait before telling me that you were my bond mate?"

I gulped, suddenly feeling very guilty. "Rand, we aren't bonded now, so at first I figured there was no point in telling you."

"No point to telling me?" he repeated incredulously. "That should have been the first thing out of your bloody mouth!"

"I didn't want to upset you," I said in a soft voice.

"Why would you think I'd be upset?"

"I was just worried that maybe you wouldn't take it well. I knew how much you suffered when you thought your bond mate was dead. I just didn't think it was a good idea to bring that up again, not when I wanted to focus on our future, on what we could be together."

"I would have come to terms with the information eventually, but now I have to deal with the fact that you kept this to yourself. It doesn't bode well for your role as Queen."

"What does my being Queen have to do with this?"

"Because everything you think and do, every action you take is a test, Jolie. A test of your character. How can you hope to be a strong and powerful monarch when you couldn't even admit this to me?"

I gulped. "I figured no harm, no foul." As soon as the words were out, I regretted them.

Rand shook his head and laughed acidly, like I just didn't get it. "No harm, no foul? Are you kidding?"

"No, I'm not kidding," I said archly. "Rand, I didn't want to tell you because I was protecting you. I was thinking of what was best for you."

"Did you honestly think I couldn't handle the truth? That I wasn't strong enough?"

"No, of course not. I just . . . just thought you would be happier not knowing. I mean, why would I want to hurt you?"

"I've lived through a lot, Jolie, and I've dealt with ugly situations and uncomfortable truths many times. I can handle anything as long as I know where I stand, as long as there is transparency." He paused for a second and then shook his head. "I thought you and I were far beyond this, that we respected each other enough to say anything."

"I do respect you, Rand. I just . . . I just didn't want to hurt you."

"You should have left that decision to me," he said and his lips were tight. "If we don't have honesty between us, what do we have?"

"I'm sorry," I admitted and sounded defeated. "I honestly thought I was making the best decision."

"As Queen, you will be put in much tougher situations and you'll be forced to have much more difficult conversations."

"And I will handle them when the time comes," I spat out.

He shook his head and paced forward a few steps, his hands fisted at his sides. "For over one hundred years I've had to wake up every morning feeling as if there is something lacking in my life, as if there is a part of me that is empty. Sometimes I lie awake at night trying to remember, forcing myself to conjure up at least one memory of my lover, but of course I never succeed." He paused for a moment or two and then faced me again. "Don't you think I would have welcomed the idea that this woman was you all along, and she wasn't dead? Don't you think it would have been an incredible consolation to me to know that I was given a second chance?"

Some of the anger within me abated as I considered the situation from his perspective. And the remaining anger turned to guilt as I realized this was my fault.

"Again, I'm sorry." I shook my head. "I don't know what else I can say."

"You're not a little girl. Sorry can't erase the fact that

you should have respected me enough to tell me." He turned away and I could see the strain in his shoulders.

"Rand, of course I respect you." I approached him and placed my hand on his shoulder. "I respect you more than anyone I know."

He turned to face me again and lifted my hand from his shoulder, only to release it coldly. "You have a funny way of showing it."

"Please, Rand."

"If you don't mind, I'd like to excuse myself and get back to my . . . work."

It was like he'd slapped me. Mortified, I suddenly felt all of two feet tall and quickly shrinking, reduced to mere inches by the man I loved with all my heart. He wanted nothing more to do with me. It was as obvious as the frown on his face.

"Rand, this can't be it," I said in a small voice.

"There's nothing more to say, Jolie."

"You aren't the least bit happy to know it was me all along?" I demanded.

He glanced at me again with hardened eyes. "I've been so preoccupied by the fact that you had no intention of ever telling me, I admit, I have found little cause to celebrate."

That was enough for me. I showed myself out, slamming the door behind me. I took the steps two at a time, wanting only to escape, to get as far away from Rand as I could. Things were suddenly crystal clear for me.

My life was no longer my own—I'd been put into position of Queen even though I'd never fully accepted it. The man I loved didn't support me and probably never would. It was time to take matters into my own hands. It was time to stop taking orders and start giving them. It was time to live my life the way I wanted to and that was exactly what I intended to do.

Thirteen

I lurched backward as Gwynn plunged her blade into my gut. It was strange but I couldn't feel any pain—nothing but numbness. Wrapping my hands around the hilt of Gwynn's dagger, which was protruding from my stomach, I stared up at her in shock. The smile she wore was so cold, so calculating, it sent shivers down my spine. In a split second she burst into ash before me, leaving only Sinjin standing there, panting as he stared at me with eyes that were haunted and pained.

Suddenly I was sinking. I could feel my circulation slowing along with my heartbeat. I didn't have the strength to remain upright, and I hit the ground hard. Then all I was aware of was the feeling of arms enveloping me with the promise of protection. I gazed up into the face of an angel . . . Rand. He knelt over me, cradling my head in his arms. He was crying.

I tried to say something, to tell him I wasn't afraid and that I loved him, but I could only gurgle as I choked on my own blood. And my eyelids were so incredibly heavy, I couldn't keep my eyes open even though Rand begged me to. It was pretty obvious that I was losing the battle. I let my eyes close and relished the darkness, the feeling that I was suspended in a sea of black . . . I was gliding—submerged in what felt like Jell-O, only hot. In fact, the Jell-O stuff was so scorching, it felt like the sting of a thousand pins pricking my skin. I opened my eyes and blinked a few times, but the scenery made no sense to my muddled brain.

I was drifting through a river of what appeared to be lava, bright orange, red, and yellow. The acrid scent of sulfur permeated my nose every time the river bubbled up, looking like it was burping. I started to panic, wanting only to free myself from the scalding liquid. I fought against the current, trying to extricate my arms, but it was like trying to free myself from tar. I had a sudden sympathy for the dinosaurs. And like good old tyrannosaurs, brontosauruses, and stegs, I was about to become extinct in a river of molten heat. I had to wonder why I wasn't already dead . . .

Then I felt a drop fall on my head and looked up into what seemed to be the ceiling of a cave, calcified with stalactites. Dripping off the stalactites was some sort of black, gelatinous goo. Another drop of the revolting stuff landed on my head and began dribbling down my forehead into my eyes. I blinked against the intrusion, and the inky goo left my eyes to travel down my cheeks, feeling like a snail's trail.

The sounds of shuffling came from above me, and I made the mistake of glancing up again. Plastered on the cave's ceiling were what looked like rows and rows of bat-like creatures. Every now and then they shifted to stretch out their rubbery wings as they stared down at me with glowing red eyes. How I'd missed them before, I had no idea.

I didn't realize I'd screamed until it was too late. Immediately the air was thick with a flurry of winged creatures, dropping from their perches and flying headlong into one another or the cave walls. Some of them fell into the river and got swallowed up with a reeking burp. One of them fell alongside me and, in an attempt to free itself from the lava's grip, reached out its scaly claws and climbed onto my shoulder, pulling itself out of the ooze like some primordial being. I tried to shake it off but it latched on to my shoulder with rows of tiny, sharp teeth. I could feel their serration as they sunk into my flesh . . .

My eyes flew wide open and I sat bolt upright, still shaking my shoulder to rid myself of the hideous creature. It took me a second or two to realize I was at home in the master bedroom of Kinloch Kirk. I slowly inhaled while reassuring myself that bats with glowing red eyes were not about to consume me.

No, it had merely been a nightmare and nothing in this room had wings or glowing red eyes. Furthermore, nothing in this room was going to eat me . . .

I glanced down at Plum, who was lying just beside me. She stretched and lifted her head, as if wondering what the hell had gotten into me.

"Sorry, Plummy." I groaned and shook my head as I thought about the fact that my subconscious must have been seriously stressed out to plague me with a dream like that.

A sudden breeze fluttered into the room and wrapped itself around me before dancing with the drapes on my French doors. A man's shadow suddenly came into view on the balcony and I gasped.

"Who . . . who's there?" I demanded, holding my hands together and concentrating on manifesting a ball of energy between them—something I could unload on the intruder.

He stepped into a ray of moonlight and I immediately recognized Sinjin. I dropped my hands and the blue light of energy I'd been creating fizzled with a pop as the sensation of warm relief suffused me.

"God, Sinjin," I started, releasing a deep sigh.

He stood there, silhouetted against the breaking waves of the ocean beyond my balcony, lit only by the moonlight. Pressing his hands on either side of the doorway, he regarded me with an amused smile. "I apologize for frightening you, my Queen."

"Never mind," I said in an irritated voice. "What the hell are you doing out there?" With his customary black attire, I found it difficult to see him. "You need to wear something other than black. You look like a floating head."

Sinjin shrugged with a chuckle. "As I said, I apologize for intruding but I am merely doing the job for which I was hired."

"What?" I demanded, albeit none too graciously.

"I am protecting you, as befits my role of sentry."

I pushed the duvet away and watched Plum jump down from the bed with an irritated meow as she showed herself out of the bedroom. I grabbed my robe from the chair beside me and covered myself. I'd been wearing my usual sleepwear—boy shorts and a short-sleeved tee with nothing on underneath it. I wasn't naked but I also wasn't exactly dressed for company. And it was cold in my room and everyone knows what the cold does to a woman's breasts. Judging by the look on Sinjin's face, he knew it too.

"Would you prefer I leave?" he asked, prying his attention from my bust back to my face.

I looked up at him and immediately shook my head. After that horrible nightmare, I wanted nothing more than some company, even his. "No, please stay."

He smiled warmly at my invitation and faced me with a question in his eyes. "Very well. May I come in?"

As a vampire, he didn't have to ask permission to enter my abode; he was just being polite.

I nodded and watched him enter my room, his strides purposeful as he walked up to the end of my four-poster bed. He wrapped his hand around one of the posts and I couldn't help but gulp. Even though he looked like he always did, tonight there seemed to be something different about him. I couldn't put my finger on it but he just appeared to be the embodiment of sex. Not that he wasn't always the embodiment of sex, but somehow it was amplified tonight.

"Were you in the midst of a night terror?" he asked in a soft, caring voice.

"Yeah, you could say that," I answered as I approached the fireplace and, conjuring a fire, stood before it, warming myself. I could feel Sinjin's presence behind me, and when I felt his hands on my shoulders I didn't try to elude his grasp. It was as if I needed his strength, his reassurance. Probably realizing I wouldn't fight him, he began to rub my shoulders, massaging them.

"You are upset, my Queen."

"Please don't call me that," I said quickly, suddenly realizing the appellation of "Queen" was something I didn't really care for. I liked it better when he called me "poppet" or even "love." Even though I had to admit (at least to myself) I didn't like it when he called other women "love." "Call me poppet please."

He chuckled, no doubt reminded of the time when he and I first met and I'd told him not to call me poppet, that I hated the name. Funny how things change . . .

"Very well, poppet." He paused and seemed to focus his attention on my shoulders. His grip was strong, to the point of almost being painful—but not quite. "Tell me what is bothering you."

"How do you know I'm bothered?"

"You wear your tension."

I sighed again, wondering where the hell I should start. There was a long-ass list of things that were bothering me and most of them had something to do with the most stubborn, frustrating warlock I'd ever met. Of course, I wasn't about to confide my Rand dilemmas to Sinjin. I'd learned once before that Sinjin couldn't keep a secret—and I'd learned it the hard way. Granted, the one time I shared my Rand problems with Sinjin I hadn't actually been in a normal frame of mind. In fact, I'd been out of my mind, drugged on Sinjin's blood. I'd opened my big mouth and told Sinjin about the first time Rand and I had nearly bonded and how Rand had suddenly stopped before sealing the deal and had, instead, taken a cold shower. Of course, that situation turned ugly when Sinjin, intending to hurt Rand, announced he would never fail me in bed. So, yeah, long story short—I'd learned my lesson and wasn't about to repeat the mistake.

"I'm lonely," I said in a small voice and realized how absolutely true my words were. I was lonely in the depths of my soul, missing Pelham Manor, missing 1878 Rand and my present-day Rand, whom I'd grown to love so well.

"Why are you lonely, love?"

"I feel as if I'm living in a place I don't recognize and becoming something I don't know. I never wanted to be a Queen and yet, here I am, with a crown stuck to my head."

"I see." Sinjin took a step closer to me until I could feel his thighs brushing against my butt. He wrapped his arms around me and I relaxed into the strength of his chest, realizing I needed a shoulder to cry on, someone to listen. I needed a friend.

"I miss Pelham Manor and Christa," I continued, my voice sounding hollow.

"And the warlock, no doubt?"

I nodded but said nothing more. I didn't want to think about Rand or I might just turn into a blubbering, ridiculous mess.

"This is all new to you, poppet," Sinjin whispered. His breath raised goose bumps along my neck.

"Yes it's new, but I don't think that's the problem." I

paused as I felt his fingers tracing my stomach, underneath my shirt. "Behave please."

He chuckled and dropped his hand, taking mine captive instead.

"It is difficult now but it will not always be so. *Perfer et obdura, dolor hic tibi proderit olim.*"

I turned around and looked at him askance, wondering where the hell he came up with this stuff.

He chuckled again. "It is Latin, from Ovid. Translated, it means: Be patient and tough, someday this pain will be useful to you."

I shook my head, suddenly amused by the fact that Sinjin was a complete enigma. I never knew what he was going to say or do. "Let me guess, you used to be a monk or something?"

"Not quite, love, although I did and still do have an appreciation for ancient Latin."

I nodded but remained quiet as I enjoyed the feel of his immense hands when they returned to my shoulders and started massaging me again. I was suddenly struck by the thought that Sinjin could break me like a twig if he wanted to, and yet his touch could also be so comforting, so caring . . .

"Sinjin?"

"Yes, poppet?"

"Do you think I'm meant to be Queen?"

"Of course." There was no hesitation on his part.

"What I mean is, do you think I can be the Queen that Mercedes needs me to be and the Queen that everyone is counting on?"

Sinjin stopped massaging me and took hold of my arms, turning me around to face him, a look of consternation on his face. It was an expression I didn't recall him ever wearing. "Jolie, it is human nature to doubt oneself. That is one of the reasons I appreciate the fact that I am no longer human."

I laughed as he stared down at me and traced the outline of my face. I closed my eyes at the feel of his touch; when I realized what I was doing, I immediately opened them again. Sinjin was so incredibly handsome, so incredibly sexy. I was suddenly shocked that I'd never really considered him as a front-runner in the race for my affections. Of course, I suppose I had in a way, but he'd always been overshadowed by Rand.

Even now he was overshadowed by Rand.

"You are a novice and have much to learn," he continued.

I pried my thoughts away from Rand and back to the question at hand. "I'm afraid I'll never learn everything I need to."

He glanced down at me with a smile. "Will your path be difficult? Most probably. Do I believe you can handle it? Most definitely." He smiled again and leaned into me until I thought he might kiss me. I took a step backward.

"Sinjin," I warned.

He seemed to ignore me and brought his face to my ear, whispering. "You must trust in yourself, love."

"Thank you," I breathed and felt my heart flutter when Sinjin didn't pull away from me. He was so close, his breath sent shivers up my shoulders. I closed my eyes again. I couldn't help it.

"You shape the monarchy as you see fit, poppet. Do not be afraid to imprint it with your stamp. Make it your own."

He pulled away from me and clapped his hands together as if his job here was now done. I suddenly felt cold by his absence—which was strange considering he, himself, was cold. I wrapped my arms around myself and offered him a smile.

"I have news for you," he said, facing the balcony amid the sound of the crashing waves as they kissed the rocks below Kinloch Kirk.

"News?"

He turned to me and nodded. "Bella has agreed to assist us in reanimating her legion. She will be delivering the names of her dead shortly."

"Is there anything you can't do?" I asked with a laugh. "How in the heck did you manage that?"

He arched his brow at the question. "I can be . . . persuasive."

I frowned. "Care to enlighten me?"

"I offered her two options—assist us or die."

I just shook my head, actually feeling sorry for Bella. I knew she'd harbored a definite attraction to Sinjin—that much had been more than obvious when she'd kidnapped me and I'd watched her interact with him. Of course, it was hard to be female and not fall for Sinjin . . .

"When did you manage that?" I asked. Bella had only been relocated from Pelham Manor to Kinloch Kirk two days before. She was being held in a guest house set away from the main property—still confined by magic and guards.

"Earlier this eve," Sinjin answered.

"I'm impressed."

"I only aim to please, poppet." He paused. "I will never fail you."

"Sinjin," I began and then was at a loss for words as I thought about the fact that this man had always been there for me. Whenever I needed Sinjin, he showed up at my beck and call. "Thank you."

He bowed slightly and turned to leave. "I must feed, love."

I nodded, swallowing down my reaction to the thought of him feeding. Feeding for a vampire could and usually was a very sensual experience. Sinjin was no different. Once he asked if it bothered me when he fed from women and joined them in bed and I had to admit it did. I just prayed he wouldn't ask me that question again.

I escorted him to the door. As he opened it, and stepped outside, I found myself grabbing hold of his arm. He turned around in surprise and glanced down at me with a furrowed brow.

"I think you have a bad rap," I said and released him. "What's more, I think you like having a bad rap." I swallowed hard, wondering how to say what I wanted to say, wondering if I could get it out. "I just want you to know, I don't believe it—I don't believe any of the bad things anyone has ever said about you."

"Love . . ."

"No, you've always been nothing but kind to me and you've always protected me and stood up for me." I caught my breath, trying to understand where I was going with all of this. "I guess what I'm trying to say is that your friendship means a lot to me, Sinjin."

He arched a brow and studied me in a very detached way, as if my words didn't please him. "You view the world through rose-colored lenses."

"What do you mean?" I asked, taken aback. "When someone thanks you for your friendship, Sinjin, it's only courteous to acknowledge it," I finished with a nervous laugh.

He shook his head, and his gaze was piercing as he stared down at me. "Do not paint me into what you wish me to be."

"I haven't and I don't," I answered even though I was confused by his response. Why would he fight the notion of being a good person? What was he trying to hide?

"Very good," he said, but his jaw was tight. He turned to leave but I gripped his arm again, nervously moving my hold down to his wrist.

"Explain what you mean."

He licked his lips and glanced away from me for a few seconds. When he faced me again, his eyes seemed to have darkened in color, seemingly drenched in something that looked like anger or passion.

"I am a creature motivated by my own self-interest."

I shook my head. When he attempted to step away from me, I tightened my fingers around his wrist. "That's what you want me to believe. That's what you want everyone to believe but I know it isn't true."

He shook his head but said nothing for a few moments. "The truth can be painful."

"If that's the case, then why are you my friend? What do you want from me?" I demanded and released his wrist, allowing him to retreat, if he so chose. He made no motion to leave and instead eyed me again with his intense expression.

"I do not believe I must make that more clear than I already have, poppet. You already know."

I shook my head and stood my ground. "No, I don't. I know what you want me to think of you and the image you try to project, but as I said before, I don't believe you."

In an instant Sinjin threw the door closed and pushed me against the wall inside my room. He was suddenly in my face. And he didn't look happy. His hand was around my throat, his fangs protruding.

"I want you," he seethed and I hadn't even realized his hand was cupping my butt until he squeezed it. "I want this."

"Sinjin," I breathed, then promptly forgot what I was going to say.

"I want all of you," he continued and his eyes were hard as they stared down at me.

Before I could respond, he released me and instantly seemed to regain control of himself again. He opened the door and disappeared into the hallway. It took me a second to catch my breath. Even then, my heartbeat continued to pound inside my breast until I thought for sure I'd pass out.

After Sinjin's visit, I couldn't fall back asleep. In the morning I found myself replaying the events of the night over and over in my head, trying to make sense of them. I couldn't deny the fact that there was something about Sinjin that drove me wild. He was just so unpredictable and sexy. But at the same time, he was a wild card. And that threw me off—I was Jolie Wilkins, someone who thrived on routine and preparation. And Sinjin was the opposite of that. He was spontaneous chaos dressed in impulse with just a touch of anarchy. And as if that weren't enough to steer me away from him, there was always Rand.

Rand.

Just thinking of him caused the figurative dark clouds to hover over my head. A macabre feeling had been bubbling up within me like a disease, a feeling that said everything with Rand was over and dead. Any love he had for me had been trampled by my own cloven hooves.

Thoughts of Rand led to thoughts of my 1878 Rand, and I wanted to cry. I'd failed him, failed in the one promise he'd asked of me—that he and I would be reunited in the here and now. Suddenly the desire to return to that time when Rand freely and totally loved me and I him suffocated me. I just wanted—no, needed—to go back to how things had been . . . way less complicated and love was all that mattered.

But now that love was dead. I didn't know why, but there was an absolute surety within me—as if there were no question on the subject. Maybe it was because I'd never seen Rand so upset, so hurt. But I'd also imagined he'd see the positive—that I had been the only woman he ever loved. And what about the stupid idea that love outweighed everything else?

Whoever came up with that lie deserved to be shot.

I closed my eyes against the onslaught of sadness that overtook me and fisted my hands as I swore to myself I would shelve this guilt. The situation remained what it was and there was nothing I could do to control or change it. I had to let it go.

Rand would live the way he wanted to live and if that meant he wouldn't support me, wouldn't love me, and wouldn't be with me, then so be it. My responsibilities now were more important than my personal relationships. It was time I stood up and became the Queen I knew I could be. Sinjin was right—I had strength enough.

At the sound of a knock on my door, I reached over from my stance against the wall and opened it. Mercedes poked her head in and smiled warmly as she entered and closed the door behind her.

"How do you like Kinloch Kirk?" she asked.

I glanced around my room, with its matching poster bed, armoire, writing desk, and vanity. All of the furniture was made of a light-colored knotty pine, which gave it a natural, rustic sort of feel. But the room was anything but rustic. Its plush white carpet, whitewashed brick fireplace, and the translucent curtains, which danced in the ocean breeze, made it pristine and lovely. It was altogether stunning in its simplicity.

"I love it," I said. "You did a great job furnishing it too."

Mercedes beamed and her green eyes seemed to take center stage in her pretty face. She looked like she was twelve years old and had just exceeded her teacher's expectations. It was an expression I'd never seen on her before—something that didn't seem to jibe with the centuries-old prophetess. But if anything, it made me fonder of her.

"I am in the process of hiring live-in help to assist in the daily management of your estate," she said.

"What, like a housekeeper?"

Mercedes nodded. "Numerous housekeepers, a cook, and a butler. And of course all those hired will be creatures among your kingdom rather than humans."

"Yeah, that makes sense," I said, thinking about the fact that human help probably wouldn't be okay with the fact that they were living among witches, wolves, vampires, and the fae.

Mercedes cleared her throat as if to say we were now moving on to heavier topics.

"Mathilda informed me of the magical shield that was put on you. We believe your gift should have returned. Would you be available to try again this evening?"

I nodded, but my thoughts weren't on reanimations at the moment. Instead I reflected back to my conversation with Sinjin. I now felt absolutely sure that I would make this monarchy my own. I was the Queen and as the Queen, I would run my domain as I saw fit. First things first: I needed to make a few announcements.

"Mercedes?"

She glanced up at me curiously.

"I wish to call a meeting, and it is a very important one. Will you please tell everyone in our kingdom to be here in one week's time?"

"Of course. I will deliver your summons by way of magic."

"I must address my people as their Queen, and I would like you to make my introduction."

Mercedes nodded. "Will you require any help in preparation for this . . . meeting?"

"No." I shook my head. "I have it covered."

She glanced at me curiously but her expression could

not hide her satisfaction—as if she was pleased I'd finally stood up to embrace my calling.

"It is imperative that all creatures are present. Not just their representatives," I continued.

"You must have news of some importance?"

I nodded. "Yes, I have announcements that everyone in our union will need to hear."

Mercedes beamed at me. "It seems you have finally accepted your destiny?"

"I feel I need to take the so-called monarchy reins and now I'm doing just that," I answered furtively, doubting Mercedes would still be happy once she knew what I was going to say. Well, even she had to wait until our entire kingdom was in attendance. That gave me a week to smooth out my thoughts and write my very first speech as Queen of the Underworld.

"Where would you like your subjects to assemble?"

I shrugged and glanced out my window at the open miles of Scottish moors. "Wherever they will all fit. I'll leave the particulars to you."

Mercedes nodded and, with a humble bow, smiled. "I remain at your service."

"Thank you." Instantly I felt like the strong Jolie I knew I could be. It was as if something had evolved inside me—something tough and angry. Without even verbalizing it in my head, I made a vow to myself to stop being a vacillating monarch. Now I was in it all the way, and I planned to make the throne mine.

"Jules?" It was Christa's voice coming from the hallway. I faced Mercedes with surprise.

"Ah, yes, I forgot to mention you have a visitor."

"In here, Chris!" I yelled just as Christa poked her head into my room and glanced around curiously. It was the first time she'd been to Kinloch since Mercedes had finished furnishing it.

"This place is the bomb!" Christa said with a big smile.

Mercedes nodded with a quick curtsy to me and a smile to Christa, and then she left the room, closing the door behind her.

"I'm so glad you came to see me!" I embraced my closest friend, who hugged me back, then pulled away and took a look around the room, before throwing herself on my bed.

"Are you loving it here?" she asked.

I thought about the question momentarily before deciding to shelve the negative. I wasn't going to focus on it anymore. From here on out, I intended to be so positive, people might accuse me of taking Prozac.

"I'm very happy," I said, smiling. Then it occurred to me that Christa might like to move from Pelham Manor. "You know, you can move in with me. You don't have to stay at Pelham Manor with Rand anymore. I know you're his assistant but . . . you could always be my assistant again?"

She nodded but it was a half-assed nod and by the look on her face, there was something she wanted to tell me. "I'm, uh, I'm actually moving in with John."

"Oh, wow," I said, shocked. "When did he ask you to do that?"

She hesitated for a moment or two, then beamed. "Last night. The same time he asked me to do this." She held up her left hand, where a diamond engagement ring gleamed at me.

"Chris!" I screamed, as bolts of surprise and happiness rampaged through me. I flung my arms around her. "You're getting married?!"

"Yes," she said with tears in her eyes. "We haven't set a date yet."

"I'm so happy for you," I said, tears already streaming down my face. It was the truth, even though I was also envious—wishing my life could be as picture perfect as Christa's seemed to be. But I was beyond ecstatic for my best friend . . . And John was a good guy—well, wolf. "Are you . . . okay with wolf babies?" I asked, not really sure how to phrase the question.

She laughed and nodded emphatically. "I'm okay with all of it, Jules. I love John like I've never loved anyone before."

"That is the best news I've heard all week," I said. Then I remembered that John was American and so was Christa. My heart dropped. "Does this mean you're moving back to the United States?"

She shook her head. "I told him we have to stay here, that I won't leave you."

I was quiet for a minute or two as I thought about her words. "Chris, you don't have to stay here for me. I appreciate the fact that you're thinking about me but you have to do what is right for you . . . both."

She shook her head. "Nothing you can say will get me to leave you, Jolie Wilkins. You and I are in this together. We're a team or have you forgotten?"

I laughed and grabbed her hand, squeezing it. "No, I haven't forgotten."

And I truly meant it.

Fourteen

It was the evening of my big day. A cold ocean breeze rustled through the trees, and with the clouds obscuring the full moon, it looked like a spooky Halloween night. Although it wasn't All Hallow's Eve, it was only a matter of minutes before I would have to appear on the balcony of the Green Room of Kinloch Kirk to address my kingdom. I paced back and forth in my bedroom, so nervous it felt as if my heart were trying to best its own record of beats per minute. I closed my eyes and deeply inhaled for ten seconds, after which I took another ten seconds to exhale. Then I remembered the index cards clutched in my hand and flipped through them.

You can do this, Jolie. It's just a simple speech, I reminded myself.

At the sound of a knock on my door, I glanced up. "Come in."

The door opened and Sinjin entered, dressed in a suit. And, yep, it was black. He offered me a quick bow and a practiced smile. He looked business-like, dapper, and radiant.

"Are you nervous?" he asked.

I nodded as I thought about the waves of apprehension roaring inside me. "Is everyone outside?"

"All your subjects are assembled outside the Green

Room as you requested." Sinjin smiled, adding, "All three hundred of them."

It felt like something deflated inside me—our legion was just so small. I hadn't done my duty to reanimate all our soldiers and the notion of reanimating Bella's seemed like a faraway dream. We had to increase our numbers. Still, for now I'd focus on the three hundred standing just outside.

The Green Room was the theater of Kinloch Kirk. I liked to refer to it as the "theater room" because inside, it was designed to emulate a Greek amphitheater—a half circle with rowed seating. But tonight no one was seated in the amphitheater—there were too many in my kingdom to fit. Instead they were assembled outside, awaiting my balcony address. And as its name suggested, the Green Room was painted green—not emerald or anything loud, but a nice sage.

"Good," I replied, sighing as I geared myself up.

"You will be fine, poppet," Sinjin said as he wrapped his arms around me. I rested my head against his chest and held on to him as if he alone could see me through this.

"Wish me luck. I think I'm going to need it," I muttered.

He pushed away and glanced down at me with a sincere smile. He almost looked human. "Poppet, you are the epitome of loveliness. Aphrodite would be envious."

"Thank you." I laughed but it had a high-pitched, edgy sound to it. I glanced down at myself and exhaled again slowly, hoping to release some of my pent-up energy.

I was wearing a two-piece suit, the color of steel. The pencil skirt ended just above my knees, and to polish it off, I wore high black boots over black tights. My jacket was tailored and ended at my waist. With my black silk shirt beneath it, I probably looked more like a salesperson than a Queen. But *c'est la vie*. I wore my long, straight blond hair down, with only a headband to hold it off my face. And I kept my makeup simple—pinkish glossy lipstick with mocha-brown eye shadow, black liner, and mascara.

"So where's my scepter and wand?" I asked with a smile.

Sinjin didn't have the chance to reply because a sudden knock came on the door. He glanced at me momentarily before turning to address the intruder.

"Announce yourself," he called out.

"It's me," trilled a woman's voice. I couldn't quite place it. I looked up at Sinjin and noticed that his posture was a bit less rigid.

"Enter," he said simply.

I watched as Klaasje poked her head in from the hallway. She smiled at Sinjin then, upon seeing me, immediately dropped into a curtsy. I couldn't really say I responded, though. I was still so caught up in the fact that Sinjin knew her well enough to recognize her voice without seeing her. And the fact that she announced herself with the very personal "it's me" had me wondering about the nature of their relationship—I mean, it was obvious they'd had one in the past but was that still the case? And furthermore, why did I care? Sinjin and I were nothing but friends, pals, buddies . . .

"Are you ready, my Queen?" Klaasje asked me.

I glanced at Sinjin in slight confusion, wondering why the hell Klaasje was up here to begin with. Then it occurred to me that Queens needed attendants . . . and I have to admit I wasn't thrilled in the least that Klaasje was mine, that is, if indeed she was.

"I have employed Klaasje as one of your protectors, my Queen," Sinjin said.

"But you are both vampires," I said, thinking of any argument I could make.

"I have arranged for your protection in the daylight as well," Sinjin said and glanced at Klaasje with a secretive smile, as if they were in on some inside joke. I hate inside jokes.

"Who?" I demanded.

"Wolves, my Queen," Sinjin responded. "I hand-picked those I believe to be strongest and fastest."

As long as Trent wasn't among them, I guess I didn't care. Still, as to Klaasje sharing the duty of my protection with Sinjin in the evenings, I couldn't say I embraced the idea. And I was sure it had everything to do with the fact that I was jealous. Well, not jealous so much as curious about the relationship between the two of them. But that was fodder for another day. Right now, I had a speech to deliver.

"May I escort you, my Queen?" Sinjin asked, glancing down at me as he offered his arm.

I nodded and accepted it, smiling a courteous thank-you at Klaasje as she opened the door for me. Flanked with Sinjin on one side and Klaasje on the other, I traversed the hallway toward the Green Room.

I felt like a bundle of raw nerves, anxious energy eating away at me until I thought I might short-circuit. I felt Sinjin's hand on mine and glanced at him in surprise. He mouthed, *You will be fine*, and I just smiled my thanks, nodding even though I doubted his words.

What if I got up there and totally freaked out? What if my mind went blank and I forgot what I was going to say? Granted, I had index cards with my notes on them, but what if I suddenly developed lockjaw and couldn't speak?

Stranger things have happened, right?

We entered the Green Room and my heart was beating so fast, I felt like I was going to become airborne. Mercedes met us and offered me a smile. She was dressed in a three-piece suit that had a look similar to mine, only hers was vivid blue. And she seemed to be in a very fine mood, wearing a perpetual smile as she spoke with Sinjin and Klaasje. Once she'd double-checked the directions she'd given Sinjin, Mercedes took a deep breath and faced me.

"My Queen," she said, bowing low. "Are you prepared to meet your subjects?"

I nodded as I watched her aura radiate outward in a sudden burst of rainbow colors. Usually Mercedes kept her aura under wraps—most otherworldly creatures can't control their auras, but Mercedes can. Apparently it takes a lot of energy to allow her aura to glow in its natural rainbow state so she keeps it hidden. The only time it comes out is when she's either doing magic or boasting. Somehow I had the feeling she wasn't in a bragging mood.

She stood directly before me and took my hand in hers, giving me what felt like an electric shock as her energy coursed up my hand and into my arm. She closed her eyes and her mouth twitched as I imagined she was chanting the lines to whatever spell she was casting on me. Then she opened them, dropped my hand, and stepped away.

"Let me guess, you possessed me with Winston Churchill's ghost to help with my speech?" I joked even though part of me hoped the answer was yes.

Mercedes shook her head as if I should know better. "I bespelled you so your voice will carry when you are speaking. Otherwise not everyone will hear you."

I nodded and said nothing as she turned toward the balcony. She took the five steps separating her from the double doors and glanced back at me.

"Showtime."

Then she pulled them open and took a step onto the balcony. I couldn't really hear what she was saying—not because she'd failed to magick herself a louder voice but because I was so nervous, I couldn't focus on anything besides my rampaging heartbeat.

At the sound of clapping, Mercedes turned to face me, announcing that it was my turn to take the stage. I took a deep breath to steady myself and then started forward. As I approached the doors, I could see the throngs of creatures below, so many of them, I suddenly felt crowded, claustrophobic.

I took another deep breath and forced myself onward, feeling like I was en route to the hangman's platform. Once outside, I braced myself on the balcony and observed the people of my kingdom.

"Behold your Queen," Mercedes announced and turned to face me with a smile. Before me, the people of my kingdom all bowed or dropped into low curtsies.

"Hello," I began, my voice wavering, echoing as if from unseen speakers. It was as if my words were suddenly carried by the wind, transported to those standing farthest from me. Immediately people started another round of their curtsies and bows. I didn't know why but I was suddenly even more nervous than before.

I wasn't sure what made me do it but I had this indescribable sudden urge to glance to my right, just below the balcony. And that was when I saw him.

Rand.

I couldn't quell the shock that flared through me. My eyes locked on his and I couldn't break free; I was physically unable to pull my gaze away. Rand merely stared back at me. There was no expression on his face—it was just placid and beautifully calm as always.

While Rand might have appeared to be calm and peaceful, I was another story, at least on the inside. It was like I was waging war with myself and neither side was winning.

What is he doing here?

I tried to root my feet to the ground when I started feeling top-heavy.

Jolie, snap out of it, dammit! I screamed inwardly, begging myself not to completely lose it.

But the fact that Rand was standing directly below me was the final straw that broke the witch's broom. I felt incredibly hot, like my fitted suit was suddenly compressing me like a boa constrictor. My heart continued its roller-coaster beating and it was all I could do to concentrate on breathing.

Why is Rand here? Has he come to judge me? Has he come to rebel against whatever it is I have to say?

I ignored the questions in my head and tried to focus on the notecards clutched in my sweaty hands but my mind wouldn't allow me. I felt as if I was about to have a breakdown. Then it suddenly dawned on me that the last time I'd had a panic attack while en route to the battlefield in Scotland, there had been someone who had helped calm me down, someone who had offered me solace.

Sinjin.

I turned back, searching him out inside the Green Room, and spotted him immediately. He stood behind me and probably realized I was about to shit myself in front of three hundred people. He said nothing but his eyes were piercing and in their ice-blue depths, I could read his confidence in me. I took a deep breath and for a moment just continued to find strength in his eyes.

Almost immediately I felt a trickle of assurance break through the dam of self-doubt. My anxious heartbeat began to slow down.

I can do this. My voice echoed through my head and feeling suddenly stronger, I offered Sinjin a quick smile of gratitude before facing my legion again.

"Welcome and, um, thank you for coming," I began as I noticed how quiet everyone was—all their eyes on me. I felt a lump forming in my throat and cleared it, hoping I could also swallow the frog. "I . . . I called this meeting because I thought it, uh, was important for you all to know who I am and why I'm standing here before you now."

I took a deep breath and glanced down at the note-card in my trembling hands before returning my attention to my subjects.

"I am Jolie Wilkins and I am . . . I'm also your Queen." Another deep breath. "But I never chose to be your Queen or anyone's Queen." There were a few rounds of "What did she say?" and a look of *Huh?* was basically plastered on everyone's face. I cleared my throat again and forced myself to continue. "This position was thrust upon me and I've had no alternative but to, um, rise to the occasion and fulfill my role."

The people in the audience were confused, their faces uneasy. No doubt they were wondering where the hell I was going with all this. And if they were curious, Mercedes had to be crapping herself right about now. But there was no way in hell I was about to turn around to find out.

"I don't agree with the philosophy of monarchy," I continued, starting to feel the fire of my words. "And while I have accepted my responsibility and I'm, um, obviously addressing you as your Queen tonight, I will only continue in this position if I can lead . . . the way I want to—my way."

More furrowed brows and sideways glances echoed throughout the audience, but I didn't allow them to interfere with my speech. I absolutely refused to look at Rand, not when just the sight of him had nearly thrown me entirely off course.

"So without further ado," I persisted, "I'd like to enlighten you all as to my plans for . . . um, what that will entail." I glanced down at the next card and then back to my people again. "I propose that the world be divided into territories and using your guidance . . . um, by that I mean your votes . . . you know, like if you were voting for the president?" Then it dawned on me that not everyone here was American. God, where was good ol' Winston when you needed him? This was becoming painful. "Anyway, I, uh, I'll assign a leader to each territory. You can live wherever you want to live and of course you can bring your families with you," I finished.

I inhaled deeply and tried to talk myself out of running back into the house and hiding out in my bedroom for the rest of my reign. No, I would get through this. I flipped through three notecards, realizing I'd gotten ahead of myself.

"Magistrates will, uh, be elected from each territory, and these magistrates will travel to Kinloch Kirk monthly to represent the needs and concerns of their citizens. Um, your magistrate will be your voice—like your representative—to ensure that all of you are content with how everything is going."

I took a deep breath and noticed that the expressions of concern among the audience had little by little melted away; instead smiles highlighted each face. And I didn't think they were entirely due to the fact that my speech delivery skills were seriously lacking and probably pretty amusing. Even though I'd promised myself I wouldn't, I glanced at Rand.

And, surprisingly, Rand wore a smile. My head felt light again, but from—relief. It wasn't that I thought he'd forgiven me about the bonding stuff or anything as big as that. But his smile felt like sunshine, warming me from the inside out.

I cleared my throat again and with newly found confidence floating through me, I hurried to my conclusion. "I ask all of you now to accept my terms. If you object to anything I've said or you prefer a more traditional monarchy, I, um, will stand down. I'll have to . . . stand down."

As soon as I finished, someone started to clap. It quickly rippled through the audience and resulted in unanimous applause. Everyone rose to their feet, stretching their arms high above their heads. I could have mistaken it for the closing ceremony of the Olympics or something—like I was Apolo Ohno skating my ass off. But, no, I was still Jolie Wilkins, Queen of the Underworld. And the only other thing of which I felt certain was that I would never be in demand as a public speaker . . .

The people of my kingdom offering me their undying support, I could feel tears starting in my eyes, tears of pride and optimism. I held up my hands and tried to quiet the buzzing throng as I fought to restrain my emotions. The last thing I wanted to do was collapse into a blubbering mess.

"Are there any questions?"

Another woman waved her hand and I nodded in her direction, giving her silent permission to speak.

"Those on Bella's side who were killed?" she began. "Will they also be brought back to life?"

Someone else added. "Aye, I had heard that too."

A woman nodded and turned to face the others before bringing her attention back to me. "My brother fought and died for Bella, but he never endorsed her cause. He was just frightened to refuse her."

I swallowed hard. "We are in the process of securing a list of Bella's fallen soldiers and we will be reanimating them."

"How does Bella know who lived and died if she is imprisoned?" someone called out.

"We are relying on the help of our magic to assist us in determining those who survived and those who . . .

did not." At the appearance of a few frowns, due, no doubt, to their disapproval of reanimating our enemies, I continued. "All of Bella's soldiers will be obligated to take the same oath each of you did as well as drink the truth serum to ensure the safety of our kingdom."

"No more questions, please," Mercedes said, suddenly appearing beside me and ushering me back into the Green Room. "Thank you for your loyalty and support," she said in conclusion as she closed the doors tightly.

"I imagine that didn't go quite the way you hoped it would," I said in a small voice, not really sure what else I could or should say.

Mercedes faced me but she didn't seem angry. "I am not in a position to criticize. You must rule your kingdom as you see fit."

I was surprised, expecting her to read me the riot act. Mercedes dropped into a curtsy and left the room. I didn't have any time to weigh her reaction because Sinjin was suddenly before me.

"You did well," he said.

I shook my head and offered him an incredulous expression that said I didn't believe him by a long shot.

A large smile widened his beautiful mouth. "Perhaps your next tutorial will be in public speaking."

It wasn't like I thought I'd done a good job addressing my people, but I was happy I'd done it and even happier it was over. It had been an hour or so since my speech and after telling the house staff to take the night off, I was alone, relaxing in my bedroom, watching *How Clean Is Your House?* on TV. I'd changed my tailored suit for gray sweats and a pink UCLA sweatshirt.

Just as Kim Woodburn was advising me on how to clean a stovetop with vinegar, there was a knock on my door.

"Come in," I called out, not even glancing over to find out who was at the door. Instead my attention was consumed by how well vinegar could cut thirty-year-old grease.

"Jolie."

It was Rand.

I craned my neck in his direction so quickly, I felt an explosion of pain straight up the back of my neck. I quickly magicked it away but there wasn't anything I could do about my frantic heartbeat. Well, maybe there was, but I wasn't sure slowing my heart rate by way of magic was really in my best interests.

"Hi," I said dumbly.

"May I come in?" he asked, and I realized he hadn't come in yet. I nodded and he entered, closing the door behind him. Then he turned to face me.

He was wearing dark brown pants and a dark green sweater. His hair looked as if it had been freshly cut, but there was a bit of shadow beginning to cover his cheeks and chin. He was beautiful.

"I . . . I came to congratulate you," he said and rubbed the back of his neck awkwardly—like he was as uncomfortable as I was.

"Oh, thanks," I responded, not knowing what else to say. "You mean for my stellar speech?" I added with a self-conscious laugh, hoping to alleviate the tension in the room.

Rand nodded and offered me a quick smile. "You did very well."

"Thank you," I said in a small voice.

He eyed the armchair beside my bed and glanced up at me. "Do you mind if I sit?"

"No, go ahead," I said, surprised that he wanted to stay.

He sat down and the heady scent of his aftershave

danced through the air, teasing and tempting. I managed to keep my cool, though. Or at least I think I did.

"I think it took a great amount of courage and integrity to do what you did today." He paused for a second or two. "I'm sure it wasn't easy to announce your plans as Queen and I'm proud of you for doing it. I also think your ideas are very honorable and just."

I swallowed hard. "I've told you all along that this didn't have to be a monarchy in the old-fashioned sense, that we could shape it . . . together."

Rand nodded and his lips were tight, as if he was deep in thought. "Yes, I realize that now more than I did before."

I couldn't help the surprise that tinged my voice when I responded, "Wow, was my speech that good?"

Rand laughed and shook his head. "Perhaps not in your delivery but in your meaning."

"I admit I was surprised to see you in the audience."

"Why?"

I shrugged. "I thought you wanted to be a renegade?"

"I was curious as to what you had to say . . ."

I suddenly felt like I wanted to cut to the chase, wanted to find out why he was here, what he was doing in my room. "Rand, why did you come?"

Rand expelled a pent-up breath of air. "When I was listening to your speech, I was struck by the fact that my being a renegade will not benefit anyone. I can do much more good working with you than against you."

"I never imagined you were against me?"

He nodded. "Perhaps that was too strong a word. I seem to be putting my foot in my mouth." He paused for a few seconds, as if searching for the best way to communicate his thoughts. "What I came to ask you, Jolie, is whether or not you would consider the role of a chief advisor, someone who could work hand in hand with you . . . someone who could help you."

"And let me guess, you want to submit your application for the job?"

He chuckled. "I would like to offer my services, yes."

I nodded, thinking it sounded like a good idea. "Then you accept me as your monarch?"

He was quiet for a second or two and then nodded. "Yes, I do."

"And how would you envision this role?"

He shrugged. "As I mentioned before, I was in the employ of Queen Victoria so I'm very well versed in the minutiae of governance. I could offer my service and guidance should you ever require them. I know the politics of the various creatures of the Underworld; I've done negotiating, leading, and organizing of factions in the past. I could help you navigate through situations that you might not be familiar with, give you insight into certain situations so you can make the most informed decisions." He took a deep breath. "I would never overstep my boundaries and I would absolutely recognize your rightful place as Queen of the Underworld."

The idea actually sounded incredibly good—I knew nothing about ruling and Rand did. And not only that, but I also admired him greatly. The only thing that worried me was the fact that we'd be working so closely again—and we hadn't exactly resolved the issues between us. And as to the whole bonding argument we'd had? Hmm, that was a matter I didn't feel like discussing—not when I was still flying high from my first public speaking event. And besides, I didn't always want to be the one bringing up our relationship. If Rand wanted to make things work, the figurative ball was in his court. I was tired of playing relationship tennis.

"I realize things aren't exactly comfortable between us at the moment," he started. I had to wonder if he'd been reading my mind.

"I wasn't going to bring that up."

He dropped his gaze to his long legs and stretched them out before him, leaning into the chair with a heavy sigh. "I care about you, Jolie."

"I care about you too, Rand."

He leaned over with his elbows on his knees and appeared to gaze at something outside my window. There wasn't anything out there but the pitch darkness of night. He faced me and smiled sadly. "Now that you are Queen, things are going to be different."

"What does that even mean?" I demanded, my voice irritated.

"It means there will be pressures on you and every decision you make, personal and otherwise, will be in the spotlight. Your life is no longer your own, Jolie."

"How does that affect you and me?"

He swallowed. "I'm a private person."

I shook my head as annoyance snaked through me. "Maybe it's best to just focus on the fact that we both want what's best for the Underworld."

"Said like a true monarch," Rand said sadly.

Then he stood up to leave as if his whole purpose in coming to my room was to offer some garbled, bizarre observation and then just disappear into the black night. Never mind; tonight I wasn't in the mood to fight. No, I was sticking with my new plan, which was to rule my kingdom my own way. My focus from here on out was only going to be on the Underworld. I wasn't going to bother myself with Rand and his hang-ups.

"Have a good night," I said dismissively and turned toward the TV again, only to see the credits of *How Clean Is Your House?* Damn men and their bad timing.

Rand didn't say anything more but obediently showed himself out. The sound of the door closing made me sad, but at the same time I actually felt proud of myself. Strong and feminine. Hmm, maybe Queen Elizabeth had it right when she declared herself the Virgin Queen. Maybe I'd follow in her footsteps. I mean, it's not like it would be tough because I was already a Queen and basically an uncommitted virgin now . . .

I was asleep and dreaming but aware of the fact that I was dreaming. Even being aware of the dream state, I didn't seem able to control the images flowing through my mind. Memories . . . memories of a time when I had battled a dragon—well, really the fairy Dougal. Dougal was first-hand man, or fae, to Odran, and the only reason Odran had ever agreed to become our ally against Bella was the fact that I'd bested Dougal in magic-to-magic combat.

As the dream dragon glared down at me with his glowing red eyes, fear pounded through me. It didn't seem to make any difference that I knew how this feat ended—with me the victor—nope, fear was fear and didn't seem to care about the details. But any fear I felt was nothing compared with the fear in Rand's eyes.

And Rand suddenly took the spotlight of my dream-scape as memories intercepted my unconscious mind and swirled together until I was reliving a time long gone.

"What's going on?" Rand demanded.

I started toward him. "It was the only way, Rand."

"What was the only way?" He grabbed my shoulders, shaking me as if trying to get the words out faster than I could say them. "What the hell have you done?"

"She's agreed ta defend herself against my best fairy," Odran said.

Rand glanced up at him, fire spitting from his eyes. "No, your fairy will kill her."

Odran nodded glumly. "Aye, Ah've told the lass boot she is determined."

Rand faced me again. "Jolie, you will die, do you understand?"

"I just have to defend myself," I said, repeating what I'd been telling myself over two hundred times already.

Rand shook his head. "It doesn't matter. His strongest fairy could kill you without even trying." He faced Odran again. "Call this off, Odran, Jolie won't fight your fairy."

Odran shook his head. "I cannae call it oof, it tis doone."

"Goddammit!" Rand yelled and then immediately fell silent, his eyes pensive. His jaw was so tight, it twitched. "Let me take her place."

"Rand, no." This was my fight. "I have to do this."

Odran shook his head again. "I grow tired ah this argument. Either step aside or I'll 'ave ye restrained."

Rand's eyes were wild. "Jolie, run. Run as fast as you can."

No sooner did he say it than two fairies grabbed his arms, pulling him away from me. Rand's face was an angry mask, outrage etching his lips and eyes. He broadsided one fairy with a burst of magic but as soon as he did so, another four surrounded him, all of them livid. Tears blossomed in my eyes as I watched him struggle to free himself.

"Run, Jolie," he yelled, still flailing against his captors but I couldn't run, couldn't escape.

Jolie, just focus on protecting yourself. Focus on nothing else, do you understand? Rand's voice broke through my thoughts.

At the sound of his voice, tears sprang to my eyes. *I'm sorry. I didn't realize what I was getting into.*

That doesn't matter now, just focus on protecting yourself.

Okay, I will.

I don't know what he plans on doing, but don't be frightened; don't let anything take your focus away from your own protection. Whatever he does, you must ignore it.

I woke up sweating. I tried to shake away the memory of the horrible creature Dougal had turned into, but the images continued to pound through me. When I remembered back to that fateful day, the way the heavens had loosened an onslaught of rain, thunder, and lightning, I was amazed that I'd even come out of it alive.

But as with most of the difficult situations I'd experienced in my life, the person who had always stood by my side and helped me get through was Rand.

Fifteen

A few days after Mathilda had unstopped my magical block and a day or so after my speech, I found myself standing just outside the front entrance to Kinloch, beside Rand and Mercedes as Mathilda looked on. It was the time of reckoning—now we would learn whether or not my abilities had been restored.

The moon shone in the sky and was full and round, acting like an orb of light. Multitudes of stars sparkled around it. I wasn't sure why, but I found them reassuring. Maybe it was just wishful thinking.

"His hat," Mercedes said and offered me the clothing from one of the deceased members of our legion.

I nodded and accepted the black ball cap, clutching it with shaking hands. I didn't know what would happen if I wasn't able to reanimate this fallen soldier—what would that mean for my powers—would it point to the fact that they were extinct?

Calm yourself, Jolie. It was Rand's voice.

I didn't turn to look at him but offered my hand, which he quickly accepted, closing his fingers around mine. Mercedes took my other hand, the one with the ball cap in it, and I shut my eyes, concentrating on the task.

Just go about it the same way you always have, Rand continued.

I nodded but didn't respond. I was still annoyed over our last encounter. Instead I focused on the blackness of my eyelids, praying my magic would take over, praying I'd open my eyes to view the battlefield of Culloden.

When it appeared nothing was happening, I opened my eyes and found Rand, Mathilda, and Mercedes all staring at me expectantly.

"Nothing," I grumbled.

"Try again," Mercedes said resolutely.

I nodded and, taking a deep breath, closed my eyes again, sinking into inky blackness. I focused and then focused some more but couldn't keep the sudden fear that I'd lost my abilities from the forefront of my mind.

"What if something happened to me?" I said. "What if something irreversible happened?"

"We removed the block, child," Mathilda said in a small voice. I felt her soft and small hand on top of mine as she patted it consolingly. "Abandon your fears."

It was more a command than anything else. And when I closed my eyes again and actually felt something akin to relief flooding me, I had to wonder if Mathilda hadn't bewitched me, hadn't slipped me her version of a fae Quaalude. But I also wasn't about to argue, not when I could finally relax and actually focus on my magic, focus on the darkness that would hopefully take me back to a time when my victim was still alive.

Even though the blackness wasn't fading, I didn't lose hope. I clenched my eyes shut even tighter and begged my powers to kick in, begged my abilities to take over. And then it was as if lightning ricocheted through my mind, the darkness suddenly intercepted by a bright flash of light, and I was where I'd hoped to be . . . on the battlefield.

The hat in my hand began to tremble and I felt myself propelled forward, toward a man who was on the ground, barely moving. As I got closer, I realized he was actually a vamp. It looked as if he'd been attacked by another vamp, a huge and open gash in his throat. His blood had already soaked the majority of the ground beneath him, but he wasn't dead. I could tell by the hollow but alive look in his eyes.

I approached him and leaned down onto my thighs, reaching for him. As soon as I touched him, light blazed up around me and I shielded my eyes against the garish infiltration.

When I opened them again, I found myself standing beside Rand and Mercedes. And beyond them, Mathilda stood beside a vampire. A vampire who faced me and smiled, revealing the fact that he was very much alive . . . or as alive as the undead can be.

It was the night after I'd managed to reanimate the vampire, and my panel of representatives was assembled around my dining room table for our first meeting in Kinloch Kirk. My panel comprised Odran and Mathilda, Trent and John, Mercedes, Varick, Sinjin, Klaasje (whom I hadn't assigned as one of my representatives but apparently the Queen's defensive force went wherever she did or maybe wherever Sinjin did), and, of course, Rand.

Rand sat at the far end of my oblong maple table. He leaned back in his chair as he regarded everyone around him quietly even though there were numerous conversations rolling around the table. I sat at the head and glanced at Rand only to find him staring at me. I smiled a quick and uncomfortable hello before looking up at the grandfather clock in the corner of the room, which announced, in a baritone *ding-dong,* that my meeting had begun. I actually felt relieved to be able to focus on my meeting instead of the dark pools of Rand's eyes or the way he'd neglected to shave his stubble and, consequently, looked deliciously roguish. Nope, I was no longer going to focus on anything having to do with Rand.

I was sticking with the promise I'd made myself that I'd focus only on my responsibilities to the people.

After all, I was now the fully committed Virgin Queen.

My sex life aside, I was excited to chair this first important meeting. It was like I was embarking on a new chapter in my life—the decisions and choices we agreed on today would affect all of our lives moving forward. And it was a good feeling to know how important I was. My opinions mattered not only for my own future but for the futures of hundreds of Underworld creatures. While that thought was a scary one, it was also invigorating.

"Thanks for coming," I began as I poured myself a glass of water, passing the jug to Trent, who sat beside me. "I wanted to address a few concerns." Then I turned to the papers on the table in front of me and passed them to Odran, who happened to be sitting on the other side of me. "Take one and pass them down the row, please," I said when it looked like he assumed they were all for him. Didn't fairies have to attend grammar school? I mean, hello, that was so third-grade.

"Ah, aye," he said and then seemed to wrestle the sheets between his large fingers.

"Need some help, big guy?" Klaasje asked with a laugh as she took the papers from Odran and passed them out to everyone else. I didn't miss Odran's smile or the sight of him pillaging her body with his eyes. I also didn't miss her hip shimmy as she passed Sinjin—or his smirk. I felt something climb up into my throat, something that felt like jealousy, but I grappled it back down. I had no reason to be jealous of Sinjin's relationship with this beautiful girl, er, vampire. Irritated with myself, I glanced down at the piece of paper before me and read off the first item on the list.

"I would like an update on what is happening with the Lurkers."

I glanced at Mercedes, who nodded, clearing her throat. "I have created a task force to research the Lurkers as you requested." (I hadn't really requested it—it had been her idea all along. But anyhoo . . .) "And what they have reported back to me is of great interest."

"Wonderful," I answered as I offered her an expression that said, *Please continue.*

Mercedes glanced around the table as if to make sure she had everyone's attention. Really, she always had everyone's attention. I think, in general, everyone was afraid of her.

"First, it is important to inform everyone here of those who make up this task force. I appointed eight creatures, all of whom I believed to be the best candidates: a female witch, three male vampires, two female weres, and, lastly, a male and a female fairy."

"Aye, Anwien and Marmion are amoong the best warriors o' my fae," Odran added.

Sinjin chuckled. "I would say the vampires chosen for the position were also the best but that would be a lie as the best are already employed in the Queen's defense." Then he faced Varick and said, almost as an afterthought: "That statement of course includes you, my elder."

Varick said nothing, but nodded, as if he approved of Sinjin's deference. I was about to smile but then I heard Klaasje giggle and the smile dropped right off my lips. I glanced over at her beautiful blue eyes and gorgeous, thick dark hair and wished I were a bigger person.

Mercedes glanced at the two of them and then faced me with a raised eyebrow, like she didn't appreciate the joking. Go, Mercedes.

"I heard they had to take tests," Trent chimed in with a bit of a chuckle, like he would never be caught dead taking a test. And maybe that made sense—I wouldn't exactly describe him as the sharpest wolf in the pack.

Mercedes faced him and her expression hinted that she wasn't amused. "Yes, I wanted only the best creatures for the position. I hand-selected those who appeared the most promising and then further narrowed the group based upon their test scores. I tested not only their IQs but also their reaction times in combat situations, their ability to think outside the proverbial box in strategy preparation, as well as their ability to defend themselves."

I nodded, impressed. Really, everything Mercedes did was impressive. She was some prophetess. "Sounds like you did a really good job, Mercedes, thank you."

Mercedes smiled her pleasure. "As to the information we have found thus far, we've had reports of Lurker activity all across the United States as well as Europe, which leads us to believe they are not located in any one place but spread out.

"And from a report given to me by the witch Freida, they are in training both day and night."

Suddenly I was worried about the tactics of the task force. The last thing I wanted was torture on my hands. "How are you getting this information, Mercedes?"

"Mostly through interviews with anyone who has had interactions with the Lurkers, my Queen. We have paid especially close attention to those who were killed by the Lurkers and were subsequently reanimated. And with fae magic, we were able to re-create scenes to observe their strategies during combat. Based on that, we were able to learn much about them."

Good, torture apparently wasn't a part of the equation. Relief.

"And your plans moving forward?" Rand asked.

Mercedes nodded but said nothing right away, as if Rand's question wasn't so easy to answer. Finally she took a deep breath and turned toward me. "In order to learn what we need to, we must capture a Lurker."

Odran nodded immediately, as if he'd been waiting for someone to say as much. "Aye. We need ta stoody them."

Rand nodded as well but said nothing more. Everyone around the table fell silent as their gazes settled on me.

"If our Queen endorses this approach, we will move forward," Mercedes finished and looked at me expectantly.

"I do think it is . . . necessary," I began before hesitation captured my voice. "But please instruct your team to try to do so without hurting anyone. I want it to be known that we will kill only when we have no other choice," I finished with as much authority as I could muster.

Mercedes merely nodded and said nothing more. Realizing this topic was now at its end, I glanced at the agenda and moved to the next question, eyeing Sinjin. "Sinjin, you informed me that Bella had agreed to help us reanimate her dead soldiers?"

Sinjin nodded. "I did, my Queen."

I couldn't help but notice that Rand's gaze narrowed on Sinjin and his jaw was tight. He looked like he was in fight-or-flight mode, just waiting for one wrong word to set him off. Rand shifted in his chair as if he couldn't get comfortable. Then it suddenly occurred to me that maybe I was just painting him with jealousy that didn't exist—maybe he wasn't bothered at all by Sinjin— maybe he just had a wedgie.

"And where do we stand?" I asked, reminding myself to pay attention to the agenda—not Rand and his foul mood.

Sinjin nodded. "Bella will provide me with a list of her deceased. She is creating that list as we speak."

We still hadn't managed to reanimate the entirety of our legion, but we were getting closer.

I faced my agenda again and sighed, knowing this

next point would be a hard sell. "Due to the fact that Bella has agreed to work with us, I believe we should give her a second chance."

"Jolie," Rand started but his voice was lost in Odran's.

"Bella shouldna be alloowed ta live," he said, his hazel eyes burning. He bashed his fist onto the table as if to reiterate his objection. His long, wavy blond hair fell off his shoulders as if it, too, were shocked by his violent display.

"Watch yourself," Sinjin growled, his eyes narrowed on Odran.

"Watch yer oown self, fang face."

"Okay, enough, we're all adults here," I started, alternating my glares between Odran and Sinjin. "I will not order Bella's death," I said resolutely. "I will not have her death on my hands."

"She can be controlled." Sinjin steepled his fingers in his lap as though this conversation did nothing but bore him. "Bella is a threat, yes, but she is a threat that can be managed."

"Said like a true womanizer," Klaasje added with a laugh but it was somehow a sad laugh, as if she thought it was a shame.

Sinjin smiled slightly, like he was amused by her comment. His eyes met mine and his smile widened.

"Jolie," Rand started again. "Bella is a severe threat, no matter what anyone else says. She's a danger to your existence."

"Randall, the Queen is protected both night and day," Sinjin announced in a tone that implied Rand was an idiot.

Rand's eyes burned with anger as he glared at the vampire. "Where Jolie is concerned, I don't trust anyone. Not Bella and certainly not you."

I was getting extremely irritated with all the testosterone in the room. "Rand, I don't have an alternative. We can't keep Bella locked up forever, and I don't want to kill her."

"She needs to die," Trent said with finality before glancing up at me. "If you don't want to order it, then maybe someone else should."

"No," I rebutted as I angrily stood up. I pushed my chair out and walked to the window, which overlooked the craggy shore below. I was the Queen and on this point, I would not waver. Bella would not be executed. Not on my watch. I turned to face everyone in the room again. "I will not have Bella's death on my conscience, especially since we'd be killing her in cold blood."

"Perhaps we should hear what the witch has to say for herself," Mathilda suggested in her soft cadence.

"Would you like me to call for Bella, my Queen?" Mercedes asked, glancing up at me. I turned toward the window again, wishing the puffins that flew in and out of the rocks had an answer for me.

Finally I faced the room and nodded. "I'd like to offer her the opportunity to become a citizen of our kingdom."

Mercedes stood up and started for the door. "Very well."

Jolie. It was Rand. *Please don't trust Bella.*

I refused to look at him. Instead I watched Mercedes open the door and disappear into the hall. *What choice do I have? Do you think we should just kill her?*

Of course not. But at the same time, I don't believe you should embrace her like she's your long-lost friend.

I glanced at him and frowned. *That's exaggerating.*

But you get the gist?

Until someone else can come up with a better solution, I think this is the only way forward. Besides, she will take the truth serum and the oath just like all her soldiers did.

Truth serums and oaths aside, I don't trust her. Jolie,

sometimes you have a very optimistic and, dare I say it, naïve perspective regarding the world.

I narrowed my eyes. *Is that all you have to say?*

Will you please just trust me on this? Don't give Bella the benefit of the doubt, Jolie. At the very least she'll disappoint you. At the very most—

Rand didn't have the chance to finish his statement because Mercedes suddenly appeared at the door again. She stepped inside and to the right, as the two weres who had been guarding Bella walked into the room, with her between them. Sinjin was immediately beside me and in another second Klaasje flanked my other side. They were bodyguards bar none.

Bella was beautiful—she always had been—but her beauty was created of hard lines and a general angularity. There was nothing soft and feminine about her. Her oval face finished in a square jaw, and her full lips were frowning at the moment. Her hair was a deep, dark brown but also had a reddish tinge to it. Adding to this her olive complexion, she could definitely be described as "exotic."

As to her figure, she was tall and curvaceous, built according to the hourglass, the quintessential ideal of feminine beauty. But there was a blight on Bella's beauty—there always had been. It was tainted by the perpetual scowl on her face, tainted by the ugliness of her personality.

Bella didn't say anything for a second or two and, instead, just wore an anxious, unhappy expression. Her gaze traveled around the room, as if she wanted to take stock of all who were present.

"Hi, Bella," I greeted her.

She turned her ire-filled eyes to me and looked me up and down in an age-old bitchy way.

"Why did you order me here?" she demanded finally,

crossing her arms against her chest as if it were her last defense. "My list of soldiers is not complete."

"I suggest ye speak with respect to yer Queen," Odran spat out in disgust.

She glanced at Odran indifferently before gazing back at me. She remained mute and raised her brows as if to say she wasn't impressed.

"I am inviting you to become a member of our society," I said as I took a few steps away from the table. When Sinjin started to close in on me, I looked at him and shook my head. I didn't want a shadow . . . or two. "I don't imagine you want to be locked up forever?"

"No, I don't."

I nodded, trying my best to seem unthreatening. I wasn't sure I was succeeding. "I'm trying to give you the chance to live a good life."

"Go on," she said. Some of her anger seemed to have dissipated, although she didn't drop her arms from across her chest.

"I appreciate your help in reanimating your fallen," I continued.

Bella looked at Sinjin. "It wasn't like I had much of a choice."

Sinjin glanced at me and shrugged.

"At any rate, I appreciate it and I'd like to return the favor," I finished.

"If you'd like to return the favor, then let me live my life outside the monarchy. Let me be a renegade like Rand always was," she spat out. Her eyes found Rand. "And where do you stand in all of this now? Are you still a renegade?"

Rand frowned and his face was stoic, placid. "Jolie's vision of monarchy is drastically different from yours."

"You never believed in any form of monarchy," she retorted. "You must be screwing her."

"You do not disrespect the Queen!" Mercedes ordered, shocking the hell out of me and probably everyone else in the room. "You are extremely fortunate she has decided to spare you."

Mercedes' rainbow aura was in full effect and the blue and purplish sections seemed to glow the brightest, revealing her anger. Bella appeared to shrink a bit in front of the furious prophetess. I'm sure she was intimidated. Hell, I was intimidated, and Mercedes was defending me. Thank God she was on my side . . .

"You don't have the option to be a renegade," I said simply to Bella. "You either become a member of my kingdom or you stay imprisoned. The choice is yours."

Bella was quiet as her attention shifted back to Sinjin. "And they have included *you* in this so-called monarchy?"

Sinjin shrugged, maintaining his expression of ennui. "I support my Queen wholeheartedly."

"Your Queen." Bella snickered. "There was a time when you said the exact same words to me."

Sinjin returned the snicker. "Except with you I never meant them."

Bella gnashed her teeth as if the lioness within her was about to make itself known. "How quickly you switch sides."

"I never switched sides." Sinjin's eyes narrowed. "I was never on yours."

"I don't think we really need to get into this now," I said, sensing that Bella's temper was about to erupt like Old Faithful. But Bella ignored me.

"So, what, are you bedding her like you did me? Winning her over with your charisma and your lies?"

Sinjin never took his eyes off Bella. I could see the imprints of sharp teeth in his lower lip.

"I am dedicated solely to the Queen and her protection is my only duty," he answered, and his accent somehow seemed deeper, stronger.

"Answer the question," Bella seethed. "Are you screwing her like you screwed me?"

"No, he isn't," I said for Sinjin when he made no motion to answer. I suddenly felt anger spiraling up my throat, constricting it until I could barely catch my breath. "Not that it's any of your damn business."

Bella faced me, her cheeks flushed, her eyes so angry, it looked as if she might burst. "And do you actually believe he's trustworthy?" She laughed acidly and faced Sinjin again. "I trusted him and look what he did to me."

"This has—" I started.

"The one truth about Sinjin Sinclair is that he's only out for himself. He doesn't give a shit about anyone," Bella interrupted.

Before I could blink Sinjin leapt forward, and in a split second Bella was in his arms, her neck braced between his fangs. All he had to do was bite down to sever her carotid artery.

"Sinjin!" I screamed. "Let her go."

"I should sink my fangs into you and kill you," he seethed, glaring down at her.

She said nothing but gulped down her fear. Instantly Odran and Rand were beside Sinjin. Rand was first to grasp his arm; Odran took the other.

"Release her," Rand said in a tight voice.

"It is yer Queen's command," Odran reiterated.

Sinjin retracted his fangs. In another second he pushed Bella away and took a step back, shaking himself loose from Rand and Odran.

"You will never again compare yourself to Jolie," Sinjin warned, staring at Bella as his chest heaved, which was odd considering Sinjin didn't breathe, couldn't breathe. He must have just been super pissed off. "You are nothing but a blight. If you ever so much as look at your Queen with anything but respect, I will finish you."

Bella's eyes narrowed. "So you could kill me just as easily as you bedded me?"

Sinjin returned to the table and took a seat, brushing himself off as if nothing had happened, and he hadn't just humiliated Bella in front of all of us.

"I believe the answer is quite clear," he finished.

And then Bella did something that surprised me. She laughed. Granted, it was sour and dripping with sarcasm, but it was a laugh all the same.

"You are such a fool," she said. I gulped as I glanced at Sinjin, hoping he wouldn't attack her again. "I actually feel nothing but pity for you."

"I can't imagine why," he replied in a droll voice, as if he was doing her a favor by continuing to listen to her.

Bella nodded like she was going to give him an earful. "Because you're in love with a woman who's in love with another man."

Sixteen

Dear Ms. Diary, phew . . . I really don't know what to say about that whole situation with Bella last night, er, today—I can't even seem to keep track of time. I just checked the clock and it's four a.m. so I guess that means our meeting with Bella ended early this morning (just a few hours ago as a matter of fact).

I'm actually pretty upset with Sinjin because I feel like he spurred Bella on intentionally—like he wanted to hurt her. I tried to go to sleep once the meeting ended but I've been up all night thinking about it. I wonder if the fact that Sinjin had to feign loyalty to Bella in the past—and in doing so had sex with her—really offended some deep-down part of him in that labyrinth of mystery and subterfuge he calls his heart. (And I won't even get into the ways their sexcapades offended and still do offend me. Let's just say it's a visual I desperately try to avoid.)

As to whether or not Sinjin really was shamed by his relations with Bella—it's all just speculation. It could be nothing more than me pinning Sinjin with remorse and regret where none truly exist. And really, what man wouldn't want to have sex with a woman as beautiful as Bella? Even if she is the spawn of the devil? I just can't really understand why Sinjin acted with such passionate vehemence toward her. Was it to protect me? To prove something? Because he honestly hates her? As usual, I'm never really sure what Sinjin is up to or what his true intentions are. What I can say is that Sinjin acted without thinking and now I'm sure Bella isn't going to want to have anything to do with us. And based on his show of . . . anger toward her, I also wonder if he's the best candidate to procure her list of deceased soldiers. Hmm, maybe I should pass that duty to Rand instead.

Rand . . . Nope, won't even spare a thought for him. Not going there.

Moving right along . . . one of the other things that I can't seem to eradicate from my mind was when Bella said Sinjin was in love with me. I mean, I know she said that to lash out at him, but I don't know what to make of it, all the same. After Bella said it, there was total silence in the room and it seemed like everyone was suddenly admiring my floors. I glanced at Sinjin and he was staring Bella down, looking like he'd tear her apart if he had the chance. And, honestly, if we hadn't been in the room, I think Bella would have been a goner.

And Rand. After Bella announced that Sinjin was in love with me and I was in love with another man, Rand's attention had been riveted on the view outside the window, like he didn't even want to be in the room. And as for me? I still don't know what to think about the whole situation. But I do have this gut feeling in the core of my being that says Sinjin really isn't in love with me. He's in lust with me, yes, but I have the feeling that if I ever gave in to him and actually had sex with him and played the part of the enamored girlfriend, he'd want nothing more to do with me. I just can't see Sinjin as the relationship sort of guy—there's something about him that screams instability and unreliability. Nope, he's the guy every woman loves to pine after in the hope she can tame him, domesticate the stallion into an ideal husband. Ha, good luck!

No, Sinjin isn't truly in love with me but there is something he wants from me . . . Is it just power, glory, control? Maybe all of the above?

Back to last night. I've never really seen Sinjin angry before, and that side of him freaks me out. He's usually the cool, calm, and collected sexy vampire with a smart-ass quip for just about everything. But last night he was none of those things. His anger was combustible and so . . . unlike Sinjin. And that thought leads me to my next: What is Sinjin really like? Maybe the image he shows all of us is completely opposite the person he really is. Why would he be hiding behind a façade, though?

And I still have no idea what his intentions are or what his agenda is. The fact that I have no clue bothers me—probably more so than it did before. I don't like having a wild card in my kingdom. As the Queen, it's my responsibility to weed out threats and extinguish them. And while I don't and never would believe that Sinjin is a threat to me or my realm, the fact that I don't know what his end goal is or what he wants is, in itself, a threat.

I believe there is an answer. And I believe that answer resides in Mercedes. What does Sinjin want from the prophetess? Why the secrecy between the two of them? As Queen, it is my responsibility to make sure they're on the up-and-up. I've got to think beyond myself now, I have to represent the interests of my people . . . And that is just what I intend to do.

The other day Christa mentioned in passing that she'd seen Mercedes and Sinjin in a heated argument on the beach just below Kinloch. Even she said she thought their acquaintance odd because she couldn't imagine why (and neither can I, for that matter) Mercedes would have anything to do with Sinjin. Yes, Sinjin could be plotting something and might need Mercedes' assistance, but why would Mercedes have anything to do *with him? It's not like she needs Sinjin—she's the prophetess, for God's sake! Unless . . . could it be that my prophetess and my bodyguard are having an affair?*

I feel silly even saying it because it's not like dating isn't allowed among my subjects. I would never fault them for being together or force them to separate. I mean, I don't like the idea of it at all because . . . I don't know why (well, I probably do but just don't want to admit it).

The more I think about it, though, the more implausible it seems. Would Mercedes really put up with Sinjin? I can't imagine that she would. Mercedes is too strong, too smart, and too powerful to have anything to do with him—especially not when he so openly flirts with Klaasje. And speaking of Klaasje and Sinjin, I can't help but wonder what the nature of their relationship is.

This is silly—I'll just drive myself crazy thinking about the what-ifs. And furthermore, none of this (as in the personal-relationships aspect) should bother me because I've got a new focus for my life, Diary. I don't know that I've told you, but I've sworn off men yet again. Yes, there was a short time a few months ago when I swore off anything with a penis but I guess I wasn't wholehearted in my approach. Well, I am now. I'm wholehearted, decided, absolute, and final in my decision.

I am going to focus all my energies, all my attentions on my kingdom, and I'm going to become the best Queen I can be.

Who knows, maybe I'll even end up on the cover of a Wheaties box someday.

I put my journal down and decided to get some fresh air. I hadn't been able to sleep all night, not after the scene with Bella. Now the dawn was just stretching her fingers across the moors of Kinloch Kirk. The sea crashed against the rocks below my window, beckoning me to listen to the songs of the thrushes, to watch the puffins make their homes in the rocks and just be grateful for being alive.

I stood up and—glancing down at my sweats and T-shirt—decided it was too cold outside for my current garb, so I grabbed my down jacket. Scotland was much colder than England, since it was so far north, and it was even colder living along the coast. I closed my bedroom door behind me and immediately noticed the two werewolf guards posted just outside my door. Both of them eyed me suspiciously. I just smiled.

"I'm going for a walk," I said simply and started forward as they immediately fell into step behind me.

Glancing back at them, I shook my head. "I'm going alone."

The first guard, a burly guy of maybe thirty with blond hair, eyebrows, and lashes, vehemently shook his head. "Majesty, your safety is our priority."

So they were going to make me do this the hard way, were they? I just smiled and imagined a burst of light consuming both of them, starting from the center of their bodies and working its way outward until it encompassed them entirely. Then I thought the words: *You do not see me and believe me to be inside my room. When I return from my walk, this charm will be shattered.*

As soon as I'd thought the last word, they returned to their post just outside my door and resumed whatever conversation they'd been having prior to my entrance. Ah, it was good to be a witch.

I faced the staircase and continued forward, silently appreciating the fact that no one aside from my guards was awake at this early hour, not even the house staff. My vampires were asleep in their special rooms in the basement of Kinloch Kirk, safe from the marauding sunlight. Everyone who'd attended the meeting last night had spent the night at Kinloch, in its multiple guest rooms. Now it appeared that they were still cradled in the arms of slumber. And that suited me fine. When your life was no longer your own, there was something to be said about sharing the early morning with no one but the ocean, the moors, and a few birds.

I hurried down the stairs and exited the double front doors, taking a deep breath of crisp North Sea air. A cold breeze whipped through the Scottish moors on either side of me, causing the heather to shimmy and flutter. A few of the bell-like purple flowers freed themselves to dance with the breeze and tumble over the cliffs, only to be swallowed up by the gyrating sea.

And I suddenly had the horrible thought, the unrealistic anxiety of wondering if I, too, would end up like those little balls of purple flowers: caught up in the winds of monarchy, forced to dedicate my life to something that might eventually come crashing down around me—something that might drown me in the waters of responsibility.

What if I couldn't be the monarch everyone expected me to be? Or what if Bella's soldiers ended up rebelling against us? What if truth serums and loyalty oaths weren't enough? Worse, what if the Lurkers decimated us? What if I couldn't protect my kingdom, dooming it and everyone within it to a miserable death?

"Why are you awake so early?"

I nearly lost my footing and had to stabilize myself against the balustrade of the path that led to the beach below Kinloch Kirk. I glanced in the direction of Rand's voice and found him standing on the shore just below me.

"I could ask the same of you," I answered, still clutching the balustrade as I slowly made my way down the perilous path, hoping I wouldn't slip on the sand-covered wooden steps.

"I couldn't sleep."

Glancing down at him, I could see the truth of his words in the dark circles beneath his eyes. His messy hair was mute testimony to the fact that he'd been tossing and turning. Well, join the club.

I reached the beach and decided to take off my shoes—no use in filling them with sand. I unlaced both sneakers and stood up again, balancing on one foot while I attempted to free my heel with the other one. "That makes two of us."

Rand nodded and took a seat on a nearby rock, regarding me with a smile that seemed strange—amused maybe. "May I join you?"

After removing both shoes, I tossed them at the base of the steps leading back up the cliff and nodded, wondering why in the hell he wanted to accompany me and further, what in the hell we were going to talk about. There were so many elephants between us, I was afraid they'd stomp one another to death.

I didn't say anything, though. I just watched Rand slip off his leather shoes and stack them neatly beside mine, which lay across the landing beneath the pathway, a sock peeking out from one sneaker, the other sock unaccounted for. And that was us to a T—Rand was orderly and disciplined and I was the one who threw my shoes aside, not caring if I lost a sock along the way or if I tracked a bunch of sand into the house.

"Interesting meeting last night," Rand said once we'd started walking.

"Yeah, you're telling me. I wonder if we're ever going to get Bella to come through now. Damn Sinjin . . ."

Rand nodded and bent down, retrieving a piece of what looked like sea glass. It was baby blue. He rotated it in the palm of his hand before throwing it curveball style so it skipped off the water a few times before disappearing beneath the surf.

"He was hard on her, strangely so."

There were a few seconds of silence in which the crashing of the waves against the beach seemed louder than I'd ever remembered it and the shrill calling of the blackbirds had more in common with the song of the harpies than any songbird I could think of.

"Rand, why are we doing this?" I asked as my feet stopped and my toes seemed to grow roots into the sand.

Rand blinked in surprise. "Doing what?"

I shrugged. "Why did you want to walk with me? If you were just asking to be polite, I think we're beyond that now." There was a part of me that wasn't interested in small talk—a part of me that didn't have time to play games with Rand anymore—a part of me that wanted to just cut away the fluff in order to get to the truth.

He nodded and ran his hand through his hair but said nothing.

"And why have you stopped shaving?" I added, wondering why the hell his facial hair suddenly mattered to me.

He touched his chin as if he wasn't aware that there was more than a few days of stubble and faced me with tired eyes. "I suppose I forget daily activities when I'm absorbed in my thoughts."

As soon as he finished the statement, the rough, dark brown hairs on his chin, cheeks, and upper lip began to recede into his beautifully tanned skin and the roguish Rand I'd actually begun to appreciate was replaced with the model-perfect one I knew so well.

"And I'm not just being polite," he added. He started walking again, so I took his lead. "That is to say, I wanted the pleasure of your company."

"Why?" I demanded.

He cleared his throat and appeared altogether uncomfortable, his gaze riveted on the sand. He lifted his face and turned toward me. "Because I care deeply for you, Jolie."

I sighed and was suddenly grateful for the fact that we hadn't decided to take a stroll beside the cliffs of Kinloch Kirk; I probably would have pushed him over by now. Rand was frustration wrapped in a nice little package, tied together with stubbornness.

"I thought you were still mad at me about the whole bonding situation," I said in a hard voice. I was tired of beating around the proverbial bush. There would be no more bushes in my life—I was going to pull out my cutters and turn those out-of-control shrubs into manageable topiaries.

"You know me very well by now, Jolie." He glanced at me earnestly as he stopped walking. I stopped as well and a small ocean wave wrapped around my ankles, the frosty foam pricking my skin with its salty coldness.

"I think I do but sometimes you still throw me for a loop," I said, feeling like I might drown in the chocolate oceans of his eyes, so I focused instead on the sea itself.

"Well, I'm certain you are well aware of the way in which I tend to overanalyze most things and how . . . cerebral I am."

I glanced at him again. "Yes, Rand, I'm well aware of all your shortcomings."

He chuckled and looked out at the ocean thoughtfully before returning his gaze to me. "What I am trying to tell you is that my anger over you not telling me you were my bond mate has since abated."

"So you've forgiven me?"

He nodded. "Yes and not only that, but I am . . . thankful to know that you always have been the only woman in my life."

"What?" I asked, at a complete loss, feeling my eyebrows knitting together. A queasiness of something that felt like irritation crept up my gut and took a firm hold of my stomach. "I just decided to be the Virgin Queen and you're telling me this now?"

Rand frowned at me in confusion. "The Virgin Queen—as in Queen Elizabeth?"

I shook my head, wishing some of my thoughts wouldn't verbalize themselves—I'd intended to only think that one. Whatever. "Never mind that," I snapped. "What are you trying to tell me?"

"That I'm sorry I reacted the way I did."

"Okay," I said and started walking again, shaking my head over the fact that men were so frustrating. It had to be true that men and women were from completely different planets, different galaxies even. It was like Rand's train would always leave the station as soon as I arrived—a classic case of bad timing.

Suddenly remembering Rand's bizarre reaction to my first speech from the Green Room, I faced him again. "And what the hell were you talking about when you said that things will be different between us now that I'm Queen?"

He nodded, as if he were remembering the conversation himself. "There will be . . . other obligations on you now, Jolie." He took a deep breath. "As Queen, you will be expected to unite our species," he finished as if that were news.

I felt irritation and impatience eating away at me. I'd wanted to take a walk this morning to clear my head, to enjoy some time to myself, and now I had to deal with this . . . "Yes, Rand, I'm well aware of what is expected of me. That was in the job description Mercedes gave me."

"It goes further than that," Rand said. There was a little attitude to his tone, like he didn't appreciate the fact that I was being short and sarcastic with him. Well, I hadn't liked the way he'd reacted to the news of our bonding, so I guess we were tied.

"How does it go further than that?"

"You will be expected to make an advantageous marriage, and it won't be for love," he finished angrily. I wasn't sure if he was annoyed with me or with the subject.

"What the bloody hell are you talking about?" I demanded, realizing I sounded just like him.

He braced both of my arms, turning me to face him. His eyes burned, and for a split second I thought he might kiss me. Instead he swallowed hard. "There has been talk, Jolie. Talk about the Queen taking a husband, a King, as a show of unity."

"That is the dumbest thing I've ever heard." I tried to beat down the irritation that was already rampaging through me. "And, furthermore, why haven't I heard anything about this? Shouldn't I be the first to know?"

Rand shook his head and dropped his hands from my arms. "You'll find that in many instances you might be the last to know." He sighed deeply. "At any rate, I wouldn't be surprised to see the subjects of your kingdom coming out of the woodwork to offer you their hands in marriage with the hope of uniting a stronger kingdom."

"Well, I won't do it," I spat back as irritation turned to fury. "I'm the Queen and I'm not about to marry anyone. It's bad enough that my entire life has been derailed to unite this kingdom and I've basically had to forfeit my personal life. This is going way too far."

Rand just nodded, but I could tell he wasn't convinced by my bravado. He didn't believe that this would go away so easily.

"And what do you think of all of this?" I demanded finally, wanting some sign from him, something to show he would fight this ridiculousness beside me, that he still loved me and wanted to be with me.

Rand seemed taken aback and took a few seconds to respond. "I obviously don't like it."

"So if I have your support, then end of subject," I answered, silently bemoaning the fact that his answer hadn't been the one I'd been hoping for. Back to the Virgin Queen for me. I started forward again but stopped when I realized Rand hadn't budged. I glanced back at him and he shook his head.

"I don't think it will be as easy as that. In a way your life has basically become the property of your kingdom."

"What?"

He inhaled deeply. "That's one of the reasons why I have always been against monarchies. I dislike everything they stand for. The only reason I agreed to become your chief advisor and the only reason I'm here right now is because I care deeply for you and I believe you can make a change, Jolie. I believe you can rule judiciously and democratically."

But I wasn't really interested in drafting another version of the Constitution. What I was interested in was why in the hell people were deciding my future—and worse, were doing it without my knowledge.

"I'm simply not going to agree to any of this," I said. "It's not like they can force me to get married."

Rand nodded. "That is true, though they can be . . . forceful with their recommendations."

"And besides, who are 'they'? Where did you hear this?"

Rand shook his head. "Not from any one person. It's been a theme as of late."

"So let's just say for the sake of argument that it was a choice that was forced on me . . . Why wouldn't you just marry me?" The words were out of my mouth before I had the chance to think them through and, in so doing, swallow them.

Rand nodded as if the idea wasn't foreign to him, as if he wasn't surprised. "I would not be considered a strong enough ally."

"You've already worked this out then?"

He nodded and his jaw was tight, his eyes piercing. "Of course I have. That was the first thought that entered my head—that I could ask for your hand. But I already know my offer would be regarded as worthless by Mercedes because we're of the same species. Furthermore, you and I would have little hope of producing future monarchs."

But according to Mercedes, I *wasn't* a witch. I opened my mouth to say something, then closed it. I didn't know what I was, and I until I did, there was no point in saying anything to Rand. For now I wanted nothing more than to return to the safety and solitude of my bedroom, where I could open my journal and spill my figurative blood all over the pages.

Seventeen

After finalizing the reanimations of our own legion and receiving Bella's list of deceased soldiers, we managed to reanimate thirty of her legion over the next few days. I had to suffer through another lesson, this one on etiquette (more specifically, the proper protocol for writing letters, including addressing them, what the salutation should be, and what the closing should be). It was now the end of the day and the sun had already crawled back down the sky, making room for night to spread her dark cloak. I found myself exhaustedly sitting on the couch in my living room trying to unwind by watching an episode of *Peep Show*.

Instead a knock sounded on the door. Before I could budge from my sloth-like demeanor, my butler, whose name was Cassius and who had also been a member of Odran's fairy kingdom in Scotland, materialized in true fae style. He opened the door with a great show of gallantry and subservience, bowing low to our visitor. Once I heard a mumbled, thick brogue, I realized it was Odran. Great. Just great.

"May I present the King o' the fae, mah Queen," Cassius said in a thick Scottish accent, his bushy red mustache moving in time with his lips. Cassius was an odd one—he never wanted to talk to me except about the operations of Kinloch Kirk, and even then he was so rigid in his posture and speech, it was like talking to a corpse experiencing rigor mortis.

"Hi, Odran," I said.

"My Queen," Odran said with a wide, bright smile while rolling his arm across his stomach and bowing like never before—something entirely too practiced and artificial.

"Why the surprise visit? I hope everything is well in fae?" I asked, turning the television off as I started for the entryway, while wishing I could spend my evening watching the hilarious exploits of Jeremy and Mark.

"Aye, Yer Highness, all is well, thank ye fer askin'," Odran responded, clearly avoiding the subject of his reason for visiting. He glanced behind himself impatiently. "Doolan, where be ye?"

I craned my neck, trying to find out who the hell Doolan was and what the hell he was doing at Kinloch. Well, it turned out that Doolan was one of Odran's warrior fae, only this evening he wasn't armed with weapons. Instead he appeared to be carrying more than an armful of colorful silks, satins, and beaded tapestries. Behind him, he toted a purple velvet bag overflowing with jewels, more fabrics, as well as enormous lilies, roses, and tulips. Flowers of that size were only possible in the realm of the fae. Strewn behind Doolan were the entrails of still more flowers, which had unfortunately not survived the trek from Odran's BMW to my doorstep.

"I bring gifts fer ye, ma Queen," Odran said and bent over into another deep bow.

"Why?" I asked, my eyes narrowing as the puzzle pieces began to fit into place. So Rand had been correct all along—there was going to be a mad rush for my hand in marriage. Well, little did everyone know that I wasn't going to accept any of them, Doolan bearing gifts or not.

"Ta celebrate yer loveliness, ma Queen," Odran lied.

I just shook my head and faced Cassius. "Can you see to it that all gifts are put in an empty room somewhere? I don't have the energy to deal with this right now."

Then I left Odran, Cassius, and Doolan standing in my entryway surrounded by enormous daffodils, rubies, and silk damasks.

"My Queen."

It was Sinjin. I paused, halfway up the stairs already, and turned to face him. "Will you accompany me please?" I asked. Really it was more of a command.

Sinjin said nothing but bowed his head in mock deference and started up the stairs behind me. Once we were shoulder-to-shoulder, I glanced over at him. "What the hell is going on with all this marriage business?"

"Marriage business, poppet? I do not understand."

Just as he finished speaking, I heard a commotion from downstairs and peered over the wooden balustrade to find that Trent had arrived with one of his wolves and, of course, more useless shit. I had to laugh inwardly at Trent's nerve—did he seriously think he had a chance in hell with me after what I'd already gone through as his so-called girlfriend? Well, the answer was pretty apparent by the fact that he was even here. I shook my head and started for my bedroom, Sinjin beside me.

"Haven't you noticed all the hullabaloo, Sinjin?" I asked and approached the window at the far west side of my room, one that overlooked the driveway to Kinloch. Opening the blinds, I focused on the entryway, which was desolate now, with only the remnants of strewn flowers coloring the ground. Maybe Odran and Trent would be the only two morons I'd have to deal with in this idiotic mission for my hand.

"I am not aware why the fairy and wolf have shown up, love," Sinjin said and took a seat in one of my armchairs as he eyed me up and down appreciatively.

I glanced at him and frowned. "You definitely don't have any problem making yourself comfortable, do you?" Before he could respond, I added: "You seem to be the only person, well, besides Rand maybe, who treats me as more than just a Queen."

"How so, love?" Sinjin asked but the half smile on his face said he knew exactly what I was talking about and, more, that he enjoyed the fact he was allowed such intimacy with me.

"I could name a million instances but let's just settle for the fact that you didn't ask me if you could sit in that chair. Plus right now you're looking at me like I'm naked."

Sinjin threw his head back and chuckled heartily before looking at me as if he could seduce me with just his eyes. "I can be whomever you choose me to be, love. Although I was of the belief that you liked me as I am?"

I sighed and shook my head, well aware that I was allowing Sinjin too many liberties where I was concerned. "Yes, I guess I do."

"Then you must come to terms with the fact that I want nothing more than to see your naked body." He leaned forward, and the smile was suddenly absent from his face, replaced with his fangs. "My one desire is to taste your flesh, to . . ."

"Enough, Casanova," I said with a subdued laugh. I glanced out my window again, this time catching the image of Varick as he stepped out of a Rolls-Royce.

"Son of a bitch."

"What disturbs you, love?"

I continued peering outside my window like a nosy old lady intent on spying on her neighbors. "Just that all of the creatures of the Underworld have arrived en masse to propose marriage to me."

Sinjin made no other remarks, and somehow I had the feeling that he knew more about this whole situation than he was letting on. But at the moment, that wasn't the topic on my mind. Instead I turned to face him and, leaning against the windowsill, tapped my fingers against my lips, studying him.

"As your Queen, I can make demands of you, right?"

Sinjin nodded, his eyes sparkling and his fangs even longer than they had been. "Of course."

"And if I make a demand of you, you must respect my order and do as I say?"

He nodded again and stood up, his immense height intimidating. He walked toward me and I felt myself melt into the windowsill, as if I knew I shouldn't allow him to come so close. When he continued his approach, I held my hand out against his chest, stopping him.

"As my Queen, no matter what you command of me, it is my responsibility to see to your . . . desires."

I smiled, not dropping my hand from his chest. Somehow I knew if I did, Sinjin would take it as an open invitation to kiss me or . . . more.

"Good." I took a deep breath. "I order you to tell me what you've been discussing with Mercedes in your secret meetings."

The smile on Sinjin's face immediately faded and his fangs retracted as his entire posture went rigid. I actually wanted to laugh at the transformation. He'd been so confident that I was about to invite him into my bed. Instead I had demanded that he tell me how many cookies he'd stolen from the cookie jar.

"I'd hoped your interests followed a different direction," he muttered.

I shook my head and crossed my arms against my chest. "No more wasting time, Sinjin. I order you to tell me what's going on between you and Mercedes."

Before he could say another word, we were interrupted by a knock on my bedroom door. Just as I was about to answer, it opened and Mercedes stuck her head in. I had to wonder why she didn't even wait for me to respond before entering . . . it was as if she knew what I'd just demanded of Sinjin. Hmm, it was almost like they had some sort of special connection with each other—one could sense when the other was in a dire situation. Well, if Sinjin didn't come out with the truth soon, he *was* going to be in a dire situation.

"Your subjects have assembled downstairs, my Queen, and they demand an immediate meeting," Mercedes said rather breathlessly.

I narrowed my eyes and frowned. "They can wait, Mercedes. I have important information I'm discussing with Sinjin."

Mercedes spared a glance at Sinjin before facing me again. And I could read nothing in her expression. "I believe it is of prime urgency, my Queen. They are beginning to argue with one another."

"Un-freaking-believable," I muttered. Shaking my head, I started for the door before turning back to face Sinjin. "Don't think you're getting out of this."

He looked taken aback but immediately smiled coolly and adopted an expression of nonchalance. "Why should I think such a thing?"

I didn't answer, just started down the stairs with Mercedes at my side. "What the hell is going on?"

"Apparently your subjects have come to insist that you take a partner in marriage," she answered.

I paused at the base of the steps and studied her. "Am I supposed to believe you had nothing to do with this?"

Mercedes frowned and secured a tendril of her dark hair behind her ear as her green eyes sparkled out at me in apparent irritation. "I had nothing to do with it at all."

I eyed her as if I didn't believe her, but there was nothing in her countenance that hinted of dishonesty. "Why do I have to put up with this crap?"

"Because you are the monarch," Mercedes answered, ushering me down the hallway. "I have ordered your visitors to await you in the library, my Queen."

I nodded and then stopped walking, facing her squarely. "And what do you think about my marrying? Do you think it's a good idea?"

She cocked her head to the side and silently considered my question. "I do not believe it is a bad idea. It would be a vehicle to unite all of the creatures in your kingdom if you were open to marrying outside your species."

And there was the nail in the coffin for Rand, just like he'd guessed. I couldn't help but wonder if Rand would make a case for himself; at the same time, I hoped he would. But no use in worrying about that now.

I faced Mercedes. At her inquisitive expression I just sighed and opened the door to my library, surprised to find ten people waiting for us. Mercedes walked in front of me to show that she would take the lead in chairing the meeting, which was fine by me.

"Please sit down," she said and it was like playing musical chairs as everyone scrambled for an available seat. I glanced around the room, recognizing some faces but not all of them. There was Odran and Doolan and some other fae man I didn't recognize, Trent and his wolf escort, Varick and Klaasje, she in her usual shadow form. Before I could switch my attention to the others in the room, Sinjin casually sauntered in and stood beside Klaasje. I offered him a hesitant smile before facing the remaining three men in the room. They stood in the far corner; I didn't recognize any of them.

"Would you like a chair?" Varick asked me.

I shook my head and leaned against the mantel of the fireplace that dominated the middle of the library. I glanced around, surprised that Mercedes had managed to fill the shelves along each wall with so many books.

Maybe they weren't books at all but just a mirage. But that was a mystery for another day.

"We understand that—"

Before Mercedes could finish her statement, the door opened and in walked Rand. And suddenly the darkness inside me gave way. The birds of my soul started singing while insects chirped from nearby rosebushes and a smiling sunshine did a happy dance between puffy white clouds while "Hallelujah" played in the background.

Rand had come to save me. He'd realized I might end up with one of the buffoons in this room and he wouldn't allow it. Yes, he was missing his white steed and some shiny armor but he was my knight, all the same.

His eyes seemed to dart around the room until he noticed me and nodded in salutation, offering me a slight smile. I returned it, even adding a little wink, like I was in on his plan. He raised his eyebrows in what appeared to be surprise before heading to the back of the room, playing the role of silent observer as he leaned against the wall.

Suddenly the unhappy thought occurred to me that Rand might not ask for my hand because he really wanted to marry me but just to save me from having to marry someone else. Of course, I was the Queen, and as far as I was concerned, there was no way in hell I was going to marry Odran, Trent, Varick, or one of the strangers in the room. And surely Rand had to know that?

Mercedes glanced at Rand and frowned, as if she wasn't happy to see him. Then she picked up where she'd left off. "It is our understanding that each of you is here either to represent your own wishes or the wishes of your master—in asking for the hand of our Queen in marriage."

I felt myself flush with anger at the thought that no one, aside from Rand, had warned me about this ahead of time. No one had come to me and asked how I felt about it before they arrived at Kinloch and demanded to be heard. Well, they would be heard all right, and then *I* would be heard.

I gulped down my anger and glanced at Rand, who stared back at me with a slight smile on his lips that said, *I told you so.* I just frowned and muttered something under my breath, turning back to the spectacle that was my life lately.

"Each of you will have no more than ten minutes to make your intentions known," Mercedes continued. She seemed so prepared for this impromptu meeting, I had to wonder whether she hadn't known this was coming.

"Odran, King of the fae, will you please approach our Queen with your proposal," Mercedes said.

Odran nodded and stood up. With Doolan and the other fairy guy behind him, he lumbered forward and faced me.

"Ma Queen, I humbly beseech ye ta accept ma ooffer of matrimony. I bring with meh the strongest of yer allies, the fae." There was a humph of general discord among the others, probably a reaction to his statement that the fairies were my strongest allies, but Odran didn't seem to notice. "Ye an' I go back a loong way, ma Queen, and ye have always known ma true feelings fer ya."

Yeah, those true feelings went no farther than his desire for a fun romp in the sheets. Yes, Odran was the King of the fairies and very powerful in his own right but he was also the King of man whores.

Apparently pleased with his short speech, Odran stepped back and nodded to Doolan as the smaller man stepped forward. "Mah King offers ye many gifts, mah Queen." Then he plopped the purple velvet bag before me and we all watched as it untied its own gold brocaded draws, opening to reveal the cornucopia I'd witnessed earlier, when Odran appeared in my entryway. There was a rustling in the bag and I leaned over to investigate further. Two white doves flew out, circled the room, and then disappeared in the air as if they'd never been.

I clapped even though I didn't feel like it. No use in being rude. It would be rude enough when I turned everyone down and told them never to pull another stunt like this again.

Odran and his posse took their seats again. Mercedes resumed her role of auctioneer.

"Will the wolves please step forward," she said.

Trent nodded and started to stand up, but before he could open his mouth, the rage inside me suddenly broke through the surface and I just couldn't control myself. "You're kidding, right, Trent?"

"Kidding?" he repeated, looking baffled, like it never occurred to him that it probably wasn't a good idea to ask me to marry him after our previous relationship ended with him dumping me. Yeah, probably wishing you hadn't dumped me now, huh, wolf boy?

"Sit back down. I won't even listen to you," I said as dispassionately as I could, which wasn't very dispassionately.

Trent grumbled something incoherent but sat back down all the same. Next the three strangers stood up and started forward. The one in the center, a middle-aged man with dark skin and a receding hairline, separated himself from the other two by taking a few steps closer to me. His purplish eyes glittered like amethysts in his face. He had to be over six feet tall and had the physique of a swimmer. With his incredible eyes and full lips, he was handsome in an exotic way. I mean, he had nothing on Rand or Sinjin, but he was a looker all the same.

"My Queen," he began in an accent that totally threw

me, "I know I have not made your acquaintance as of yet but I wanted to introduce myself and offer my proposal." His English was flawless but it was the type of English you definitely learned as a second language, the Queen's English—textbook English, not conversational.

I just smiled, not really knowing what else to say or do.

"I am Tabor, King of the demons."

I felt my stomach rise up into my throat. King of the demons? I hadn't even known there was a King of demons.

He took another bow and I offered my hand . . . um, I mean literally, not in the figurative sense. "I am very pleased to meet you, King Tabor," I said and when he accepted my hand and kissed it, surprise stirred in my stomach. So demons could also be lady charmers. It seemed every creature in the Underworld had some sort of charisma attached to him.

"It pleases me greatly that you and your people have joined our cause," I said, actually appreciative of the fact that I could properly address someone who controlled the demons—as I mentioned before, I really didn't have much knowledge of them. Hopefully I could maintain a friendship with Tabor. I definitely wanted the demons on my good side.

Tabor nodded. "We support you and your monarchy wholeheartedly, and it is my wish to also support you as your lover and husband."

At the thought of making love to a demon, I pulled my hand from his and nodded again with a slight, hesitant smile. Hopefully he wasn't going to be too bummed out that I wasn't prospecting for a demon lover or husband.

"A marriage between us would firmly cement the union between the witches and the demons," Tabor continued. His eyes suddenly glowed red, then immediately returned to their amethyst purple. It sort of freaked me out but no one else seemed to be bothered by it so I figured I shouldn't be either.

"Thank you for the offer," I said and watched him take his seat as Mercedes reined control of the room again.

"Is there anyone else who would like to plead his case?" she asked.

I glanced at Rand and noticed that his attention was on Tabor, his expression hard and his eyes narrowed as if he didn't trust the demon. I cleared my throat, wondering if maybe Rand hadn't heard Mercedes, hadn't recognized his cue. He glanced at me and then at Mercedes as she repeated her statement. Still, he made no motion to do anything. I felt as if I'd been slapped right across the face.

Wasn't he going to ask for my hand? Wasn't he even going to try to win me away from all these creeps? Was he really going to feed me to the fairies, wolves, and demons?

"I will state my case," Varick said and suddenly stood up.

I glanced at him and before I could say *Stake yourself,* Sinjin suddenly let out a hair-raising growl and launched himself at Varick, dragging his master down to the floor. They rolled around for a few seconds before Varick separated himself from Sinjin. In a split second he shoved his palms into Sinjin's chest and thrust the younger vampire away from him. I could hear a groan of protest as Sinjin flew through the air. His back hit the wall so hard, the room shook. Sinjin fell forward but braced himself against the floor, on his hands and knees.

"Sinjin!" I cried out as I took a step forward to make sure he was all right. But Mercedes' firm grip on my arm prohibited me from getting any closer.

"You gave me your word that you would not ask for

her hand," Sinjin growled at Varick as he stood up and leaned against the wall.

"Have you lost your mind!" I screamed, trying to yank myself out of Mercedes' vise-like grip.

But Sinjin's eyes never strayed from his master. In their narrowed depths, I could see hatred.

I glanced at Varick and found him standing in the middle of the room, his arms crossed against his chest, austere in his apparent indifference. "You have acted outside your class." Varick paused for two seconds. "It is none of your business whether or not I propose to our Queen."

With another growl, Sinjin lunged at Varick again, and then I completely lost sight of them both. They were moving so quickly, their vampire speed prevented me from tracking them with my naked eye. But while I couldn't see anything more than a few wisps of color here and there, I could hear them. The air was thick with the sounds of gnashing teeth and blows against flesh.

"Sinjin!" I screamed out again before turning to face everyone in the room. "Someone do something!"

"'Tis between master an' servant," Odran said while firmly shaking his head.

"That is bullshit," I railed back and glanced at Klaasje, noticing she was worrying her bottom lip and gripping her arms against her chest.

"Help him!" I screamed, hoping she understood that I meant Sinjin.

"I can't," she answered, shaking her head. She refused to look at me. "Varick is my elder."

I started forward but Rand's voice in my head stopped me.

Jolie, no! They will kill you!

And as if his words weren't enough to keep me out of the fight, I suddenly found I couldn't move my feet. It was like my shoes were stuck to the floor with super-glue. Rand had magicked me in place.

Before I could rebuff Rand's magic, a sound like rip-ping fabric caught my attention and I blinked to find Sinjin suddenly on the ground before me. He was lying prostrate, blood covering every inch of him. I started to move toward him but my feet wouldn't oblige me. I threw an angry expression to Rand and he nodded. In-stantly I dropped to my knees beside Sinjin, afraid that Varick had killed him.

Varick took a few steps closer to us and with a thought, I erected a wall of protective energy that encapsulated us. It was a silly attempt, since my powers didn't work against vampires, but really it had been more of an in-stinctual response than a logical thought.

"You stay away from him," I screamed at Varick. As if he hadn't heard me, Varick took another step closer and I stood up, inserting myself between him and Sinjin.

"I order you to leave him alone," I yelled. "As your Queen, I order you to back away . . . now."

"He does not know his place," Varick said and glared at me, but he took a few steps away from us all the same.

Glancing at Sinjin's bloody heap of a body, I was sud-denly frightened for him—frightened for what would happen to him at Varick's hands if he survived the dam-age that had already been inflicted on him. I glanced at Varick again and swallowed hard as I realized the truth in Varick's eyes. Sinjin would suffer for his disobedience. But the degree to which he'd suffer was what was wor-rying me.

"I am hereby nullifying Sinjin's ties to you," I said even though I wasn't sure if I had the power to make such a demand.

"No, Jolie!" I heard Rand's voice and there was a

round of gasps in the room followed by total silence, but I didn't care. It was my responsibility to protect Sinjin.

"You are unable to make that command," Varick said in an even tone.

"I am the Queen of the Underworld," I shot back.

"Jolie, think about this," Rand said. He was instantly by my side but I didn't spare him a glance.

"My command is law," I said.

Varick shook his head and glanced at Mercedes as if to double-check who was right and who was wrong.

Mercedes merely nodded. "If it is the Queen's will, so it must be," she said in a small voice, the tone of which relayed the fact that she didn't agree with what I'd just done.

"I order Varick to release Sinjin of any and all ties between them," I continued, glancing at everyone in the room. "From this point onward, Sinjin is his own master vampire. He will answer to no one but me."

"You have made a terrible mistake," Varick spat out at me. He was shaking with outrage. "And you will suffer for it."

Before I could say anything more, he simply vanished.

Eighteen

JOURNAL ENTRY

The last few days have sort of blurred together in my mind, becoming like one enormous day and night with no ending and no beginning—mainly because so much has happened. And my mind is such a complete muddle, I can't focus on one subject for more than a few minutes before another one comes flying in, demanding to be heard. I wonder if this is what it feels like to lose your mind.

So, Diary, you're probably most interested in what happened to Sinjin after he was attacked by Varick. Well, thank God he ended up surviving the attack. He only required Klaasje's blood (apparently vampires can drink one another's blood and the blood of a vampire is endowed with healing traits—something I was unaware of). Anyway, Klaasje basically nursed him back to health and in so doing, she and I had some time to . . . get to know each other better.

I have to admit that I feel guilty over the way I've been treating Klaasje—I've been short with her and none too friendly. And really, she has never been anything but kind and respectful to me. Well, the ugly truth of the whole matter is that I was jealous of Klaasje because of her relationship with Sinjin. And as much as it pains me to write this now, I feel that I must. I have feelings for Sinjin and I always have. Now I can admit that

*I'm ashamed of myself because the truth of the stupid
situation is that I have no right to be jealous of Klaasje
because I don't want to be with Sinjin in a romantic
way—that is, I don't think Sinjin and I have any hope of
a future together.*

*But moving on . . . after the whole ordeal with Varick,
I ordered everyone to leave the room so Klaasje could
tend to Sinjin. At the time, Sinjin was incoherent, not
even able to sink his fangs into Klaasje's skin, so she'd
had to open her own wrist while I held Sinjin's head to
it, allowing the blood to drip into his mouth. Little by
little, his strength appeared to return; within thirty minutes or so he was able to hold Klaasje's wrist himself.*

*While Sinjin was out of it, probably dreaming of
large-busted women with prominent veins, Klaasje and
I had the opportunity for a little girl talk—a little one-
on-one time. And given the fact that I was acting like a
jealous ass, of course I pried into the nature of their
"friendship." And Klaasje had some pretty curious
things to say on that subject.*

*She admitted that Sinjin would forever hold a place in
her heart because she had loved him once, back when
they knew each other in Texas, but she firmly insisted
that she would never drop her defenses enough to love
him again. She said she recognized who and what Sinjin
was and she realized that Sinjin was incapable of loving
another person—that he just wasn't "wired that way,"
as she said. And of course I could relate to her story
myself—she had touched on the exact reason why I believe in my heart of hearts that Sinjin isn't in love with
me. Because he's incapable of it.*

*Strangely enough, Klaasje seemed happy with their bi-
zarre friendship even though she was convinced it would
never be more than it now was. Even stranger, she said
Sinjin acted differently around me—that she would*

never have imagined he'd endanger himself and rebel against Varick because of a woman. She seemed perplexed over the fact that Sinjin had seemed . . . jealous and possessive. Those were words that just didn't describe him. He wasn't that type—he was the love-'em-and-leave-'em type.

Of course I didn't know what to think about any of that and just shelved it away as a mystery I'd never unravel. Sinjin was Sinjin and I've come to realize I will never understand him or his actions. But somehow I'm okay with that, I guess.

After our heart-to-heart about Sinjin, I felt sorry for Klaasje as I wondered what it would mean to have loved Sinjin such a long time ago and be reunited with him in the here and now. Klaasje seemed to be lost in her thoughts for a little while and then she finally shook her head as she rubbed Sinjin's forehead (he was still out of it at this point) and asked him what he'd gotten himself into.

It was all very strange, and I've since replayed the events over and over again in my head until I'm so sick of them, I can't even see straight. But at least Sinjin turned out to be okay. Klaasje informed me that he would require her blood each evening; in about three to four days he'd be the same old Sinjin we all know so well.

What that meant for me was that I couldn't leave the house, because I was sans my two bodyguards (Klaasje was too weak to protect me, owing to the bloodletting, and Sinjin . . . well, I think that much is obvious). Unless I wanted to subject myself to an entourage of wolves who had been appointed as my impromptu bodyguards, I was stuck in Kinloch.

So for the past three days I've been sitting around here, playing with the cat and otherwise trying to keep myself occupied. Granted, we reanimated more soldiers in Bella's army—and I had the "pleasure" of more lessons, the most recent on the history of the werewolf. But other than those minor distractions, I've had way too much time on my hands. And having too much time on my hands sucks because it gives me plenty of opportunities to think, think, and think some more about how Rand chose not to ask for my hand. He never championed me, never played the role of white knight, riding up on his steed to steal the maiden away from the troll-faced interlopers. I know that sounds completely stupid but there is a part of me—the little girl deep down inside me—who believes in fairy tales and would love nothing more than to live that ridiculous dream. But that's all it is—an intangible dream. And one that should be destroyed, as far as I'm concerned.

I've finally come to terms with the fact that the Rand of today is drastically different from my 1878 Rand. Really, they aren't even the same person. So maybe I'll never be able to keep the promise I made to 1878 Rand about us being together in this century. Maybe we aren't fated lovers—maybe we never were. Maybe we simply aren't fated anything.

I know it probably sounds like I'm feeling sorry for myself and I guess the truth is that I am. But, Diary, I have never felt so completely alone before—so totally abandoned. Yes, I have Christa and I've always had Christa, but she has her own life.

I keep remembering my Rand of 1878, how tender he was, how our love had been so all-encompassing, so whole, true, and real . . . so completely beautiful. And the worst part is that I keep replaying in my head the memory of the moment he slid his mother's ring onto my finger and asked me to marry him. The look in his eyes had been so deep, so genuine. I experienced true happiness, true love for the first time in my entire life.

There's a void inside me now—a void that's been

sucking in all my hopes and aspirations for love. It's a darkness that's taking me over, a disease. But there's nothing I can really do to stop it. Short of returning to 1878 and living out the remainder of my years there, I don't know that there is anything that can be done to save my heart from splintering and dying.

I set my pen down and felt a sob catch in my throat as I glanced down at Rand's mother's ring, which I still wore on my left hand. I felt a tear slide down my cheek as I pulled the ring off and opened the top drawer of my desk, dropping the ring inside. As I closed the drawer, I felt like I was closing off the part of me that believed in the idealism of love, the part of me that loved Rand.

At the sound of a knock on my door, I wiped my wet cheeks against the arms of my sweatshirt. Mercedes announced herself and I begrudgingly opened the door, realizing the reason for her visit.

"I'm not going to marry any of them," I said with conviction.

Mercedes nodded as if she wasn't surprised by my announcement. "May I come in?"

I opened the door obediently, allowing her to enter.

"I do hope you have considered every angle of this issue? Weighed both the pros and the cons?" she asked.

I nodded and sighed, gazing out my window at the gray clouds that now obstructed the sun. Drops of rain began to gently fall, spritzing my window. "Yes, my mind is made up."

"Very well," Mercedes answered, offering me a brief smile before she turned to face the door. She took a few steps toward it but then stalled and faced me again. "Do you trust Sinjin?" she asked.

"Trust Sinjin?" I repeated, my tone belying the fact that I was at a total loss.

Mercedes nodded and focused on the ocean view

outside my window. She approached the window and placing her fingers on the sill, stared down at the waves as they lapped at the rocks.

"Why do you want to know?" I prodded when it seemed she'd completely gone mute.

She continued admiring the view. "Were your hopes on Sinjin?"

"What?" I asked, realizing she meant had I hoped Sinjin would ask for my hand instead of Varick. "No! I wouldn't marry Sinjin."

She turned her eyes to me with a relieved expression and just nodded, although she didn't say anything for a few seconds. "I hope that in emancipating Sinjin from his master, you realized the weight of your action?"

I hadn't really thought about the repercussions of that move so, no, I couldn't really say I did.

"Why, what's the big deal?" My voice was laced with defensiveness.

"Sinjin will be much more powerful now."

I gulped. I didn't know why but for some reason that seemed like a bad thing. "How? He's still the same Sinjin."

Mercedes shook her head and forced a smile. "Sinjin now has no one to keep him in line. That is why I wanted to know whether you trust him."

I narrowed my eyes. "I think the real question should be if you trust him."

Her shoulders bounced with surprise, as if she was taken aback. "Why should it matter if I trust him?"

I shook my head. "It seems like there's something going on between the two of you and every time I try to get an answer out of either of you, you tiptoe around the subject or avoid it in some other way."

Mercedes nodded as if she were weighing my words. "I do not trust the vampire," she said simply.

"What are your meetings with Sinjin about?" I demanded, crossing my arms against my chest.

Mercedes shrugged and stepped away from my window, coming to stand in the middle of the room, just before me. "Sinjin is after power—whether it be your power or mine. He craves control."

Knowing Mercedes, I figured she wasn't giving me the whole picture. But at this point, I couldn't say I really cared what Sinjin and Mercedes were up to. No, I didn't care because I actually had another plan for my life—another path I'd just decided on about, um, ten minutes ago.

"Mercedes," I started, searching for the right way to phrase this next part. "As your Queen, I want you to send me back to 1878."

"For what purpose?" she asked, eyeing me suspiciously.

"Because I hate my life," I said and took a few steps away from her, feeling the sudden need to escape the damning expression in her eyes.

"What do you mean?" she asked.

"It's not that I hate it," I admitted. I took a deep breath and looked at her. "I was happy in 1878. I loved Rand and he loved me. Nothing is the same now."

"It is your duty to make it the same."

I laughed, but it was an ugly sound. I looked at the waves outside my window and wished I had no responsibility other than crashing against the rocks and pulling back with the tide again. I faced Mercedes and shook my head. "I've tried to make things right in this century, believe me."

Mercedes shook her head. "Perhaps you are not trying hard enough. There is a reason, a purpose—"

"Yes, yes, yes, I know what you're going to say and I'm sick to death of hearing it," I snapped. "If this is the purpose and the reason to my life, I want none of it." I started to shake with anger. "I hate what my life has become."

"I am very sorry to hear that." But her tone said she wasn't sorry and wouldn't allow me to leave my troubles and worries behind. Mercedes would always protect the monarchy. She would always protect the kingdom.

"If you're really sorry then send me back," I finished.

Mercedes' lips pursed as her eyes narrowed on me. "And what of your responsibilities as Queen?"

I shrugged and waved away her concerns. "You be Queen. You are way more suited to the role than I ever was anyway. You're more powerful than I am. You should have been Queen from the get-go."

"You are not fully aware of your powers yet," she said.

"I don't care. Right now, you'd make a better Queen."

She shook her head. "I am not meant to be Queen, Jolie. The responsibility has always been set aside for you." She took a few steps closer to me and tried to relax her frown into a smile, which came out looking like a grimace. "Stop feeling sorry for yourself and focus on being the monarch we both know you are."

"This isn't about feeling sorry for myself," I barked although she did have a point—I was wallowing in my own misery. But no need to admit that.

"Then think no more on it."

She started for the door. I suddenly felt the tears welling in my eyes. "Please, Mercedes."

She paused for a moment more and then showed herself out of my room, closing the door behind her.

I wasn't sure when I'd made the decision or why, really, but I found myself standing outside Rand's guest room door and it took all my nerve to knock. Rand was visiting Kinloch in his position as chief advisor, not only to meet with Mercedes and me but also to help us re-animate the remainder of Bella's soldiers.

I knocked and held my breath, my heart beating in time to the sounds of Rand's heavy stride as he came to answer the door. He pulled it open and looked surprised at first, but his surprise slowly gave way to a smile.

"Jolie?"

"Can we talk?" I asked, shifting from one foot to the other as if I had to pee.

"Of course." He opened the door for me.

I hurried inside and glanced around the room, taking in the light brown of the walls and the white of the furniture. Rand's laptop was on a table positioned just in front of the fireplace. It was the only possession of his I could see.

"What's on your mind?" he started.

I stood in front of the fireplace and gazed down at the logs, covered in soot and halfway burned. "Why didn't you stand up for me?"

The frown on his face announced the fact that he had no idea what I was referencing. "I apologize but—"

"When everyone was offering marriage, why didn't you champion me?"

He shook his head. "There was no reason for me to."

"No reason?" I scoffed.

Rand's frown deepened. "You are a strong woman, Jolie, it's not my responsibility to save you."

I felt something burst inside me, something angry. "It's not about saving me."

"Then what is it about?"

I shook my head, feeling tears starting in my eyes. It had been incredibly stupid for me to come here—especially given the fact that Rand and I had to work together closely. I'd let my emotions get the best of me, and it wasn't something I was proud of. Especially not when I was Queen—I needed to be more in control of myself.

"Never mind." I turned on the ball of my foot as I started for the door. Rand grabbed my hand and pulled me back around again until I was facing him, until we were mere inches apart.

"I knew you weren't going to accept any of them," he said in a gravelly voice.

"How did you know that?"

"Because I know you."

I shook my head and dropped my attention to the floor before bringing it back to his face. "Rand, for once, I just wanted you to react emotionally, to think with your heart instead of your brain. For once, I hoped you'd stand up for me, let it be known that you're the only one for me."

I felt mortification blossom up within me at the fact that I was admitting things I usually kept inside and under wraps. But maybe it was about time I let it all out. Maybe admitting to my true feelings was exactly what I needed to do.

Rand glanced away from me and sighed deeply before looking down at me again. "I knew you wouldn't accept any of those proposals. You told me as much yourself." He took another deep breath. "And I'll be damned if my marriage proposal were ever to be lumped in with the likes of Odran, Trent, Varick, and the King of the fucking demons!"

I pulled away from him and shook my head, only aware of the fact that he just wasn't getting it. I started for the door again with tears bleeding down my cheeks.

"I don't know why I keep trying, Rand," I said in a small voice, refusing to look at him. "It's like you keep kicking me and I stupidly keep coming back."

Before he could respond, I left the room.

I wasn't sure where I wanted to go and took the stairs

two at a time, heading into the hallway that led through the living room and into the bedrooms belowground . . . those of the vampires. I angrily wiped the tears from my cheeks and vowed to myself that I would never expect anything of Rand again. He wasn't my 1878 Rand. He wasn't the same man I'd given myself to. The quicker I realized that, the better. Things with Rand were over. Done.

When I stopped walking, I found myself standing outside Sinjin's door, battling with myself over whether or not to knock. A plan had been coming together in my head, an escape route. But even as I stood in front of Sinjin's door, I had to ask myself if I was really going to do it.

I rapped on the door twice. It opened and Sinjin appeared in the darkness, glancing at me in surprise.

"Poppet, are you well?"

"I need to speak with you," I answered. Then it occurred to me that maybe Sinjin had a woman in his bedroom with him. "Can I come in or are you . . . occupied?"

"Of course." He smiled and opened the door just a smidgeon, forcing me to squeeze past him. When I did, I realized he was wearing only a pair of white silk boxer shorts. His chest was bare and beautiful, with its sculpted, ropy muscles.

"Um, do you want me to come back after you've dressed?" I asked, feeling decidedly uncomfortable.

Sinjin closed the door behind him and leaned against it, crossing his arms against his wide chest and smiled down at me . . . hungrily. "No."

"Oh, okay," I said and started to fidget with the zipper of my sweatshirt. Not wanting to face Sinjin in his current state of undress, I glanced around the room. It was a fairly large space, painted dark blue; the carpet was a dark gray, thick and plush, almost like walking on memory foam. A king-sized bed with a black leather headboard dominated one wall, and black side tables flanked the bed. A flat-screen television decorated the opposite wall, and it looked like Sinjin had installed some sort of high-tech sound system. It's not like I knew anything about sound systems but given that there were speakers in each corner of the ceiling, I figured it would probably be impressive to anyone who knew about that sort of stuff.

"Did Mercedes pick all this stuff out for you?" I asked, in awe.

Sinjin chuckled. "No. Had she, I imagine this room would resemble the rest of the house—a style not quite in line with my own."

Well, I guess Sinjin wouldn't like my style either because I loved the furnishings in Kinloch. But that wasn't why I was here and I needed to get to the point. I mean, I was standing in a room with a half-naked vampire.

"Thank you, poppet," Sinjin said, and his English accent was thick, sensual.

I glanced at him in surprise. "For what?"

He stood up straight from his stance against the door and approached me. When he was just in front of me, he put a hand on each of my shoulders and pushed me backward until my calves met his bed.

"Sit, you appear nervous," he said.

So I did. I sat down on his enormous bed and watched a smile of amusement spread across his mouth that said he had me right where he wanted me.

"Why are you thanking me?" I demanded.

"You freed me from Varick," he said simply. "That was a favor the likes of which I will never be able to repay."

I shook my head. "There's no need given all the good turns you've done me." I mean, there was rescuing me when Bella kidnapped me, training me to fight against the vampire Ryder, feeding me his blood . . . the list went on.

"We can agree to disagree, poppet." He studied me for a moment or two, still standing before me. "Tell me why you have come."

I dropped my gaze to my hands, which looked so small in my lap, and sighed before glancing up at Sinjin again. "I want you to take me away."

He quirked a brow and considered me curiously. "Take you where?"

"I don't care. I just want to escape." I stood up and approached the far side of his room, wishing he had a window. I suddenly felt claustrophobic. I leaned against the wall and faced him again. "I no longer want this life. I want out of here."

"Do you think that is being responsible given your—"

"I don't care about responsibility!" I railed.

Sinjin nodded as if he couldn't disagree. "And you wish for me to escort you . . . to what?"

"To a new life," I muttered as I took a deep breath. This wasn't coming out exactly like I had hoped it would. "I mean, I imagine you aren't tied to Kinloch—or to Britain, for that matter?"

Sinjin nodded. "I have no ties."

Considering that to be in my favor, I took a few steps toward him. "We could go somewhere else, then, Sinjin. We could travel the world and do whatever we want to do."

"What are you trying to escape?"

I swallowed hard. "Nothing. I'm . . ."

"Perhaps I should rephrase the question. Who are you trying to escape?"

There was no point in lying. "Rand."

Sinjin nodded and was silent for a few seconds, but he never took his eyes from mine. "I will heed your wishes on one condition."

"Which is?"

He came closer to me until no more than six inches of air separated us. "That you forget the warlock. If we are to start a new life together, I want you to give yourself to me. I want to share your bed, your body."

I swallowed hard and battled the feelings within me. I wanted Sinjin, I always had. But could I go through with it? Could I shelve my feelings for Rand and focus on Sinjin? The better question was: Could I trust Sinjin?

"Done," I said.

Sinjin smiled broadly and took the step that separated us until his chest brushed up against mine. "You do understand what that entails?"

I felt the breath catch in my throat as I forced myself to meet his sensual gaze. "I think so," I answered, so intimidated by him that it came out as a mere whisper.

"It means, my pet, that I will taste you whenever I choose, your body will belong to me, it will be my name you scream when I am inside you."

Feeling his breath against my cheeks, I closed my eyes. I couldn't help it. A flurry of butterflies started in my stomach. I tried to beat them down, tried to convince myself I could go through with this.

"Do you think about making love to me?" he asked, his breath caressing my skin as his finger outlined my neck, tracing my collarbone.

"I've always wondered what it would be like," I admitted.

He chuckled, and it was an opulent sound. I opened my eyes and found him staring at me, heat burning in his eyes. Before I could guess what he was going to do, his mouth was on mine, the points of his fangs threatening my lips. But there was nothing threatening about the way he kissed. It was powerful, hungry, and urgent. His tongue made a forceful entry into my mouth, and he gripped the back of my neck as he pushed me up against the wall.

He pulled away and chuckled down at me again. "You are flushed."

"Sinjin," I started, not even knowing what I wanted to say.

"Shall we escape then?" he asked, still wearing the devil's smile.

I nodded and he stepped away from me.

"Your things?" he began, probably alluding to the fact that I hadn't shown up with luggage.

"I don't need any of it," I said quickly. I was a witch, I could magick anything I'd possibly need.

"Goodbyes?"

"Only to Christa," I answered. "And I can't think about that now. She'll talk me out of leaving."

"Then that conversation can occur over the phone."

"Do you need to pack?" I asked as he neared the door.

"No." Reaching for the pair of pants and long-sleeved shirt draped over the chair just beside his bed, he dressed. He slipped on his black leather shoes and faced me with another practiced smile. "Shall we?"

Twenty minutes later we were in Sinjin's Mercedes SLS AMG and headed out of Eyemouth. Where we were going, I had no idea. We hadn't exactly discussed it. In fact, since getting into the car, neither of us had said a word. So many thoughts were going through my head that I couldn't even fathom the idea of having to think about what to say. As we entered the highway that led to Pelham Manor, something inside me cracked, something broke.

"I can't do this," I said in an anguished tone. After not getting a response, I faced Sinjin and his jaw was tight. "Turn the car around, Sinjin, I can't do this."

"Why?"

I sighed, long and hard. "I . . ." I had to look away

from him. I couldn't admit this next part while looking him in the eyes. "I know that I will always love Rand. Even though we aren't meant to be together, I will always love him."

Sinjin didn't say anything right away and when I forced my eyes back to his face, I immediately regretted it. He was furious; ire seemed to drip from his eyes, and his jaw was so tight, it looked like he might crack his teeth.

"I consider you an intelligent woman and yet I cannot understand how you remain so blinded and foolish when it comes to that blasted warlock!" Sinjin yelled.

I was taken aback, not expecting such vitriol from him.

"Sinjin . . ."

"When will you realize he does not love you and never will? When will you understand you are wasting your time with him?"

I glowered at him. "Turn around."

He made no motion to turn around and, instead, stepped on the gas until we were driving so quickly, the lights of the scenery around us blurred.

"You need to wake up, Jolie. You need to wake up and realize I am the best man for you."

"I'm sorry, Sinjin." It was all I could say.

Nineteen

Jolie, stop crying, dammit! I yelled at myself as I threw my door shut and collapsed onto my bed.

But the tears wouldn't subside—they just kept pouring out of my eyes as if they had a mind of their own. And really, it's not like my mind was doing anything to help curtail them. Instead I couldn't stop repeating Sinjin's words, running over and over through my head— "When will you realize he does not love you and never will?"

The sad, desperate truth about the whole situation was that maybe Sinjin was right. Maybe Rand didn't truly love me. Yes, Rand seemed to think he was in love with me and had said as much, but maybe it just wasn't the case—maybe he only thought he was in love with me? I mean, if Rand truly, deeply loved me, then why wouldn't he have found a way to be with me? Yes, there were plenty of obstacles stacked up against us, but wasn't love supposed to trump everything standing in its way? Wasn't that what all those sappy love songs were about?

I stood up and wiped my eyes against my shirtsleeve, walking toward the window just beside my bed. I glanced outside but saw nothing in the dark. Even the milky rays of the moon were hidden by a cluster of billowy, dark gray clouds. The comparison between the dark night outside and the darkness that seemed to have taken up permanent residency within me wasn't lost on me. In a sudden bout of anger I smashed my fist against the windowsill, which did nothing but ricochet pain up my arm.

"Fuck!" I screamed and then broke into another round of sobs. My entire life had entered a tailspin, like I was in the throes of a hurricane—a tempest of emotions battering me with regret, pain, and anger.

Yes, 1878 Rand loved me, and no, it was not an option to return to him. So what did that mean for me today? One thing of which I was certain was that I absolutely, wholeheartedly loved him—and yes, I wanted to be with him. In my picture-perfect notion of an ideal world, Rand was and always would be by my side. The miserable truth of the whole stupid matter was that I wanted to grow old with him. Even if we could never have children, I didn't care. Rand was enough for me.

But was I enough for him? The more I thought about it, the more I realized that I was really stuck in a tough situation. It would be one thing if Rand had admitted to me that he didn't love me and never had—then I could merely retreat and lick my wounds until they healed. I would get over it. Of that I was sure—because I was strong.

That wasn't the case, though. Rand believed himself to be in love with me, and yet he seemed unable to act on that love. Why? I really had no clue. At first it seemed to be the monarchy situation that was holding him back. Then it was the bonding situation. And really, these were just the most recent roadblocks. When we first met, it had been the fact that he was my employer! Bah!

The more I thought about it, the more I realized Rand had a serious problem—his inability to pursue what he wanted. Yes, I always knew he overanalyzed everything and weighed the consequences of every action until he was red in the face. But now actions needed to be taken. The time for thinking was over. Now it was time to act.

And suddenly my answer was obvious—I needed to hear the words from Rand's lips. If he didn't love me—if he didn't want to pursue me and allow me inside that fortress he called his heart—I was giving up. I would move on. Yes, it would be difficult, but I'd have to apologize to the figurative Rand of 1878 and then lock away those memories and my associated guilt forever.

As far as the Rand of today was concerned, he had only one more chance. He either needed to claim me or let me go.

I heard the sound of raindrops splashing against the windowpanes and glanced outside again only to watch a bolt of lightning brighten up the night sky. The brief show illuminated the rain, which was now falling in torrents. As if the lightning weren't warning enough to stay inside, the raucous round of thunder grumbled through the sky. Yet it did nothing to shake my determination.

It was now or never. Rand had to make a choice and I was going to force him to stick to it. As God was my witness, Rand was going to make a damn decision. With a renewed sense of determination, I took a deep breath, trying to prepare myself for the confrontation that was soon to occur once I got the nerve to visit Rand's guest room. Almost immediately a flood of doubt and thoughts of second-guessing myself broke through my mind.

What would I say to Rand? Would he even be in his room? What if he'd decided to return to Pelham Manor?

In this storm?

Well, maybe he has a date?

A date? It's not like Rand has much of a social life.

Okay, that's true, but what if he happened to have met someone and eagerly wanted to return to Pelham Manor to drown his frustrations about me in the eyes and smile of some new woman? What if I walked in on a super-embarrassing situation like Bridget Jones did with Daniel Cleaver and that American woman?

Thank God I'm not wearing a bunny suit.

Really, Jolie, don't be stupid—Rand isn't dating anyone.

Hmm, Rand's dating life aside, maybe I should just call him first? Maybe that's a better thing to do than knock on his door or drive to Pelham Manor?

But if I called him, what would I say? "Hi, in a total lapse of sanity, I've freaked out and I demand you tell me if you're in love with me and want to be with me?" Yeah, no.

Oh my God, Jolie, what is wrong with you? You have completely lost it. You're arguing with yourself!

I had lost it. I was standing in the middle of my room, caught between taking a few steps to the door and reaching for my cell phone. I glanced at the clock and noticed that ten minutes had gone by. I would stay firm in my decision to demand an ultimatum from Rand. It was now or never, remember?

Maybe I'd try the phone. I turned away from the bedroom door, took the three steps separating me from my iPhone, and took a deep breath as I lifted it.

"Jolie."

I think my heart stopped for a second or two and I had to ask myself if I'd just imagined Rand's voice. I mean, I hadn't even dialed his number yet. It was like I was in slow motion as I turned around and saw him standing in my room, the door still open behind him. He was panting and soaked, presumably from the storm outside.

Neither of us said anything—we just stood staring at each other like we were the stars in a silent film. I was the first to speak.

"What . . . why are you here? What happened to you?"

I started, still wondering if he wasn't just a wet figment of my imagination come to destroy my wood floors.

He didn't respond. Instead he closed the gap between us and before I could say another word he grabbed me, pulling me into his wet and cold chest. He didn't even pause before his lips were on mine and his tongue was in my mouth. I started to succumb to him, started to allow the butterflies in my stomach to take over, but then I felt something burst inside me—something that was full to the brim with frustration and pain. Tears assaulted my eyes and began streaming down my cheeks and before I knew what I was doing, I felt myself pull away from him just at the same time that I smacked him right across the face.

He reeled back and held his injured cheek, shock in his eyes.

"What the bloody—" he started.

And maybe his words were all I needed to hear because whatever was brewing in the cauldron within me was now boiling—roiling and spitting like an angry cat.

"You are a coward!" I screamed at him as I pounded my fists onto his chest in mute frustration.

"Jolie!"

I didn't dare look up at him but continued my assault on his pecs, throwing as much rage into my fists as I could muster.

"Stop it!" he ordered, trying unsuccessfully to grab my wrists.

"Why are you here?" I yelled. "Do you get some sort of perverse pleasure from fucking with my feelings?"

He finally managed to round up my fists and when he did, he held them in front of me while I attempted to wiggle out of his iron grasp. "I could ask the same bloody thing of you!" he railed at me, managing to catch me completely off guard.

"What?" I started but he interrupted me.

"What the fuck were you doing in Sinjin's car?"

"I don't have to answer to you," I spat back and struggled to free myself so I could deck him again.

He held my wrists even more firmly, and it was pretty obvious I wasn't about to free myself anytime soon. "You're right, you don't have to answer to me." Then he dropped his hold on my arms and stepped away from me, running his hands through his wet hair. "I'm sorry I came . . . I . . . just watched you get into Sinjin's car and something inside me snapped."

The thought that he had watched me leave with Sinjin was something I wasn't prepared for. But it was also something I didn't want to concern myself with—his jealousy was not my problem. I shook my head and suddenly felt exhausted. "I don't get you at all . . . your actions just never make any damn sense."

"I think they make perfect sense," he said and shrugged. "I'm jealous."

"That's just it!" I said in an angry voice. "There's no reason for you to be jealous because you don't give a shit about me!"

Rand seemed taken aback—I wasn't sure if it was due to the venom in my voice or my words. "Jolie—"

"I want you to admit to me that you don't love me and you don't want me and we won't ever be together," I said.

Rand looked perplexed. "Why?"

"So I can move on and heal and never think about you again!"

Rand shook his head. "I can't admit to any of that because it isn't true."

"I don't understand you, Rand." There was nothing left in my voice—no fight, no anger, just exhaustion. "And why the hell are you soaking wet?"

He cleared his throat and appeared to be embarrassed. "After I watched you leave with Sinjin, I was so consumed with anger, I didn't know what to do with myself. I just stood there in the rain like I'd lost my mind."

I was surprised to say the least. That wasn't like Rand. "Then you must have seen us return, what, five minutes later?"

He nodded. "Where . . . why were you . . . perhaps I would rather not know."

"Nothing happened between us, Rand," I said in a defeated voice. "I wanted something to happen but I couldn't bring myself to see it through."

"You wanted something between you and Sinjin?" Rand asked, his brows furrowing.

"I wanted to escape my life here."

"Why?"

I laughed, but it was an empty and cold sound. "Because of you. Because of the fact that I just don't know how you feel about me, why you seem to care about me and yet you never act on your emotions, why you won't just claim me."

Rand ran his fingers through his hair and exhaled slowly. "Jolie, I love you and I've always loved you. There's not an hour that goes by that I don't think about you."

"But—" I started.

"I just don't know how to deal with your new role as Queen," he said and there was something odd in his expression. Something worried or concerned maybe. "I don't have the makings for a King, Jolie. I've never wanted to be the leader of our species. I don't have your talents."

"Rand," I started.

"No, let me finish," he said firmly as he dropped his gaze to his feet. He took a few seconds and then glanced up at me again. "You should not love me. You should love someone who is good for your kingdom, someone who can advance your cause." He let out a strange sort of laugh. "I can still barely stomach the fact that I'm willingly taking part in a monarchy."

I was quiet for a second or two. "So why did you come here, why are you here now?"

He shook his head and dropped his gaze to the ground again. Apparently noticing the large puddle beneath him, he narrowed his eyes and it disappeared, his entire person suddenly dry—as if he'd never been in the rain in the first place.

"Because despite the fact that I'm convinced I'm not good for you, I'm also not going to let you go."

His voice was rough and before I could comprehend it, he grabbed my arm and pulled me into the nest of his embrace. He held me tightly and stared down at me with passionate eyes.

"I don't under—"

And then his lips were on mine and his kiss was demanding, hungry—as if he were making up for lost opportunities. Well, it was about time! Holy freaking cow was it about time.

I wrapped my arms around his neck and opened my mouth as his tongue plundered mine, mated with mine in an age-old dance. His fingers snaked through my hair and worked down my neck to my coat, which he deftly removed, letting it fall to the ground.

I pulled away from him because I suddenly wanted to make sure we were on the same page. I had to make sure that this new announcement of his meant what I needed it to mean—that he wasn't going to change his mind at some later date.

"What are you saying?" I asked, albeit breathlessly.

Rand's jaw tightened. "You want me to claim you? Then call this me claiming you."

He pulled me into his arms and lifted me, bride style, as he started for the bed.

"And you aren't going to change your mind in two

hours or tomorrow or the next day?" I asked. "Because that would destroy me."

Rand shook his head and stared down at me. "No, I'm not going to lose you. I would never forgive myself."

He settled me down on the top of the bed as I leaned on my elbows and watched him. He stood at the end of the bed, his chest rising and falling with his belabored breathing.

"Then it's you and me?" I asked. "For the long haul?"

He nodded. "You and me."

"No going back?"

"No going back."

I gulped and looked around, suddenly realizing what this meant. "And what happens now?"

He tore his T-shirt over his head, and his incredibly sculpted chest met my hungry gaze. I wanted more than ever before to run my fingers across the hills and valleys of his beautiful body. To taste the saltiness of his skin, to listen to the beating of his heart and feel his warmth.

"Now I'm going to make love to you," he said in a throaty voice.

I felt butterflies flutter up in my stomach as he approached the bed. He climbed on top and was as powerful and sleek as a lion as he moved up my body, pinning me beneath him. He brought his fingers to my face and traced my hairline, his hand disappearing behind my neck as his lips descended on mine. He kissed me much more delicately this time.

He lifted his head and when he looked down at me, he smiled.

"Shall we attempt to re-create that bond?"

I smiled back up at him. "You're on."

Twenty

I almost felt like I was dreaming—like I wasn't actually in my bed with Rand on top of me, like I wasn't wearing just my bra and panties. I'd been waiting for this moment for so long that it almost didn't seem real. And had Rand really pledged himself to me, or had that been a figment of my imagination too?

The feel of Rand's thumb pressing against the inside of my thigh while the rest of his hand gripped the outside felt genuine enough. So did the heat emanating from his body. Nope, I was pretty sure this was the real deal—stamped with a seal.

"What are you thinking about?" he asked as he stopped kissing my neck and pulled away, staring down at me.

"What do you mean?" I asked innocently.

"It feels like you're distracted."

I giggled a bit and felt a little silly as I answered the question. "I was debating with myself about whether or not this was real."

Rand chuckled and shook his head like he just didn't understand me. "Jolie, I'm real and this is real so please stop orbiting in outer space because I'd like to have you in the moment, right here beneath me."

I swallowed hard at the expression of pure lust in his eyes.

"Okay," I said sheepishly.

He offered me one more amused smile and then started kissing my neck again. His lips were incredibly soft and slightly moist.

"Your skin tastes so sweet," he whispered and nibbled on my earlobe while I giggled and ran my hands down his naked back, relishing the feel of his muscles as they tensed beneath my hands.

And I suddenly had the desire to just look at him, to soak in his beauty, to come to terms with the fact that the one man who had captured my heart when he'd first walked into my store two years ago . . . was really mine.

"Rand, I need to see you."

He pulled away from me and offered me a puzzled expression.

"Just sit up," I said with a smile and watched him obey, bracing his arms on either side of me so he wouldn't shift too much weight on my middle.

I didn't say anything as I drank in his beauty. My eyes traveled from the wave of his chocolate-brown hair, to his warm brown eyes, past dimples that betrayed the fact that he probably thought I was the strangest girl he'd ever met. His lips lit up in a half smile, highlighting his square jaw.

I allowed my gaze to continue south, to imbibe his smoothly defined chest muscles peppered with wiry, light brown hair. And still farther south—down to his rock-hard abs and the trail of brown hair that started just below his navel and acted like an arrow pointing below his pajama pants.

"Have I ever told you how beautiful you are?" I asked, glancing up into his face again.

"You asked me if I used magic to enhance my appearance when we first met."

I laughed with him and returning my gaze to his incredible body, shook my head in wonderment.

"You do realize I've been yours all along?" Rand

asked, the smile dropping from his lips. "From the moment we met, it has always been you."

He glanced down at me again, his gaze traveling from my face to my chest.

"Show me your breasts," he whispered.

I felt a burning deep down in my core—an aching, yearning need. I sat up slightly, reached around my back with both hands to unhook my bra, and slowly pulled each strap down my shoulders, teasing Rand as I moved at a snail's pace. With a smile, I pulled the satin material away until only the peaks of my alert nipples met his eyes.

He swallowed hard—I could see his Adam's apple bobbing with the effort. And then his hands were on my breasts, teasing my nipples.

"You are stunningly beautiful, Jolie," he whispered as he leaned down and took one of my nipples in his mouth. I immediately arched up against him, the burning in my core now an out-and-out fire.

Then his hands were on my thighs again, grazing the outside of my panties. I brought my hand down and blocked his from the junction of my thighs.

"No, let me see you first," I whispered, wanting nothing more than to touch him, kiss him, hold him in my hands.

He pushed away from me and stood, his eyes never leaving mine. But my eyes left his as they moved down his exquisite chest, pausing at the drawstrings of his pajamas. He was rock hard—I could see the outline of his penis straining against his pants.

"Don't be shy," I said in a raspy voice.

With that, he pulled his pants down and he was suddenly gloriously naked before me, beautiful in his raw masculinity. I felt myself inhale deeply as I gazed at him, realizing this was the first time I'd ever beheld his naked body in its entirety. Of course there had been the time that we'd had sex in 1878, but there had been more urgency then and I'd never truly seen him in all his glory.

I wrapped my fingers around him, wondering how I'd ever be able to support his girth, how I'd been able to do so all those years ago. And suddenly I was struck with the need to taste him. I dropped off the bed, dipping down on my knees as I took him in my mouth and watched him clench his eyes tightly.

"Jolie," he groaned out.

Before I'd had my fill of him, he gently pushed my mouth away. Grabbing me by the waist, positioning me on the bed, spreading my legs, he angled himself between them, his shoulders resting on my thighs.

"Quid pro quo," he said with a smile and slipping my panties to the side, his mouth was suddenly on me.

I screamed out in pleasure at the same time that I ground my heels into the bed and shot upward. Rand chuckled as he pulled me back toward him, holding my pelvis down to keep me in place.

"Rand," I whimpered. "I don't know . . . how much more I can take."

He made a throaty sound and raised himself up, watching me with a smile of amusement as his fingers danced over me, teasing me ruthlessly. He continued holding my panties to the side as he ran his index finger down the length of me. I clamped my eyes shut.

"When we bonded before," he began and then slipped a finger inside me as I bucked up. He pulled his finger out of me again and chuckled.

"You are evil," I groaned out.

He chuckled more deeply and buried his finger in me again. "At what point did you know it was happening?"

I tried to remember, to force myself to focus when all I wanted to do was lose myself in the feeling of his fingers.

"Jolie?"

"Oh my God," I muttered. "I really can't think right now."

With another chuckle, he removed his fingers and slid my panties off, spreading my legs again as he settled himself between them. The head of his erection perched at my opening.

"Are you able to think now?"

I leaned on my elbows and glanced up at him. "Are you sure you aren't a demon whose sole intention is to drive me to insanity?"

"Quite sure," he answered with the epitome of a demonic smile. "Answer the question."

I thought back, remembering the feel of Rand inside me, and the memory of our bonding rained down on me as if it had happened only yesterday. "We started bonding once you were . . ." I cleared my throat and felt myself blush. "Um, once you were in me. It happened right as we were both coming."

He didn't respond right away so I glanced up at him to find him staring down at me, lovingly.

"Don't look away," he said. Before I could question him he drove himself into me. Gasping at the feel of his invasion, I arched up and clenched my eyes shut.

"No, look at me, Jolie."

I opened my eyes and focused on him. He was watching me like a hawk as he pulled out, only to push back into me again. I wrapped my legs around him and he pushed harder.

And suddenly it was as if I'd been transported back in time, as if my Rand of 1878 was making love to me. That was when the beauty of the moment dawned on me. Rand loved me and I loved him—today, in the here and now. We were destined for each other and in a few moments' time, we would be bonded again. I finally had the man I'd wanted for so long. Rand was mine, body and soul, and I'd kept my promise.

I was surprised when something inside my throat constricted and tears started in my eyes. I couldn't even control myself as they fell onto my pillow.

"Jolie, am I hurting you?" Rand said and immediately stilled within me.

I shook my head and held him to me, embraced him like I'd never held him before.

"No," I said. "I'm just so incredibly happy. I love you so much and now you're actually mine."

Rand chuckled but lifted me into his arms, holding me tightly as he began pushing into me again. I gasped beneath him.

"Yes, I am yours," he whispered. "I love you, Jolie, and I promise to protect you forever."

I could feel myself growing wetter, hotter. I was going to come soon, I could feel it.

"I'm close, Rand."

"That's right," he said between clenched teeth, and pushed into me with renewed zest.

I arched up and threw my head back, screaming out as bliss captured me, transporting me to a place that defied words. Rand's grasp on my shoulders tightened and I opened my eyes to find his firmly shut. With a groan, Rand thrust inside me once more and then collapsed against me, his chest rising and falling in time with my heart.

I swallowed hard and wondered which one of us would bring up the obvious first.

"I didn't feel it," Rand said as he kissed the side of my face. There was something in his eyes—surprise warring with disappointment and concern.

I sighed. "I didn't feel it either."

And then I was left wondering—wondering why we'd just had the best sex of my life, and yet we hadn't bonded.

Twenty-One

Wow, Diary, I don't even really know what to say or where to begin. I guess I'm still reeling over the fact that for the first time in the last two years, well, really, for the first time since I met Rand, I don't have this insatiable need burning inside me—this question constantly plaguing me about whether or not Rand loves me, whether or not we will be together—a plague of questions that used to drive me insane.

Now my emotional seas are no longer turbulent— instead, they're calm and peaceful.

The man I've loved since the moment he first walked into my store loves me. The man I've dreamed about, the man I've lusted after, the man who has owned my heart . . . wants to be with me . . . forever. It's a feeling that's difficult to explain, a sense of absolute bliss, of complete and total happiness.

Well, I guess I can't go that far. There is one little thing that is bothering me and I know it bothers Rand too— that whole little sticking point about why we didn't bond when we had sex last night. And I do have to admit, ahem, that after that first mind-blowing session, we stayed up for the rest of the night and did it five more times. Five more times! Can you even believe that? I guess I can't call myself the Virgin Queen any longer . . .

And as to Rand and his sex drive . . . I never really had

any idea how completely insatiable my warlock is. He's so funny, Diary, because he said he was just as sexually frustrated as I'd been over these last two years. Well, even more so, because at least I had that little session in 1878 to relieve me. Well, granted, Rand did too, but he couldn't remember it and it had been over one hundred years ago for him. Of course, I'm not about to believe that poor Rand hasn't gotten any in over one hundred years, but that's not a thought that pleases me so I'll move on . . .

So back to this whole bonding deal (or not-bonding deal in our case . . .). As I mentioned earlier, we had sex a total of six times and still nothing. No fireworks, no blinding lights, no sudden unexplainable feelings, no random thoughts or words in my head . . . nothing. And I've been sitting here, at my desk in my room at Kinloch, wondering why. In fact, I can't get any of this out of my head.

I wonder if traveling out of 1878 and Rand nearly dying and Mathilda having to wipe me clear out of his brain somehow messed things up, somehow un-bonded us. And if it did un-bond us, could that bond ever exist again?

I mean, really, not being able to bond shouldn't matter that much. It's not like Rand and I would stop loving each other just because we can't bond. And furthermore, Rand said there wasn't a requirement for witches to bond in order to be together forever and he was insistent on the fact that he and I were meant to be together and that he'd "be damned if not bonding would keep me away from the woman I love."

I have to admit I'm gushing over his words right now, gushing over the memories of last night. I'm like a silly girl with a high school crush. Hmmm . . . Jolie Balfour. That looks pretty freaking awesome . . .

So I've decided to shelve the whole bonding issue for now. One of the life lessons I've learned is that when things defy explanation, it's sometimes better just to set them aside and move on rather than dwell on them and drive yourself crazy. So, bonding situation, I'm leaving you and I'm moving on. I will not let you get in the way of my complete and total happiness regarding the fact that Rand Balfour is really mine. Finally.

In other Jolie Wilkins thoughts of late, I'm nervous about Sinjin. That is to say, I know I have to tell him I'm with Rand—I simply won't put up with his apparent jealousies or his constant flirty attentions. It wouldn't be right or fair to Rand. Yes, there was a part of me and there still is a part of me that cares about Sinjin, and probably always will, but I'm not in love with him and I never have been. I wonder if I might have loved Sinjin if Rand had never been in the picture . . . but I'm not sure. Maybe I would have. Of course, that really doesn't matter now.

Nope, now I'm attached, spoken for, and I have to tell Sinjin as much. I just hope he takes it well, that it doesn't completely destroy him. Regardless of his reaction, I absolutely have to tell him. In fact, when the sun sets, that will be my mission. I'll tell Sinjin and then I'll return to Pelham Manor this evening for bonding attempt number two. Ha ha ha.

So, moving on to other topics, namely, my position as monarch of the Underworld, things seem to be at a standstill as far as the Lurkers go. Mercedes reported just this morning that our Lurker task force was still attempting to Lurker-nap one of them and that so far they've been unsuccessful. There also haven't been any other attacks to report, thankfully.

So, like that old Louis Armstrong and Ella Fitzgerald song, things are looking up. It is a great little world we live in, and that part about four-leaf clovers? Yep, that's true too.

I'm in love with a man who loves me, really, a man who adores me. I'm Queen of the Underworld and even though

I was really never happy with my destiny, I can say I'm happy now. In fact I'm happier than I've ever been.

Six hours later, the sun was saying its last goodbye before it retired for the evening and handed over the reins to the dark cloak of night. And my heartbeat increased as I prepared myself for the fact that I was going to have to do something that I knew would hurt Sinjin. I wasn't sure at what level it would hurt him but I hated the idea nonetheless.

Feeling like I had the weight of the Underworld on my shoulders, I left the safety of my bedroom and ventured downstairs, to the basement. I wasn't sure if Sinjin was in his room or already out and about, but I figured his bedroom was a good place to start.

I swallowed hard as I arrived at his door and taking a deep breath, knocked. There wasn't an answer, so after another three seconds, I knocked again.

"Looking for someone?"

I turned around and faced Sinjin, who was leaning against the wall and regarding me with amusement—a raised brow and half smile. But even though he seemed his usual, flirty self, there seemed to be a harder edge just beneath the surface—a reminder that our last run-in had been less than friendly.

"Uh, yeah, I'm looking for you actually," I said with what I hoped was a warm smile, a smile that said our past argument was forgiven and forgotten.

Sinjin nodded, but continued lounging casually against the wall as his gaze traveled down my body from my bust to my hips.

"Why are you dressed up?" he asked.

Due to the fact that I'd planned to see Rand this evening, I was wearing tight black pants and a fitted white angora sweater that ended just at my waist.

"Um, I, uh, I'm going somewhere later," I responded shakily.

Sinjin's eyes narrowed and his jaw tightened. "I see."

I felt my heartbeat increase and I was sure it had everything to do with the fact that Sinjin was looking at me like I was a piece of prime rib.

"Um, Sinjin, I . . . wanted to talk with you," I started.

He shrugged, his eyes still razor sharp. "Then talk."

I swallowed, glancing around myself. "Um, can we talk somewhere else? Somewhere a little more private?" I definitely didn't want spectators if this whole situation erupted into something ugly.

"We can discuss your concerns in my bedroom," Sinjin said before a wicked smile overtook his lips. "Perhaps in my bed?" He stood up straight and took a few steps toward me. "Or perchance you would like to have this conversation while my face is buried in your lovely breasts?"

I backed up. "Sinjin, stop talking like that."

He smiled but it was acidic. It suddenly dawned on me that he knew why I was here—he had to know. He'd never treated me so callously before. It was as if he'd given up on whatever hopes he'd harbored for us.

"Like what, love?" he asked and strode past me, opening his bedroom door and disappearing inside. I looked down the hallway and, figuring that I didn't want to get into an unpleasant conversation in the middle of my house, followed him, closing the door behind me.

"As your Queen, I demand you treat me with respect," I finished angrily.

Sinjin chuckled, but the sound was icy. "As you wish, my monarch."

So he was going to play the game of "Sinjin's being an asshole," was he? Whatever. I had one thing to say and dammit all, I was going to get it out.

"I came to tell you . . . ," I started.

Sinjin suddenly closed his eyes and opened his mouth, lifting his nose into the air as if he'd caught a whiff of something and, judging by the expression on his face, it was a whiff of something incredibly . . . good.

"What the hell are you doing?" I asked, suddenly feeling uncomfortable as I witnessed the expression of ecstasy that was in the process of pasting itself all over his face. I wrapped my arms around myself.

He opened his eyes and their usual ice bluc had deepened into something darker, something passionate. "I can smell your desire, your need."

"Oh my God," I said but the rest of the sentence fell off my tongue when he stood up and inhaled deeply again.

"I have smelled you before, love, but never anything as heady as this, as intoxicating." He took another four steps, erasing any distance between us, and I found myself instinctively retreating until my back and calves met the wall. But Sinjin continued coming and when he was directly in front me, he braced his palms against the wall, trapping me between them.

"Keep away from me," I whispered as fear began to snake through me.

Sinjin smiled, his fangs cresting his lower lip. "Your blood is calling to me, poppet."

And then I suddenly wondered if he was picking up on my desire for Rand. I'd always known that vampires had an uncanny sense when it came to reading the emotions of their prey, and it appeared Sinjin was now reading my . . . lustful needs. What he hadn't realized was that they weren't intended for him.

"Sinjin," I started and pushed him away from me.

"Let your fears go, love, I will not hurt you." And he pushed his face into my neck, slamming his body into mine as I struggled to release myself.

"Get away from me, Sinjin," I spat out, but it was as if he hadn't even heard me. "I'm in love with Rand, dammit!" I yelled finally, thinking it might be the only way to get him off me.

In an instant Sinjin pulled away from me. He seemed to study me, almost as if he were debating over whether or not I was being truthful. His eyes were livid, riddled with angst, and his fangs were longer than I ever remembered them.

"I . . . I came to tell you as much," I said much more softly, my sentence an apology in itself. I dropped my gaze to the lush carpet so I wouldn't have to witness the pain evident in Sinjin's eyes.

He pulled away from me. I glanced up to find that his fangs had retracted.

"This is not news."

I nodded and smoothed my sweater and pants down even though they really didn't need it. "Yes, I'm aware of that but if you'd allowed me to finish, I would have told you that . . ." I took a deep breath and raised my chin. "I would have told you that Rand loves me as well and that we are . . . now . . . together."

Sinjin merely nodded. There was no sign that my words had, in any way, upset him. Instead he just seemed casual—detached and indifferent.

"Then your lust is for him?" he asked and swallowed hard, his eyes suddenly boring into mine.

I didn't say anything; simply nodded. Sinjin responded by raising a brow before turning away from me and starting for the door.

"If that is all you came to tell me, please feel free to leave."

"Sinjin," I said and started toward him. "I didn't want to . . ."

"No," he answered and shook his head as if he didn't want to hear any more. But he was going to hear more. There was one more thing I had to tell him, one more subject I had to get out in the open.

"I care about you, Sinjin, I've always cared about you." I paused and glanced at the floor again, summoning up my courage, forcing the words to my tongue. I looked up at him again. "I never wanted to hurt you."

"Hurt me?" he asked and threw his head back, laughing as if I'd just told him the best joke he'd ever heard.

"Yes," I said, my voice betraying my confusion over his bizarre response.

He stopped laughing and narrowed his gaze on mine. "You have not been paying attention, poppet."

"Paying attention?" I repeated. "Paying attention to what?"

He shook his head like the joke was on me, like he'd just not only turned the tables but turned them upside down. "How many times did I tell you not to paint me with your ideals of who and what I should be?"

I shook my head. "I don't understand, Sinjin."

"That is quite apparent. It appears you never did."

I swallowed hard. "Sinjin, what the hell are you talking about?"

His jaw tightened and he was quiet for a few seconds before he turned the full extent of his blazing eyes on me. "I am not hurt nor was I ever hurt by any of your actions."

I felt relief bubble up inside me. "Oh, I . . . I'm happy to hear that. I was just concerned that maybe I . . ."

He chuckled and shook his head, as if to say he wasn't finished. "You misunderstood me all along, it seems."

"Misunderstood what?" I asked again, starting to get irritated by his attitude.

Sinjin glared at me. "In order for me to be hurt by your admission, that would require me to care about you—to have invested feelings and emotions into you, poppet. But what I have been alluding to all along, and what you have seemingly never understood, is that I do not form attachments to women, not even you."

I felt my stomach drop. Granted, I'd hoped not to hurt

Sinjin, but I hadn't considered the fact that he might hurt me. And the truth of the matter was that his words stung me to my core because I *had* cared about him and still did.

"But—" I quickly stopped myself. I didn't need to get into the hows and whys of it because none of that mattered anyway. All that did matter was that Rand loved me and I loved him.

"Do not misunderstand me, poppet." Sinjin reached for my hand, pulling me against his chest. "Yes, I have always wanted to penetrate you, and yes, I desire your body even at this moment."

I pulled my hand out of his and pushed him away. "You've said enough," I spat out and started for the door, suddenly feeling sick.

"Do not be alarmed concerning my welfare, love," Sinjin continued and chuckled again, calling out to me from his stance in the middle of the room. "I do not care if you love the warlock or if you love the fairy, the wolf, or any other creature. You can love them all at the same time for all I care."

I didn't say anything else but ran the remaining few feet to the door and threw it open, slamming it behind me as I felt the sting of tears in my eyes. It hurt to know that Sinjin had never given a rat's ass about me. But more than that, I was floored, wounded by the fact that he'd just made a total fool of me, that he'd just attempted to cut me down into nothing . . . that all he'd ever wanted from me was sex. What really hurt the most was that our friendship had never meant anything to him.

An hour later I was sitting in my room and thinking about how Sinjin had turned out to be such an asshole. I'd never seen it coming even though he had warned me all along. He'd told me not to paint him into something I wanted him to be, not to believe him to be a good and honorable person. And I'd stupidly attributed him with characteristics I wanted him to have—maybe to make the fact that I did like him more bearable, more easily digestible. I'd been so stupid, so incredibly stupid.

Well, I needed to stop thinking about it, I told myself resolutely. Instead I'd focus on the fact that I was almost packed for my weekend trip to Pelham Manor, where Rand would no doubt alleviate my hurt feelings with just a kiss. The need to see him was suddenly over-whelming, suffocating.

Screw Sinjin—he could continue living like the jerk-off that he was, but he was going to do it outside Kinloch Kirk. There was no way I was going to let him continue serving as my protector after all the nasty things he'd just said to me. Maybe Klaasje would be willing to do the job herself. And on that point, I was sure Rand would be more than pleased. After all, Rand had always barely tolerated Sinjin—truly, he had been right all along. He'd always seen Sinjin for what he was—a self-centered, egotistical, childish jerk.

I threw my backpack over my shoulder and opened my bedroom door, walking down the hallway. I took the stairs two at a time, the need to see Rand consuming me. I couldn't wait to feel his warmth, to snuggle into his broad chest and feel his incredibly muscular arms around me. I couldn't wait to smell him, to taste his lips, and feel him inside me. I opened the front door—and Plum darted out in front of me before I could stop her.

"Dammit!" I yelled and ran after her as she hightailed it down the driveway and disappeared into the undergrowth just beside the drive. And like the responsible cat owner I was, I followed her into the savagery of the woods, trying to avoid the twigs and tree limbs as they reached out and seemed intent on snagging my brand-new sweater.

"Here kitty kitty," I called in a soft voice that hope-fully didn't sound annoyed or angry.

Out of the corner of my eye, I caught a glimpse of

something that looked like a flash lighting up the otherwise dark background of the beach just beyond Kinloch. I glanced down as Plum wove herself between my legs. Picking her up, I decided to further investigate the strange light. I forced my way through more trees, eventually emerging on the other side, where a strong wind blew through the Scottish moors.

And there on the beach were Sinjin and Mercedes. And it looked like they were up to absolutely no good, partially hidden by the rocks of the coastline. They appeared to be in the midst of some sort of ritual or charm. I watched Mercedes close the circle she'd been drawing in the sand around both of them with a long, pointed stick. Then she closed her eyes and held her hands up toward the heavens, her lips moving like she was chanting. She opened her eyes and dropped her hands, at the same time glancing over at Sinjin and reaching for his hand.

And that was when I realized what the hell was going on. I had seen this before—the drawing of the circle, Mercedes facing north, west, east, and south. I'd watched Mercedes cast the same spell in 1878, moments before she'd sent me back to my own time.

I dropped the cat, who responded with an angry meow. But I wasn't concerned with Plum at the moment. My heart thudded in my chest and my breathing came in short, shallow pants. I had . . . I had to tell someone. I needed help. I couldn't handle this on my own.

Rand! I screamed his name in my head as I turned around and started running for the tree line. I thought about running down to the beach and trying to stop Mercedes but I knew I wouldn't make it in time. *Jolie, are you all right? What's wrong?* Rand's voice responded in my head, his tone fringed with worry.

Rand, I need you to do as I say as quickly as you can. You can't ask any questions because we don't have time. I need you to go to Mathilda.

Jolie . . . , Rand started and I was suddenly scared to death that he was going to drill me on the specifics. We didn't have time for specifics.

Find Mathilda!

Okay, just answer me this . . . are you hurt?

I felt my heart begin to calm and I tried to think without the hysteria that had accompanied my previous thoughts. *No, I'm not hurt, Rand. I'm fine but I need you to find Mathilda as quickly as you can.* I took a deep breath. *I . . . I know why Sinjin has been meeting with Mercedes.*

Sinjin meeting with Mercedes? Rand repeated. *What the bloody hell are you talking about?*

I had forgotten the fact that I'd never told Rand that Sinjin and Mercedes had been having secret meetings. Dammit.

Never mind that now, Rand. Just go to Mathilda. I'm on my way as well. I took a deep breath as a thought suddenly occurred to me, one that scared me to death. *If I don't get there in time . . .*

Jolie, are you in trouble? For God's sake, tell me! Rand sounded as if he was a step away from inconsolable. I could only imagine the thoughts that were going through his mind. Of course, whatever was going through his mind was probably not as bad as what was happening in reality.

Rand, please . . .

What the bloody hell is going on? If something has happened to you, tell me. I will be there momentarily.

Rand, I don't have time for your questions! I took a deep breath. *Do whatever Mathilda says you must, even if I don't get there in time. And I want you to know that whatever happens, I love you and I will always love you.*

My God, Jolie, if anything happens to you . . .

Rand, you must tell Mathilda that Mercedes is in the process of . . . of sending Sinjin back in time . . .

Twenty-two

"So what did you think of Owen?" Christa asked as she leaned against the front counter lazily.

The truth was I didn't think of Owen. Christa had made it her own personal mission to see to it that I had a date after a six-month-long dry spell. So she'd skimmed through her Roll-a-Date of men she'd casually gone out with (some of whom she'd slept with . . . well, most of whom she'd slept with), and for some reason or another she'd fixated on Owen.

"I talked to him on the phone for maybe fifteen minutes, Chris. What could I really think of him from fifteen minutes?" I asked, looking up from sweeping the floor.

"I can find out a lot about a man in fifteen minutes," she argued, her nose turned up defensively, as she started thumbing through the bills in the cash register and then summed them up on the spreadsheet I'd just printed out.

"In fifteen minutes, I can find out what his favorite color is, what his favorite food is, what his favorite position in bed is . . ." She looked up at me with a smile.

"Oh God." I shook my head.

"Come on, Jules, you gotta give me something here. Did you at least like his voice?"

I shrugged as I pulled the trash bag out of the can and tightened the drawstrings, ready to drop it off in the trash bins just outside. "Can you hand me a trash bag, please?"

Christa sighed. "Not until you tell me what you thought of Owen's voice." But she bent down and grabbed a bag from the roll underneath the counter as if to say I didn't really have to answer her question.

"I just wasn't that impressed with him. I mean, his voice was okay, maybe a little too high-pitched."

Christa frowned and handed me the bag while I shook it out and placed it neatly inside the bin.

"Did you like anything about him?" she continued.

I was quiet as I considered her question. Then I faced her squarely. "No, not really. And I don't think I could ever date anyone who says 'like' so much."

"Well, you need to get used to the fact that you should start dating again," she said with a grumpy frown.

"Let's not get into this again . . ."

"Jolie, you need to get out. You're almost thirty . . ."

"Two years from it, thank you very much."

"Whatever . . . you're going to end up old and alone. You're way too pretty, and you have such a great personality, you can't end up like that. Don't let one bad phone call ruin it."

"It's not about one bad phone call. I've had a string of bad dates, Chris. At least the last three dates I've been on were complete and total catastrophes." I didn't know what else to say—the sad truth was that I'd rather spend time with my cat or Christa than face another loser over dinner or drinks while we both searched for something we had in common that might save us from staring at each other in silence.

Feeling suddenly depressed, I gazed out at the street-lights beyond the windows of my store and watched how they highlighted the empty street. It was a Thursday night in Los Angeles in the middle of December, which was why the sun was long gone and it was only seven p.m. Christa and I should have closed up over an hour ago but our last client had taken longer than I'd anticipated. Taken longer as in she'd suddenly freaked out when I told her I could see her aura and it looked a little yellowish, which meant she might be sick and should visit her doctor to get a physical to make sure everything was okay.

Then she'd proceeded to unload on me—crying as she detailed her entire life's history including her recent divorce and how she'd decided to shack up with the first guy who showed any interest in her and who, incidentally, had given her chlamydia—something she was now on antibiotics for and something that was also the reason for her yellowish aura, which should have been pink or violet.

"Are you even listening to me?" Christa asked.

Shaking my head, I entered the reading room and started sweeping.

I heard the door open.

"Well, hello to you," Christa said in a high-pitched, sickening-sweet, and non-Christa voice.

"Good evening." His voice was deep, hypnotically so, and his accent thickly English.

"Um, we're closed," Christa started but immediately cleared her throat. "But I'll make an exception this one time."

I just shook my head as the man chuckled.

"I do appreciate it," he said.

"What can I do for you?" Christa purred, her tone more befitting the question: *Which do you prefer, crotchless panties or pasties?*

"I seem to have come across some trouble with my car," the man said. "I have a flat tire and was wondering if perhaps I could use your telephone?"

"Um, you don't have a cell phone?" Christa asked in shock.

The man chuckled. "I am on vacation in America and failed to hire a mobile phone, most unfortunately."

"Jules?" Christa called. "Is it okay if an incredibly handsome man uses our telephone?"

Figuring I should probably make an appearance just to ensure this guy wasn't a total weirdo before he took Christa off to his love shack for the night, I headed out of the reading room.

When I glanced at him, it wasn't one of those quick appraisals you usually do when you meet people and look immediately at their faces. Instead I seemed to fix-ate on his shiny black shoes, then moved my gaze up his tall and muscular body, ultimately settling my eyes on his face, which was by far the most handsome face I'd ever seen. It was angular with a well-defined nose and strong cheekbones. He looked like he should have graced the cover of some high-fashion men's magazine.

I didn't say anything for a long time. I actually don't even know for how long. I just stood there like a total imbecile and stared up at the man like I'd never seen one before.

"Um, Jolie?" Christa prodded as if to say, *Wake up, girl, you're totally embarrassing yourself.*

I shook my head, hoping to collect my wits. "I'm . . . I'm sorry. What . . . What did you need again?"

The man chuckled, and I wasn't sure if I was imagin-ing it, but it seemed like he'd just been looking me up and down . . . appreciatively. Yes, I had to be imagining it. I mean, Christa was still in the room and any man would prefer her to me.

"I have a flat tire and my car is parked just outside your store, miss," he said with a smile that about melted my insides. "I wonder if I might trouble you to use your telephone?"

"Oh," I nodded. "Yeah, sure, of course you can."

I needed to snap out of it. I mean, yes he was the

best-looking guy I'd ever seen in my life, but was I that blindsided by looks? Was I that completely and totally shallow? Usually I was the rational Jolie who said looks weren't what mattered. It was the person inside who did. Jeez, maybe I'd been living in LA for too long.

"Here," Christa said with a smile as she lifted the cordless phone from the receiver and leaned over the counter, offering him a full view of her cleavage as she handed the phone to him.

He smiled and nodded as if to say *thank you* as he accepted the phone. Strangely enough, he didn't even seem to notice her boobs, which were about to spill out of her shirt. Hmm, he was probably gay. All the best-looking ones inevitably were.

He pulled out his leather wallet and rifled through a wad of bills and credit cards, pulling out what looked like a rental car agency's card. The guy had to be loaded. If the wad of hundreds wasn't sign enough, his super-expensive slacks and sweater were a good indicator.

"I will be just over here so as not to disturb you both," he said and started dialing as he neared the far corner of the store. Once the person on the other line picked up, he started explaining his predicament.

"Are you all done?" I asked Christa, wanting—no, needing—to focus on anything but our incredibly handsome and, dare I say it, sexy visitor.

Christa nodded then glanced over at him as if to make sure he wasn't looking before she regarded me again and mouthed, *Hot damn!*

I just shook my head and offered her a raised-brow expression. She glanced over at him once more, as if she couldn't help it, and then followed me as I carried the trash to the back door.

"Oh my gosh, is he the most gorgeous thing you've ever seen?" she demanded once we were out of earshot. "I nearly had an orgasm when he walked in the store."

"Chris, do you have to be so crude?" I asked and frowned at her.

"Yeah, in this instance I do." Then she shook her head as if she was still in disbelief.

"Well, it looks like tonight is your lucky night," I offered with a smile.

"Do I look okay?" she asked and smoothed her hands down her tight, white halter top and red miniskirt. "I knew I should have worn my pink top today. It looks way better with my hair and eyes."

I just shook my head. "Chris, you look great. You're gorgeous and I'm sure he's already thinking about where he's going to take you to dinner." Well, it was a white lie—I was convinced he was more interested in what she'd be like between the sheets.

"You think?" she beamed.

"I'm sure," I said and opened the back door, heading for the trash cans in the alleyway. Christa stayed inside, which was just as well. I'm sure she wanted a little alone time with the handsome man anyway. I pulled open the bin's cover and threw the trash into it. Then I started for my store, wondering what in the hell I was going to eat for dinner tonight. I was out of Healthy Choice frozen dinners but I really didn't feel like going to the grocery store. Of course, the cat also needed more Fancy Feast . . .

When I walked back inside, the handsome man was sitting on the couch in the front entry and Christa was nowhere to be seen.

My stomach dropped.

"Um, where did my friend go?" I asked, trying to sound like I wasn't completely freaking out.

The man shrugged. "She said she had to leave to get ready for a . . ." He smirked as if he was about to say something funny. "Hot date I believe she termed it."

I felt myself swallow down a lump of dread as I fingered my cell phone, which, thank God, was in my pocket. What had this creep done with Christa? There was no way in hell she would have left without taking him with her . . . as in home for the night.

I glanced at the counter, where Christa had left her bag, and noticed that it too was missing.

"Oh, okay," I said and tried to maintain the appearance of someone who wasn't seriously about to pee herself in fear. I grabbed the broom and headed for the front door. "I'll just be out here sweeping the entry, but make yourself at home while you wait."

The man smiled at me warmly. "I will, thank you."

I nodded and tried to keep myself from running outside. Instead I walked to the front door, and when I made it through I almost wanted to sigh with relief. I started sweeping, heading farther and farther down the sidewalk and farther from the stranger's line of sight. Once I was beyond my storefront and safe from prying eyes, I immediately speed-dialed Christa.

Surprisingly, she picked up on the first ring.

"Where the hell are you?" I whispered.

"I'm on my way home. Sorry I didn't say goodbye but I totally forgot that I have a date with Ryan tonight."

I felt my heart slow down. Christa was okay and had just been a space cadet, as usual. "What about the guy here? I thought you were all hot for him?"

She was silent for a few seconds. "Well, really, what am I going to do? Ryan is already waiting for me."

"I'm glad to know you're okay, but you could have waited for me instead of leaving me alone with this guy," I grumbled.

"Oh, sorry, Jules, I didn't even think of that. Do you want me to come back until he leaves?"

I sighed, thinking I probably sounded like a baby. "No, it's fine. Have fun with Ryan."

"Okay, thanks, Jules," she said and hung up.

So it looked like it was just me, the broom, and the hottest man I'd ever seen in my life. Great, just great. Well, hopefully the rental agency people would arrive soon so Mr. Gorgeous Man could get on with doing whatever it was he was planning on doing.

I strolled back into the store and offered him a quick smile.

"Roadside assistance phoned and said they would be arriving in ten minutes. Thank you again for your hospitality."

I just nodded and glanced at the clock, noticing it was already eight p.m. When I looked away from the clock, I felt the man's eyes on me and I made the mistake of looking at him. He was wearing the strangest expression—something like amusement and maybe admiration. I didn't know why but I had the distinct feeling that he wanted to touch me. He looked like he was doing his damndest to stay seated.

"What is your name?" he asked.

"Um, Jolie, Jolie Wilkins."

He nodded with another smile that revealed perfectly straight, white teeth. "That is a very lovely name."

Realizing I was still holding on to the broom like I thought I was a witch who was about to take off on it, I started for the hall closet and stowed it away. When I turned around, the man was staring at me again. He made me uncomfortable—made me feel like he could almost see right through me. I moved behind the counter and took a seat on the stool, facing him.

"What is it you do in this store?" he asked.

I felt myself swallow down my embarrassment over the fact that I was going to admit I was a psychic to someone who probably didn't believe in that sort of thing.

"I, um, I read fortunes."

He nodded as if he wasn't surprised, his gaze straying

to the street as a car drove by. He seemed to home in on the store windows as a smile seized his lips. "I suppose I could have deduced that from your front windows."

I glanced at them and laughed. It said FORTUNE TELLER in bold white lettering right across the top of the door and the huge window beside it.

"You said you were on vacation in the States?" I asked, feeling the need to participate, considering he was trying to make conversation.

He paused for a second or two as if weighing his response. "Yes, on vacation. I am originally from Britain, as a matter of fact."

Just as I was about to ask him what part of Britain, the roadside assistance truck pulled up in front of my store, putting its blinkers on because, as usual, there wasn't anywhere to park along the curb.

"Looks like help just arrived," I said and couldn't deny the feeling of sadness that welled up within me. Which really made no sense. It wasn't like I actually thought this stranger would have any interest in girl-next-door me.

The man glanced over at the window, and recognizing the truck, stood up. "Thank you again," he said.

I just nodded and watched him walk up to the counter and hand me the phone. He paused a moment or two after I took it from him and offered me the sexiest smile I'd ever seen. His lips were so full, and they had a pink-ish hue to them. I felt my stomach begin to fill with butterflies and quickly turned around as I placed the phone in its cradle. When I turned around again, the man had already walked out of my door. The little bells hanging from it dinged as he exited.

And the most handsome man I'd ever seen walked out of my store and my life just like that.

I continued fussing around the store, telling myself I'd wait until he drove away to make sure he was okay. I wasn't really sure why I didn't just pack my things and head out now—it wasn't like the roadside assistance guy would leave him stranded—but I stayed anyway. Which was pretty stupid considering I couldn't even see his car from my store window. He must have experienced his flat tire pretty far down the street.

After a few minutes of standing around my perfectly clean and tidy store, I sighed and grabbed my purse as I started for the door, figuring I was being silly and should just go home. I definitely didn't want this guy to think I was waiting for him. Talk about embarrassing the crap out of myself uselessly.

I opened the front door and locked it behind myself.

"Excuse me again?"

I whirled around to find the handsome man seated in a black sports car. He'd pulled up just alongside me. It was a car I'd never seen before—maybe a Ferrari or something of the sort.

"Wow, that was fast!" I said, legitimately shocked.

He nodded but didn't remark on the speedy work. "I know this is quite forward of me, especially considering we are not . . . acquainted with each other, but I wonder if I may take you to dinner tomorrow evening?"

"Oh," I started in surprise before a sinking feeling took hold of me. There was nothing about me that would hold this man's interest. It would end up being an embarrassing, uneventful evening when we both realized he was completely out of my league and he really should have been with a much more beautiful and exciting woman.

"Um, I . . ."

"As I mentioned earlier, I am visiting and I do not know where to go or what to see."

He just seemed so nice, so lonely almost.

And I found myself saying something that completely floored me. "Sure, I'd love to."

The man beamed as if I'd just given him exactly what he'd wanted for Christmas. "Wonderful. May I pick you up here tomorrow evening at seven, perhaps?"

I nodded again. "Sure."

He smiled and his car started rolling forward but, seemingly remembering something, he hit the brakes.

"I apologize profusely," he began, shaking his head in apparent disbelief as another sexy and devilish grin took hold of his sumptuous lips. "Where are my manners? I have not even introduced myself."

I hadn't realized he hadn't introduced himself either. How bizarre.

"I am Sinjin Sinclair. Very pleased to meet you."

I smiled again, thinking this was the most exciting night I'd had in a long, long time. And Christa was going to pee herself when she heard that Mr. Gorgeous Man had actually just asked me out on a date.

"I'm very pleased to meet you too, Sinjin."

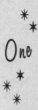

One

When the phone rang at ten minutes to seven, I wasn't surprised. Nope, I figured that Sinjin Sinclair, the most handsome and charming man who had ever stepped into my life, had probably just come to his senses and realized he didn't want to take me out for dinner after all. Maybe he'd suffered from a slight brain freeze the night before when he'd been awaiting roadside assistance at my tarot-card reading shop, and that was why he'd asked me out.

So when he phoned to say he was lost, I was surprised—not so much that his navigational skills were lacking but that he actually wanted to go through with this. Okay, I know what you're thinking—that I must look like a troll, or something equally heinous . . . Well, I'm not a troll by any stretch of the imagination, but I'm also not the girl who stands out in a crowd. I'm more the girl next door—well, at least, I live down the street from the girl next door.

Okay, I'm probably being a little too hard on myself because I have been told I'm attractive and I know I'm smart and all that stuff, but, still, I'm nowhere near Sinjins Sinclair's league.

But back to the phone call. After Sinjin said he would be at my door shortly, I hung up and then stood in the center of my living room for a few minutes like a space cadet, gazing at the wall until I'm sure I looked like a complete and total moron.

But while it might have appeared that nothing of much concern was going on in that gray matter between my ears, appearances can be deceiving. Thoughts ramrodded my brain, slamming into one another as new ones were born . . . *What was I doing? What was I thinking? What would I possibly have to talk about with a man who was as cultured and refined as Sinjin Sinclair? Moreover, how was I going to eat in front of him? What if I choked on an ice cube? Or I sneezed after taking a mouthful of salad and sprayed carrot chunks all over his expensive clothes?*

Jolie Wilkins, calm down, I finally said to myself, closing my eyes and taking a deep breath. *You are going to go on this date because if you don't, you're never going to forgive yourself. And, furthermore, Christa will most definitely murder you.*

I inhaled another deep breath and forced myself out of my self-inflicted brain coma, starting toward the mirror as I took stock of myself for the umpteenth time in the last hour. Christa, my best friend and self-acclaimed fashion advisor, had left twenty minutes ago after chastising me about my current getup. Yes, she'd tried to force me into what amounted to shrink-wrapping, complete with stiletto heels that were so narrow, they could double as weapons. Then, after that attempt had failed, she'd tried to get me to go with a flame-red corset dress that was so tight, I couldn't walk and breathing was out of the question. So yes, I'd defeated the raunchy clothing demon but I couldn't say I felt very good about my victory.

I sighed as I took in my shoulder-length blond hair and the fact that the curl Christa had wrestled into it only minutes before was now long gone. It could be described as "limp" at best. My makeup was nice though—Christa had managed to talk me into smoky eyes, which accented my baby blues and she'd also covered the freckles that sprinkled the bridge of my nose while playing up my cheekbones with a shimmery apricot blush. She'd lined my decently plump lips in a light brown and filled them with bubble-gum-pink lipstick, finishing them with a pink gloss called "Baby Doll."

There was a knock on my front door and I felt my heart lurch into my throat. I took another deep breath, glanced at my reflection in the mirror once more, trying not to focus on the fact that I was anything but sexy in my black amorphous skirt which ended just below my knees, black tights, and two-inch heels. Even though my breasts are decently large, you couldn't really tell in my gray turtleneck and black peacoat.

Maybe I should have listened to Christa . . .

Another quick knock on the door signaled the fact that I was dawdling. I pulled myself away from my reflection and, wrapping my hand around the doorknob, exhaled and opened it, pasting a smile on my face.

"Hello," I said, hoping my voice sounded level, evenkeeled, because the sight of Sinjin standing there just about undid me. There was a tornado rampaging through me, tearing at my guts, and wreaking havoc with my nervous system.

If looks could kill, I would've been pronounced dead before my head even hit the floor.

"Good evening," the deity before me spoke in his refined, baritone English accent. His eyes traveled from my eyes to my bust to my legs and back up again as a serpentine smile spread across his sumptuous lips.

"Um," I managed, meaning to add a "how are you?" to the end of it, but somehow the words never emerged.

Sinjin arched a black brow and chuckled as I debated slamming the door shut and hiding out in my room for the next, oh, two years, at least.

"You look quite lovely," he said, with that devilish

smile, as he pulled his arm forward and offered me a bouquet of red roses. "These pale in comparison."

My hand was shaking and my brain was on vacation as I reached for the roses but, somehow, I did manage to smile and say, "Thank you, they are really beautiful."

But the beauty of the roses didn't even compute—my overwhelmed mind was still reeling from the presence of this man. *Man* didn't even do him justice; he seemed so much more than that—either heaven-sent or hell's emissary.

He was wearing black, just as he had been the night before. His black slacks weren't fitted, but neither were they loose—in fact, they seemed tailored to his incredibly long legs. And his black sweater did a very poor job of covering his broad shoulders and narrow waist. Even though his body and intimidating height would have been worth writing home about, it was his face that was so completely enthralling and alluring.

Sinjin's eyes should have been the eighth wonder of the world. They were the most peculiar color—an incredibly light blue, most similar to the blue-green icebergs you might find in Alaska or the Alpine waters of Germany. They almost seemed to glow. His skin wasn't white, but neither was it tan—he must not spend much time outside because it was flawless, without the kiss of a freckle or mole.

His hair was midnight black, so dark that it almost appeared blue. Tonight, it looked longer than I remembered it being. The ends curled up over his collar, which was strange considering I'd only met him the day before and I could have sworn his hair was short. But the strangest thing about this amazing man was that I couldn't see his aura . . .

I've been able to see people's auras for as long as I can remember. The best way to describe an aura is that it's a halo-type thing that surrounds someone—it billows out of them in a foggy sort of haze. If someone is healthy, his or her aura is usually pink or violet. In those who aren't healthy, yellow or orange predominates. I had never before met anyone who didn't have an aura or whose aura I couldn't see. And what surprised me even more was the fact that I hadn't noticed his missing aura the first time I'd seen him . . . Of course I had been pretty overwhelmed by his mere presence—and that dazed feeling that didn't seem like it was going to go away anytime soon.

"May I escort you?" he asked as he offered me another winning smile and turned his body to show me his proffered arm.

I gulped as I tentatively wrapped my hand around his arm, trying not to notice the fact that he was really . . . built. Good God . . .

"Thanks," I said in a small voice as I allowed him to lead me outside.

"Are you forgetting something?" Sinjin asked as he glanced down at me.

"Um," I started and dropped my attention to my feet, attempting to take stock of myself.

Shoes were on, purse was over my shoulder, nerves were present and accounted for . . . the only thing I'd forgotten was my confidence, which was currently hiding underneath my bed.

Sinjin stopped walking and turned around. I followed suit and noticed the door to my modest little house was still open—gaping wide as though it was as shocked as I was that I'd forgotten to shut it. Not to mention the fact that my cat, Plum, could easily have snuck out, if she hadn't already.

"Oh my God," I started and felt my cheeks color with embarrassment. It had to be pretty obvious I'd completely forgotten how to function in his presence. I separated myself from him and hurried back up my walkway.

I glanced inside the apartment and noticed Plum sound asleep on the sofa. I breathed out a sigh of relief. "Good kitty," I whispered and shook my head at my inattention, closing and locking the door behind me.

"Shall we try this again?"

I jumped as I heard his voice, shocked that he was suddenly right béside me. I shook the feeling off, figuring he must have been trailing me all along. But, still, there was something . . . uncanny about it, something that set off my "Spidey" senses. I blamed it on my already overwhelmed nerves.

"Yes," I said with a nervous laugh as he offered his arm again and I, again, took it. This time, we made it to the curb where a black car awaited us. It was so angular it almost looked like a spaceship. It was the same vehicle he'd been driving the night before when he'd gotten a flat tire and had asked to use my phone. He opened the door for me and I offered him a smile of thanks as I seated myself, glancing over at the steering wheel where I recognized the Ferrari emblem.

A Ferrari . . . seriously?

I had to pinch myself. This just wasn't real—it couldn't be real! I mean, my life was composed of TV dinners and reruns of *The Office*. My only social outlet, really, was Christa. Men like Sinjin Sinclair with their fastidious attire and stunning good looks, driving their Ferraris, just didn't figure into the Jolie Wilkins equation . . . Not at all!

"I hope you do not mind that I made reservations at Costa Mare?" he asked with a boyish grin.

Costa Mare was renowned for its Italian food and even more renowned for the fact that it took months to get a reservation. "You were able to make a reservation there?" I asked in awe, my mouth gaping in response.

Sinjin shrugged. "As a rule, I never take no for an answer." Then he chuckled as if to say he was making a joke. But you know what people say about jokes—

there's always an underlying element of truth to them. It would not have come as a surprise to me at all to learn that Sinjin Sinclair was accustomed to getting his way.

For the next fifteen minutes, we made small talk—discussing things like the weather, his flat tire, and the history of my friendship with Christa. Before I knew it, we'd pulled in front of Costa Mare and Sinjin was handing the keys to the valet. Sinjin shook his head at the doorman who attempted to open my door, insisting that he would do it himself. I couldn't remember the last time a man had opened my door for me. The guys in LA weren't exactly gentlemen.

I took Sinjin's arm and allowed him to escort me into the restaurant, where the staff seemed to fuss over him like he was some great messiah. They led us through a weaving path of tables, polished marble flooring and dimly lit candles, finally designating us to a desolate table in the corner of the room that was surrounded by potted bamboos that acted as a screen from the rest of the restaurant.

"Where would you prefer to sit?" Sinjin asked me with a polished smile.

"I don't care," I answered as I waited for him to pull out my chair. He chose the seat with the best view of the restaurant, but I hadn't been lying—I really didn't care.

The host, a rotund, short man, who was probably in his late forties, offered us our menus, placing our napkins on our laps, and left us to our own defenses.

"A man should always choose his seat wisely," Sinjin started, glancing at me with a smirk.

"Why is that?" I asked, wondering what he was getting at.

He nodded as if he had a long and interesting story he was about to divulge. "In times long past, it could mean death if a man's back was to his enemies."

"And you're still practicing that I see?" I asked with a

smile, suddenly feeling increasingly comfortable with him. It was strange because I wasn't a person who was, in general, comfortable around anyone I didn't know.

"It is my duty to ensure your safety, poppet."

I wasn't sure why but the word "poppet" seemed so familiar to me even though I was sure I'd never before heard it. It was a sudden moment of déjà vu, of that feeling that somewhere, sometime, I'd experienced this exact moment. It made no sense but I couldn't help but feel haunted by it all the same.

"Well, I'm sure things are fine in this day and age," I said, trying to shake off the weird feeling. It wouldn't budge. There was just something so . . . familiar about all of this. I took a deep breath and started perusing the menu, hoping to change the course of my wayward thoughts. Feeling as if Sinjin were staring at me, I glanced up and found his eyes fastened on me. He didn't even try to hide the fact, and when I caught him, he smiled.

This one was smooth.

"Have you selected your supper?" he asked, his mouth spreading into a wide smile as if he was in on some inside joke that I wasn't privy to.

I swallowed hard, suddenly more than aware that maybe this whole date was just the setup for a one-night stand. That was when it struck me—that's exactly what it was. Sinjin was traveling from Britain and he probably wanted to taste everything the U.S. had to offer, including its women. Well, unluckily for him, I wasn't on the menu. I felt my lips tightening into a line and tried to keep my cool. But inside I was fuming— mainly at my own idiocy. Had I really been out of the game so long that this hadn't dawned on me from the get-go?

"I think so," I muttered and concealed myself with my menu.

"What is on your mind?" Sinjin asked as he pushed my menu down with his index finger, forcing me to look at him. I could feel my cheeks coloring. He had nerve . . .

"Nothing," I started and dropped my eyes.

"Please, Jolie, do not insult my intelligence."

I took a deep breath. If he wanted to know what was on my mind, he was about to get an earful. "I'm not into one-night stands," I said as stiffly as I could.

Sinjin narrowed his eyes, but the smile on his lips revealed the fact that he was amused. "A wise policy."

So he was still playing this game, was he? "Well, I think you should . . . be aware of that . . . well, in case you . . . in case you . . ."

"In case I what?"

I could feel sweat breaking out along the small of my back. He was forcing me into a corner and that damn smile was still in full effect. "In case you . . . were, uh, looking for that . . . that sort of thing."

He didn't drop his attention from my face. If anything, his eyes were even more riveting, challenging. "Is that what you imagined I was looking for?"

So he was going to make this tough on me, was he? He was going to make me spell it out for him and embarrass myself? Well, I might not be in his league, but I wouldn't be made a fool of. I was much too smart for that. "Without a doubt."

"And what, pray tell, gave you that impression, if I may be so bold as to inquire?"

"I . . . um," I cleared my throat and forced myself to look him straight in the eyes. "I couldn't figure out why else you'd be here with . . . with me tonight."

Sinjin took a deep breath and it seemed to take him forever to exhale it. "I see."

"So, if you are . . . looking for that, you might as well take me home now . . . no harm done," I finished and held his gaze for another three seconds before I picked up my ice water and began chugging it.

"Very well," he answered and his voice was tender.

I dropped the menu and reached for my purse, feeling something icy forming in my gut as I readied myself to leave. I wasn't angry, no, but I was humiliated. Strangely enough, though, relief was beginning to suffuse me . . . relief at the fact that I could end this farce and lick my wounds in the comfort and serenity of my house. After collecting my things, I stood up and noticed that Sinjin hadn't moved an inch. I glanced over at him with a question in my eyes.

"What are you doing?" I demanded.

"Perhaps I should ask the same of you?"

I swallowed hard. "I thought we were leaving?"

"Why are we leaving? We have not even ordered yet."

"But I thought," I started before my voice was swallowed up by the fact that I was at a complete loss.

Sinjin smiled up at me and shook his head, pulling out my chair. "Please have a seat, love," he said. "You misunderstood my intentions."

"But you said 'very well,'" I started, even as I took the seat and pulled myself back up to the table again.

"I was simply agreeing with your assessment of the fact that you are quite opposed to 'one-night stands' as you so fittingly termed them." He smiled again, cocking his brow. "And while I find you to be quite a delectable package, poppet, I am afraid I quite agree with you regarding the more sensual side of our association . . . for the time being, at least."

So he wasn't looking for a one-night stand? Or maybe he was so smooth, he was masking the fact that he was looking for a quick hookup and he'd put his plan of attack into action once I was no longer suspicious. I took a deep breath and lifted my menu again, wishing I'd never agreed to this date in the first place. "Oh."

"Would you be averse to the notion of . . . starting over?" he asked and leaned back into his chair as he studied me.

I felt an embarrassed smile pulling at my lips even though I still wasn't sure what his intentions were. Well, either way, it took two to tango and my tango shoes were in a box in my closet, covered with dust. "No, that sounds good."

"Very well," he said again and called the waiter over. "Ms. Wilkins . . ."

"Please, it's Jolie."

He smiled languidly. "Jolie, what would you care to drink?"

I faced the waiter and smiled. "Do you have any Riesling?"

The waiter nodded. "Yes, ma'am."

"A glass of that, then," I finished.

"And you, sir," the waiter asked, turning to face Sinjin.

"The same, please," he responded.

"Are you ready to order?" the waiter asked us both, his pen poised above the pad of paper like he was about to start a race or something.

Sinjin glanced at me and I nodded, having already figured out what I wanted. "I'd like the sea bass, please."

The waiter scribbled down my order before facing Sinjin. "And you, sir?"

Sinjin shook his head. "Nothing for me, thank you."

"Sinjin," I started, shocked that he wasn't ordering anything. "You aren't going to make me eat alone?"

He smiled. "I apologize, love, but my stomach is a bit finicky at the moment. Would you mind terribly?"

How was I going to say no to that? I shook my head and the waiter nodded, disappearing into the kitchen moments later.

"We can go if you aren't feeling well," I said.

Sinjin waved away my concern with his long fingers. "I have a bit of a stomach condition and it plagues me every now and again. Nothing to concern yourself with, love." He studied me for a moment or two and smiled again. "Where were we?"

"Um, I think we had agreed to start over."

He chuckled. "Ah, yes, starting over." His voice trailed as he apparently searched for a new topic. "Tell me about your tarot reading business."

I sighed and glanced down at my ice water. The ice had melted into tiny lumps and I submerged each one with my straw as I thought about his question. "Well, as you know, I'm a psychic," I said. Whether he even believed in that sort of thing was anyone's guess—it hadn't been something we established the night before.

"Have you always known this about yourself?" he asked, just as the waiter returned with our wine. Sinjin raised his glass. "Prost!" he said and brought the glass to his lips as I downed a swallow of the bitterly sweet wine. Before he took a swig, he set the glass back on the table and glanced over at me again. "Well?"

I smiled. "Um, yeah, for as long as I can remember. I could always see things and I just seemed to know things about people. Stuff that I shouldn't know." I wondered if I'd said too much. Usually men didn't react well to my day job—thinking I was either a charlatan or a nut job.

But there was no sign of judgment on Sinjin's handsome face. Instead, he just nodded and I couldn't tell if he thought I was full of it or not.

"I know the feeling."

I faced him, my eyes wide, as I wondered what he was admitting. "Are you psychic?"

He shook his head. "No but I have had my dealings with the otherworldly."

So he didn't think I was a liar or a Looney Toon. I breathed out a sigh of relief. And, as the relief washed over me, a feeling of disappointment surfaced. Sinjin might understand me, but it wasn't like he was going to stick around. I mean, he was traveling here on business or vacation or something.

"What about you?" I asked. "You're here for work?"

He never took his eyes from mine and there was something in their depths. Something untold, something hidden. It appeared that this man had his own skeletons hanging in his closet. I could tell just by reading his eyes.

"Yes, quite so."

"What do you do?"

He shrugged and finally averted his eyes, lifting his glass of wine as he trailed the rim of the glass with his finger. "I own my own company."

"Ah, what type of business?"

"Finance," he said quickly, somewhat dismissively, and then leaned forward, seemingly uncomfortable about discussing the specifics.

"And you're here for just a little while, then?" I hoped I didn't sound anticipative because I was all too well aware that this charade probably wouldn't last longer than tonight. Not when he had a whole life waiting for him in Britain.

God, what if he's married?

He glanced at me again and didn't respond right away, just continued looping his finger around the rim of his glass. "I am considering opening an American branch of my company. That is why I am currently here." He stopped talking for a few seconds and then smiled at me. "Perhaps I will not return to Britain—for the foreseeable future, at any rate."

I felt something happy burst within me even though it made no sense. If Sinjin decided to stay, that didn't mean we'd necessarily see each other again. And even if we did see each other once, twice, or even multiple times, he'd still have to return to Britain eventually and where would that leave me?

I shook the feelings of elation right out of me. I was getting way ahead of myself. And truly, I was just being silly, setting myself up for disappointment.